"Call a plumber when the sink is clogged, the cops when you've been robbed, but when the you-know-what hits the fan, it's time to call Repairman Jack. . . . Wilson's tale shakes, rattles, and rolls." —*New York Daily News* on *The Haunted Air*

"Like the best of Dean Koontz's work, Wilson's work combines an action/adventure yarn with a touch of the fantastic. . . . If you haven't read any of the Repairman Jack novels before, now is a good time to start. They're smart, exciting, and most of all, fun." —*The Denver Post*

"Jack is righteous!" —Andrew Vachss

BY F. PAUL WILSON

REPAIRMAN JACK NOVELS

The Tomb	*Crisscross*
Legacies	*Infernal*
Conspiracies	*Harbingers*
All the Rage	*By the Sword*
Hosts	*Jack: Secret Histories*
The Haunted Air	(young adult novel)
Gateways	*Bloodline*

THE ADVERSARY CYCLE

The Keep	*Reborn*
The Tomb	*Reprisal*
The Touch	*Nightworld*

OTHER NOVELS

Healer	*Black Wind*
Wheels Within Wheels	*Dydeetown World*
An Enemy of the State	*The Tery*

Sibs
The Select
Virgin
Implant
Deep as the Marrow
Mirage (with Matthew J. Costello)
Nightkill (with Steven Spruill)
Masque (with Matthew J. Costello)
The Christmas Thingy
Sims
The Fifth Harmonic
Midnight Mass

SHORT FICTION

Soft & Others
The Barrens & Others

EDITOR

Freak Show
Diagnosis: Terminal

F. PAUL WILSON

HARBINGERS

TOR®

A TOM DOHERTY ASSOCIATES BOOK
NEW YORK

This is a work of fiction. All the characters, organizations, and events portrayed in this book are either products of the author's imagination or are used fictitiously.

HARBINGERS

Copyright © 2006 by F. Paul Wilson

All rights reserved.

Edited by David G. Hartwell

A Tor Book
Published by Tom Doherty Associates, LLC
175 Fifth Avenue
New York, NY 10010

www.tor-forge.com

Tor® is a registered trademark of Tom Doherty Associates, LLC.

ISBN-13: 978-0-7653-5139-5
ISBN-10: 0-7653-5139-0

First Edition: September 2006
First Mass Market Edition: September 2007

Printed in the United States of America

0 9 8 7 6 5 4 3

for my sibs,

Peter
and
Lu

ACKNOWLEDGMENTS

Thanks to the usual crew for their efforts: my wife, Mary; my editor, David Hartwell; Elizabeth Monteleone; and my agent, Albert Zuckerman. Special thanks to Steven Spruill for his perceptive insights and going the extra mile.

More thanks to:

Lisa Krause for the title. The folks in the www.repairmanjack.com Forum came up with many excellent suggestions, but *Harbingers* hit the bull's-eye.

Ken Valentine and New York Joe for weaponry assistance.

Sandra Escandon, M.D., and Paul Gilson, M.D., for neurological guidance.

Stu Schiff for the world's most amazing single malts.

And super extra-special thanks to Ethan Bateman for lending me his sui generis metaphors.

Finally, a wink and a nod to the few readers out there who'll know the Wauwinet Inn's seasonal schedule.

FRIDAY

1. "Hey, Jack, can I bother you a minute?"

Jack sat at his table in the rear of Julio's. He looked up from his coffee and saw Timmy O'Brien, one of Julio's regulars. A fiftyish guy, thin, hangdog face, watery eyes, and wearing a Hawaiian shirt in January.

Julio's, an Upper West Side bar that had fought the good fight and succeeded in holding on to its working-class roots through the neighborhood's decades of legitimization, rehabilitation, restoration, and gentrification, had been Jack's hang for years. Julio always saved him a table where he could sit with his back to the wall.

"Bother?"

"Well, yeah. I mean, I know about what happened last month, and I'm really sorry for your loss. I know you've still got to be bummed, but I could really use some help, Jack."

"What kind?"

"Your kind."

Jack sighed. He'd been on sabbatical, ignoring e-mails and voice mails from prospective customers. Didn't feel he could focus enough—or care enough—to earn his fee. That was part of it. Truth was he was having trouble caring about much of anything outside his small, immediate circle. No interest, no energy, and probably drinking too much these past three weeks.

He didn't need a shrink to tell him he was depressed. But a shrink would want to give him pills, and Jack didn't want pills. He preferred beer—but not before lunch.

He couldn't find the energy to get up and get out and get moving again. What was the point? Who cared? And when he got right down to it, did anything he did, anything he'd *ever* done, matter in the long run? Had he ever made a difference?

He wondered.

But Timmy looked so needy. Jack wasn't ready to venture outside his self-circumscribed world of Julio's, Abe's, Gia's, and his own place, but maybe he could make a few suggestions.

He pointed to the seat across from him.

"Shoot."

As Timmy settled his butt in the chair and his draft on the table, Jack reviewed what he knew about the man.

A dozen years ago Timmy had been an advertising hotshot, near the peak of the copywriter heap. Lots of money, but too much of it going up his nose. His agency had been on the short list for a big Citibank account and he had this idea that he was sure would clinch it for them. He'd once shown the Julio's gang a mockup of the ad.

A big, neon-bright lettered cross with tiny letters below it:

$$
\begin{array}{c}
\blacksquare \\
\textbf{J E S U S} \\
\textbf{A} \\
\textbf{V} \\
\textbf{E} \\
\textbf{S} \\
\text{at CITIBANK}
\end{array}
$$

Everyone here at Julio's had thought it was way cool, but the new Timmy said he had no idea where his old self had come up with such a stupid idea. The agency brass had told him to forget it, but coke-fueled grandiosity mixed with his own hubris had convinced him that this was the only way to go. So against all advice and all orders, he'd pitched it to the bank officers, telling them that though he knew it would be controversial, that very controversy would make Citibank a household name.

The officers agreed, but figured the bank's name would be associated with other words in those households—like "hell-bound" and "damned" and "sacrilegious."

The multimillion-dollar account went elsewhere. And soon after, so did Timmy.

After bottoming out a few years later, he put himself in re-hab, joined NA, and cleaned up his act.

But the clean and sober Timmy was not the same man. The guy who'd had his finger on the pulse of America's wants—who'd even created some of those wants—could never quite localize that throb again. He was still in advertising, but work-ing far below the apogee of his heyday. Always a little out of step—like the Hawaiian shirt—ever functioning just outside the norm. No longer big-time, resigned to be forever small-time.

In other words, a prototypical Julio's regular.

But Jack didn't remember ever seeing him here before five o'clock. And a morning beer—even if it was late morning—wasn't like the new Timmy. Something had to be bothering him.

"It's about my niece."

"How old?"

"Fourteen."

"Oh, man."

A problem with a fourteen-year-old girl. That could mean anything from promiscuity to drugs to being an all-around wild child. None of which Jack could help with.

Timmy held up a hand. "Now, now, I know what you're thinking, but it's nothing like that. Cailin's a good kid. She goes to Mount Saint Ursula, scholarship and all—straight-A student, field hockey, the whole thing."

"Then what is it?"

"She's gone."

"Ran off?"

"I told you, Cailin's not like that. But this morning, some-where between her house and school, she disappeared."

"This morning?" Jack shook his head. "Hell, Timmy, she's been gone, what, four hours? She's probably off with her boyfriend."

"Except her boyfriend's in school."

"What do the police say?"

"Same as you: Hasn't been gone long enough. If someone had seen foul play, that'd be a different story. But with kids running away all the time, they're pretty blasé about the whole thing. Like, 'Yeah-yeah, come back when it's been a coupla days.' So I'm coming to you, Jack."

Jack sighed. He could see Timmy was worried, but he had to lay out a few facts of life.

"I don't do missing persons, Timmy, especially a hot case. And there's a very good reason for that: I can't. I don't have the resources. I'm just one guy, and the cops are many. And they've got all those computers and databases and people from *CSI: New York*."

"But they're not using them!"

"The other thing is, I'm not a detective. I'm a fix-it guy."

"Well, then, fix this."

"Timmy—"

"Damn it, Jack!"

Timmy slammed his palms on the table. His beer mug and Jack's coffee cup jumped. The midday regulars looked over, then went back to their drinks and talk. He lowered his voice.

"My sister's going nuts, Jack, and so am I. I never had kids—two wives but no kids. Cailin's been like a daughter. I couldn't love her more if she were really mine."

That struck a nerve. Jack knew the feeling. He had the same relationship with Vicky.

"What do you think I can do, Timmy?"

"You know people, and you know people who know people—people the cops don't know."

"As in, 'I've Got Friends in Low Places'?"

"You know what I mean. Put the word out—a sort of street-level Amber Alert. I'll pay a reward—five hundred, a thousand, my apartment, anything." His throat worked as his voice choked. "I just want her safe and sound. Is that too much to ask?"

It might be, but Jack supposed he could make a few calls. Timmy was a regular here, and Julio's regulars tended to watch each others' backs. How could he say no?

"Okay, I'll call some people." He kept his phone list at home. A quick walk from here. "But five hundred won't be enough."

Timmy spread his hands. "I know you don't come cheap, but like I said: anything."

"What I'm trying to tell you is we're venturing into What's-in-it-for-me Land. Some of the guys I call, and most of the guys *they* call, aren't going to pass the word around out of the goodness of their hearts. They're going to need incentive."

"Name the figure."

Jack had done this before and knew it had to be set up so, in case of success, everyone along the chain walked away with something. What he'd tell his first-line contacts was that if someone in their contact string found the girl, they'd get the same reward as the finder. This would go down the line: If A tells B who tells C who tells D who finds the girl, all four get the same reward. Five hundred bucks apiece seemed like a good incentive—one that looked better and better as it moved down the chain, ballooning to a bonanza by the time it reached the street people.

"Probably cost you twenty-five hundred, although it might go as high as five."

Timmy slumped with relief.

"Done. I can't think of anything better to spend it on."

"Got a pen?" When Timmy handed him one, Jack grabbed a napkin and readied to write. "What's she look like? What was she wearing?"

"She left the house in a blue coat over a typical Catholic girls' school outfit. You know: white blouse, blue sweater, blue-and-white plaid skirt, blue knee socks."

Jack shook his head. "Got to be a gazillion kids dressed like that in the city."

"Yeah, but they don't have Cailin's hair. It's bright red—all natural—and wild. She's always complaining about how nothing she tries will control it."

"Got a picture?"

"Sure." Timmy fumbled in a back pocket for his wallet. "You thinking of posting it around?"

Jack shook his head. He had neither the time nor the manpower for that sort of canvassing.

"Just want to see her face."

Timmy wiggled a wrinkled photo out of his wallet and passed it across.

"Taken maybe a month ago."

Jack stared at the girl in the picture. Cute kid. Round face, freckles, red and green bands on her braces, and a Santa cap squished on her wild red mop.

"You weren't kidding about the hair."

"She goes on and on about it. She'll wear you out with her constant carping about it, but . . ." He wiped an eye. "I'd give anything to be listening to her right now."

Jack rose and clapped him on the shoulder.

"I'll get on it. Can I keep the photo?"

"Sure. Long as you need it."

"No promises, Timmy, beyond making the calls. It's a long shot."

Timmy grabbed his hand and squeezed.

"I know, but you're all I've got right now."

Jack waved good-bye to Julio and stepped out into the cutting January wind.

Long shot? Who was he kidding? More like hitting a dime at a thousand yards with a Saturday night special.

2. "Look," Vicky said from where she'd planted herself before the monitor. "I think she's smiling." She was endlessly excited by her impending state of sisterhood.

Jack found the scene vaguely shamanistic. Gia lay on a recliner in Dr. Eagleton's office while a technician angled the magic wand of a fetal ultrasound this way and that over the skin of her swollen, lubricated belly.

She'd popped just before the first of the year. Through careful clothing selection she'd managed to hide it during the first two trimesters, but now she looked undeniably pregnant. Her face had filled out some, but her hair was as short and as blond as ever.

Jack's eyes strayed back to the grainy image on the monitor, melting in and out of the darkness as the ultrasonic flashlight swept over the baby. A big head, a little body, a chain of vertebral beads and, in the center, an opening and closing black hole—the heart.

Jack stared, fascinated. His child—his and Gia's.

"How's the pregnancy going?" the tech said.

Her name tag read LIKISHA. A twenty-something black girl with a Halle Berry smile and hair shorter than Gia's.

Gia opened her mouth to reply but Vicky spoke first.

"She has to sprinkle a lot."

Likisha frowned. "Sprinkle?"

Vicky looked up from the monitor and smiled. "You know—number one."

He loved her big grin. She had dark brown hair—her father's color, he'd been told—woven into a long single braid, and her mother's blue eyes.

The two women in his life.

"Ah." The Halle Berry smile appeared. "Number one. Got it."

"But don't worry," Vicky added. "She doesn't have diabetes. Doctor Eagleton checked her for that."

"That's good." Likisha turned back to Gia with a bemused expression. "How about—?"

"She gets lots of backaches too," Vicky said, eyes back on the monitor. "But that's normal for the third trimester."

Likisha's voice rose an octave as she stared at her. "How old are you, girl?"

"Nine."

"Going on forty." Gia's smile betrayed her pride in her little girl.

"But how—?"

"She reads a lot. Constantly. Sometimes I have to tell her to stop reading and go out and play. She's become a junior obstetrician since she learned I was pregnant."

Jack said, "And she'll be going for her junior pediatrician badge after the baby's born."

"Hey!" Vicky cried. "She's sucking her thumb."

"*He*, Vicks," Jack said.

"*She*," Gia said.

Jack shook his head. "We haven't established the sex yet, and that looks like a he to me." He glanced at the technician. "What do you think?"

"Can't say for sure—not with the way she keeps that umbilical cord between her legs."

"*His* legs. Okay, then. What's your best guess?"

"I'm not supposed to guess. But if I was guessing, I would guess it's a girl."

Jack feigned offense. "Sure. You women already outnumber us, but does that satisfy you? Noooo. You want me to be the only male in a house full of women."

Likisha smiled. "Only way to go."

"Do you know for sure the baby's *not* a boy?"

She shook her head. "No. But you do enough of these you develop a sixth sense. And my sense is saying 'girl-girl-girl.' "

Jack turned to Gia. "You two worked this out beforehand, didn't you."

Gia smiled that smile and winked. "Of course we did. We're sisters in the international feminine conspiracy to take back the world."

Likisha raised a fist. "Sister power!"

Vicky mimicked her. "Sister power!" Then she turned to her mother. "What's sister power?"

"Any names picked out?" Likisha said.

Jack said, "Jack."

Likisha shook her head. "Not very feminine."

"Emma," Gia said, smiling at Jack. "At least we agree on that. And Emma she will be."

Jack groaned, then turned serious.

"But whatever—he or she—the baby looks okay, right?"

Likisha nodded. "Typical thirty-two-week-old fetus with all the standard equipment in working order."

Jack let out a breath. So far—except for a near miscarriage—an uneventful pregnancy. And he prayed it would remain that way. His life otherwise had been anything but—a marching band of bad news. He didn't know if he could handle any more.

His cell phone vibrated against his thigh.

"Excuse me."

He'd made his calls for Timmy, made his reward promises, and left Julio's number. Then he'd picked up Gia and Vicks and brought them here.

He stepped out into the hall and checked the caller ID: Julio.

"What's up?"

"Hey, Meng. Louie G. call. He say he got son'thin." Julio read off a number.

"Thanks."

Jack punched it in and listened to the ring. Louie Grandinetti ran a produce supply in the west twenties. He also ran numbers. He'd give odds on anything and everything. If the meek ever inherited the earth, Louie would be making book on how long they'd keep it.

"Yeah?"

"Louie? Jack. Got something?"

"Got a runner who told some grate sleepers to keep an eye

out. One of them thinks he saw something. Might be useful, might be nothing. The guy's an old bearded dude they call Rico. Told him to hang around Worth and Hudson. You were interested you'd stop by."

Down near the financial district. Didn't seem likely, but you never knew.

"Thanks. I'll check it out."

"And should this pan out . . ."

"Don't worry. I'll be stopping by with a token of my esteem."

"Luck."

"Yeah."

Jack felt a little tingle of anticipation. Maybe, just maybe . . .

He ducked back into the ultrasonography room, where he found Gia sitting up and adjusting her clothes.

"Gotta run."

"Where?"

"A little business."

Her eyes narrowed. "Really? Nothing rough and tumble, I trust."

"Nope. Missing kid. Strictly arm's length."

"I've heard that before." She reached out her hand and he clasped it. "Only two months to go, Jack. Please be careful."

"I will. I promise. If I locate the kid I call nine-one-one and walk away."

"Promise?"

Jack held up his three middle fingers, palm out.

"Scout's honor."

She smiled. "You were never a Scout. When did you ever join anything?"

"I'm joining you as soon as Abe comes through for me."

Gia looked at him, locking her eyes with his. They held the stare, then she nodded.

"A little business could be good for you, Jack. You look a lot livelier right now than you have since . . ."

She didn't have to finish.

Jack kissed her. "You can get home okay?"

She laughed. "I'm pregnant, not crippled."

Jack glanced over at the monitor where Vicky still stared at the image of the baby frozen on the screen.

"Pretty soon, Vicks."

She turned to him, grinning. "Likisha's getting me a picture so I can take it to school!"

"Can I get one too?"

"Really?" Gia said. "What for? To show around Julio's?"

"Someday I'll bore people with photos of my kids, but this one's just for me. I want to be able to take it out and look at him whenever I want."

"*Her.*"

3. Jack hopped out of the cab at Hudson and Worth and looked around. He hadn't taken time to change. Kept the jeans and beat-up bomber jacket he'd worn to the doctor's. He noticed a bearded guy on the corner. A ragged-cut square of cardboard with a crudely printed message dangled from his neck.

> *Micky Mouse stole my car*
> *Need $$ to go to Orlando*
> *and kick his ass*

The guy could have been anywhere from forty to seventy. A flap-eared cap covered much of his head. A dirty, gray, Leland Sklar–class beard hid pretty much everything else. He wore what looked like a dozen layers of sweaters and coats, none of which had seen the inside of a washing machine since the Koch administration. He jiggled the change in the blue-and-white coffee container clutched in his gloved hand.

Louie had said look for a beard hanging around Worth and Hudson. This could be him.

"Cool sign," Jack said. "How's it working for you?"

"A gold mine," he said without inflection. He kept his eyes straight ahead. "Get 'em to smile and they part with some change."

"Mickey's got an 'e' in it."

Still no look. "So I been told."

"You Rico?"

Now he looked. "Yeah. You Jack?"

"Hear you saw something."

"Maybe. Heard there was a reward for finding a red-haired kid, so I been keeping my eyes open."

"And?"

"Follow me."

He led Jack around a couple of corners, then stopped across the street from an ancient five-story, brick-fronted building.

"I seen three guys carrying a red-haired girl through the cellar door over there."

The building looked deserted. The scaffolding and boarded-up windows said remodeling in progress.

Rico said, "Lucky thing I was looking that way because it happened so fast I'd'a missed it."

This didn't sound good, even if she wasn't Timmy's niece.

"What was she wearing?"

"Couldn't tell. Had her wrapped up in a sheet but I saw her head. Had Little Orphan Annie hair."

Jack pulled out Cailin's photo.

"This her?"

"Never saw her face, but the hair's pretty much the same."

"When did all this go down?"

"Soon as it started gettin' dark."

"I mean what time?"

"Ain't got no watch, mister."

Jack did. He checked it: 5:30. Full dark now. Sunset came between four-thirty and five these days, but the streets started to murk up before that. She could have been in there for an hour or more.

"Struggling?"

"Nope. Looked asleep. Or dead maybe."

Cailin or not, he'd have to go take a look. As he stepped toward the curb Rico grabbed his arm.

"Don't I get my money?"

"If it's the right girl, yeah."

"How's about a little advance? I'm a tad short."

Jack nodded toward the sign. "I thought that was a gold mine."

"Traffic's been light. C'mon, man."

Jack fished out a ten and gave it to him. Rico checked it, then grinned, showing both his mustard-colored teeth.

"Bless you, sir! I'm gonna use this to buy me a nice bowl of hot chili!"

Jack had to smile as he crossed the street.

Right.

He approached the rusty, wrought-iron railing that guarded the stone steps to the cellar. He leaned over for a look. Light filtered around the edges of the chipped and warped door at the bottom. But no window.

He stepped back and looked around. To his right he saw an alley just wide enough for a garbage can. In fact, two brimming cans stood back to back at the building line. Behind them, faint yellow light oozed from a small, street-level window. The alley dead-ended at a high brick wall.

Jack placed a hand against each of the sidewalls and levered himself over the garbage cans, then knelt by the window. He wiped off the layer of grime and peered through. Took him a few seconds to orient himself, to make sense out of what he was seeing.

"Shit."

A naked red-haired, teenage girl lay strapped to a long table. Jack didn't need to pull out the photo again. He recognized her. Cailin wasn't moving. Her eyes were closed. Could have been dead, but the duct tape over her mouth said otherwise. Didn't need to gag a corpse. She looked unharmed.

Three lean, shaggy-haired men dressed in jeans and sweatshirts hovered around her. Two stood watching as the third drew on her skin. Looked like he was using a black Sharpie to trace weird free-form outlines all over her body. The pattern reminded Jack of Maori tattoos, but much more extensive.

On the wall behind them someone had painted an inverted pentacle in a circle.

Jack nudged the window and felt it move. Slowly, carefully, he eased it inward but it wouldn't pass the inch mark.

"Come on, Bob," said one of the watchers. "What's taking so long?"

"Yeah," said the other. "Get it fucking done."

"Get off my back!" Bob said. "This has got to be done *right*! I do a half-assed job, it's all for nothing."

"Nothing?" The first one nudged the second and grinned as he stared at Cailin's naked body. "Oh, I wouldn't say that."

The second guy thought that was real funny.

Someone needed to bring this party to a screeching halt. The window was too small to fit through, but he could pull his Glock and break the glass. Or he could go around front and kick in the door.

He'd promised Gia to stay arm's length and do the 911 thing, but he couldn't count on the cops getting here in time. Had to go in.

He'd reached the garbage cans and was just about to hop over them when a big black Chevy Suburban chirped to a halt at the curb before the building. Jack ducked as three men dressed in black fedoras, black suits, black ties, and white shirts stepped out. Despite the darkness, all wore sunglasses. They were either trying to look like the Blues Brothers or the mythical Men in Black from UFO lore.

Or like the two similar-looking characters Jack had dealt with last spring.

The three made a disparate group. One was huge, one short and skinny, one somewhere between.

They looked like they knew where they were going as they crossed the sidewalk and hurried down the cellar stairs. When Jack heard them kick in the door, he scrambled back to the window.

The trio with the girl had heard the sound of the door—how could they not?—and drawn long knives.

The three men in black burst in with drawn pistols.

"Who the fuck're you?" said the artist.

The big guy pointed a suppressed H-K Tactical at him and fired. The bullet hit him in the nose and flung him back against the table. He hung there against Cailin's body, then slithered to the floor, very dead. The other two immediately dropped their knives and raised their hands. But the big guy wasn't impressed. With no hesitation and no sign of emotion he shot each once in the head.

Phut!
Phut!

"Damn you, Miller!" the middle-size guy shouted. "What'd you do that for? What's the matter with you?"

Miller holstered his pistol. "Just improving the gene pool."

"What about the plan? Tag them and track them, see where they hang out. See if there's any more like them. Remember that? Ever occur to you that they might have been useful alive?"

"Buncha fucktards. Nothing useful ever coming from them." The corners of his mouth curled up in a barely notice-able smile. "Least not now anyways."

The medium guy shook his head. "All right, let's wrap her up and get her out of here."

"Let Zeklos do it. He's gotta be good for *something*."

The third, a buck-toothed weasel guy, shot him a venomous look, then approached Cailin.

What the hell?

Jack could still call the police, but the group would be long gone before they got here. Besides, he wanted to know what was going on. Who were these guys? And what did they plan to do with Cailin?

He pulled a knit cap from his jacket pocket. Had an idea of how to find out.

4.   Cal Davis averted his eyes from the girl as Zeklos began unstrapping her from the table. He wanted to stare at her, the red pubic fuzz, the small pink-tipped breasts. He didn't like the feelings bubbling up from his core.

"She breathing?"

"Yes," Zeklos said. "I should leave the tape?"

"Definitely."

He didn't want her making a racket if she came to.

He looked at Miller staring at the girl. Didn't even bother with a corner-of-the-eye sneak. Just flat out stared.

Goddamn loose cannon.

"This really pisses me off," Cal told him. "You could have waited till I pumped them a little."

Miller shrugged, still staring at the girl. "The O told us we had to get here and stop them." His smile blinked like a faulty neon sign. *Bzzt*: on. *Bzzt*: off. "We're here, and they're stopped. End of story."

Typical Miller.

"Okay," Zeklos said. "She is ready."

Cal looked and saw that he'd wrapped her in a sheet from the top of her head to her soles. She could have been a carpet except for the twin bulges of her breasts. He turned back to Miller.

"All right. I'll go up and check topside. Zeklos gets the car door. When I give the signal, hustle her up and put her in the front passenger seat. I'll take the wheel."

Miller frowned. "Why do I have to carry her?"

"Because you are beast of burden," Zeklos said, his accent thicker than usual.

Miller cocked a fist and stepped toward him. The little man

flinched and backed up a step, almost tripping over one of the corpses. Miller smiled—*bzzt*—and lowered his fist.

Cal gritted his teeth. "Need I remind you two lover boys that we have an unconscious teenage girl and three corpses on our hands at the moment. I'd prefer not to have to explain them."

Zeklos sulked. "He keeps pulling the rope of anger."

Miller shrugged and gathered up the girl. Cal followed Zeklos up the steps. As the little man crossed to the car and opened the door, someone started yelling.

"Where's my money, damn it? I want my goddamn money!"

He saw a bearded demento with a sign around his neck standing by the rear bumper, pounding on the tailgate.

"My money, goddamn it!"

Cal looked up and down the sidewalk. Cold night. Not many pedestrians, and none of them close. Just the hobo.

Perfect.

Always good to be seen by at least one person, and the loonier the better.

He signaled Miller in the stairwell.

"Let's go!"

As Miller hit street level with his bundle, Zeklos left the door open and hustled around the front of the car to the street side. Cal followed.

And still the bum rattled on about his goddamn money.

As Cal slipped behind the wheel, Miller folded the girl onto the floor in front of the passenger seat. Cal started the car and had it moving as soon as Miller hit the rear seat beside Zeklos.

The hobo got in one more thump against the tailgate and then he was a dwindling, fist-waving figure in the rearview mirror.

"All right," said Zeklos, rolling the "r" harder than usual. "Now that we have girl, what we do with her?"

"Right good question," said a voice from the rear that belonged to neither Miller nor Zeklos—unless one of them had developed a Southern drawl.

Cal instinctively hit the brakes and looked in the rearview.

He saw Miller sitting stiff and wide-eyed, saw Zeklos turning his head.

"Eyes straight ahead," the voice snapped. "And you—driver man—keep on a-movin'."

Cal complied. All he could make out in the rearview was part of a third silhouette behind Miller.

The guy drawled on. "Ah've got the muzzle of m'Glock pressed against the base of Miller's skull here. Kinda wish Ah could add a sound effect, like cocking the hammer, but as you boys pro'ly know, Glocks ain't got no external hammer. But Ah've got the trigger safety depressed and Ah'll put one through Miller as quickly as he did those three creeps a few minutes ago. Quicker, maybe. So, 'less you want to be puttin' in a call to Mister Wolfe, Ah suggest y'all stay calm and do what yer told."

Cal felt sweat begin to collect in his armpits. This guy knew their names. And he knew what Miller did in the cellar. How? Unless he'd been there, or had a video camera hidden, or was one of the Satanists—

But he'd called them creeps.

Cal slowed his dervishing thoughts. Never mind who or why or how. Deal with the now. That was how he'd been trained.

What could he tell about this guy? Only his voice to go on. Caucasian male for sure. Between thirty and forty, he guessed. But that growly accent didn't ring true. Sounded like a bad imitation of Andy Griffith. Which meant he was probably a northeasterner hiding his roots.

Didn't matter if it sounded phony, though. It did the trick: If someday any of them ever heard his real voice, they'd never recognize it.

With a stab of chagrin Cal realized that the bum banging on the tailgate hadn't been crazy. He'd been shouting at their visitor.

Okay. Be cool. Lighten things up a bit.

"What'd you do? Rip off that old wino's change cup?"

The guy ignored him.

"First thing we do is collect all the bang-bangs. Driver man, you hand yer purty H-K over yer shoulder butt first. And be real easy 'bout it. Nuthin' cute."

Hell, he even knew what they were packing.

"Then skinny here will hand it back to me the same way."

Cal did as he was told, followed by Zeklos and Miller surrendering theirs.

"Ah do appreciate it," said the guy. "Hey-hey. Forty-fives. Big 'uns. But Ah guess y'all'd want subsonic rounds if you're gonna use suppressors."

This guy knew his stuff.

"Now, Ah know y'all got backups, so send them back too."

A minute later all three backups were out of reach.

"Good. We're off to a fine, fine start. I love these Suburbians, don't you? So roomy in the back. Why looky here—bags o' street clothes. This what you wear when you're out of uniform? I think I'll just nab one of these here shoppin' bags. Right accommodatin' of y'all to make it so handy."

Definitely a put-on accent.

From the rear came the sound of their weapons dropping into a bag.

"Okay," Cal said. "You're holding all the cards now. What do you want? If it's the girl, forget it. We gave you our guns, but you don't get the girl without killing us. All of us."

"Is that so? Mighty brave. But Ah'm right curious about yer plans for that sweet young thang there."

"Fuck off," Miller said, obviously forcing the words through clenched teeth.

Cal's first instinct had been to say the same, but he'd feared it might set something off. He bunched his shoulders, tensing for the gunshot.

But none came.

"Now that's right dispolite, Mister Miller," the guy said. "One more remark like that and Ah'll have to put a permanent stop to yer mouth. And then I'll move on to yer little friend here and see how anxious he is to have his teeth bucked out more than they already is. Damn, boy, that's some set of chompers you got there. Ah bet you could eat corn on the cob through a picket fence."

Cal had to smile despite the situation. He'd never heard it put that way, but the guy was dead on the mark.

"So Ah'm asking y'all one more time: What was yer plans for the girl?"

Hell, might as well tell him.

"Get her back to her family."

"Really now. Well, that's right white o' you. And how was you plannin' to do this fine thing?"

"Leave her on a park bench, call nine-one-one, and keep watch till the cops showed."

"Fine idea! Let's do 'er!"

The response caught Cal off guard. If this guy wanted the same thing they wanted, why was he doing this?

Obviously he hadn't known their plan. Cal found that faintly reassuring: At least he didn't know everything.

But he seemed cool with the plan. Which meant he was looking out for the girl. And that put them on the same side.

So weird. His training had prepared him for dealing with an enemy who had the drop on him. But a non-enemy . . . ?

"Where we a-goin'?" the guy said.

"We ride around and check the parks until we find a bench where we can do a discreet drop off."

"All right then, y'all stay straight ahead here on Worth. We'll check out Columbus Park when we come to 'er."

This guy—definitely a New Yorker.

They cruised Worth, passing the Javits Federal Building on the right, and came to a park on the left. Looked deserted. A wrought-iron fence ringed the perimeter. Benches had been placed outside the fence in alcoves along the sidewalk.

"Turn onto Mulberry," the guy said. "And go slow."

Cal complied.

As they approached one of the bench alcoves the guy said, "Okay, stop. Them benches look like good 'uns. We'll put 'er there. Driver man, you'll do the honors."

Cal pulled into the curb and hurried to the passenger side. One quick look around to make sure no one was nearby, then he bundled the girl in his arms and hurried her over to the bench. He stretched her out and pulled the sheet down to expose her face. If she stayed out here like this too long she'd freeze to death. But if Emergency Services did their job, she'd be in the back of an ambulance long before.

It occurred to Cal then that he could simply take off and leave the ersatz Southerner with Miller and Zeklos. *Then* what would he do?

He shook off the idea. *Yeniçeri* didn't run out on each other. No one, alive or dead, was ever left behind.

He hopped back into the front seat and got the car moving.

"Make the call," the guy said. "Then let's find us a place where we can sit and watch."

Cal found a spot near the corner of White and Baxter that gave them a clear view of the bench. A minute after they'd settled in he saw a figure strolling by. The man stopped at the bench, bent for a closer look. Cal watched him fumble his cell out of a pocket and start hitting buttons. That done, he took off his overcoat and draped it over the girl.

This city had a bad rap for being rude and uncaring. Yeah, it had its share of creeps, but it also housed millions of good Samaritans.

5.   An ambulance finally arrived and they all watched until it loaded the girl and roared away.

Now what? Cal thought.

The guy must have read his mind.

"Okay. We got 'er done. Now let's move this party up to Canal Street."

"What for?"

"That's where you're a-droppin' me off."

Dropping him off . . . Cal liked the sound of that.

They reached Canal, bustling despite the cold.

"This here looks good. Pull over and pop the tailgate."

"And what if I don't?"

"Then I step over some twitchin' bodies and go out a side door. Yer call."

Cal pulled over and popped the tailgate.

"I'll drop this bag o' guns off in a trash can about a block upstream. You can pick 'em up there."

As the guy turned to go, Miller swung an arm back and grabbed the sleeve of his jacket—just a few fingers' worth. In a blur of motion the guy had the muzzle of the Glock between Miller's eyes.

"Miller, no!"

"That's right, Miller. Y'all've played real nice up till now. Let's not go ruin it."

Cal tried to see his face but could make out only a few features in the darkness back there. His hand snaked toward the courtesy-light button, but he pulled it back. Not a good idea to startle the guy while he had a gun to Miller's head.

"Not ruining anything," Miller said softly. "Just want to

know where I can get in touch with you, so we can, you know, grab a beer, get acquainted."

"You can't."

"Who are you?" Cal said. Not that he expected an answer.

"No one."

"Who're you working for?"

"Me."

And then the guy was out of the car and walking away with his shopping bag.

"After that son of a bitch!" Miller said.

Cal's sentiments exactly. But backing up on Canal was out of the question. So was a U-turn. Had to be on foot.

He jumped out of the car and hurried along the sidewalk, angling this way and that through the pedestrians. Miller started out behind but soon took the lead. Cal could tell by the bunch of his huge shoulders that he was in a barely contained rage, ready to grab and toss aside anyone who got in his way. People must have sensed that because they veered out of his path.

They collected stares, and why not. Three guys in black suits and hats and dark glasses barreling along the sidewalk.

"Hey!" said Zeklos from the rear. "I have found them!"

Cal turned and saw him by a trash can holding a Gristedes shopping bag. He reached Zeklos first and had the bag tucked under his arm by the time Miller arrived.

"Gimme mine," Miller said.

Cal shook his head. "Not here."

Miller's face reddened. "I want—"

Cal nodded toward the subway entrance on the corner.

"He's gone. We'll never catch him now."

Miller surprised him by smiling—a real smile lasting more than a nanosecond. "That's what you think. And that's what *he* thinks. But you're both wrong."

"Care to enlighten me?"

"You know those RF transponders we were gonna use to trace the creeps?"

"Yeah. So—?" And then he understood. "You stuck one on him?"

"Damn straight. When I grabbed his coat."

Cal had to smile. "Miller, sometimes you really surprise me."

"Not as surprised as this asshole when we show up at his front door."

Zeklos was rubbing his mouth.

"My teeth are not so bad as he say, yes?"

6. What a weird night.

Jack sat alone at his table in Julio's. After training up from Chinatown he'd stopped in to do some thinking over a brew or two. Halfway through his first and still hadn't found any answers.

For a while there he hadn't been sure he'd ever make it back, not with how Rico had almost blown it. He'd seen Jack climb into the rear of the Suburban and decided it was time to collect his money.

But the suits had been too intent on getting the girl into the car to pay any attention. Just another sidewalk crazy.

The suits . . . those three guys . . . armed to the teeth with quality heat and about as ruthless as they come. What were they—vigilantes?

And what was it with the black suits and fedoras? Some sort of uniform?

What Jack really wanted to know was where they'd gotten their information. They'd burst in as if they knew exactly what they'd find. But the question was, had they been there to interrupt some sort of ceremony and save the victim, or was it Cailin in particular they were protecting? Was there something special about her?

And who the hell sent them? Timmy?

Just then the man in question turned from the bar and, cell phone in hand, all but fell over himself rushing to his table.

"Jack! My God, Jack, you did it!"

"Did what?"

Timmy sat and lowered his voice. "My sister just called. They found Cailin out cold on a park bench downtown."

"Great! She okay?"

"Yes! That's the beauty part. She was drugged but she's out of it now. No sign of being, you know, molested or anything. The only thing out of line was her clothes were missing and someone had drawn these designs all over her body. Really weird-looking stuff, according to Sally."

"Well, that's great news."

"Trouble is the cops want to take pictures of the squiggles and Sally's fighting them. They say it's a clue and it's evidence, she says she's not going to have pictures of her little girl in the buff floating around every precinct locker room in the city." He puddled up and sniffed. "Thanks, Jack."

"What makes you so sure I had anything to do with it?"

"Come on, Jack. You bullshitting a bullshitter?"

This was always a problem when he did something for someone he knew—something they might want to brag about. *Yeah, I told this friend of mine and he took care of it for me. Just like that.* And then people want to know who the friend is. Most of Jack's fix-its involved means and methods that his paying customers preferred not to be connected with, so they kept mum.

Just as Jack would keep mum and let that good Samaritan get all the credit for finding her. The downside of that was he'd have to pay Louie and the two or three connections downstream from him—including crazy Rico—out of his own pocket, probably to the tune of a couple of grand.

But it was worth it. Jack hadn't felt this alive in weeks.

"You put anyone else on her trail, Timmy?"

"You're the only guy like you I know."

Jack didn't know whether to believe him or not.

"Well, Tim, maybe she was kidnapped by some mad doodler who wanted her to be a living work of art."

"Doodler? Guy's a sicko."

Okay. He talked like the snatch was a solo act and he'd just used the present tense. Obviously he didn't know what had gone down in that basement.

Timmy was staring at him. "You *sure* you didn't have anything to do with this?"

Jack lifted a hand, palm out. "I made some calls, but Timmy I swear I did not put your niece on that bench."

"Okay, then." He rose and extended his hand. "But thanks anyway for trying. I've got to get down to the hospital. I—" Timmy stopped, frowned, and pointed to the bench next to Jack. "Hey, you got something stuck on your coat."

And then he was heading for the door.

Jack looked down at his bomber jacket and saw a black, dime-size disk stuck to the leather. He pulled it off and held it up to the light.

Damn thing looked like an electronic bug or—

He went cold.

Or a tracking device.

And if so, he'd led them here.

But maybe not yet. Maybe he still had a chance.

Timmy, he thought as he hopped from his seat and hurried toward Julio's front door, you just paid me back more than you'll ever know.

7. Cal rode shotgun with the mobile tracking receiver on his lap while Zeklos drove and Miller hung over the backrest, watching the blip on the tracker.

"Looks like Upper West Side," Miller said.

Cal nodded as he studied the screen. Things looked good. They were stuck on Amsterdam and 70th in the perpetual traffic jam where Broadway pushed through on a diagonal. The transponder was signaling from almost dead ahead. The guy hadn't moved for maybe ten minutes.

"Mid eighties is my guess."

Zeklos said, "It will not be long now."

They'd already had the tracking receiver in the car because the original plan—before Miller killed them—had been to follow the three mouth breathers to others of their breed. But the black suits were a problem, so they'd stopped long enough for a change. The suits had their uses, but not when sneaking up on somebody who might have an eye out for them. They'd chosen nondescript civvies from the collection in the back of the truck, but layered. Who knew—they might have to spend some time out in the cold.

"My guess is he's home."

Miller leaned back.

"Isn't that nice. Probably warming his feet by a fire. Hope he's comfy. He's about to have company."

"Yes, he is, but no shooting unless you have to. I want to know who this guy is and where he fits into the big picture."

"Fine," Miller said, "but he's got some dues to pay for sticking that gun in the back of my neck."

Miller . . . a goddamn loose cannon. And Zeklos . . . Zeklos had competency issues.

"Look, he could have pulled the trigger, but he didn't. He didn't mess with the girl and he gave us back our hardware. We're no worse for the wear. Not even a scratch. So ease up."

"Nobody does that to me and walks away scot-free."

"Yes," said Zeklos. "And I do not forget what he has said about my teeth."

Cal ground his own teeth.

"You guys got the best look at him. Remember anything else about him?"

Zeklos shrugged. "Average-looking man. In the middle of his thirties perhaps. Leather jacket and jeans."

"Wasn't very big, I can tell you that," Miller said.

"Short?"

"Nah. In between."

"Great. An average-looking, average-height guy in his midthirties dressed like a zillion others like him. What happened to all your observational training?"

"His knit hat—it was pulled low," Zeklos said. "That hides very much."

"We're going to have to be right on top of him before we know it's him."

Zeklos said, "I will know him when I see him. And then we see who has bad teeth."

Cal turned back to the screen and saw something he didn't like.

"Damn! He's moving again."

Miller bungeed up against the backrest. "Where?"

"Looks like downtown. Make your next right, Zek. Maybe we can head him off."

Crosstown was a slow go, but when they hit Central Park West the transponder was signaling from the right.

"He's downtown from here. Go!"

The trouble with these RF trackers was they didn't give you a good idea of distance to the object. Could be three cars ahead, could be a mile.

They followed the signal down Broadway and had just passed Times Square when it suddenly veered to the left and then behind.

"Stop!"

The truck was still moving as Cal jumped out with the tracking receiver in hand. He ran back and watched the blip veer right. He looked up and saw a guy in an overcoat getting out of a cab.

"There he is!"

The guy looked up, surprised, then terrified as Miller and Zeklos closed in on him.

"Wait," Zeklos said. "This is not him."

Miller was shaking his head. "Yeah. Too tall."

"Check the driver," Cal said.

Miller yanked open the door and hauled out a confused and frightened-looking black guy babbling in some foreign tongue.

Strike two.

But the tracker said the transponder was here.

Cal checked the rear of the cab, the fenders, the trunk lid, the license—

There. A black disk stuck to the license plate. Cal ripped it off.

The bastard.

"Let them go, guys." He held up the disk. "Looks like we've got a player on our hands." An idea struck. "You!" he said to the passenger, who still had a deer-in-the-headlights expression. "Where'd you catch this cab?"

"C-C-Columbus."

"*Where* on Columbus?"

"The eighties, I think."

"You *think*?"

"I wasn't watching. I kept walking as I looked for a cab."

Cal turned back toward the car. "All right. Columbus in the eighties. That's where we're going."

Zeklos moaned. "We will never find him."

"You're probably right. But who knows? We may get lucky."

8. The obvious move would have been to go home and keep his head down. But Jack wanted to know if the suits had been able to triangulate on him. If so, they'd either wait outside Julio's to grab him, or follow him home.

So after sticking the disk on that cab's license plate, he'd returned to the table and kept an eye on the door and front window.

Half an hour passed with nothing. Then an hour. Good. Looked like he'd been lucky. But just to be sure, he'd duck out through the back alley.

He was reaching for his jacket when he saw a familiar face pop into view outside the front window.

Jack ducked his head as alarm dieseled through his gut. What had they called the little guy? Zeklos? Whatever. No mistaking his Freddie Mercury overbite. They'd found him.

Or had they? They hadn't seen much of him, didn't even know his hair color. Maybe . . .

No, had to assume the worst.

So much for luck.

He rose and strolled to the bar where he motioned Julio over. The muscular little man leaned close. A cloying odor preceded him.

Jack winced. Where did he find these colognes?

Julio frowned. "You don' like my new scent, meng?"

"It exceeds your usual standards. You should buy another bottle and throw them both away." Jack leaned closer. "Might be a little trouble."

Julio glanced around and smoothed his pencil-thin mustache with a thumb and forefinger.

"Yeah? Who?"

Jack had been watching the window from the corner of his eye, and now he saw Miller's face pop up and down.

That nailed it. They'd found him.

"They're outside. Probably three of them. Might come in, might not. But it wouldn't hurt to get folks properly arranged."

"Okay. I spread the word. Where you gon' be?"

Jack looked around. Good question.

"Lend me your zapper."

9. Cal watched Miller dodge a cab as he hurried back from the bar across the street.

"Him all right."

"Did I not tell you?" Zeklos said.

Cal said, "Did he see you? Either of you?"

Miller shook his head. "He was too busy talking to the bartender."

Zeklos stared across the street at the bar. "It is a strange place, yes? All of the plants in the window, they are dead. Why hang plants if one is not going to care for them?"

"Worry about that later," Cal said. "Let's find our vantage points and wait for him to come out."

Miller was still shaking his head. "Uh-uh. We go in in uniform and drag him out."

"Listen to me," Cal said, fighting a burst of anger. "I'm team leader and I say—"

"You were team leader for getting the girl. That's over and done. Now there is no team. We're just three yeniçeri out to find out who's screwing with us."

He'd been seeing a steady decline in yeniçeri discipline in the last year. Here was further proof.

Cal turned to Zeklos. "What do you say?"

Zeklos shrugged and looked away. "I do not wish for hours to stand in this freezing cold."

Cal found himself speechless for a few heartbeats. Zeklos hated Miller. Cal couldn't believe he'd take his side on anything. But then again, it was pretty damn cold.

Miller clapped his hands. "I guess that's it then. Let's get into uniform."

"Why not just do it now—as we are?"

Miller shook his head. "No way. This is a public appearance and I want it known that this jerk was hauled away by men in black."

Cal sighed. "All right. But one of us should be stationed at that alley over there, just in case there's a back way out."

"Good idea," Miller said. "Zeklos—think you can handle that without screwing up?"

The little man glowered at him. "You are driving the car of obnoxiousness, Miller."

He turned and started across the street.

"You forgot your suit," Miller said.

Without turning, Zeklos raised his right hand and gave the single-digit salute.

"You've been coming down pretty heavy on him. Lighten up."

Miller snarled. "Everybody cuts him too much slack. He's a fuck-up. We trusted him with that simple hit-and-run last November and he blew it. He should be working in Home Depot or something."

They returned to the Suburban where they struggled back into their black suits, ties, hats, and sunglasses.

Back on the sidewalk Cal gave himself the up and down, then Miller. They both looked rumpled.

"Not exactly our usual clean, pressed look."

"It'll do." Miller pulled out his H-K and checked the breech. "What do you think: yes or no to the suppressors?"

"Yes. They're scary."

"Okay. Let's do it."

"Do what, exactly? What's the plan? We need to be synched up before we go in there."

"We'll keep it simple. We go in guns out. You keep everyone down—maybe crease one or two if they start to look restless—while I grab the asshole and haul him out. We jump in the car, blindfold him, then take him Home where we can work on him. Good enough?"

No. It was cowboy stuff. Cal preferred a more finessed approach.

"I'd rather let him come to us. Grab him out here."

Miller turned on him. "Look. I'm going in. Either you're with me or you ain't, but I'm going in."

Discipline . . . going, going . . .

Cal sighed. "Okay. Let's go."

He let Miller take the lead, and nodded to Zeklos standing at the mouth of the alley. Then they were through the door and standing just inside it with their pistols waving back and forth.

"This is gonna make you think you're in a bad movie," Miller shouted, "but if everyone sits quiet, no one gets hurt."

Cal scanned the room. To the right nothing but empty tables, a jukebox, and the dead plants. A couple of guys at the bar along the left wall. Another dozen-fifteen guys sat at tables arranged in a semicircle across the middle of the room. No one to either side . . . everyone in front of them. Something wrong with this picture but he couldn't say just what.

"Which one is he?"

Miller looked around. "Fuck! I don't—"

Cal froze at the unmistakable sound of a hammer being cocked—no, *many* hammers cocking.

Pistols had appeared all over the room—semiautomatics and revolvers of all shapes and sizes and finishes.

Cal's saliva turned to dust.

Now he knew what had bothered him: The arrangement of chairs and tables allowed for perfect field of fire on the doorway.

"I missed that," someone said. "*Who* won't get hurt?"

"Say hello to my little fren'," said a voice to his left.

Cal glanced over and found himself looking down the barrels of a sawed-off ten-gauge coach gun. This close they looked like the entrance to the Midtown Tunnel.

"Okay, easy now," he told the little guy with highly developed muscles and a very low temperature in his eyes. "Eeeeeeasy."

"Be happy my little fren' don't say hello first. She speak double-ought."

Cal didn't know if the guy was putting him on with the accent, but did know a sweat had just broken out all over his body. What kind of place was this? Like an armed camp. It gave him a surreal feeling, like he'd stepped into a saloon in the old West.

He lowered his pistol and raised his empty left hand.

"Our mistake. Sorry." He took a step back. "We'll be going now."

Miller didn't budge, still had his muzzle pointed toward the room. Cal grabbed his arm and squeezed.

"I said we'll be going now."

Miller seemed to come out of a trance. He lowered his pistol and together they backed out the door. Derisive laughter followed them into the night.

"What the fuck?" Miller said through clenched teeth.

Cal's sentiments exactly. "Great plan."

"Hey, how was I to know? You ever been in a place like that? You ever even *heard* of a place like that?"

"Maybe in Deadwood."

"Fucking humiliating."

Yeah, it was. Cal wondered if his face looked as red as it felt.

"At least we got out with our skins."

"Since when was that ever enough?" Miller raised his pistol. "I've a mind to go back in and—"

"Don't be an idiot. If the bartender's ten-gauge doesn't cut you in half, the rest of them will Swiss you."

"We don't even know those were real guns."

"Oh, they were real all right. But where was our guy? Hiding or ducking out the back? He wouldn't know we left someone stationed outside."

The Miller smile buzzed on and off. "Hey, right. Let's—"

Miller froze as he glanced over Cal's shoulder. Cal turned and realized why: Zeklos lay crumpled across the mouth of the alley.

10. Jack sat in the back of an idling cab upstream from Julio's. He'd flagged it after using Julio's stun baton on the buck-toothed guy.

Good plan to watch the alley. Not good if the guy you were watching for had already slipped out of said alley.

Jack simply could have walked away then, but figured they'd keep looking for him. He wanted to send them packing, so he'd zapped Zeklos. It had been almost too easy. The guy had been so focused on the alley that he hadn't heard Jack come up behind him.

Now he watched as they helped their staggering third member to the Suburban.

Time to go home, guys.

As the Suburban lurched away from the curb, Jack tapped on the plastic screen between him and the cabby.

"Go."

He sat back and wondered again about these guys. They'd worked like a well-oiled team downtown, but up here they looked more like the Three Stooges.

The cabby's license said his name was Ibrahim Something-or-other, and he was good at tailing. He kept two or three cars behind, changed lanes back and forth, letting other cabs slip behind the Suburban. Anyone watching for a tail wouldn't have a chance of making them. Jack wondered if in his pre-immigration life Ibrahim might have been an operative of some sort in Kabul or the like.

The Suburban reached the West Side Highway and took it all the way down to the tip of Manhattan, then entered the Brooklyn-Battery Tunnel.

Jack couldn't remember the last time he'd taken the Battery, but he had memories of it being shabbier. Looked like they'd spruced it up—the tiled walls seemed pretty clean and the ceiling looked new. A *long* tunnel, curving this way and that under lower New York Harbor.

The toll was on the Brooklyn side. The Suburban didn't have E-ZPass but the cab did, which meant Jack was through the toll first.

"Go slow, Ib. Let them pass you."

They did, and led them straight into Red Hook.

Jack had never been to Red Hook; looking around he could see why. Lots of dock but little else. Poor, dirty, unkempt, but old too. So old and ill-maintained that a few streets still had their original cobblestones; Jack's head hit the taxi's ceiling a couple of times as they bounced and jounced along.

Red Hook had a slapped-together look, without a hint of a plan or continuity. As if buildings from all over the city, from all eras of its history, had been teleported here and plopped down willy-nilly.

But the worst part: almost no traffic.

"Be careful here, Ib," he told the driver. "We're going to stick out. Put on your off-duty light and give them a couple-three blocks lead. Try paralleling them."

That proved difficult. Most of the streets were one-way, but a lot T-boned into others, necessitating a quick right or left. But Ibrahim was good. Paralleling the Suburban placed Jack two blocks away, which was not a bad thing. He figured he could give them a longer leash here. Red Hook was small and bounded by water on three sides. On their present course they couldn't get too far too fast without landing in the East River.

The Suburban stopped in front of a small, three-story brick warehouse across the street from Red Hook Park. WHOLESALE FURNITURE was printed in faded white letters across its front.

Jack dropped to his knees on the floor.

"Keep moving."

Peeking out the lower edge of the window he saw the three of them—the little guy under his own power now—walking toward the warehouse door. Miller stopped and stared.

Jack ducked lower as they passed. And as he did the skin on the front of his chest began to itch and burn. But the sensation faded almost as quickly as it had come.

He had Ibrahim stop out of sight around the corner.

Decision time: Cab home and check this place out tomorrow, or watch now?

He decided to give it an hour.

He handed Ibrahim a hundred-dollar bill and had him drive around until he found an unlit stretch on the edge of the park with a view of the building. Jack noticed that all the windows—at least all he could see—had been bricked over.

Strange.

"Okay, Ib. Get comfortable."

The headlights went out, the engine and heater stayed on. The Ib-man snored. Jack watched.

11.   The Oculus sat up in bed. What had awakened him? He heard faint echoes of the yeniçeri arguing on the ground floor, but they argued a lot lately.

Had Diana called to him?

He rose from his bed and padded to her door. He eased it open and saw the thirteen-year-old sleeping peacefully in her bed.

He started back to his own bed.

What had—?

And then he froze as an odd feeling crept over him.

Fear?

No . . . something else. Something wonderful.

Someone special was nearby. His proximity—his very existence—was momentous.

The Oculus had assumed his existence, but now, to have it confirmed . . .

A lump formed in this throat. After the terrible events of the past few years, he'd fallen into despair, almost given up hope. But now he knew all was not lost. They still had a chance.

He sat cross-legged on the bed, closed his eyes, and waited.

12. "I want you out!" Miller shouted.

Cal stood with the six yeniçeri who'd pulled guard duty tonight, listening to Miller rage at Zeklos.

They'd gathered on the first floor of the warehouse that made up the Northeast Home. It had once been the New York Home, but that was when there had been more Oculi. And more yeniçeri.

The concrete floor lay open around them. The windows had been bricked up. The far right corner was walled off into a lounging area, with lockers, easy chairs, TV, microwave, and fridge. The top floor—the third—was laid out the same.

The Oculus and his daughter occupied the middle level.

A good, solid, defensible structure. Cal would be sad to leave it, but staying in one place too long these days was inviting disaster.

As soon as they'd returned from Manhattan, Miller had called the three guards down from the top floor. He'd said he wanted a brief confab, but it turned out to be a dump-on-Zeklos session.

The guy in question stood apart, shoulders slumped, head down, staring at his shoes.

Miller had a point, but Cal felt sorry for the little guy. Blackball him? Was Miller going to push it that far? The procedure was in place for banishing an incompetent or uncooperative yeniçeri, but Cal had never seen it used. He knew Miller hadn't either.

"You're a complete fuck-up! We gave you a simple job to do—watch the alley. Just watch it and if you saw the guy, hold him until we got there. That was all. You got the job because I thought even you couldn't fuck up something that simple. But you did. Royally. I've had it!"

"The very same would have happened to you, Miller," Zeklos said without looking up. His voice was low, barely audible.

"I don't think so."

"You would have made same mistake as I. I did what I was supposed to: I watch alley. But none of us—you included— guess that he was already out on street. He would have snucked up on you just like me."

Miller sneered. "He might have *tried* to, but I'd've caught him. I'd've been watching three-sixty."

Zeklos gingerly rubbed his neck where the stun gun had burned him.

"He hurt me. He knock me out. I have soil my pants and had to change them. Is that not enough? I should not be eating the corn of humiliation too."

Miller's laugh had a nasty edge to it. " 'Corn of humiliation'? Where do you come up with this shit? Is it some sort of Romanian thing?"

Cal had heard enough. Miller needed to vent, and justly so, but Zeklos had suffered enough.

"Okay, let's all take a breather and cool off. By tomor—"

"Tomorrow, hell!" Miller said. "This guy's a menace, not just to anyone who gets stuck working with him, but to the MV itself. I want him out. As soon as we can get a quorum together, I want a vote so we can settle this once and for all."

This wouldn't be happening if the Twins were still around. The matter would have been brought before them for a decision. But they'd disappeared almost a year ago and command structure had been slowly going to hell ever since.

"That's pretty harsh," Cal said. "And I don't think you've got the support."

"Oh no?" Miller turned to the other yeniçeri. "You all remember last November, right? The first time we let Zeklos solo. A simple hit and run. Nothing to it, right? But what does he do? He screws up!"

Zeklos, head still down, said, "The steering . . . it fail me."

"No," Miller said, jabbing a finger at him. "*You* failed. The target is still walking around! You blew that window of opportunity and we haven't had another." He turned back to the other yeniçeri. "Am I right or am I right?"

"Damn right!" said one of the guards.

"Yeah," said another.

Cal noticed that it was Hursey and Jolliff doing the talking. Both were part of Miller's claque. When off duty they followed him around like dogs.

The divisiveness was more fallout from the Twins' absence. Cal had tried to fill the void but he had no mandate.

"And why is he here? Think about it: His Oculus was killed."

"Not fair, Miller," Cal said. "*Lots* of Oculi have been killed in the past year, not just Zeklos's."

"Yeah, but Zeklos is here, alive and well, while all of his Romanian yeniçeri brothers are dead. How do we explain that?" He pointed at Zeklos. "Where were you—hiding under a rock?"

Finally Zeklos lifted his head. His eyes blazed.

"I was at home. I had illness, much illness!"

"Yeah, sure. We'll have to take your word on that. But the fact remains that your Oculus is dead and you're not." He held up his index finger. "That's strike one. Then you screwed up the hit and run." A second digit popped up. "Strike two. And tonight you let that guy get away." A third finger joined the others. "Three strikes and you're out."

Cal saw other heads nodding—all six now.

Miller was making a good case. Things didn't look good for Zeklos. But then, this was hardly a quorum.

And yeah, Zeklos wasn't the sharpest knife in the drawer, but blackballed? What else did the guy have?

About as much as I do, Cal thought. Nothing.

He raised his hands. "Let's not be too hasty here. We don't have to resort to such extreme measures."

He glanced at Zeklos and cringed inside at the light of hope in his eyes. How long would that last?

"What's extreme?" Miller said. "You're either in or you're out, part of the team or not. No in between."

"Just hear me out." He turned to Zeklos. "Zek, you've got to know you've been screwing up. Even you have to admit that."

Zeklos's gaze returned to his shoes as he nodded.

Miller said, "Well, then, I guess it's unanimous."

Cal shot him a look. "What I'm proposing here is something like a tune-up. Go back to training camp for a refresher."

Zeklos's head snapped up. "But I am yeniçeri!"

"Of course you are, but sometimes our skills get rusty. It can happen to the best of us."

"I cannot go back to b-b-be trainee!"

"Consider it like baseball. Just think of it as getting sent down to the minor leagues for a while." Cal looked at Miller. "Will that satisfy you?"

Miller shrugged. "As long as he's out of here."

"I do not know this minor league," Zeklos said with a trace of defiance. "But I know I am full yeniçeri, and I do not go back to play with children."

Cal locked eyes with him. "If you don't, Miller's going to call a vote. And then you might not be *any* kind of yeniçeri."

Come on, Zeklos, he thought, trying for telepathy. I'm offering you a chance. Take it.

Instead, Zeklos's eyes took on an *Et-tu-Brute?* look. Then he squared his shoulders and looked around.

"I am going home."

"Okay," Cal said. "I know it's a tough decision. Think on it, then come back in the morning."

Zeklos didn't nod, didn't shake his head. He simply turned and walked out the door.

13. Jack straightened in the backseat when he saw someone step out of the warehouse. The skinny little buck-toothed guy they'd called Zeklos started walking away.

He rapped on the plastic barrier and startled Ibrahim out of his doze.

"Get ready to move."

They watched him until he turned right a block and a half away.

"Let's go."

"Follow him? But there is no traffic. He will see us."

"Just drive around. I'll stay down. Third time you pass him—if it comes to that—ask how to get to some street."

Jack slouched low in the seat as the cab started to move. He scratched his chest as they passed the warehouse. The skin had started to itch and burn again but, as before, quickly passed. He wondered about that but let it go.

"You are not a killer?" Ibrahim said.

The question startled Jack.

"Why do you ask?"

"I see this movie—*Collateral*—where killer takes taxi to killings. It is directed by Michael Mann. I am liking this film, but I do not want to be driving a killer."

Jack had to smile. "No, not a killer. Just need to talk to one of these guys alone. That's all. Just talk."

They turned onto Columbia, a wider, busier two-way. Good.

Jack peeked through the rear corner of his window as they passed Zeklos. He walked with his head down, his hands in his pockets. The picture of dejection. Someone wasn't having a good day.

"Is this an exciting thing you do?" Ibrahim said.

"Not very."

"Oh. That is too bad."

"Hey, exciting isn't always fun."

After what Jack had been through lately, unexciting was a major plus.

"I think maybe you could tell me what you do here and I can write screenplay that I sell to movies."

"Screenplay?"

Had he somehow made a wrong turn and wound up in L.A.?

"Yes. I sell it to Hollywood. Maybe Michael Mann direct."

"Maybe he will. If he does, you'll be set for life."

As Ibrahim did a wide swing through the neighborhood, Jack switched his focus to the street signs they passed, trying to orient himself. Most had names; he'd have preferred numbers. As they returned, going the opposite direction, Jack snapped out of his slouch.

Where'd he go?

They'd reached the fringe of what might pass for a business district. All the stores were closed, but a triangular Red Hook Lager sign glowed in the window of a bar on the right.

"Wait here. I'll look inside."

When Jack reached the door—the place called itself the Elbow Room—he pulled it open only a couple of inches. And there at the bar, tossing back a shooter of something, sat his guy.

Jack peeled off another C-note as he hurried back to the cab.

"Here." He handed it through the window. "Find a place nearby to wait and I'll give you Ben's twin brother."

"How long?"

"Give it an hour."

"I don't know . . ."

"How many weeknights you make this much an hour?"

Ibrahim agreed to wait. Jack took his cell number and headed back to the bar.

14. The Oculus's eyes snapped open.

No!

After growing momentarily stronger, the wonderful feeling, the sense of a special presence, had faded as quickly and mysteriously as it had come.

Why? Why hadn't he come forward? He must know he'd be welcomed.

Or had he been there at all? The Oculus didn't think he'd imagined it, but circumstances were so dark and dire right now . . . perhaps wishful thinking on his part.

No . . . he'd felt what he'd felt, sensed what he'd sensed. But it was gone now.

It almost seemed as if someone or something was teasing him.

The Oculus laid back and hoped that whoever it was would return. And soon.

They needed him.

15.   Whoa, Jack thought as Zeklos downed his sixth shot of Cuervo Gold in twenty minutes. Either he's a competition drinker or he's got sorrows to drown.

Jack figured on the latter.

He'd slipped in and situated himself with his back to the weasel and the rest of the room, but opposite an ancient Miller High Life sign. It showed a red witch drinking a beer as she rode a crescent moon. He'd chosen this particular sign because it was mirrored, allowing him to watch without being seen as he nursed a beer.

Wasted subterfuge, it seemed. Zeklos sat with his head down, his attention fixed on his drinking. Only time he'd look up was to signal for another. Jack probably could have sat one stool away and never been recognized. Didn't speak to anyone, and no one spoke to him. A good indication that he wasn't a regular.

Six shots seemed to do it for the guy. He rose, tossed a few bills onto the bar, and made for the door. Not exactly staggering, but definitely weaving. Jack gave him a minute, then followed.

He spotted him going back the way he'd come. Heading for the warehouse? No, he stayed on Columbia and kept going until he came to a cluster of three row houses standing alone midblock; any neighboring buildings had been demolished. Zeklos stopped at a narrow door on the end unit, keyed it open, and stepped inside.

Jack crossed to the far side of the street and watched to see if a light came on. It did: second-floor window on the left.

Okay. He strolled back across the street, fishing his lockpicking kit out of a pocket. He'd brought it along in case he had to bypass a lock or two to get to Cailin. Lucky thing. Though it hadn't been necessary then, it would come in handy now.

He stepped up to the door, glanced around—no one in sight—then checked out the lock.

And groaned.

A Medco Maxum. The place must have been ripped off in the past and someone opted for extra security. These were bitches to pick. Even with a gun it would take him a lot of fiddling before he got it open—*if* he got it open—and all that time he'd be exposed to whoever passed by.

The units to his right each had a fire escape fixed to the front, but not this one. Had to have one somewhere. City code demanded it for buildings three stories and up. He walked around the left side and found it: a classic cage-and-diagonal-ladder model. Less light back here too. Perfect.

He couldn't haul down the sliding lower ladder—the racket would wake the dead—so he examined the wall under the escape. The building was brick and old. Somewhere in time someone had decided to paint it green. A lot of that had chipped off, leaving the original red peeking through. Gave it a real Christmasy feel.

Finally he found what he needed: A slightly protruding brick at knee level.

He wedged the outside sole of his boot atop the tiny ledge and leaped. His hands found the railing. Slowly, carefully, quietly he pulled himself up to where he could climb over the top into the cage.

That done, he peeked through the window and found an empty bedroom, lights out. The illumination leaking from the hall showed a single dresser and an unmade bed. Jack tested the lower sash and smiled when it rose. He eased it up, slipped inside as quickly as he could, and shut the window. Cold air would give him away.

He pulled the Glock from the small of his back and held it at the ready. His plan was simple: Get the drop on Zeklos and see what info he could squeeze out of him.

He peeked around the doorjamb and found the man in question sitting at his kitchen table. Tears ran down his cheeks.

He'd positioned the muzzle of his silenced H-K under his chin. A finger trembled on the trigger.

Jack leaped into the room and grabbed the barrel, angling it away. The weapon discharged. Plaster puffed and a silver-dollar-size pock appeared in the wall.

He snatched the pistol from Zeklos's fingers. The little guy looked up at Jack, stunned at first, then recognition dawning in his tequila-glazed eyes.

"You!"

Baring his Nutty Professor teeth he leaped at Jack with fingers curved into claws. Jack delivered a hard palm jab to his solar plexus. Zeklos gasped, lost his balance, fell back into his kitchen chair. For an instant Jack thought he was going to come back at him, but instead he doubled over and vomited. Once. Twice.

Swell.

The reek of bile and partially digested tequila filling the air was almost as bad as Julio's latest cologne.

While the guy was dry-heaving, Jack popped the magazine from the H-K and ejected the chambered round.

Once the heaving stopped, Jack pulled a chair opposite him—not too close—and sat.

"So, Mister Zeklos. What makes you want to try some do-it-yourself brain surgery?"

Zeklos raised a sweaty face the color of lemon sorbet and gave him a wide-eyed stare.

"How do you know my name?"

Some sort of East European thing slipped through the booze slur, but Jack couldn't place it any closer than that.

"I'm psychic. There, see? I've answered your question, now you answer mine."

"What have I to live for? I am going to be kicked out of MV because they do not think I deserve to be called yeniçeri."

"Yeni-whatti?"

But Zeklos was in his own little world.

"My life is a cabbage roll. No-no. My life is tripe soup. Last year I lose my fathers and now this. MV is my world, my family. Without it I have nothing. No place to go, nothing to do. Damn Miller! Damn him!"

Dissension in the ranks . . . good to know.

"It is all your fault!" His voice rose as he glared at Jack and rubbed the burn marks on his neck. "I am in disgrace now! I am mowing the grass of life."

What?

"All because of you!" Color was returning to his face. "You make me look the fool and now they say I am not yeniçeri!"

That word again.

"Yeniçeri—what's that?"

Zeklos leaned back and clammed. He seemed to realize he'd said something he shouldn't have.

Jack nodded. "Okay. You don't want to explain, fine. But then tell me how you three wound up in that basement tonight."

Zeklos shook his head.

Jack raised his Glock. "Hey, I've got a gun and you don't. I ask, you answer."

Zeklos sneered. "You wish to kill me? Be my visitor."

It took Jack an extra second or two to figure out the "visitor" bit.

Yeah, kind of hard to threaten to kill a guy who'd been in the process of offing himself. Not much leverage here.

"How about I not kill you? Like maybe start with a kneecap or two?"

Zeklos paled but shook his head. Undersized and funny looking, yeah, but the little guy had guts.

Which left Jack in a bit of a quandary. He could follow through with his threat but didn't think he had the stomach for it. Wouldn't be the first time he'd kneecapped someone, but that had been a mix of personal with business. This was neither. This was . . .

What the hell *was* this?

Jack wasn't sure. He'd wound up here because Zeklos and his buddies hadn't let matters slide after their downtown dance. Jack's curiosity had been piqued before that, but he could have lived without knowing any more about them. Now he was interested. Very much so.

But whatever the situation, Jack decided it wouldn't be a

bad thing to have this cashiered yeni-something available as a potential resource.

Rising, Jack grabbed the H-K and stuck it behind his belt. Taking it served a double purpose. It took away Zeklos's suicide tool—of course his backup was somewhere around or he could have a good length of rope stashed anywhere—and gave Jack an excuse for a return visit.

"I'm going to borrow this for a while. Be cool. I'll get it back to you when you're in a better mood."

"Do not come back. You disarm me, you embarrass me, you loose my bowels, and you make fun of my teeth. You are a terrible man and I do not ever wish again to see you."

"Yeah, it's been a rough night, hasn't it," Jack said as he backed toward the door—couldn't see any reason not to take the stairs down to the street. "But we all have those."

He stopped as his fingers closed on the knob.

"At least tell me one thing, okay? Those curlicues that the jerk in the cellar was drawing all over the girl. What did they mean?"

Zeklos stared at him. "Was blueprint."

"Blueprint for what?"

"For cuts they would make."

Jack had been afraid of that.

16. As the credits began to roll, Jack stopped *The Big Lebowski* disc and turned off the TV. He was about halfway through a chronological Coen brothers festival. He'd seen them all before but had never realized how many of their films featured Steve Buscemi.

He rose, stretched, wandered to the window. He stared down at the still and silent street three stories below his brownstone apartment. Nothing happening down there. Too late and too cold.

But as he was turning away he saw what looked like a puff of smoke drift into the cone of light beneath one of the street-lamps across the street. It dissipated so quickly he wasn't sure he'd really seen it. So he waited. A few seconds later another faint white cloud drifted into the light, and he realized it wasn't smoke. It was breath.

Someone was standing in the shadow of the tree directly across the street from his apartment.

Jack squinted through the window, wishing it were cleaner. He made out a silhouette that looked male. But beyond that . . .

He couldn't say for sure what the guy was doing there, but Jack sensed he was watching . . . watching Jack's windows.

One of those guys in the black suits? Had he picked up another transponder at Zeklos's place?

He clenched his teeth. His apartment was his sanctum. Fewer than half a dozen people knew where he lived. If they'd followed him home . . .

No. Couldn't have. The only physical contact he'd had with Zeklos was a single gut punch. He'd stayed a couple of feet away during the rest of his visit.

And then the figure moved, turning and walking out of the shadow into the cone of light. Jack couldn't see his face but knew by the way he walked—he was using a cane but didn't seem to be leaning on it—and by the slight stoop of his shoulders that he was old. And big. Anything beyond that was hidden by his homburg and bulky overcoat—both dark brown instead of black.

Jack watched until he was out of sight.

What the hell? Jack had never seen that old dude before, but he knew—didn't know how, but sure as hell *knew*—that he'd been watching these windows.

SATURDAY

1. Jack felt pretty decent as he stepped through the Isher Sports Shop's front door. Livelier physically and lighter mentally than he had in weeks. The clear, bright morning sky and brisk air didn't hurt, but he had to give the credit to yesterday. It had been a tonic. Cost him a few thou, but well worth it.

Back in the game.

He wended his way through Isher's towering, overstuffed shelves where dust collected like snow on a glacier. Probably because the stock rarely moved and never turned over. Abe's real business was conducted from the basement, so he didn't spend much time prettying up the teetering farrago of objects to be struck and objects with which to strike them and protective equipment to protect the strikers from being struck.

He found Abe in his usual spot behind the rear counter.

"Brought you a surprise," he said as he approached.

With a flourish he placed a bag of chips on the scarred wooden counter.

"*Nu?*" Abe said. "Doritos? What for?"

Abe wore his unfailing attire: black pants and a bulging white half-sleeve shirt. Jack was waiting for the day when one of the buttons popped off. Be cool if a chicken materialized and gobbled it in midair.

"Breakfast."

Abe's eyebrows lifted toward the bare expanse of his upper scalp. His expression shifted between shocked and offended as he placed a pudgy, short-fingered hand over his heart.

"Doritos you call breakfast?"

Jack hid a smile. Time for their ritualistic dance.

"Sure. Breakfast is just the first meal of the day. Break . . .

fast. You break your fast." Jack nodded toward Abe's belly. "Although in your case, fasting might be an alien concept."

Abe shook a finger. "Breakfast is the most important meal of the day. French toast is breakfast. An Entenmann's Brownie Crumb Ring is breakfast. A bagel and a schmear is breakfast. Doritos are not breakfast."

"Never know till you try."

Jack held the bag out to him. Abe stared as if it contained decayed human body parts.

"It's open already. A half-eaten bag you bring me?"

Jack had bought it with the intention of opening it here, but he'd started sampling on the way over.

"Not half. Only a quarter or so." He shook the bag. "Come on. One."

Abe took it and read the logo as he pulled out a chip.

"Nu? A 'Wow' Dorito? I've heard of these."

He held the yellow-orange chip between thumb and forefinger, examining it like a philatelist contemplating an addition to his collection.

"They've been around for years," Jack said as he grabbed a couple and crunched them. He reached for the morning's *Post*. He wanted to check for any news about last night's goings-on downtown.

"Really, Abe, they taste surprisingly like the real thing. I mean, considering they're fat free and all."

Abe made a face. "Fat free, shmat free. Always with the no fat."

"For you, not for me. I don't worry about fat, but we've got to watch out for that sputtering ticker of yours."

"It's not sputtering!" He looked offended again. "It never sputters."

"Yeah, but it will be." Jack reached across the counter and patted the ample belly. "And maybe fat free can shrink this."

Abe looked down at the vast expanse of his white shirt and pointed to the orange smear of Dorito dust left by Jack's fingers.

"Oy, now look what you've done."

"First of the day," Jack said. Abe tended to keep a record of his daily food intake on his shirt. "It'll have company soon enough."

He crushed a broken chip and let the crumbs fall to the counter. A blue-feathered streak appeared and immediately began pecking at them.

"See? Parabellum likes them, and parakeets don't have to worry about bulging waistlines."

Abe shook his head. "I don't know. It says here it contains Olestra."

"Yeah. Instead of fat. That's why they call it 'Wow.'"

"I hear they call it 'Wow' because that's what you say on your many trips to the bathroom later."

Jack gave a dismissive wave. "Trash talk from the food nazis. But even if true, think of it as a bonus: Reduce your cholesterol and cure your constipation problem in one swell foop."

"I don't have a constipation problem."

"And you won't have to worry about one if you eat these."

Abe stared at his chip, then at his pet.

"Oy. Parabellum doesn't have a constipation problem either. Just the opposite already. Now—"

"Stop stalling and try it."

"Well, maybe just one." He shoved the whole chip into his mouth and chewed slowly, thoughtfully. "Not bad." He wiggled his fingers toward the bag. "But I can't give an educated opinion after just one. I'll have to try another."

They shared the bag, crunching as they started in on the papers.

Jack said, "Have you seen anything about three shot-up bodies down in the financial district?"

Abe read every New York paper, plus a few from Washington and Boston.

"I should ask how you know such a thing and the papers don't?"

Jack told him the story from its start in Julio's to its end in Red Hook.

"Such a busy night. No wonder you're Mister Sunshine."

"I've never been Mister Sunshine."

"This is true."

"The thing is, I've got this feeling it's not over with those guys—and I don't mean the dead oxygen wasters."

"Because you don't know their game?"

"Bull's-eye. Being bugged like that creeped me out. Got a way I can keep it from happening again?"

"Just the thing."

He slipped off his stool and stepped into the storage closet behind the counter. Jack heard rummaging noises and a few words he assumed to be Yiddish curses. Then, red-faced and puffing, Abe returned to his stool. He placed something that looked like an undersized radio/cassette player on the counter.

"Here. A TD-seventeen. Not a state-of-the-art sweeper, but just what you need. Detects any RF signal between one and a thousand megahertz."

Jack picked up the little black box, fiddled with the aerial and the sensitivity dial. Looked simple enough.

"Great. Put it on my tab. How come you stock this up here instead of downstairs?"

"Downstairs is crowded enough already. I should stock something legal downstairs?"

Jack thought of something as he stuck the sweeper in his pocket.

"Last night . . . the little guy called himself a *yennasari* or something like that. Any idea what he was talking about?"

Abe frowned. "Doesn't ring a bell."

That increased Jack's frustration. He needed some sort of handle on these guys. Abe had a degree in anthropology and a minor in languages. If he didn't know . . .

"Unless he was using a form of janissary."

"Who can say? What's a janissary?"

"The janissaries were bodyguards of the Turkish sultan, his household troops back in the day of the Ottoman Empire. If I remember correctly, they were started in the fourteenth century. The Turks began conscripting Christian boys from the Balkans, converting them to Islam, and training them as soldiers. These became janissaries."

Jack shook his head. "These guys weren't Turkish. Not even close."

Abe rolled his eyes. "The janissaries were disbanded already. Back in the eighteen hundreds. But it's become a generic term for any sort of elite military force. How come you don't know this?"

"Hey, I'm a dropout, remember? But now it starts to make sense. These guys behaved like a team, were well armed, and the little guy, Zeklos, was devastated that he was being kicked out. Said he had nothing to live for. If you were raised since childhood to be part of a team, and then got kicked out . . . yeah, you might want to put a bullet through your brain."

"Speak for yourself."

"He also talked about something called *emvee* being his world. That ring any sort of bell?"

"Emvee?" Abe shook his head. "Could be initials. But M-V initials could stand for anything from motor vehicles to music video to the Maldives to whatever. Oy. Such possibilities. It gives me an ache in the head."

The phone rang. Abe bent to check the caller ID.

"This I have to take."

Jack waved and headed for the door. Things to do.

2.   He'd gone maybe half a block when he heard someone calling his name. He turned and saw Abe waving from the store's front door.

"Jack! Come back! Such news I've got!"

So Jack went back.

"What's up?" he said as he followed Abe's bustling form back to the rear of the store.

"That call was from a contact overseas—the one who's been working on your resurrection."

"Why didn't you say so? I would have waited."

"I didn't know if it would be good news. I didn't want to get your hopes up."

Hopes up? They'd just shot into orbit.

Impending fatherhood called for changes—momentous changes—in his legal status. Right now that status was zilch. The various and sundry governments—federal, state, and local—wheeling around him had no clue that he existed. Since his birth he'd stayed under their radar—by happenstance as a teenager, by design since he'd slipped into the city fifteen years ago.

But to be a real and true father to the baby, he had to be a citizen. Sure, he could love it and nurture it just as much in his present nonexistent state, but Gia had brought up a wrenching scenario: What if something happened to her?

The possibility had never occurred to Jack, mainly because the idea of anything bad happening to Gia was inconceivable. She would always be there.

But her point had been nailed home last November when she'd told him how a speeding truck had come within inches of splattering her all over Park Avenue.

Gia's death, as unthinkable as it seemed, and as remote a prospect as he could imagine, was not beyond the realm of possibility. Jack knew losing her would leave him emotionally devastated, but the ripples from her death would have far-reaching effects.

The baby would have no father of record. Jack—using his real surname for the first time since he'd gone underground—might be listed in the hospital birth records, but couldn't be listed anywhere else. The guy in question had never filed a 1040, so the IRS would be eager to talk to him. But Homeland Security would be even more interested. A man without an identity, with no official record of his existence . . . if that didn't start the word "terrorist" flashing red in their heads, nothing would.

He might be able to straighten it out without doing time, but that would take years. And during those years, Vicky—who he considered his adopted child—and his natural child would be living with Gia's folks back in Iowa. Jack had never met them, but he was sure they were good people. And as such they'd want to keep their grandchildren out of the clutches of someone as unsavory as Jack. Vicky would be forever lost to him—with no blood tie, he was out of the picture for her—and he'd have to fight for his own child. A custody battle for the baby would be ugly and inevitably go against him.

The only way to prevent that horror show was to become a real person—be reborn as someone with a clean slate. Someone with no relatives, no legal baggage.

Abe's idea had been brilliant: Assume the identity of someone overseas, a dead someone who wasn't listed as such. A nobody with no family to come looking for him.

Where would one find such a man?

"What did he say? Did he find someone?"

Abe nodded as he slipped behind the counter and fished out a yellow legal pad.

"You're going to be Mirko Abdic."

"Who is?"

"Was. He was a Christian Croatian gofer used by an associate in Bosnia during the war—a street kid he took under his wing. Used him to deliver messages when the communications broke down—a frequent occurrence according to him. Young Mirko was captured and tortured and killed by some Muslim Serb militia. My associate tracked them down and learned his fate. Since no one was asking or even cared, he neglected to report Mirko's death."

"But was his birth recorded? You never know in these Third World countries."

"Recorded. My associate checked."

"Criminal record?"

Abe shook his head. "Never arrested. If he'd lived longer, I'm sure he'd have had a long one. And since he was born and baptized a Christian, he won't be scrutinized like a Muslim."

Jack thought about that. A few minutes ago the plan had been an abstraction, a possibility. Now that it was a reality, Jack wasn't sure how he felt. Relief that a solution had been found, but tinged with a certain inescapable dismay.

"This I know you know," Abe said, studying him, "but you have many changes ahead of you."

"Tell me about it. *Everything* is going to change."

"Not everything. You'll still be Jack, just with a different name."

"I might still be Jack, but I can't be Repairman Jack."

"And that will be a terrible shame."

Jack shrugged. "Maybe, maybe not. Maybe it's time to hang it up and start a new chapter."

"You're mixing metaphors already."

"Yeah, well, it's simply too dangerous to stay in the fix-it trade."

Not just to him, but to the family he was about to have.

He'd always tried to work his fix-its at arm's length, keeping his head down, never allowing himself to be seen. In the ideal fix, the target never even knew he'd been fixed. Just chalked it up to a run of bad luck and cursed the fates instead of Jack.

But every so often, no matter how carefully he planned, something went wrong. Like that old saying: *Want to make God laugh? Tell him your plans.*

Sometimes he was seen, which meant someone knew his face—or thought he did. Jack used various disguise techniques—wigs, mustaches; something as simple as cotton pledgets stuffed between the gums and the cheeks gave a face an entirely different look—but he always ran the risk that someone looking for him would wind up on the same block. If the old target spotted him and followed him home . . .

"You're maybe thinking about Cirlot?"

Jack nodded. He'd fixed Ed Cirlot but it had been one of those cases where he'd had no choice but to show his face. Because of Jack, Cirlot wound up in jail. When he got out he'd come looking.

"He gave me a bad time. But I was living alone in my apartment. No one in danger but me. What if he'd followed me to Gia's?"

"Let's not think about that. The fact that it's happened only once is testament to the care you take."

"Once is too many. That's why I can't risk making new enemies. Repairman Jack is dead, long live . . . what's his name again?"

"*Your* name." Abe glanced at his yellow pad. "Mirko Abdic." He made a face. "Oy, such a name. You're going to have to change it as soon as you can."

"Right. Along with my spots."

His whole life . . . upside down. Becoming a citizen, joining the herd and allowing the politicos to fleece him along with the rest of the sheeple . . . the prospect made him ill.

But it had to be done. The baby hadn't been Jack's idea, and it hadn't been Gia's, but the little guy—it *had* to be a he—was on his way and Jack wasn't going to let anyone get between him and his child.

He sighed. "Okay. How's this going to work?"

"Details still have to be fine-tuned, but plans are in the works to smuggle you into Sarajevo toward the end of the month. A nonstop trip? No. Circuitous at best. But once you're there you'll assume the identity of Mirko Abdic. A temporary visa has been applied for—"

"Legal?"

"Of course. Isn't legit the whole idea? To be legit you must have a legit visa. After you get here you can marry Gia in time to be the baby's legal father. Then you apply for a green card.

Later you can apply for citizenship and the circle will be complete."

"It's a thing of beauty, Abe."

"Your admiration and veneration I accept. But it's not over yet. Still some kinks to be ironed out. The biggest will be language. You'll have to pass through whatever outward-bound security they have over there without speaking a word of the language."

Jack didn't like that.

"Couldn't you have brought me in as a Brit or an Aussie? I could fake 'rine in Spine' and 'shrimp on the barbie.' "

"Their record-keeping is too good. We needed a country with a recent period of anarchy and chaos to provide an inventory of unreported deaths. This is the best way. The language problem will be worked out."

Jack believed that. He had implicit trust that Abe would not send him off until he was satisfied that every detail had been nailed down.

So why did he feel so queasy?

3. Gia sat in the Sutton Square house kitchen and stared at Jack. She'd held back her tears as long as she could, but finally they began to flow.

"It's true? It's really going to happen?"

Jack nodded. "Seems that way. Still some details to be ironed out, but we should be able to tie the knot early February."

They sat across the table in the old-fashioned kitchen. Even though she and Vicky had been living here for almost a year and a half, Gia refrained from calling it *her* kitchen. Legally, the tony townhouse still belonged to Vicky's aunts, but Nellie and Grace were never coming back. In a few years it would be Vicky's, but until then . . .

She looked down at her cooling cup of tea as she felt a sob building. She'd been on an emotional roller coaster since the start of her third trimester—up, down, happy, sad, energetic, exhausted in rapid succession, occasionally all at the same time. And that growing sob . . . she bit it back but it broke free.

Jack reached across the table and grabbed her hand.

"What's wrong, Gi? I thought you—"

"Nothing's wrong. Absolutely nothing. Except that I've turned your whole life upside down."

"No, you—"

"Go ahead. You can say it. If I hadn't been careless with my pills that one month, you wouldn't have to go to all this trouble. You'd still be doing your fix-its and leading your life the same way as before."

She'd never been guilt-prone, but now she was drowning in it. Jack had said he was going to find a way to change his life for the baby. And though he always kept his word, the idea had remained an abstraction until this morning.

"Oh," he said. "And I had nothing to do with the baby, I suppose?"

"Well, sure you did, but—"

"No buts. The past is past, the baby is now. He wasn't planned—"

Gia couldn't help it. "She."

"Let me rephrase: The baby wasn't planned, right, but we haven't been pointing fingers because there's no one to point to. So don't go pointing a finger at yourself. Things are what they are. We deal with it. End of story."

Gia agreed in principle, but couldn't get past the enormity of Jack's sacrifice.

He rose and took the seat next to her, then drew her onto his lap.

"Look." He slipped his arms around her. "Here's the way I see it. I've always known I couldn't keep up the Repairman Jack thing forever. It's not the kind of scene you can play indefinitely. I mean, can you see me wearing Depends while I'm meeting customers in Julio's?"

Gia laughed through her tears. "That's taking things to extremes, don't you think? Just a little?"

"Maybe, but the thing is, I've had a good run, and a lot of good luck. I've made a nice piece of change. At some time in the not-too-distant future I was going to have to call it quits anyway. So why not now? Why not quit while I'm ahead . . . before I slip up and regret it? Opt to go out upright, under my own steam."

It made a lot of sense, but didn't ring quite true. Jack was giving up the cherished, under-the-radar lifestyle he'd worked at all his adult life. He might in time convince himself that it had been the smart thing to do, the best thing to do, but she knew it was costing him dearly.

Which reminded her of why she loved this strange, driven man.

She wrapped her arms around his neck and squeezed.

"I feel as if I'm robbing the world of something unique and precious."

"You're doing nothing of the sort. I'm a grown-up and this is my decision. I don't have to tell you I wish we had a different system—in a lot of ways—but this is the one we're stuck with. My approach has painted me into a corner that won't allow me to claim paternity. I can't change the system so, for the baby's sake, I've got to adapt."

She hugged him tighter.

"I wish there was an easier way. I hate the thought of you sneaking into a foreign country—Yugoslavia of all places."

"Yugoslavia is no more. It's Bosnia-Hurtstogoweewee now."

"Whatever it's called, I'm worried."

"You always worry about me."

"Yes, I know. But at least here in New York you're on your home turf—you *own* this city. It's your playground. You know all the rules. But a foreign country . . . where you don't even speak the language . . ." She tightened her grip. "I hate it. If anything happens to you . . ."

He gave her a squeeze. "Nothing's going to happen. In a week or so you're going to have a foreign houseguest with a funny name."

"What was that name again?"

"Mirko Abdic."

"That's got to go. We don't want to saddle our little girl with a name like Emma Abdic."

"You mean *Jack* Abdic. Or maybe we could go for Arnold Abdic."

"That's not even funny," she said, but laughed anyway.

It felt good to laugh. She just hoped they'd have something to laugh about when all this was over.

4.   Instead of a cab, Jack took his own wheels to Brooklyn this time. And instead of the Brooklyn Battery Tunnel, he decided to cross the East River on the Williamsburg Bridge.

Mistake . . . at least in a car as big as Jack's.

Checkpoints had tightened on bridges and tunnels since what had come to be known as the LaGuardia Massacre. Before that, the heavy scrutiny had been directed at vehicles entering the city. Appeared they'd expanded that to those leaving.

His big black Crown Vic's trunk—fittingly enough for a car that got negative miles per gallon—was huge, big enough to house a whole Al Qaeda cell and their favorite caprine squeezes. Apparently that made it something to look out for.

Jack's stomach turned sour as a cop at the entrance to the span signaled him to pull over.

The big, bored-looking white guy with five-o'clock shadow before noon strolled up to Jack's window. No hurrying for this guy.

"Good morning, sir. May I see your license and registration?"

This was bad. Very bad. Jack's IDs, though the best money could buy, were bogus. The registration would pass muster, but he didn't know if the John Tyleski license he'd been using would withstand a computer check. Ernie the ID guy was good, but no one was perfect.

With moist fingers, Jack dug the license out of his wallet, the registration out of the glove compartment, and handed them over.

The cop thanked him and turned away, studying them as he

headed toward a kiosk by the curb. Halfway there he stopped and returned to Jack's window.

"These don't match."

Here we go.

"Yessir. I drive and run errands for Mr. Donato."

"We're talking Vinny Donuts here?"

"Yessir."

The cop looked around, then handed the cards back.

"Okay. You got anything in that trunk I shouldn't see?"

Nothing but some of Jack's burglary tools, and they were hidden in a canvas bag in the spare well.

"Not a thing, sir. Mr. Donato is a loyal American citizen."

"Yeah. Okay, pop it so I can take a look."

Jack did. The cop made a cursory examination—going through the motions—then slammed it shut.

He slapped the roof and said, "Have a nice day, sir."

"I will now," Jack muttered once his window had rolled up.

He crossed the bridge slowly, letting the adrenaline work its way out of his system as he blessed the day he'd come up with the idea of cloning Vincent Donato's car. Mr. Donato, sometimes called "Vinny Donuts" and sometimes called "Vinny the Donut," was built like Abe and ran certain ventures of dubious legality out of Brooklyn. Jack had bought a black Crown Vic identical to Vinny's and had Ernie make up an identical registration card and plate.

The inspiration had been mothered by necessity: Someone with no love for Jack had traced the plates on his previous car to Gia, putting her and Vicky in jeopardy. Now should anyone trace his plates they'll find themselves dealing with a hard guy notorious for a bad attitude.

He'd returned to his normal steady state by the time he reached the BQE and took it down to Red Hook. The big Vic sailed along the pocked pavement as if it were velvet.

Across the river, Lower Manhattan gleamed in the winter sunshine. The city looked so clean from over here. Almost pristine. He wondered when someone would discover the three anything-but-pristine corpses in that cellar.

He rolled into Red Hook, found Zeklos's apartment, and

parked out front. Then he leaned back, watched the pedestrians, and waited.

After twenty-five minutes a middle-aged man carrying a grocery bag stepped up to the building door. As he fumbled for his key, Jack hopped out and came up behind him. When he unlocked the door, Jack reached past him and held it open.

"I got it," he said.

The guy looked at him, suspicion in his eyes.

"You live here, bud?"

Jack held up his own shopping bag and loosed his most charming smile.

"Staying with Zeklos. Y'know, Two-B?"

"You mean the ghost?"

They stepped into a tiny vestibule, and then Jack followed the guy up the stairs.

"Why you call him that? He's a good guy."

"Maybe so. But nobody hardly ever sees him. You hear him go in and out, but it's like he's invisible. Like a ghost, y'know?"

Jack knew. He'd been living that way for the past decade and a half: slipping in and out unseen. A ghost in the machine.

A ghost soon to be exorcised.

Jack laughed. "Well, trust me, he looked pretty solid last night."

He held his breath as they reached the second-floor landing. A three-story building . . . he prayed this guy lived on the third.

As Jack turned right into the hallway he waved and said, "See ya."

The guy said, "Yeah. And say hello to the ghost for me."

Then he started up the next flight.

Perfect.

Jack took his time ambling down to 2-B. When he reached it he glanced back to check that he had the hallway to himself. He did. He knocked.

"Mr. Zeklos . . . delivery." No answer, no sound from within. "Mr. Zeklos . . . Candygram." Still no response.

He'd been checking the door as he knocked. A tight jamb. That made a plastic shim approach a little tougher. The no-name knob lock would be a snap to pick; the Schlage deadbolt above it would be tougher, but no match for his pick gun.

Another check of the hallway and Jack went to work. The knob lock wasn't even set—Zeklos depended entirely on the heavier Schlage. Sensible choice. Three minutes of raking with the gun, a twist of the tension bar, and he retracted the bolt.

He put his hand on the knob and pulled his Glock. Three possibilities on the other side of that door: an armed and angry Zeklos, a dead Zeklos, or no Zeklos.

Jack wasn't looking for a fight. Plan A was to talk to Zeklos if he was home and unarmed, try to pump him a little. If he was home and alive and locked and loaded, that would trigger Plan B, which was to get out of here with as little fuss as possible. If not home, shift to Plan C.

He moved to the side, crouched, took a breath, and pushed open the door.

"Zeklos? You there?"

From what he could see from his angle, the place looked empty, sounded empty, *felt* empty.

Jack ducked inside and did a quick check of the bedroom and bathroom—no one.

He pulled Zeklos's H-K from the shopping bag and wiped it down. Would have been nice to have access to a crime lab— check out Zeklos's prints, see if he had a record, or a gun license, or if Zeklos was even his real name. But he didn't, so low tech would have to do.

Part of the low-tech approach involved head games. That was where Plan C came into play.

He wiped down the pistol and placed it on the kitchen table. Then, keeping his gloves on, he pulled out a pen and notepad and wrote:

> Sorry I missed you.
> Catch you later.
> J

He slipped that under the pistol and made his exit.

He smiled as he bounced down the stairs. The last thing Zeklos would expect was the return of his weapon. Losing it had to be a crushing blow to the ego of someone who considered himself a yeniçeri. Now that he had it back he might be a little less defensive and a little more forthcoming about his buddies in black.

And then again he might not.

Head games . . . such fun.

5. Now what?

Jack sat in his car and stared out at the street. He'd started the engine but hadn't put it in gear. He'd budgeted a longer time frame for Zeklos. What to do with the excess?

Well, since he was in the neighborhood, why not drive by the yeniçeri warehouse and see if anything was shaking?

He took a roundabout route, scanning the sidewalks for familiar faces—always better to see first than be seen.

A couple of turns and he had the warehouse in sight. The bricks of the walls looked battered, weathered, and faded, but the ones filling the window frames looked new.

Nobody out front.

A quiet day in crummy Red Hook.

As he approached the three-story building he felt the same itching, burning sensation across his chest as last night, intensifying as he passed the front, fading as he left it behind.

What the hell?

6. "Don't you think you were perhaps a little harsh with the man?"

The Oculus sat behind the desk in his study and faced the two yeniçeri, Miller and Davis. They stood before him, feet apart, hands behind their backs. Both wore casual clothes—the yeniçeri imposed no dress code at Home—with Davis in jeans and a sweater and Miller in a gray warm-up.

The Oculus had been downstairs a few moments ago and noticed a dejected-looking Zeklos packing the contents of his locker into a battered suitcase. After learning the situation, he'd called the two principals here to discuss the matter.

"He's a menace," Miller said. "He should be kicked out pure and simple without fooling around with half measures."

The Oculus didn't particularly like Miller as a person—and he sensed he wasn't alone in that—but no one could doubt his devotion to the MV and to his job as one of the Oculus's protectors. And after what had befallen his brother and sister Oculi around the world, he needed all the protection he could get.

"I agree that Zeklos is a liability at this point," Davis said, "but I don't think he's broken beyond repair. I think he's simply lost his edge." He glanced at Miller. "He needs a tune-up, not a bullet."

"He's not fixable and should be dealt with according to the Code."

Davis turned to Miller. "You want to pull the trigger on him? Would you like that? Would that make your day?"

"You do what has to be done."

It pained him to see such dissension. More, it frightened him. An effective MV needed solidarity to perform its duties of protection and eradication. If not for his daughter, the Oculus would have had the MV focus on its eradication responsibilities. But with Diana here, he wanted them in top form as protectors as well.

He could only suggest. Although his opinions carried weight, the yeniçeri were an autonomous organization with their own rules and set of procedures—which seemed to be breaking down since the loss of the Twins. They would listen, but in the end they would make their own decision.

The Oculus raised his hands. "Gentlemen, may I make a suggestion?"

"Of course," Davis said.

"I favor the middle course." He saw Miller's features harden so he focused his attention on him. "I say that purely as a matter of practicality. After the recent depredations, the MV is not exactly flush with yeniçeri. You need every man you have. To throw one away at this juncture—"

"Is losing nothing," Miller said. "We can't count on him."

The Oculus shook his head. "Yes, but—"

He froze. That feeling—the same as last night—had returned, as strong as before.

Davis stared at him with a concerned expression. "Something wrong?"

"No . . . something right, I think. I hope. I pray."

He told him about last night's unique sensation, how it had burst upon him, and how it had faded away.

"And now it has returned."

He closed his eyes as the feeling grew stronger.

"What's it mean?" Davis said.

The Oculus looked at him. "That someone special, someone we've been looking for, is near."

Miller's eyes widened. "The Sentinel?"

"I . . . I'm not sure, but this feeling is so . . . so beckoning that it might very well be the Sentinel. Or an emissary."

"Where?"

The feeling was strong now.

"Outside! He's right out front this very moment!"

He wished now that they hadn't bricked up the windows.

"The roof!" Davis said.

But as he followed Miller and Davis up the stairs, the Oculus felt the sensation begin to fade.

No! Not again!

He reached the roof and stared down at the traffic three floors below. Half a dozen cars in sight. The source was moving away . . . it had to be in one of them, but he could not tell which. He wanted to scream *Stop!* But to whom?

Anger tinged his desperation. Why was he being taunted like this? To what end?

He waited for the inevitable moment when the feeling would evaporate as if it had never been.

There it went . . . fading . . . fading . . .

And then the fading stopped. The feeling remained faint, but steady.

"Is he gone?" Davis said.

The Oculus shook his head but said nothing. He concentrated on the sensation, centered on it. It remained faint . . . faint . . . and then . . .

A little stronger . . . and then stronger still . . .

"He's coming back! We can't let him get away!"

"Which way's he coming?" Miller said.

"I don't know. I can't tell. But I'll know when he's close. And then you must follow him. Find him and bring him to me."

7. The itching and burning had faded to next to nothing by the time Jack turned a corner two blocks from the warehouse. He pulled over and unbuttoned his shirt. No rash, but the usually pink scars on his chest, a matched troika of ten-inch ridges running diagonally from up near his left shoulder down and across his right pectoral, looked red and swollen now.

He ran his fingers over them. Hot.

His chest muscles tightened. Considering the nature of the creature that had left these souvenirs, this was not good.

Had to be related to that warehouse. The scars seemed to react whenever he got near it.

He leaned back and thought about how he'd landed here. Anyone else would see it as a string of coincidences.

Timmy's niece is kidnapped. Timmy—just like Jack—happens to be a regular at Julio's. Jack just happens to be present when the dudes in black appear. A little cat-and-mouse action leads him here, to a place that causes an angry reaction in his scars.

Coincidences? Not likely. Especially since he had it on good authority that there would be no more coincidences in his life.

Which meant he'd been led here.

But by whom? And for good or ill? Check that: *Whose* good or ill?

Part of Jack—the more primitive brain centers devoted to self-preservation—urged him to slam the car into gear and get the hell out of here.

Good idea. Smart idea.

But let's think about that.

No one knew he was here. No one was aware he even knew

about the place. Driving by too many times might raise a flag if they had security cameras aimed at the street.

But he could walk by.

Once. Just once.

He'd worn a midweight Jets hoodie under his bomber. Pull a knit cap down to his eyebrows, wrap a scarf around his neck and lower face, pull up the hood, add a pair of sunglasses, and he'd be unrecognizable. Wouldn't work in warmer weather, but here in January he was just another guy shielding himself from the cold.

So that was what he did. When he finished the wrap-up he checked himself in the rearview mirror.

Call me Griffin.

He adjusted the Glock in the nylon holster in the small of his back, then stepped out and walked to the corner. After a quick survey, he put his head down and into the breeze, then started toward the warehouse. Figured he might as well go for broke and walk right past the front door.

With each step the discomfort in the scars increased but he kept moving, determined to see how bad it would get. By the time he came even with the door he felt as if his chest were on fire.

And then the door flew open and half a dozen men jumped out, swarming around him with drawn pistols—all suppressor-equipped H-Ks. Miller's massive presence was unmistakable among them.

Shock slowed him. How had they known? How could they possibly have known it was him?

He went for his Glock but a muzzle jammed against ribs.

"Don't even think about it."

So he lashed out with fists and feet. Got in a few good kicks and punches, caused some pain, picked up some for himself. Desperation added extra strength and speed—if they got him inside he'd be cooked—but despite his efforts they soon had him down. He felt his Glock pulled from its holster. Then they lifted him, one man to each limb, and carried him kicking and twisting through the door.

The farther inside they took him, the worse the burning across his chest. But questions about how he'd screwed up took over. They'd been waiting for him. No way they could have recognized him . . . unless one of them had seen him changing in the car.

His scarf had slipped up over his eyes during the melee so he saw very little of his surroundings as he was carried to a chair and slammed into it. His backup was yanked from its ankle holster, then his legs were released, but his arms remained stretched and pinned behind him.

"Hey-hey," said a voice. "He's got a Kel-Tec backup . . . a P-eleven. That's a keeper."

"Let's have a look at you," said another voice, this one vaguely familiar. Probably Miller's.

The scarf was pulled away, taking the shades with it, and Jack found himself gazing up at Miller—out of uniform, but as mean looking as ever. And big. Jack hadn't appreciated his size before. He didn't quite qualify for a Stonehenge upright, but he looked like he could sub for a lintel. His eyes held all the warmth of photovoltaic cells, and they flashed when he saw Jack's face.

"Fuck! Look who it is!"

Look who it is? Miller's surprise didn't make sense. Hadn't they known who they were snatching?

Miller's smile undulated like a worm, allowing glimpses of mottled, steel-gray teeth as he looked behind Jack.

"Hey, Davis. You won't believe this."

A guy with short blond hair, a receding hairline, full lips, and bright blue eyes—he'd been driving the SUV last night—stepped into view. He too did a double take.

"I'll be damned."

Jack didn't get this. They hadn't known it was him.

He glanced around. They'd seated him in a dingy, wide-open space. No natural light through the bricked-over windows. One of his attackers limped back and forth, rubbing his knee. Another had a swollen lip.

"We'll *all* be damned if we don't figure how he found us." Miller leaned close to Jack and bared his teeth. "But not as damned as this piece of shit."

Jack locked eyes with him. "Ooh, my midi-chlorians are all atwitter."

After the few seconds it took for that to register, Miller

made a fist the size of a softball and cocked his arm. Jack steeled himself for the blow. This was going to hurt.

But Davis grabbed his arm.

"The O didn't say anything about working him over."

Thank you, O, whoever you are.

"But he didn't say not to."

He shook off Davis's hand and completed his swing. Jack was ready by then. At the last second he ducked and angled his head toward Miller. The punch landed on the crown of his skull, rattling his brain and vibrating down his spine. Lights flashed in his vision but quickly cleared. Hurt like hell, but Miller hurt worse.

"God *damn*!"

Jack looked up and saw the big jerk clutching his hand against his chest. Fury lit his eyes as he reared back his leg.

"You lousy son of a—"

"Stop this immediately!"

A new voice. Jack turned and saw a middle-aged man in a long robe gliding toward him. He sported long silvery locks and his face glowed with a beatific expression. Looked like somebody who could have been right at home in the Heaven's Gate pilot seat.

Oh, hell. A cult.

Were any comets due?

"He must not be harmed."

A little late for that. Jack was already hurting—big time. Fire, hotter that ever, blotted out his headache as it raked across his chest. He felt as if he were being branded.

"He's the one we told you about," Davis said. "The guy who interfered with last night's mission."

The guru or whatever he was—the "O" Davis had mentioned?—smiled as if he'd known this all along.

"From what you told me, I don't think 'interfered' is a fair assessment. He did not interfere with the purpose of your mission, which went as planned, did it not? I'm sure he involved himself only out of concern for the child's well-being." He focused his smile on Jack. "Is that not right?"

Jack couldn't have answered if he'd wanted to. This was his

first close-up, straight-on look at the guru, and what he saw locked his tongue.

His eyes . . . all black . . . not a trace of white . . . like holes into interstellar space.

He'd seen eyes just like that—or at least thought he had—last year.

What the hell had he got himself into?

"It's all right if you don't answer," the guru said. "I understand that you didn't expect to be hauled in here like a side of beef. I apologize for that, but I saw no other way."

Miller's steel eyes blinked. "*You're* apologizing to *him*? You're the Oculus, he's . . . he's . . ."

Obviously Miller was at a loss as to who the Oculus—Jack figured that was what the "O" stood for—thought Jack was. He wasn't alone.

The guru never took his black eyes off Jack.

"Nevertheless, Mister Miller, I am apologizing."

Jack didn't know what to make of this guy. The Oculus, whatever that meant, had an imperturbable, celestial air about him. He wasn't just plain old laid-back, he was Dilaudid-with-a-Jack-Daniel's-chaser laid-back.

"Please release him."

As the two behind let go of his arms, Jack decided this guy might not be so bad. The first thing he did was rub his chest where three soldering irons were at work.

"You're going to let him walk?" Davis said.

"If he wishes."

Jack rose. "I wish."

He had to get out of here before his scars burst into flame.

The Oculus raised his hand. "But not until you and I have had a chat."

Jack rubbed his scars again.

"Maybe I'm not in a talking mood."

Miller cocked one of his Belgian-block fists. "I can fix that."

The Oculus was watching Jack, his eight-ball eyes fixed on his chest.

"The scars are burning, aren't they." It wasn't a question.

How did he know about the scars? On other occasions certain people had seemed to be able to look through his shirt and see them, but those folks had been on the wrong side.

What side was the Oculus on?

"We can't let him go," Miller said. "He knows too much. He's found Home. He'll lead others—"

"No, he won't."

Miller's face reddened. "You can guarantee that?"

Not once had the Oculus's gaze shifted from Jack. "Yes. Because you see before you the Heir."

The hush that followed was absolute except for the ticks of water moving through the heating pipes.

Something about the word, its implications, and the uppercase *H* Jack sensed in the pronunciation, sent a sour chime echoing through his head.

Miller recovered first. "Bullshit!"

"Tradition has it that the Heir will bear the scars of the Otherness when he makes his presence known." The Oculus's black eyes fixed on Jack's. "Show them. Let them see your scars."

Jack shook his head. "I don't think so."

He'd been assessing his position during the blather. Six guys—all yeniçeri, he guessed—plus the Oculus formed a rough circle around him. No, wait. One more hovering on the fringe: Zeklos. But he had a suitcase in his hand and didn't look engaged.

How to get out of here . . .

The Oculus looked like a powder puff, but the others . . . the way they moved, the way the two who had been holding his arms remained behind him, blocking his way to the door, spoke of training and professionalism.

He could try, but his chances of getting past them and to the street were slim. And then if the door was locked . . .

"I am not giving an order," the Oculus said, "I am making a request. Please show them your scars."

Jack couldn't read those onyx eyes, but he sensed something in the tone that said, *It's important that you do this.*

Well, why not? Probably feel good to get some cool air against the heat.

"Okay. Since you put it that way."

He pulled off the Jets jacket and threw it on the chair. He untucked and unbuttoned his flannel shirt but didn't take it off. Instead he pulled up his T-shirt.

Everyone stared. Someone gasped, someone said "Jeez," someone said "Holy shit."

Jack looked down and repressed a gasp of his own. He'd never seen the scars so red.

"Mister Tucci," the Oculus said. "Please dim the lights."

A dark-haired yeniçeri walked to the wall next to the door and turned a rheostat. As the overhead lights faded, Jack watched his scars.

They began to glow a dull, ember red. What the—?

He heard Davis say, "I'll . . . be . . . damned."

Jack's sentiments exactly. It was this place. Had to be. But what here could cause this?

He heard a sound and looked up to see Zeklos's open-mouthed stare. He'd dropped his suitcase.

"Thank you, Mister Tucci," the Oculus said. "That will be fine."

As the lights came up, the glow faded. But the burning remained as strong as before.

Jack pulled down his T-shirt. He went to button up his outer shirt but quit after trying the first button. Didn't want to put his shaking fingers on display.

"Somebody want to tell me what the hell is going on?"

The Oculus smiled. "I shall be more than happy to, Mister . . . ?"

Jack hesitated, then figured what the hell.

"Jack . . . just Jack."

"Very well, Jack. We shall adjourn to my quarters and—"

"Just a goddamn minute," Miller said. "No way we're going to let him get you alone."

"I have nothing to fear from this man."

"I'm not so sure about that. He waltzes in here—"

Jack had had about enough of Miller. "You call that waltzing? Who taught you to dance—Godzilla?"

Someone snickered. Miller threw a glare past Jack's shoulder, then turned to the Oculus.

"It's our job to keep you safe. And until I'm convinced you're safe with a guy caught sneaking around Home carrying a couple of nines, I'm his Siamese twin."

"I agree," Davis said. "Dangerous enough to allow you alone with him, but Diana's up there too. Too risky."

"Very well. You both may come along if you wish."

Davis nodded. "We wish. But I want to know one thing first: What made those scars?"

The Oculus raised his right hand and raked the air before Jack's chest with his index, middle, and ring fingers.

"A rakosh."

"Oh, come on!" Davis said. "They don't exist."

The Oculus turned to him. "Common knowledge in the outside world says we don't either."

"But I thought they were just bogeymen the Twins made up to scare us when we were kids."

The Twins? The words rocked Jack.

"Oh, they are quite real. Or at least they were." Back to Jack. "Are you responsible for their disappearance?"

"All but one."

Another hush.

Finally the Oculus nodded. "I see. I've sensed one somewhere to the south. And only the man who killed them would know that one still lives." He turned and started walking away to Jack's left. "Come. We'll be more comfortable in my quarters."

"I've got a *lot* of questions," Jack said.

"And I have the answers . . . at least most of them."

Jack wanted to hear those answers—maybe he'd finally connected with someone who didn't speak in riddles and non sequiturs—so he followed.

Davis and Miller tagged along.

8.   The Oculus's second-floor office was spacious but spare. Despite the open space, it had a mausoleum feel. Maybe because of the bricked-up windows. He seated himself behind a desk and pointed toward a padded swivel chair opposite.

Miller and Davis stationed themselves behind and to either side of Jack, standing like soldiers at parade rest. Jack's head and neck still ached, but his scars didn't burn so much. Were they getting used to the place?

The Oculus leaned back and steepled his fingers. His black eyes fixed on Jack.

"Now . . . Jack. Tell me all about yourself."

Yeah, that'll happen, he thought. Right after Steely Dan does a Christmas album.

"I'm just a guy who's been in the wrong place at the wrong time now and then. I thought you were going to answer *my* questions."

"Very well. Ask away."

Jack leaned forward. "Who the hell are you people?" He jerked his thumbs over his shoulders. "How did these guys know what was going down in that basement, and why did they care? What—?"

The Oculus smiled and held up his hands. "One at a time, please. Let's start at the beginning. I assume you know about the Conflict."

Jack sensed another uppercase letter. "You mean between the Ally and the Otherness?"

The Oculus nodded. "Good. Then I don't have to explain. It's so difficult to explain."

Jack could appreciate that. After all he'd been through, all he'd seen and experienced in the past year and a half, he still found it difficult to accept the idea of two incomprehensibly vast cosmic forces locked in an eternal war Out There. "Ally" and "Otherness" were human designations. No one knew their real names—maybe they had none.

The kicker was, rather than being the grand prize, humanity and its corner of reality were a two-dollar chip in a high-stakes game that spanned the multiverse. And apparently chips changed hands now and then. Neither side could call itself a winner until it had all the chips. There might never be an overall winner, but the game went on. And on.

And although Earth wasn't a particularly valuable chip, the stakes here were high. Higher than high: the ultimate.

Right now humanity was in the Ally's pocket. The Ally was an indifferent landlord—did minimal upkeep but didn't charge rent. The Otherness, on the other hand, had renovation plans, inimical changes that would suck the life out of humanity and turn the planet into a surreal hell.

Or so Jack had been told.

"How about explaining who you are," Jack said. "Start with whose side you're on."

The Oculus looked offended. "Why, the Ally's, of course. I am one of the Oculi."

Well, that cleared up a lot.

"Which is?"

"A network of men and women around the globe who act as conduits to whatever tiny part of itself the Ally has assigned to watching this particular possession. I am, so to speak, one of the Ally's eyes."

"You chose this?"

"No. It chose me. Oculi interbreed. When we die, our children take our places."

"How long has this been going on?"

"We began a long, long time ago. Before recorded history. Back in the First Age."

Jack jerked his thumbs over his shoulders again. "Where do these yeniçeri fellas fit in?"

The word had the desired effect: shocked silence.

Nothing wrong with keeping them off balance wondering how much he knew.

Miller broke it. "The fuck is this guy?"

The Oculus glanced at him. "I told you: the Heir."

"Like hell. The Heir is going to be chosen from the yeniçeri."

The Oculus remained impassive. "Apparently not." He returned his attention to Jack. "How do you know about the yeniçeri?"

Might as well come clean.

"I overheard the word. I gather it's a form of janissary, correct?"

A nod. "Correct. From the Turks who institutionalized the practice."

Thank you, Abe.

"Which means these guys were kidnapped as kids and—"

"Not kidnapped. That was the Turkish corruption of the practice. The heritage of these men long precedes the Ottoman Empire; it stretches all the way back to the First Age. By tradition they are culled from the world's foundlings and orphans, children sentenced—by misfortune or malice or parental callousness—to brief, miserable lives."

"Brutish, nasty, and short."

"Precisely. They are plucked from that fate, given a home, and educated in a wide array of skills and knowledge, including the arts of combat. They graduate to become members of the Militia Vigilum."

Militia Vigilum . . . that explained the emvee. Sort of.

"You've got me on that one."

The Oculus's smile carried a touch of condescension. "The Militia Vigilum were ancient Rome's corps of firefighters. The designation is apt. As a group these yeniçeri have had many names through time. The original, from the First Age, is unpronounceable, but a form of firefighting is one of their major duties, so they adopted Militia Vigilum. When the Otherness starts a fire, they douse it."

"And Cailin was a fire?"

"Was that the child's name? Yes, she was going to be sacrificed to the Otherness in a most painful fashion."

"How did you know that?" This had been bugging Jack since last night. "How did you know where she was?"

A small smile. "I am one of the Ally's eyes of this world . . . its vision. When it sees fit, it sends me visions—we call them Alarms. Sometimes they concern fires to be doused, and sometimes . . ." The smile faltered, then faded. "Sometimes of dangers that require preemptive action. Sometimes we are required to start fires."

The Oculus didn't look too happy about that part of the job. "Preemptive how?"

"Figuratively speaking, it shows me a lit cigarette butt in a woods, then shows me a foot grinding it out."

"How about a little less figuratively?"

"It's not the sort of thing I wish to discuss. At least not yet. Let's talk of other matters."

"Okay, then. So those three cockroaches were worshipping the Otherness?"

"Not directly. The Otherness neither needs nor wants worshippers. No Otherness religion. It prefers to work sub rosa, through other religions."

"Okay, but what did those guys expect to get in return for slicing up Cailin?"

The Oculus shrugged. "Who can explain beliefs? Some people are sensitive to the Otherness and, wittingly or unwittingly, do its work. The results are satanic cults and fanatical offshoots of established religions."

"The Islamic nuts."

"Goat humpers," Miller said.

The Oculus shook his head. "Not just Muslims. Look at the Crusades. Religious zealots are fertile ground for the Otherness. Ironic, isn't it. The fanatics think they're serving their religion when all the while they're strengthening the means of its ultimate demise—pushing closer to the destruction of all religions. Nine-eleven provided a bonanza for the Otherness . . . the deaths, the pain, the terror . . . a nectar of chaos to feed it."

"Sounds like it's winning."

The Oculus nodded. "It is, I'm afraid. Here, in this Home building, lives a squad of the Ally's firefighters, part of its army on earth, protectors of the Oculi and warriors against the Otherness. But it's a shrinking army."

"Don't tell me you can't find any abandoned children."

"No, that's not the problem. There are fewer Oculi than ever as well."

"Which means what? The Ally's losing interest in this place?"

Part of Jack hoped that was true. Maybe he'd get his life back. But then another part of him quailed at the thought of humanity—and that meant Gia and Vicky and the baby—facing the Otherness alone.

The Oculus looked away. "Perhaps. I can't be sure, and I can't explain it, but that is what I sense."

"Maybe it's found a more interesting marble for its collection. Like Jupiter or Saturn. They're a lot prettier."

"No, only living worlds are prized. It's almost as if the Ally thinks we're dying here, and so it devotes less and less attention to us. Perhaps because it's seeing less and less activity."

Jack couldn't buy that.

"Humanity's bigger and more active than ever."

"I said *seeing* less activity. For the past three years someone has been systematically killing the Oculi, and many yeniçeri along with them."

Now came Jack's turn at shocked silence.

This explained the yeniçeri paranoia. And he had a pretty good idea who they feared.

"Is the person behind this—?"

The Oculus's hand shot up. "Do not name him. He knows when his name is spoken and seeks out the speaker."

Jack had heard this before. It struck him as Harry Potterish, but he respected the sources and so he abided.

"Okay. The one I'm thinking about . . . his name begins with R, am I right?"

The Oculus nodded. "It's safer to call him 'the Adversary.' "

"Where's the Sentinel while all this is happening?"

Jack had been told, but he wanted to see if these folks knew.

The Oculus gave his head a sad shake. "No one knows. He hasn't been heard from for almost half a millennium. No one has an explanation."

Jack had been told that someone named Glaeken used to be the Defender, or Sentinel as these folks called him, but he was just a man now—an old man with no powers. But Rasalom didn't know that. And Jack hoped he never found out, because he guessed that being the Heir meant he'd have to step into Glaeken's shoes should the need arise.

The Oculus said, "But how do you know of the Adversary?"

"We've met."

Jack heard sharp intakes of breath from the Oculus and Davis.

Miller said, "He's shitting us. Or if he isn't, it proves he's not the Heir. The Adversary would never let the Heir live."

Jack shook his head. "He says killing me would be doing me a favor . . . would spare me some misery to come."

Jack's stomach clenched and unclenched in the ensuing silence. He remembered Rasalom's words. How could he forget? They'd been branded on his memory.

Physical pain is mere sustenance. But a strong man slowly battered into despair and hopelessness . . . that is a delicacy. In your case, it might even approach ecstasy. I don't want to deprive myself of that.

He'd lost the last two surviving members of his family in the past month. Was that what Rasalom had meant by "slowly battered into despair and hopelessness"? Jack had been depressed afterward. But hopeless? Despairing? Not even close.

Jack didn't know how, but he was convinced that Rasalom had been behind those deaths. Maybe not directly responsible, but involved. The result was unrelenting rage—at Rasalom, and at the Otherness.

"What's he like?" Davis said.

"Just a guy. He doesn't wear a cape or have a vulture sitting on his shoulder. Pass him on the street and you'd never give him a second thought. Just an ordinary, everyday guy . . . until you look in his eyes and he lets you see what's going on in—"

"Daddy?"

Jack glanced to his right and saw a chunky preteen girl standing in the doorway. She had blond hair, blue eyes, a pimple on her chin, and an open book in her hands.

"What is it, Diana?"

"Can you please help me with this algebra problem?"

The Oculus smiled. "What were you told about interrupting meetings?"

She looked down. "Sorry. But I'm just not getting it."

"It's hard at first, I know. Keep trying. I'll be in as soon as I finish here."

She smiled. "'Kay."

When she was gone the Oculus turned back to Jack.

"My daughter. I took her out of school when the Adversary began killing off the Oculi. Now I homeschool her." He smiled ruefully and shook his head. Jack couldn't read those eyes, but he sensed the man's love for his daughter. "I never realized what an awesome responsibility it was."

"What about her mother?"

"Dead. A fire in a Midwest Home. The Oculus there and her son—our son—were killed. I had taken Diana to raise, so she was spared. But our boy . . ." His mouth twitched. "He would have taken his mother's place had he lived, just as Diana will take mine, but . . ."

Jack wondered about that. Diana had normal blue human eyes. Would she develop her father's black eyes as she got older?

Whatever. Jack had had enough of this for now. His scars still itched but had stopped burning. He still had questions, but he felt too much like a prisoner here. He needed to walk free, get back to the real world, feel New York City pavement beneath his feet.

He stood.

"Okay, you help your daughter while I—"

The Oculus shot to his feet. "You're not leaving!"

"That's the plan."

"But there's so much I wish to know! About the Sentinel—"

"Wouldn't know him if I tripped over him." He turned toward the door. "Bye."

Miller stepped in front of him.

"Not so fast. You'll go when he says you can go."

Jack turned to the Oculus, checking Davis's position as he moved. Close enough for Jack to land a side kick to his knee hard enough to bring him down if it came to that. Miller wouldn't be so easy. Miller wouldn't be easy at all.

And of course, they were armed and he wasn't.

Better be cool.

"Am I a prisoner?"

"No, of course not, but—"

"Then I'd like to go."

"But you were led here for a purpose—to join us."

Right. He'd get on the sign-up line right behind Godot.

"I'm not much of a joiner."

"But there's so much we need to discuss."

"We'll make a play date. Now, can I leave peacefully or do things have to get ugly?"

The Oculus sighed. "Very well. But please come back."

Jack wanted a repeat too, but more on his terms. Not as a captive audience.

"We'll work something out."

He turned back toward the door but Miller still blocked it. He glared past Jack at the Oculus.

"Are you out of your mind? He knows all about us now. We can't let him go!"

"We can," the Oculus said. "And we will."

"This guy's a fake. He's not the Heir."

"But he is."

"What have you been smoking? The Heir will come from the yeniçeri."

And then Jack got it. If anyone was going to be designated the Heir, Miller had expected to be him.

"Hey, Miller," Davis said. "Cool it."

Miller pointed at the Oculus. "I signed on to protect him. That doesn't mean I have to kiss his ass. This is a bad move and I take no responsibility for any damage this guy winds up doing."

He turned and stomped out of the room.

Jack turned to Davis. "You have some things of mine, I believe."

Davis nodded. He looked embarrassed. "Yeah. Come on. I'll get them for you."

9. Jack walked a circuitous route from the warehouse, stopping every half block to check for bird-dog action. He didn't spot anyone and was eventually satisfied that he was on his own.

Not necessarily a good sign. They'd bugged him once. Why not again?

A direct route to the car would have run two blocks at most. Jack stretched it to six. When he reached the Crown Vic he stopped long enough to retrieve the TD-17 from the glove compartment, then resumed his walk.

As he moved he turned on the detector and immediately got a positive for an RF signal. But that could be coming from anywhere around him. He turned down the sensitivity until it stopped, then wanded himself with the little gizmo. No response. He notched up the sensitivity and tried again. Still nothing. He kept pushing it up until he found a signal, but it didn't seem to be coming from him. Most likely RF pollution.

Okay. Maybe he was clean. The only way to be sure was to run a check in the car.

He trotted back, hopped in the front seat, and watched the indicator light as he shut the door. It went dark. He opened the door again and it lit. Just pollution. He started the car and avoided the area around the warehouse as he headed back to the BQE.

Not a bad morning's work. He'd come to Red Hook to learn a little more about the yeniçeri and wound up learning a lot. He'd also wound up with a bruised scalp and a sprained neck. Small price.

Still had a lot of questions though.

Like who had started the yeniçeri. He had a feeling being a yeniçeri was both a day job *and* a night job. So who funded their training and paid their expenses?

But a bigger question—the biggest—was about this Heir thing. He'd heard from more than one source that he'd been drafted into this war. He'd hated the notion then and liked it even less now that he was being called the Heir. Heir to the Sentinel's job? What did that entail? How did you defend against a cosmic force like the Otherness? It all seemed so crazy.

Maybe being Sentinel meant going toe to toe with Rasalom.

Not a comforting thought. Rasalom had been creepy the first time Jack had met him, but the second time he'd been downright scary. So much more powerful—walking on water, paralyzing with a gesture.

How am I supposed to stand up to that?

The whole hero thing made him queasy. He wasn't a hero. He didn't want to be a hero. Okay, for Gia and Vicky and the baby he'd be a hero if the need arose, but as for the rest of humanity . . . he didn't want that responsibility. Couldn't handle it. He was just Jack. Just a guy.

Even worse was the knowledge that his life was no longer his own. Every move seemed scripted. Even this morning. The Oculus had come right out and said it.

You were led here for a purpose—to join us.

Was that the way it worked?

But how? The creeps just happened to snatch the niece of a regular at Julio's, a guy who was sure to ask Jack for help. So he gets involved. And because of that he crosses paths with the yeniçeri. They all play cat and mouse for a while, culminating in Jack's arrival at the warehouse.

You were led here for a purpose—to join us.

Led by whom? Did the Ally use Otherness types to do its work, or was it the Otherness pulling the strings? Would his involvement with the yeniçeri somehow disrupt whatever unity they had—there didn't seem to be a whole hell of a lot of that as it was—and lead to the death of the Oculus?

It made him dizzy.

Why me? What's so special about me?

The BQE was stopped dead, so he took surface roads. While waiting at a red light he turned on his phone and found a message from Abe. He had more news. That meant they needed another face to face.

Two in one day. Wow.

10.   "All you've got to do is get yourself to South Florida," Abe said. "From there everything will be taken care of."

During the few hours they'd been apart Abe had accessorized his wardrobe with a mustard stain on his white shirt and a sprinkle of powdered sugar on his black pants.

"Can you be a little more specific than 'taken care of'? What's going to be taken care of and by whom?"

"My Balkans contact. We'll call him Mischa for now."

"For now?"

"With his real name, of course I trust you. But him, I don't know. I've vouched for you but that doesn't mean he'll want you to know the name his mother gave him. If he does, he'll tell you. If not, it's Mischa. Professional courtesy."

"Gotcha. All right, I'm down in South Florida. What next?"

"Before you go I'll be given the number of a slip at a marina in Palm Beach. You go there first thing Tuesday morning and the owner of the boat in said slip will take you across to the Bahamas and drop you off on West End, one of the out islands."

"How far is that?"

"About seventy miles. He'll be piloting a sport fisher that can make the trip in three hours."

"Déjà vu."

"Yes. Reminds you of a similar trip you made with your brother last month, I'll bet. Only this is much shorter."

Right. Bermuda had been 650 plus. After that, seventy was around the corner.

"From said island you'll be ferried into New Providence where one of Mischa's associates will sneak you aboard a cargo plane."

"Not in a crate I hope."

"Not so bad as that, but a pretty stewardess you shouldn't expect. Brown bag it if you want to eat."

"Seems kind of roundabout, don't you think? Why don't I just call the Ashes and have one of them fly me straight to the Bahamas?"

"Because this is the way Mischa wants it done. It's the procedure he uses for moving certain commodities back and forth between here and Sarajevo or Kosovo. Everyone knows their parts. Like a well-oiled machine it works. He doesn't like to mess with a winning formula."

Jack shrugged. He understood. Perfectly.

"Okay. It's his show. The plane takes me to Bosnia-Hurtslikegonorrhea. Then what?"

"Not so fast. You're expecting a nonstop? Don't. The first plane takes you to Nouakchott International Airport."

"Jeez. Where the hell is that?"

"Mauritania."

"Swell."

"Less than an hour you'll be there. Then it's onto another cargo plane to Sarajevo. *That's* when you'll be crated up. Another of Mischa's associates will get your crate through customs and truck you to a warehouse where you'll meet Mischa himself. And that's when you'll pay half the fee."

And a hell of a fee it was.

"He's agreed to take Krugers, right?"

"Yes. Of course." Abe smiled. "They're as good as gold."

"Ha-ha. How long am I there?"

"A day, two at most. Mischa will settle you into your new identity, get you through immigration, and you will fly to JFK tourist class on Bosnia Airlines."

"And that will be it."

"That will be it."

"Next week I'll be Mirko Abdic."

"Next week you'll be Mirko Abdic."

Something squeezed in Jack's chest.

11. A customer for Abe's real line of merchandise came in so Jack left them to their dealing. His headache had faded but still nagged him. His stomach felt sour.

This called for a beer.

He was halfway to Julio's when his cell phone rang: the man himself.

"Julio. Just on my way over."

"Maybe you shouldn't, meng. One those gun guys from last night showed up."

Jack stopped walking.

"The big one or the smaller?"

"Smaller."

Davis.

"What's he doing?"

"Just sitting at the bar, drinking a draft. He let me pat him down. Say he don't wan' no trouble. He's clean but I dunno. I look outside, don't see nobody, but maybe you better stay away."

Hell with that. Julio's was his hang and he wanted a beer in Julio's.

"See you in a few."

If it had been Miller he might have thought twice, but Jack had sensed a core of decency in Davis. Question was, what did he want? Talk? Okay, Jack could talk. He still had questions.

But just the same, certain precautions were called for.

He made a slow approach to Julio's, checking all the cars and nooks and crannies. But he didn't stop there. He ambled a block past the front door, still checking.

No one. At least no one he could make.

As he stepped inside he spotted Davis at the bar. He wasn't in his suit and was just polishing off his draft. Without breaking stride Jack tapped him on the back and motioned him to follow. He led him to his rear table where he assumed his usual back-to-the-wall position, eyes on the door. Davis pulled out a chair opposite him and dropped into it. He thrust out his hand.

"Cal Davis."

Jack shook it. "Jack. What are you drinking?"

"Stella. Didn't expect to find it on tap in a dive like this."

Dive . . . Julio would have liked that. He worked hard keeping his place a dive. And Davis had passed the first test: He didn't drink Bud or—God forbid—Bud Light.

Jack signaled to Julio for two Stellas, then leaned toward Davis.

"I hear you want to talk."

"Yeah." He ran a hand across his short blond hair and put on an affable smile; Jack didn't know how real it was. "Interesting morning, huh?"

"Very. What do we talk about?"

The beers came then and Davis lifted his in a toast.

"To lots of interesting mornings."

Jack had a sense that Davis was trying to soften him up, charm him. Jack wasn't in the mood for charm.

"Interesting is personal. And it's something of a curse to the Chinese."

Another smile. "Touché."

"Talk."

Davis sighed. "Nothing too serious to say. Just want to see if I can persuade you to throw in with the MV."

"I gave my answer."

"I know." Davis lost his smile and leaned forward. "But 'I'm not a joiner' doesn't cut it. This isn't about you or me or the Oculus. The stakes in this battle go way beyond us. They impact on everyone you know and love."

"You don't get it: I've never worked with anyone. I don't know how. I'd be more of a hindrance than a help."

"That's a cop-out." He jerked a thumb back over his shoulder. "Your Puerto Rican friend behind the bar, the one who's got one eye on me and the other on the sawed-off he keeps under the bar. He and everything he knows and loves are at stake. How about your attachments? Got a girlfriend, a wife, kids?"

All of the above—sort of. But wasn't about to tell Davis.

"My business."

He shrugged. "Fair enough. I don't see you doing the Ward Cleaver or Jim Anderson thing, but what—?"

"Let me ask you something," Jack said. "The Oculus—and speaking of the Oculus, does he have a real name? You know, like Joe or Tom or Fred? I don't see his mother leaning out the back door shouting, 'Ocky, dinner's ready!'"

"His mother was an Oculus, and she did have a name for him. But as with all Oculi, that fell by the wayside once he assumed the role. We address him as Oculus but out of earshot he's 'the O.'"

"Okay. The O says I'm the Heir. What exactly does that mean?"

Davis gave him a wide-eyed stare. "You mean you don't know?"

Jack was sick of hints—he wanted a full explanation. Maybe he could squeeze one out of Davis.

"Nope. Heir to what?"

"Why . . . the role of Sentinel."

"And just when does that happen?"

"Should something happen to the Sentinel, something final, you will step into the role."

"Swell." That was what he'd gathered. "But I'm just a regular guy. I can't fight the Otherness . . . or the Adversary."

"When you're elevated to the part, you'll be changed. You'll have . . . powers."

Jack didn't want powers.

"All right. How many of these Sentinels have there been?"

"Only one."

Jack blinked. "One? That would mean he's . . ."

"Immortal. Right."

This was crazy. But then, everything had become crazy. The world he knew now was not the world he'd grown up in.

Davis added, "Immortal in the sense that he can't age. But not invulnerable. He can be killed."

Jack shook his head. Me? Immortal? He couldn't buy it. It was the stuff of fantasy novels, and he didn't like fantasy novels. Never happen.

"What planet are you from, Davis?"

"This one. But I've peeked behind the veil—and so have you—and seen the real world, the one that's hidden from the vast bulk of humanity. We both know truths that would drive many of them over the edge."

"Maybe we're over the edge."

But Jack didn't think so. He'd fought through a ship full of nightmares, seen glowing bottomless holes in the earth, and fought the frightful things that rose from one of them.

"We're not. But you not knowing you're the Heir . . . makes me wonder if the Oculus might be mistaken."

Jack tried not to sound hopeful. "Why's that?"

Davis frowned. "The Heir is supposed to be molded since birth to be the Sentinel. That's why we've always assumed he'd be one of the yeniçeri."

Here was an opening Jack had been waiting for. He pounced.

"But aren't all you guys, in a way, molded from birth to be something?"

"Yeah, but the Heir would be different. He would face the Otherness and come away scarred but alive." He stared at Jack's chest. "You fit the scarred part, but . . ."

"But I haven't been molded."

"I gather not."

Now the question Jack had wanted to ask ever since he'd seen the Oculus's eyes.

"Who molded you?"

Davis shifted his gaze to his beer. "Two wonderful, inspiring men."

"Are they related?"

Jack had started to say, "Were" but switched to the present tense at the last instant.

Davis's head snapped up. Suspicion sparked in his eyes.

"Why do you ask?"

Jack shrugged. "No particular reason. Something in your tone . . . like they're a father-son team or something."

He held his breath, hoping Davis would open a door by saying a certain word.

"They were brothers—twins."

And there it was, lying on the table. The Twins . . . Jack had butted heads with them last April.

" 'Were'?"

A nod. "They're gone. The Twins sensed the Otherness preparing for a major coup and went to put a stop to it. Neither has been seen or heard from since."

For a few seconds he was afraid Davis would begin to cry. Jack looked away, not just to cut off the sight of the man's welling eyes, but to keep his own from giving anything away.

The Twins . . . two identically odd-looking ducks in black suits and fedoras and dark glasses. They were gone—for good—because of Jack. He hadn't realized until the end what side they were on. But that wouldn't have changed matters: It had been him or them.

He shook his head. No good guys in this war, just black and different shades of gray.

Davis said, "We always assumed—*they* always assumed—that one of them would be the Heir."

That explained something. Right after their deaths he'd felt a change, as if some mantle had fallen onto his shoulders. He hadn't understood then, but he knew now: The Ally was saying, Okay, they're gone because of you, so you take their place.

"You said they sensed the Otherness preparing a coup. You mean the Oculus, don't you?"

He shook his head. "They had the sight as well."

That explained the weird black eyes he'd spotted on one of them.

"They raised us, trained us . . . they were like foster fathers."

And that explained Zeklos's odd plural when he mentioned losing his fathers.

"That's another reason you should throw in with us. We can protect you."

Jack had to say it: "Like you did the Twins?"

Davis's eyes flashed. "They tended to operate on their own. Sometimes they'd bring yeniçeri along, but they saw themselves as a two-man team. If we'd been along maybe they'd still be alive. They wouldn't let us protect them, but you . . . we can take your back."

"It's not me I'm worried about."

Davis smiled. "So you don't live in a vacuum after all. You have people you care about. Who?"

"You'll never know."

"I don't care to. But look at the big picture: By joining us you could make the world a safer place, and that means safer for them."

A low blow, but one that hit home.

On the other hand, from what he'd seen so far, these guys didn't seem much of a threat to the Otherness. The Ally needed a better team on its side if it was going to beat the Adversary.

"What makes you think you're having any impact?"

Davis rubbed his jaw. "I'm sure we didn't impress you last night, but we lost our center and a good deal of our focus last spring when we lost the Twins. Your involvement might center us again."

"And what would Mister Happy Face say about that?"

Davis smiled. "Miller? He'll hate it. He's headstrong and impulsive, and flies off the handle too easily, but he's dedicated to the cause. You've only seen his dark side."

"Right. Like he's got a light side."

Davis frowned. "Well, come to think of it, if he does, I've never seen it. But he'll go along with whatever the Oculus and the majority decide."

"But I shouldn't turn my back on him?"

"Like they say, you can choose your friends but you can't choose your family. Miller is family—all yeniçeri are brothers—so I won't bad-mouth him. He's got his faults. One of them happens to be a vicious streak about a mile wide, but he's an in-your-face type. Your back will be safe. It'll be your front you'll have to watch."

Davis finished his beer and grabbed Jack's empty mug. "This round's on me."

Jack leaned back and watched him as he headed for the bar. Something likable about Davis, something trustworthy.

But he couldn't see joining the MV and working with them. Couldn't see himself working with anybody.

But that was the old Jack. And the old Jack was about to disappear and reemerge as Mirko Abdic.

Maybe Mirko Abdic would need something like the Militia Vigilum.

Jack didn't know. He decided not to make a decision either way. He'd temporize with Davis—make no promises but not slam the door—and think on it.

Everything, it seemed, was changing.

12. Gia shook her head and bit her lower lip. " 'The Heir'? I don't think I like the sound of that."

"We're on the same page there."

They sat on the Chippendale sofa in the Sutton Square library that also served as a TV room. A *Seinfeld* episode that must have been in its ten-thousandth rerun was playing, but no way Jack could dredge up any interest. Same for Gia.

"So, if this Sentinel dies, you'll be taken away from us?"

The words stunned Jack. He hadn't seen it that way. Davis had told him he'd be changed, given powers . . .

"No way I'll leave you."

But would what he valued and cared about change as well?

She clutched his arm and leaned against him. "Even so . . . let's hope this current Sentinel, whoever he is, lives another couple of thousand years."

Jack couldn't tell her that he'd been told that the current Sentinel—so far the only Sentinel—had retired from his job and his immortality, and was nearing the end of his days.

So it was only a matter of time.

Jack resisted the urge to jump up and start kicking holes in walls. His life was no longer his own, goddamn it. He hadn't signed up for this. Why couldn't the Ally have chosen someone who was slavering for it? Like Miller.

"But what if he *is* killed?" Gia said. "What if you have to take his place? What will you do?"

"Absolutely nothing. If nominated, I refuse to run, if elected I refuse to serve."

"Passive-aggressive isn't your style."

"What else can I do? In this case the only way I can fight back is to refuse to participate."

"But if you're needed—if the Otherness starts something only you can stop—are you just going to sit back and watch? That's not you."

Jack sighed. She was right. He couldn't see himself doing that. Especially if it endangered Gia and Vicky and the baby.

"But that's all speculation at this point," she said. "This Militia Vigilum you told me about is here and now. What are you going to do?"

Jack trusted his instincts and they said *Avoid*. But he'd learned to trust Gia's instincts as well.

"If you were choosing for me, what would you say?"

She pursed her lips and didn't speak for a few seconds. Then she let out a breath.

"I'd give them a try."

Jack winced. "Ouch." If he'd known she was going to say that he wouldn't have asked. "Why?"

"Purely selfish, personal reasons. I know you're a lone wolf. I know you don't like to explain things. I know you like to act on instinct if something goes wrong and you can't do that if you have to explain it to someone else. I know you think the risk of something going wrong is directly proportional to the number of people involved."

Jack smiled. "So you *have* been listening."

"Of course. And all that said, I still hate you working alone. Just like I hate you traveling to Europe alone."

"I won't be alone. Abe's contacts—"

"You don't know them and they don't know or care about you. If signals get crossed or a connection is missed, you'll be alone in a foreign country where you don't speak the language and don't have any papers."

Jack had thought about that, and the bad-news possibilities formed a cold lump in his gut. But he couldn't let Gia know.

"I'll be fine."

She shivered against him. "Maybe you shouldn't go. Maybe there's another way."

"Maybe there is, but Abe has spent months setting this up and I trust him like I trust you. But getting back to the MV, they won't be any help to me in the Balkans."

"I was thinking on a more day-to-day basis. Your methods are like walking a high wire without a safety net. This MV group could be your safety net."

Jack cleared his throat. "The problem with a safety net is that it's a very human tendency to be less sharp, less focused if you know it's there. You might become a smidge cavalier about falling because hey, no biggie . . . the net's there to catch me. Net or not, I don't want to fall. Ever."

"Okay, here comes the personal, selfish part: I'd worry a lot less if you had something, someone to fall back on."

"Kind of a moot point, isn't it. I'll be pretty much retiring from fix-its once I become Mirko Abdic."

"But you can't retire from this war you've been drafted into." She bit her lip. "Maybe this invitation to join the MV is a sign."

That took Jack by surprise. He leaned back and looked at her.

"A sign? Since when do you believe in signs?"

"Why not? I never believed in ghosts until one tried to kill the baby. I never believed anything like the Lilitongue could be possible, but it was only a few weeks ago that it invaded this house and wouldn't leave. So why not believe in signs?"

A wave of guilt swept over him as he considered what she'd been through because of her relationship with him.

"Case made. In spades. But what makes you think it's a sign?"

She raised her shoulders in half a shrug. "I'm not sure. The timing, I guess. Becoming Mirko Abdic . . . it will give you a legal identity, make you a card-carrying citizen. You won't be a lone wolf anymore. You'll be a member of a pack, part of something larger than yourself."

"Yeah. I know." That had been the hardest thing to accept about this whole plan. "But let's get back to signs. What does the MV have to do with my new—?" And then he saw it. "Joining something larger than myself. And the MV is another larger something."

He found the symmetry vaguely unsettling.

"Right. So even if you're no longer Repairman Jack, you're

still involved in this insane war. That's not going to stop, and it's not something you can take on alone. It might wind up that you need them and their Oculus as much as they need you."

"I don't—"

She punched him lightly on the arm. "Come on, Jack. Even the Lone Ranger had Tonto."

Maybe she was right, but he couldn't see himself becoming a card-carrying member of the MV.

"I'll think on it."

"Give it a try. Mix with them awhile. If it's not a good fit, you walk away. If you think it has possibilities, you hang on awhile longer. Where's the downside to a trial run?"

Good question. But it didn't make the decision any easier. He guessed he'd—

"Mom! Mom!" Vicky came running in holding out her right fist. "Look what happened!"

She opened her hand to show them.

At first Jack didn't know what he was looking at: white, boxy, smaller than a Chiclet, with reddish discoloration on one side. Then he recognized it.

A tooth.

"It just came out!"

Gia gripped Vicky's jaw. "Let me see. Is this the one that's been loose?"

Vicky nodded as she opened wide and stuck the tip of her pinkie into an empty socket in her left upper jaw. "Righ' 'ere."

"That's great, honey. Looks like you made another five dollars."

Vicky grinned. "No, this one's worth ten. At least!"

Jack slapped his forehead. "Ten bucks for a tooth? Where are the pliers? I'm going to pull all mine out and—"

"It's only for teeth that *fall* out, silly."

"Yeah, but ten dollars! The Tooth Fairy only left me a quarter when I was a kid."

Gia gave her daughter a sidelong look. "You got only five dollars for the last teeth."

"Yeah, but those were incisors and canines. This is a molar. It's worth double."

Incisors and canines . . . how did she know this stuff?

Gia smiled. "Where does it say that?"

"In the Tooth Fairy Rule Book."

"Well, if you can show me that, I'll believe it. Otherwise I think the Tooth Fairy will think five is plenty."

"Aaaw."

13.   Jack hung around until after Vicky went to bed. They gave her half an hour before creeping upstairs to check on her. They found her curled into a ball under her covers, her long-lashed eyes closed, her hair, released from its braids, fanned out like a dark cloud on her pillow. The picture of innocence.

Gia gently slipped her hand under the pillow and extracted the tooth from its resting place. Then she pulled a five-dollar bill from her pocket.

"You're not giving her ten?" Jack whispered.

Gia smiled. "Five's plenty. She knows there's no Tooth Fairy but she's a little operator who likes to see how far she can push the game. Don't worry. She expects five, so she won't be disappointed."

Jack felt his throat tighten as he watched her slip the bill under the pillow. Everything pointed to dark days ahead. He had to find a way to protect these two—make that three—from whatever was coming. But how?

He felt leaden and inadequate as they tiptoed out of the room. Maybe he should look into the MV. Maybe they'd have a way.

"Meet you downstairs," Gia said. "I have to make a quick trip."

"To 'sprinkle'?"

She smiled. "Yes, but don't worry—I don't have diabetes."

"So I've been told."

As Gia stepped into the bathroom, Jack fished a five out of his pocket and tiptoed back into the bedroom where he added it to the stash under Vicky's pillow. As he turned and started back out, he heard a little voice behind him.

"Thanks, Jack."

14. After he got home, Jack sat by his front window and watched the sidewalk across the street. He stayed up till after midnight, but the watcher never showed.

SUNDAY

I. Cal Davis watched Miller yawn.

"Tired?"

Miller gave him one of his patented flat stares. "What do you think?"

They sat at a card table, playing gin. Cal had just won the latest round, but they'd been fairly even through the night. The *long* night. He glanced at his watch: 7:30. Only half an hour left to the shift. He probably looked as tired as Miller.

"I think I'm glad. I hope you're exhausted."

Miller's stare morphed into a glare. "What's that supposed to mean?"

"Just what I said. Because you're the reason we've had to go to twelve-hour shifts."

"Bullshit."

No—truth. And Miller knew it. Sending Zeklos down to the minors had screwed up the customary eight-hour rotation. They'd already been too shorthanded to do that right, and the loss of Zeklos had tipped the apple cart.

The Oculus killings and attendant yeniçeri losses had thinned the ranks—and not just by death. Some of the less devoted members of the corps had turned tail and run. For a while those who remained had hunted them down and terminated them, but now they didn't have enough manpower for that.

"We could have kept Zeklos for guard duty and just not sent him out on ops."

Miller snorted. "He'd have found a way to mess that up too."

Cal shook his head. "You're really something, man."

"And as for the shift change," Miller said, jabbing a finger at him, "the twelve-hour deal works out better. Sure we're stuck with longer shifts, but now we've got more flexibility. We might even be able to start taking vacations again."

Cal heaved a mental sigh. Vacation . . . when was the last? Long, long time. That had been in Aruba. He'd found an array of unattached women down there. A true paradise.

Maybe Miller was right. Maybe the twelve-hour rotation would work out.

The door chimed. Miller rose and checked the video monitor.

"Well, well, well. Look who's here."

"Zeklos?"

"No. The Oculus's new best friend."

"The Heir?"

Cal suppressed a grin as he jumped up and joined Miller at the monitor. Yep. Here he was, waiting on the step.

His talk with Jack yesterday must have worked. Cal had come away thinking he'd failed—miserably. Talking to the guy had been like having a heart-to-heart with a wall. Hadn't shown the slightest trace of interest. Either he had an A-class poker face, or something had changed his mind.

"You can call him that," Miller said. "I think he's a phony. What's he doing back here?"

"The O invited him, remember? And so did I."

Miller wheeled on him. "You?"

"Yeah. Tracked him down yesterday and pitched him on throwing in with us. My silver tongue must have worked its magic."

"You mean your shit tongue. I thought we were done with this jerk."

"Buzz him in."

Miller shook his head. "Let him cool his heels."

Cal reached past him and pressed the door release.

"Now."

2. Jack was about to hit the CALL button again when the lock buzzed open.

He gripped the knob with a gloved hand, but hesitated to turn it.

Big decision, this. Joining up with these guys, with any guys . . . it didn't feel right. He'd thought on it all night and had arrived at the conclusion that Gia had a point: The Otherness was too big to face alone. So where was the downside of giving it a try? If he didn't like it, or they didn't like him— Miller, he was sure, had already made up his mind about that—he'd walk away. At least he'd have given it a shot.

He rubbed his chest with his free hand. The burning and itching had returned, but not as severe as yesterday. Maybe the scars were getting used to the place.

He turned the knob and heard a bell as he pushed through. Took his eyes a few seconds to adjust from morning sunshine brightness to the dimmer light within. When they did he found himself facing Davis and Miller and two more yeniçeri he hadn't seen before. Davis and Miller had empty hands, but the other pair had their pistols out as they moved his way from the partitioned rear of the space.

Davis gave them an all-clear wave. "It's okay, guys." Then he turned to Jack with a smile. "Welcome back."

Miller scowled. "What are you doing here?"

Jack looked at him. "And a gracious good morning to you too, Mister Miller."

"You didn't answer my question."

"Back to have another tête-à-tête with your fearless leader. You okay with that?"

Miller said nothing but his scowl deepened.

Davis turned to one of the yeniçeri. "Tell the O that the Heir is here."

As the guy headed for the stairs, Jack heard a chime. Davis stepped back and looked at what Jack assumed to be a monitor, then jabbed a button.

The lock buzzed, the bell rang as the door opened, and in stepped Zeklos.

Miller threw his hands in the air. "The rat-faced boy joins the bunco Heir. Now my day's complete."

Zeklos's eyes darted back and forth, hunting for a friendly face, or at least one not overtly hostile. Jack felt sorry for the little guy.

"Zeklos," Davis said, his expression neutral. "What's up?"

"I am going to Idaho camp."

"Fuck!" Miller shouted. "You hear what he just said?" He pointed at Zeklos. "That's why you're outta here!"

Zeklos took a step back. "What? What did I say?"

"You just mentioned the location of a training camp!"

"But he is Heir."

Jack said, "And 'Idaho' isn't exactly a pinpoint location."

Miller's pointer swiveled toward Jack. "You stay out of this! This is a yeniçeri matter!"

"A bully is a bully, yeniçeri or not."

Miller took a step forward. "You mind your own fucking—"

"Easy," Davis said, grabbing a tree-trunk arm. "Can't we all just get along?"

While Miller gave Davis a long, hard glare, Jack glanced at Zeklos and found the little guy staring at him with an odd look in his eyes. Jack could almost read his mind: First this guy returns my gun, then the Oculus calls him the Heir, and now he sticks up for me.

Although that hadn't been Jack's intention—bullies just plain pissed him off—he figured he'd made a friend. Zeklos appeared to be on the outs with everyone else here, but he still might prove to be a source for another slant in the workings of this enclave.

Finally Miller turned back to Zeklos.

"If you're going back to camp, what are you doing here?"

"They cannot take me until next week."

"So?"

"So . . ." His Adam's apple bobbed. "So, until that time, I do not have anyplace else to go."

"Let him hang around," Davis said.

Miller gave him a disgusted, you-are-such-a-pansy look and turned away.

Jack shook his head. The MV sure as hell looked like it needed some leadership. Wasn't anyone in charge here?

The yeniçeri who'd been sent upstairs returned.

"He wants to see him right away."

"Shit," Miller said, shaking his head. "Okay, but we pat him down first."

"I don't think so."

"Sorry," Davis said. "No one but yeniçeri are allowed to be armed in the presence of the O."

Jack thought about that. Not unreasonable. For now.

"Okay." He pulled the Glock from the small of his back and his PK-11 from his ankle holster. "But this is the last time I give up my iron. I'm either trusted or I'm out of here."

Miller flashed his non-grin. "Then you're outta here."

"That'll be up to the O," Davis said. "Let's go."

3. The Oculus met them at the door to his office, smiling as he shook hands with Jack and fixed him with an inky stare.

"I'm so glad you decided to join us."

"Not quite yet. There's still a lot I want to know."

He ushered Jack into the room.

"Of course, of course. That's only right and sensible."

The four of them situated themselves as before: The Oculus behind the desk, Jack in the chair, Davis and Miller on flank.

"What do you want to know?" the Oculus said. "Simply ask and I'll tell you whatever I can."

Jack leaned back. "Davis and I had a little talk yesterday and he told me about the Twins. Who were they, where'd they come from, where do they fit in all this?"

The Oculus steepled his fingers. "I'm not sure."

Here we go with the evasions.

"I thought you were going to answer my questions."

"I can tell you only what I know. No one knows much about the Twins—they weren't exactly forthcoming about their origins or their mission. But I'll tell you what I've pieced together over the years."

"Fair enough."

"As I told you, the yeniçeri were started by the Sentinel back in the First Age, and he maintained them from prehistory through the Dark Ages. For some unknown reason he abandoned them in the sixteenth century. The Oculi stayed on watch, but for five hundred years they received virtually no Alarms. During that time the yeniçeri ranks withered due to lack of need."

Jack gestured left and right. "Looks like some folks didn't get the message."

"That's where the Twins come in. They appeared seemingly from nowhere in nineteen-forty-two and restarted the yeniçeri camps."

"Why then?"

"I wasn't an Oculus then, but my parents were, and they told me they'd both sensed something awakening in the world, something they'd never felt before in their lives."

A disturbance in the Force? flashed through Jack's head, but he decided it might be impolitic to share it.

"Can you be a little more specific?"

The Oculus shook his head. "No, because they couldn't describe it. Neither could the other Oculi, but they all felt it on the same day: May third, nineteen forty-one."

"Obviously something happened that day . . . way too early for Pearl Harbor . . . doesn't anybody know what?"

The Oculus shook his head. "For years we conducted detailed studies of that date, in all countries, all cultures, but have found nothing. It had something to do with the Otherness because, after centuries of dormancy, it became active again. Every Oculus sensed its renewed activity. Then, less than a year later, the Twins appeared and began gathering recruits for the yeniçeri."

"But that means there was no Militia Vigilum then. So who put out the fires?"

"For decades after the Twins' appearance there were relatively few, but gradually increasing in number. While the yeniçeri were growing and learning, the Twins did the firefighting themselves. They always wore sunglasses, white shirts, and black suits, ties, and fedoras. They'd show up, take care of business, then leave. They tried to be discreet but were spotted often enough to spawn the myth of the 'Men in Black.'"

Jack smiled. "So, the Men in Black had no connection to UFOs or the CIA."

"Not in the least. The first new generation of yeniçeri was trained and ready when we—the Oculi and the Twins themselves—sensed a brief explosion of Otherness activity somewhere on Long Island. The date was recorded: February eleventh, 1968. The Twins and a squad of yeniçeri from this

Home fanned out through the island but the source faded quickly and was gone before they could locate it."

An explosion of Otherness on Long Island . . . not the first time Jack had heard about that. He knew the location: the village of Monroe. He also knew that a cluster of deformed babies was born there nine months later. And Monroe was where the Twins had bought it last year.

But he couldn't say so. They'd want to know how he knew, and no way he could tell them.

"So," Jack said, trying to keep all this straight, "the Sentinel disbanded the yeniçeri but the Oculi stayed on watch. Why is that?"

A shrug. "Who is to say? Although we share a common goal, we Oculi operate independently of the Sentinel."

"Who's been AWOL for five hundred years. Any chance he might be dead?"

Jack heard a sharp intake of breath from Davis and a grunt from Miller.

"If he is," Miller said, "then you're a fake, because the real Heir would have already taken his place."

"He's not dead," the Oculus said. "I sense his presence . . . but so faintly. He's still with us, but I don't know where. And I don't know why, in this dark hour, he hasn't shown himself and given the Ally's disciples someone to rally around."

"Morale's pretty bad, huh."

"None of your business," Miller said.

Jack glanced at him. "It wasn't a question."

The Oculus shook his head. "We are losing by inches. I don't understand the Adversary's strategy. Killing off the Oculi limits the Ally's vision in this world, but in no way diminishes its power. But I sense it may be just a part of a multifaceted long-range plan."

"Maybe killing you off is a bigger part than you think," Jack said. "As I understand it, he's also killing off the MV. The combination means fewer eyes to spot the fires, and fewer firemen to put them out."

"That is why we live in the equivalent of an armed fortress. It used to be we could . . . could . . ."

He wavered in his seat like a drunk.

Davis stepped forward and leaned on the desk. "Is it an Alarm?"

The Oculus covered his black eyes with a trembling hand. "Yes."

Davis turned to Jack. "A warning from the Ally."

Right. The timing seemed just a bit too convenient. He knew the guy was trying to sell him on joining up, and Jack had been listening. But if he thought—

With a cry the Oculus fell out of his chair and landed on the floor. He began to writhe, shake, and shudder.

Jack jumped to his feet and started toward him, but Miller put out a restraining arm.

"Leave him be."

"Yeah," Davis said. "It's like this every time. We have to let it run its course."

4. The Alarms are always silent, yet they never come alone. Pain is their devoted companion. This is why he dreads them. Icy blades stab his brain as lights strobe behind his squeezed lids. He feels the world tip beneath him and, though he instinctively reaches for the edges of his desk, he knows he's going to fall.

A scene leaps into view . . . an empty subway platform . . . smoke roiling from one of the tunnels . . . on the tiled wall: WEST 4TH.

That fades to gray . . .

Then his inner vision lights with a street scene. He recognizes the New York Public Library in the background. A sudden burst of flame and flying debris obscures the building as a bus explodes.

More gray . . .

Then another subway with another smoking tunnel. He makes out 59TH ST on the wall.

Yet more gray . . .

Then a man standing in the center of the crowded main floor of Grand Central Station . . . the man explodes, the blast tearing those nearest to pieces, the ball bearings and nails and screws he embedded in his explosives dropping those farther away.

Gray . . .

And then a car midspan on the Brooklyn Bridge . . . it explodes . . .

Gray again . . . much longer than before . . .

And now half a dozen men in the front room of a shabby apartment . . . they are cramming bars of claylike material into the pockets of work vests . . . through the glass of the window behind them a bridge is visible over the roof of the building across the street.

And then the pain fades along with the light and the visions . . . and all becomes dark again.

5. Jack listened with a growing sense of dread as the Oculus described his visions.

When he'd stopped his seizure and come to, Miller had helped him back to his desk where he now sat, looking pale and shaken.

"They're . . . they're going to paralyze the whole city," Davis said in a hushed tone.

Jack agreed. Subway nexuses like West 4th and 59th Street, a bus, a railway center, a bridge . . . and those might be just a sampling. But even if they were the whole plot, these bombings would affect the entire city—much more so than the London bombs affected the Brits. Those hadn't played out against the backdrop of the fall of the Trade Towers or the LaGuardia Massacre. New Yorkers didn't have the history of terrorism the Brits had suffered from the IRA. Millions of people, afraid to step on a train or a bus, would stay home. The city would grind to a halt.

Miller kicked a wall. "Where do we find these fucks?"

"I . . . don't know."

That set Jack back.

"You don't *know?* Last time you told them Cailin's exact location."

The Oculus had the heels of his palms pressed against his temples.

"You have to understand, these Alarms are like short-wave radio. The reception isn't consistent. Sometimes it fluctuates and the images fade in and out. Reception last time was excellent: I saw the intersection, saw the front of the building, saw the cellar door. But this time . . ."

"You said you saw a man in a room . . . anything about the

room that'll give us a clue? Like, if maybe he belongs to Wrath of Allah?"

The Oculus lifted his head. "Wrath of Allah? Why them, rather than Al Qaeda?"

Jack didn't want to get into the personal score he had to settle with Wrath of Allah.

"They did LaGuardia. It's the same kind of MO."

The Oculus shook his head. "No, no posters or anything. Just a room . . . bare walls . . . wait. Out the window, to the left, I saw a bridge—and not too far away."

"The Brooklyn?"

"No, it was arched, two levels—"

Davis and Jack spoke in unison: "The Verrazano."

Jack said, "Day or night?"

"Day. Bright sunlight outside."

"Where was it angling from?"

"From above and behind it, I think . . . no, I'm sure. The side toward me was in shadow."

Jack said, "Could be Bay Ridge."

"Yeah," Miller said softly, menace edging his voice. "Lots of mosques in Bay Ridge. And only a few miles from here."

But something about this bothered Jack.

"So am I to take it that the Ally is anti-Islam? Pro-U.S. and anti-Arab? When did it become politicized?"

Miller laughed. "Yeah, that's right—the Ally is a Republican."

The Oculus cleared his throat. "The Otherness feeds on anything that causes fear, pain, and discord. As does the Adversary. The Ally warned us about nine-eleven, but we weren't able to find the culprits in time."

"You mean you didn't call it in?"

"Of course we did—to the FBI, the CIA, the NYPD—but we didn't know who or when. So our warnings were ignored. Obviously."

"Why did the Ally choose you? 'Cause you're in New York?"

"For major conflagrations, all Oculi receive the same vision. For minor occurrences—like the girl—only I, being the nearest, would receive that Alarm. In the nine-eleven matter, a number of us in the Eastern states donated yeniçeri to the search."

Miller held up a thumb and forefinger, a quarter inch between them. "Missed the fuckers by this much."

"Oh, what a feast that must have been for the Adversary," the Oculus said. "I was also shown the pain and fear caused by the terrorism in Iraq after the conquest, but there was nothing we could do to prevent that."

As awful as 9/11 had been, the LaGuardia Massacre had had much more of an impact on Jack's life.

"What about LaGuardia?" Jack said. "Were you warned about that?"

The Oculus lowered his gaze to the desktop. "In a way."

"But you couldn't prevent that either?"

"Prevent it? No."

"We *can* do something to prevent this," Davis said. He turned to Jack. "You with us?"

This was all moving too fast. He'd come here to learn a little more about these folks, but now he was being pressured into joining them on an operation.

He didn't like it, but how could he say no?

These bombings would hurt the city more than 9/11 and LaGuardia combined. Unlike Jack, the city had already bounced back from LaGuardia. In both cases people could tell themselves that they worked in a bagel shop or a bookstore or a sweatshop and that no one was going to fly a plane into those places, or hose them with machine-gun fire. The average Joes and Janes could figure they were too small-time to be a target.

But this tactic would have a wider effect: If the subways and buses and trains and bridges they rode on every day could be blown up, so could they.

If the Oculus's visions were real and true—and Jack still needed convincing on that score—he couldn't walk away.

"Let's just say I do tag along. What's the plan?"

Miller's smile flickered on and off. "Simple. Find 'em, finish 'em, and forget 'em."

"Like in that cellar the other night?"

"Right."

Davis said, "Except there's a lot more at stake here than a little girl."

Jack saw the *find 'em* part as a major problem. He turned to the Oculus.

"How much time do we have?"

"I don't know. The visions have no time sequence. For instance, in the matter of the girl, I was shown her after they'd finished with her." He shuddered. "That was what would have happened had we not intervened."

"So we may have a day, a week, a month?"

"I wish I could say. The nine-eleven warning came on September second."

Jack had a feeling this warning would be equally fruitless. Finding an Arab terrorist cell in Bay Ridge . . . good luck.

But what did they know so far? The northern flank of the Verrazano Bridge was visible from the cell's window. That narrowed the area to Bay Ridge's western rim.

Not narrow enough. Not nearly enough.

"Are these Alarms ever repeated?"

The Oculus shook his head. "Never."

Swell.

"Okay, can you remember seeing anything else through that window? Anything at all?"

He closed his black eyes and leaned back. "Let me see if I can reconstruct it."

For a while the only sound in the room was breathing, then the Oculus's eyes popped open as he stiffened in his chair.

"The building across the street. I saw the bridge across its roof. It had a redbrick front."

Jack suppressed a groan. Probably ninety percent of the buildings in Bay Ridge had redbrick facing.

"Anything else? A funny chimney, a crazy antenna, a satellite dish—anything to make it stand out?"

"No, just—wait. The cornice! The building had a faded yellow cornice carved with a drape flanked by two inverted hearts."

Jack rubbed his vaguely itchy scars. "West Bay Ridge, in

sight of the Verrazano, across the street from a redbrick building with a pretty specific cornice design." He looked at Davis and Miller. "That sounds doable to me. How about you?"

Davis and Miller nodded.

Jack sighed. Looked like he'd just become a double secret temporary yeniçeri in the Militia Vigilum.

But no black suit. No way was he climbing into a black suit.

6. After they'd finished arguing the suit issue, after Davis and Miller had changed into their uniforms, and after Jack had his heat back in his holsters, they were ready to go.

Davis held out a pair of sunglasses. "At least wear the shades."

Jack had no problem with that. He took them and checked them out, turning them over in his hands. Sleek black frames, slight wraparound.

"Okay. Sure."

"Put them on."

"I'll wait till I get outside."

Davis grinned. "No, try them. They'll surprise you."

Jack slipped them on and—

"Whoa!"

The room had barely darkened. He took them off and checked the lenses, but from the outside they looked impenetrably black. He'd seen photochromic lenses, even owned a pair once, but this was different.

"How do they do that?"

Davis shrugged. "Don't know. They're something the Twins came up with. Pretty cool, huh?"

Jack put them back on and looked around. Almost like not wearing shades at all.

"Hot."

"The O is calling other Homes for reinforcements, but we can't wait."

Jack spotted Zeklos standing off to the side, watching them. The longing look on his face tugged at Jack.

He turned to Davis and jerked a thumb at the little guy.

"What about Zeklos? Why not bring him along?"

Miller overheard that.

"No way. He's out for retraining. Besides, he's a menace."

"But he's got two good eyes," Jack said, and left it at that, hoping Davis would pick up the ball.

He did: "Yeah, Miller. Right now we can use all the eye-balls we can get."

"I told you—"

"Would you be saying that if the Twins were here?" Davis said, showing some heat. "You going to let your personal feel-ings pave the way for another nine-eleven? You want to win this one or not?"

Miller stood silent a moment, staring at Davis, then Jack, then Zeklos, then back to Davis.

"All right. He's another set of eyes, but that's all. He doesn't suit up and if we have to make a move, he stays put."

Davis turned to Zeklos. "That okay with you?"

Zeklos nodded, then glanced at Jack. Something like love glowed in his eyes.

7. After a lengthy, contentious discussion, with most of the heat coming from—of all people—Miller, they yielded to Jack's logic: A four-way split on foot would be the most thorough but would take the longest; pairing off in two cars would allow for only one dedicated observer per car, since the driver had to be watching the street. All four of them in one car would provide three sets of eyes to comb the cornices.

So it came down to Davis driving the Suburban with Miller shotgun, leaving Jack and Zeklos in the back.

Jack studied a Brooklyn map as they drove to Bay Ridge. He couldn't see how anyplace east of Sixth Avenue could have the view of the bridge the Oculus had described, so they started near the waterfront at Shore Road and Fourth—on the edge of John Paul Jones Park—and began working their way upriver and inland from there, snaking a winding course along the streets and avenues.

Bay Ridge was a typical New York melting pot. People of all races, all shapes and sizes. The usual delicatessens, tae kwon do studios, travel agents, restaurants, bars, and bodegas lined its streets. A BP gas station, a limo service, Domino's Pizza. Jack noticed a store awning that proclaimed itself a Tea Room and sported Arabic script.

While they waited at a red light at 99th and Third, two women wearing scarflike hijabs crossed in front of them, each pushing a baby carriage.

Miller said, "Oh, yeah. This is the place."

Davis turned onto Third Avenue. "I think we're too close to the bridge here."

Jack agreed but didn't feel the need to say so.

They were making progress, but to Jack it seemed maddeningly slow. If only they knew how much time they had.

To his right, Zeklos peered out his window, studying the edges of the passing roofs. Jack kept a look out his side but also kept an eye ahead. Not an easy task with Miller's hulking carcass jammed in front of him.

They kept doing their switchbacks, working the grid. On Third Avenue, between 92nd and 93rd, ahead and to the left, Jack spotted a three-story redbrick building with a cornice that might fit the Oculus's description. He wouldn't know until they were closer.

He nudged Zeklos and pointed. The little guy looked, then turned to Jack, eyes wide. Jack nodded and pointed to the front seat.

Zeklos hesitated only a second, then he leaned over the seat and pointed through the windshield.

"There is something!"

Davis slowed the car and craned his neck for a look. Miller leaned forward, doing the same.

"You know," Davis said, "that could be it. Good eye, Zek."

Zeklos glanced at Jack and said, "It was really—"

Jack gave him a hard nudge and shook his head.

Miller growled. "If he spotted it, you know it's wrong."

"Pull over," Jack said.

Davis stopped in an empty space before a fire hydrant and idled. Jack jumped out and looked at the building that faced the cornice. They could have been twins—three-story, brick-fronted apartment houses, but the second lacked a cornice.

He leaned close to Davis's open window.

"Give me your cell number."

Davis jotted it down.

"Okay. Drive around and keep looking while I check this out."

"Since when does he give orders?" he heard Miller say.

Jack walked away before he heard Davis's reply.

A mini-mart advertising Te-Amo cigars and lottery tickets occupied the building's street level. The residential door stood to the left. He stepped up onto the front stoop and began pressing random call buttons. Finally a tinny voice spoke from the speaker.

"Yes?"

Jack pressed his hand over his mouth and pushed a garbled mishmash of syllables through the fingers.

"What?"

He repeated the mishmash.

"Fuck it!"

The buzzer sounded and he pushed the door open. Once in he bounded up the stairs to the roof door. It warned that an alarm would sound if he opened it, but he couldn't find any contacts. He pushed it open and . . .

Silence.

To assure he wouldn't get locked out, he took off a shoe and used it as a wedge. Then he walked to the parapet and stared at the roof across the street.

The scene matched the Oculus's description: redbrick front, drape-and-inverted-heart cornice, and beyond that, angled to the south . . . the Verrazano Bridge.

The Arabs were somewhere below his feet. He hoped they belonged to Wrath of Allah . . .

He felt the darkness well up inside at the thought of them. He wanted—*needed*—to get one of those sons of bitches alone and extract a little information.

He unclenched his fists and let out a long slow breath. That could be dealt with later. Maybe. Right now . . . step one completed.

Jack called Davis. "I think we've found it."

"Excellent!"

"What's the next step?"

Jack knew what his next step would be, but he thought it best to let Davis and Miller think he was deferring to them.

"Come on down and we'll figure it out."

Not what Jack had in mind.

"Fine, but I don't know if I can get back in. How about this? I hang around up here and see if anyone goes in or out."

"But you don't know the apartment."

"The building's got four per floor: two front and two back.

The only place you can see the roof across the street is from the third floor. That puts our guys in one of the two front apartments."

"And if someone comes out?"

"You guys grab him or follow him or whatever you think you should do." Jack hoped they'd follow him. "You any good at bird-dogging?"

"Miller's the best."

Jack nodded to himself. Okay. He'd planted the *follow* seed.

Davis said, "What if someone goes in?"

"Then I come downstairs, let you in, and we pay them a visit."

"Sounds like a plan. Hang on." Some muffled conversation followed—Davis obviously had his hand over the speaker—then, "Okay. We'll try it for a while. But if nothing happens, we'll bust in."

"Which one?"

"Both."

"Okay. And hey, send Zeklos up with a pack of cigarettes."

"What the hell for?"

"I need an excuse for hanging out in the hall."

8.   Ten minutes later Jack opened the front door for Zeklos, who handed over a pack of Marlboros.

Jack stared at the pack. "Filtered? I want manly, unfiltered ciggies—Camels, Lucky Strike, Pall Mall."

"I do not think they make those anymore in this country."

As Zeklos turned to go, Jack grabbed his arm. "Hey, why don't you keep me company?"

Zeklos glanced at Jack, then back to the street.

"Miller told me drop these off and come right back."

Jack raised his eyebrows. "And your point is . . . ?"

Zeklos paused, then nodded and gave Jack a buck-toothed grin.

"Yes. Fuck Miller."

They headed up to the third floor where they sat on the chipped tile and leaned against the wall near the top of the stairwell. A mélange of sounds and odors swirled around them: a little opera, a little hip-hop, an argument, a child being scolded, frying bacon, boiling cabbage, sautéing onions.

Jack opened the Marlboros and offered one to Zeklos.

He shook his head. "No, thank you. I am quitted."

"I never really started, but we've got to look like we have a reason for hanging out in the hallway."

Zeklos took one and stuck it in his mouth. Jack did the same, then pulled out a disposable butane lighter.

"If you are quit, how do you have lighter?"

Jack shrugged. "Never know when you're gonna need fire."

He lit Zeklos's, then his own, and took a drag. And got a head rush. And coughed.

"Now I know why I never liked these things."

He'd simply pretend to inhale.

Zeklos lowered his volume. "Can I ask you something?"

"Go ahead."

"Okay. I want to know . . ." He seemed hesitant. "I want to know what is your amusement."

"Amusement? Oh, you mean game?"

"Yes. That is it. You stop me from killing me, but you take my, um, metal, which make me feel worse."

"Well, I didn't want to have wasted my time."

"I understand. But then you return it."

"Because it was yours, and I figured if you were still alive by morning you'd most likely stay that way."

Jack didn't mention the part about messing with his head.

"But then you take my part this morning, and then you ask me to come along to search. Why is this?"

Jack had felt genuinely sorry for him, but that hadn't been the whole reason. He needed an asset, and Zeklos had been part of the inner circle before being pushed outside. Might be more forthcoming than the others if Jack needed more information.

And Jack had one more reason.

"Well, I haven't known Miller long, but I do love pissing him off."

Zeklos laughed. "I like you . . ." His voice trailed off. "What should I call you? 'Heir'?"

"You do and you're going straight back to Miller. Jack will do just fine."

Jack figured they'd seem less suspicious if they jabbered about something while they waited. So he started an ersatz argument over the relative merits of American football versus Romanian football—known over here as soccer.

They were each on their third ciggie—making sure to pocket the butts—when a young brunette, her waitress uniform visible within her open coat, stepped out of an apartment to their left. She stopped in her doorway, giving them a wary look.

"Sorry about the smog," Jack said with what he hoped was a reassuring smile. "My sister won't let us smoke in her place."

She said nothing as she locked her door and hurried past them to the stairs.

Jack crossed 5C off his mental list.

Halfway through cigarette number six, with Jack's tongue taking on a funky feel, his TracFone vibrated. He pulled it out and checked the readout: Abe.

Must be important. Abe usually left voice mail unless he had something that couldn't wait.

"Gotta take this."

Why not? He wouldn't say anything meaningful to anyone else.

Zeklos shrugged.

"Hey, Abe. What's up?"

"Just heard from my Balkan associate. Tuesday's the day."

"So soon?"

"Why wait? You want I should put him off? May be a while before he can line up all these ducks."

"No, I guess not." The day after tomorrow. Scary. "Tell him to expect me."

"Your first leg starts at six a.m. The location of the dock slip I'll give you later. The reason I'm calling is you'd better make plans to fly out tomorrow so you can be bright-eyed and bushy-tailed Tuesday morning."

"Okay, Abe. I'm a little tied up today."

"On a Sunday you work? You should be resting for your trip."

"Bye, Abe."

As Jack cut the connection, a swarthy type with a close-cropped beard stepped out of 5A. Jack gave him a careful once-over. The guy wore a snug blue nylon warm-up. No tell-tale bulge of a loaded vest.

He closed his door and glared at them.

"You are not to be smoking out here," he said with a thick accent.

Jack decided on a more New York response than he'd offered the waitress.

"What's it to you, pussy face?"

The guy flinched as if he'd been slapped, but quickly recovered.

"You could start a fire."

Yeah, he thought. Bet you're extra worried about a fire.

"Yo, Achmed, I'll start a fire in your ass you don't shut up and get outta my sight real quick."

The guy's lips tightened but he said nothing. Instead he double-locked his door and stomped down the stairs.

"Hey," Jack said, nudging Zeklos. "What say we order some takeout?"

Had to be careful what he said because his words would echo down the stairs.

Zeklos caught on immediately. "Of course. Pizza would be very good at this time."

Jack dialed Davis's number.

"Yo, Angelo's? Need a large pie to go."

"What?" Davis said. "Jack?"

"Yeah. Pie to go. You deaf?"

"I assume you're telling me someone's coming down."

"You got it."

"We'll be ready."

"Okay. And don't lose my order."

Jack flipped his phone closed and stared at the door to 5A.

Zeklos whispered, "We should go in?"

Jack thought about that. "Let's wait a little. Maybe someone else will show."

9.   After twenty minutes of nothing but thinking about his impending trip to the Balkans he decided the time had come to give the door a try.

He signaled Zeklos to draw his weapon and crouch to one side of the door. Glock ready, Jack crouched opposite him and knocked.

No response.

He knocked again. Harder.

Nothing.

One more time: "Hello? Falafel-gram!"

Had to be empty. Who could resist that?

He pulled on a pair of thin leather gloves. Time for the autopick.

The two Yales yielded quickly. Now what?

Zeklos raised his eyebrows. "Booby trap?"

Jack shrugged. Made sense: Blow up their explosives if the wrong person found them. But would the door be boobied, or just the explosives inside?

Jack thought back to the bearded guy as he'd come through the door. He hadn't been particularly careful as he'd shut it. He'd even jiggled the knob after keying the locks. A good sign, but it didn't mean a whole helluva lot.

Had to risk it. The stakes were too high.

He waved Zeklos away. "Get back by the stairs. I'm going to peek inside."

Zeklos shook his head. "No. You get by stairs. You are Heir."

No time to argue about it. Jack turned the knob and eased the door in a fraction of an inch, then another, and another . . .

Finally it opened enough to allow a sliver-view of a ratty

couch. A little further and he saw the whole couch, then the window. He stepped to the side and gave the door a gentle push. It swung in on creaky hinges, revealing an empty front room.

Jack signaled to Zeklos and they both went in low, pistols before them. Two bedrooms to the left—empty.

Except for pizza boxes, burger wrappers, and scattered papers, the damn apartment was empty. No sign of explosives, no primers or timers. *Nada.*

Jack prayed they were in the wrong place.

He positioned himself before the window and looked out. He saw the north edge of the Verrazano to the left, the drape cornice of the brick building across the street, just as the Oculus had described. But no plastique-stuffed vests.

Zeklos pointed to the side wall. "Look at this."

The scrawl had registered with Jack as he'd entered but he'd had other things on his mind. He checked it out now.

Giant-size Arabic script had been scribbled with a black Sharpie. It meant nothing to Jack.

"You read that gibberish?"

Zeklos shook his head. "I have enough trouble with English."

Jack pawed through the debris looking for diagrams, photos, timetables, a list of names, a computer, anything that would provide a hint of whatever they'd planned. But these weren't amateurs. They knew better. Keep it in your head.

But Jack kept rummaging. Wouldn't feel right if he blew off any possibility.

He came across a pair of calendars—last year's and this. He flipped through the first and found occasional time numerals combined with Arabic scrawl. Probably meeting times. No help there. In the later one the January page had a few notations in the first two weeks, then a blacked-out box.

The fourteenth.

And no notations after that.

Jesus!

"Tomorrow's the day! Got to be. They're out there with their vests and their car bombs right now."

Made sense. Monday morning rush hours were the worst of

the week. If you wanted to wreak maximum panic and damage, that was the time to do it.

Shit.

Jack thumbed the recall button on his phone. Davis answered.

"That guy who left here," Jack said. "Tell me you're still on him!"

"Better than that. We've got him—as in Miller's standing here with his foot on his neck."

"He wearing a vest?"

"No. What's the problem?"

"The apartment's empty."

"That's okay. He led us to the stash. You wouldn't believe what they've got here."

He gave Jack an address on Richmond Terrace in Staten Island.

10.

"Guy didn't have a clue he was being followed," Davis was saying. "No decoy maneuvers, nothing. Led us a straight shot over the bridge to here. Even unlocked it for us." He gestured around him. "You believe this?"

Jack didn't want to believe what he was looking at.

He and Zeklos had headed for the island as soon as they found a cab. Something about the Richmond Terrace address rang a bell, and then Jack remembered that one of last year's more interesting customers had a business there.

Richmond Terrace ran along Staten Island's north shore. A heady mixture of brine and fumes filled the air. At its southernmost end it started off scenic and well kept, with waterfront promenades and views of the Manhattan skyline. But it rapidly deteriorated from there, devolving into junkyards and chop shops and plumbing supply warehouses sprinkled among the piers and dry docks. Between the tugboats and through the forest of cargo cranes along the waterfront, the northern stretches offered a breathtaking view of Bayonne's tank farms just a short hop across the river.

A truly desolate stretch of road—overgrown fences, rotting wharves, graffiti-scarred buildings, potholed pavement—a place where small businesses come to die.

Jack's instincts had told him it might not be a good idea to have the address logged in the cab's record, so he'd told the driver he didn't have an address and to cruise Richmond Terrace until they saw the place they were looking for. When they'd passed the address—a self-storage cubicle farm—he let the cab drive on until they reached Sal's Salvage, Inc. They'd got out there and walked back.

North Shore Self Storage occupied a waterfront plot that

used to be a dry dock—some of the docks and bays still remained. After finding the yeniçerimobile in the parking lot, he and Zeklos had searched around until they spotted Davis standing in front of one of the units. He'd rolled up the corrugated steel door to let them in, then rolled it three-quarters down after them.

Jack instinctively reached to remove his new sunglasses and realized he didn't have to. They'd adjusted to the lower light.

He stared at the four black, fifty-five-gallon drums arrayed on the concrete slab, then turned to Davis.

"Tell me they're not full of—"

Davis nodded. "Yeah. Semtex A."

Zeklos gasped. *"Dumnezeule!"*

Jack didn't know what that meant, but it probably echoed his own shock. His gaze wandered to the bound-and-gagged figure on the floor. Miller stood over him.

"What do we know about him?"

Davis shrugged. "His license says he's Shabbir Something-or-other at the address where you spotted him. But who knows if that's legit."

Probably as legit as Jack's license.

"Why the gag?"

Not as if the guy was going to yell for help.

Miller said, "Couldn't stand listening to any more of his Allah bullshit."

Allah . . .

Jack knelt and ripped the duct tape from the guy's face, taking a fair amount of beard with it.

"Hey! Shabbir! You with Wrath of Allah?"

He spat at Jack. "I am a soldier of God! I am of the Omar Sheikh Martyr Brigade!"

"Never heard of it."

Davis said, "Omar Sheikh is the animal who beheaded Daniel Pearl on videotape. The Pakistanis sentenced him to hang for it, but they haven't got around to it yet."

Jack stared at Shabbir. "How can he be a martyr if he's not dead?"

"The traitors are offering him up to appease America!"

Jack shook him. "Forget that. Wrath of Allah—the ones who gunned down those people at LaGuardia. What do you know about them?"

"They too are soldiers of God! They are heroes!"

Jack remembered the litter of dead he'd seen around the baggage carousel—remembered one death in particular—and wanted to throttle this piece of crap. With no little difficulty he resisted the impulse and jammed the duct tape back over his mouth.

"What do we do now?" Zeklos said.

"We?" Miller shook his head. "There is no 'we' as far as you're concerned. Just me and Davis."

"Don't forget Jack," Davis said.

A glare was Miller's only reply.

"I don't know about you guys," Jack said, "but I think the best course is to tape him up, take off, and call the feds."

Miller sneered. "Yeah, right. So they can take him to the Gitmo Country Day School and give him a special diet and a Koran and a cleric and an ACLU asshole to hold his hand. You know how I'd handle these guys—the few who somehow survived? They'd get a cinderblock box smaller than this, no window, and a hole in the floor. And special diet? They'd get a special diet: Every day I'd whip them up bacon for breakfast, sausage for lunch, and pork chops for dinner—no substitutions, please. Eat or starve."

"You wouldn't get any argument from me," Davis said. "But we're not at Gitmo and this guy obviously isn't working alone. The feds can use him to find the rest of his posse."

"We don't need to find his posse." Miller waved his arms at the drums. "We've got their toys, and without their toys they can't play."

Jack said, "The Oculus saw them stuffing vests with plastique."

Davis pointed to the corner. "They're over there. Six of them packed full, salted with one-inch wood screws and ready to go. But that's small-time stuff. Take a look at this."

He led Jack to the nearest drum and lifted its lid. Jack

looked inside. He saw reddish gunk up to the three-quarter level. A cell phone lay on top. A wire ran from the phone into the gunk.

Jack felt a jolt of alarm as he leaned over the rim. He knew that wire led to a detonator or two.

"I hope to hell that phone is turned off."

"It is. Every barrel's rigged like this. And don't worry, I made sure all the phones are off."

"Then they're all set to go."

Jack could see how it would go down. They load the drums into car trunks, stall the cars on bridges near a support or mid-shaft in a tunnel or two, hitch a ride away, and then call the rigged cell phone. The ringer sends a current to the detonators and *BLAM!*—collapsed tunnels, and bridges with severe structural damage.

And rampant panic.

Jack said, "The Oculus saw suicide bombings, but these are rigged for remote detonation. Which means they're probably saving the suicide vests for the buses and subways, *after* they've blown the cars."

Davis was nodding. "And that means they don't have bod-ies to spare. They've got half a dozen vests here. Probably means only half a dozen in their cell."

"Smart," Jack said. "Keep it small. Keep it tight. Fewer chances of a leak or a screw-up."

Davis turned back to Miller. "Jack's right. This is way too big and too well planned for our little crew. We're stretched to the limit as it is. We've got to turn him in."

Miller shook his head. "I'm sick of jawing about this."

He kicked the Arab onto his belly and stomped hard on the back of his neck. Jack heard the *crunch* of shattering verte-brae. The guy twitched once and then lay still.

"Now *you're* a martyr," Miller said.

Jack felt nothing for the terrorist. He didn't know how much blood he had on his hands when he died, but he'd have been bathing in it if he'd had his way. And if Jack had found out that he'd been part of the LaGuardia Massacre, his own foot would have been on that neck.

"For Christ sake, Miller!" Davis shouted. "That's the second time—!"

They all jumped as the dead man's cell phone began to ring.

"Must be Allah calling to tell him he ain't getting his seventy-two virgins."

Davis was still fuming. "Why the hell did you do that?"

Miller's lips parted into what he probably thought was a beatific smile. Not quite.

"I just want peace is all. You know how I hate arguments. And now there's nothing to argue about."

This is why I work alone, Jack thought.

11.   Jack listened to Davis and Miller dicker to a compromise: They wouldn't call the feds yet; instead they'd watch the storage area and make the call when the terrorists showed. Miller wanted a vantage point far enough away that they wouldn't be seen and scare them off.

"That way we nab them all," Miller said. "I'll feel better about that."

Jack was thinking about how long it would take the agents to get to Staten Island from the FBI field office in downtown Manhattan. On a Sunday night, with flashers going, pretty damn quick. Even quicker with a copter.

After surveying the lay of the land they decided the best watch nest was the roof of a ten-story apartment house about half a mile inland. It promised a clear view of the storage lot and of this cubicle in particular.

If tomorrow was indeed detonation day, the terrorists would have to load up today or tonight. More likely tonight.

They left Miller to watch the cubicle while Jack, Davis, and Zeklos raced to Red Hook for field glasses and food for the surveillance. Jack pulled his handy-dandy tool kit from his trunk, then the two of them headed back to Staten Island sans Zeklos.

"I had to side with Miller this time," Davis said. "Zek's not going to contribute anything to the surveillance, so he shouldn't be along."

Jack said nothing, but the lost look on the little man's face had followed him all the way back to the car.

The apartment building was a brick-faced, low-income box. Getting in was easy: Someone had broken the lock on the front entry doors and so they waltzed right through.

The door to the roof, however, presented a problem.

NO EXIT
ALARM WILL SOUND

Jack checked its edges and found the magnetic contact sensor along the top. It had been crudely installed, leaving the wires exposed.

Davis grunted. "Probably works about as well as everything else in this place. That is, not at all."

"I wouldn't want to count on that," Jack said. "This is too important."

He heard a metallic *snikt!* behind him. He turned and saw that Miller had flicked open a knife. The overhead light reflected off the four-inch blade.

"Just cut the wires and forget about it."

Jack grabbed his arm as he raised the knife.

"That'll only work on an open-circuit model. This is probably closed."

Davis frowned. "So what?"

"Open circuit means there's no flow-through of current. The circuit is held open by the magnetic contact on the door. Opening the door removes the magnet and the circuit snaps closed, sending a signal to the alarm. Cutting the wires works just fine for them. But the closed-circuit model has continuous flow-through. Cut the wires and you're busted. Almost everything's closed circuit these days. How come you guys don't know this?"

Davis shrugged. "Stealth isn't a big part of our MO."

"So what do we do?" Miller said. "Stand around with our thumbs up our asses while those Islamic turds load up their cars?"

"We can jump the wires, but that takes time. So let's try this."

He opened his tool kit and checked through the side pockets until he found a quarter-size disk. He held it up.

"This little doodad is an NIP magnet—don't ask me what the letters stand for. The important thing is there's ten pounds of lift in this baby."

He slipped the disk between the magnet and the sensor. It

snapped up against the sensor, keeping the circuit closed. Jack pushed open the door.

"We're in business."

He turned to find Davis and Miller gawking at him.

Davis pointed to the tool kit. "What's that? A Felix the Cat bag? What else've you got in there?"

"This and that."

Miller's eyes narrowed. "You've got your uses, mister. But where'd you learn so much about burglar alarms?"

"Heir school. Let's go."

12.   Jack adjusted his stiff, cold fingers around the field glasses. His eyes burned from staring through the powerful lenses. Davis had brought along a Leica Duovid model. The 12× magnification gave a clear view of the Arabs' unit but the image swam with the slightest movement. He had to rest his elbows on the parapet to steady the binocs.

Six hours of taking turns watching the storage farm and still nothing. The sun had quit early, but the half moon in the cloudless sky gave aid but no comfort. A chill wind had sprung up, ferrying damp salt air from Newark Bay, making surveillance a frosty chore. So much so that they took half-hour shifts on the parapet, with the off pair huddled on the stairwell to keep warm.

At least the cold would keep Shabbir's body from stinking. They'd stowed it under a blanket in the rear of the Suburban. Didn't want the discovery of his earthly remains to spook Allah's henchmen before the feds could catch them.

If not for the cold he might have enjoyed the view. Not for what he could see of Staten Island, but what was around it: the Statue of Liberty and the glow of Lower Manhattan . . . sans the Trade Towers. Despite the years, Jack still hadn't acclimated to their absence. And here he was, on the lookout for members of the same tribe of shits responsible.

He shook off the rage. That wasn't the way to go now. Anger was a great fuel but also a distraction. No cowboy stuff tonight. They had to do this right.

Jack checked his watch: nine minutes to go before his turn for a warmth break. He rubbed his eyelids, then fitted them back into the eyepieces. He'd become so used to seeing no activity that it took a few seconds for his brain to register the battered sedan pulling into the self-storage lot.

It did two slow circuits under the lights of the empty lot before stopping. A short, swarthy male got out and looked around.

Jack adjusted the focus. This could be it.

After a moment or two the guy started up one of the lanes, but not the one with Shabbir's unit. Jack wasn't ready to give up on him. The guy was playing it smart, moseying around to see if he had company. The unanswered calls to Shabbir had to have shaken up the cell.

Jack watched the guy wander up and down a number of aisles before stopping at the unit in question. More furtive looks around and then he bent over the combination lock. Seconds later he was rolling up the door.

Got him. But only one. Had to be at least four more to account for the six vests.

The guy stepped inside. A flashlight beam flickered on and off a couple of times, then he stepped back out and got on a cell phone.

A minute later three more rust buckets wheeled into the lot. Had to be them.

Jack trotted over to the door to the stairwell and pulled it open.

"They're here."

Miller was the first out. He grabbed the binocs as he dashed past. Jack and Davis followed him to the parapet.

"Well, well," Miller said, peering through the Leica. "Will you look at this."

"I'd love to," Davis said, "but you're bogarting the glasses."

Miller didn't seem to hear. "We've got four dune monkeys walking toward our deceased friend's bin where a fifth awaits."

"How're they acting?" Davis said.

"Real cautious." Miller lowered the glasses and handed them to Davis, then fished in his pocket. "Time to call the Fibbies."

"Tell them to hurry," Davis said as he peered through the

glasses. "We might have to step in if they don't get here in time."

Jack glanced at Miller and watched him hold down a single button on his phone. He'd put the FBI on his speed dialer?

And then Jack realized what was going down.

He reached for Miller's phone. "Miller! No!"

But too late.

The night sky turned to day as a deafening blast shook the building and almost knocked them off their feet.

Jack watched a ball of flame mushroom into the sky, lighting up the whole north shore and Bayonne as well. The self-storage farm looked like Ground Zero. He could feel the heat from here.

Miller grinned into the flames. "Oops."

"You son of a bitch!" Davis shouted.

Jack saw how it had gone down. While he'd been waiting alone Miller had turned on one of the phones, copied down the number, and entered it into his speed dialer.

Jack's shock yielded to fury.

"Do you have any idea how many innocent people you just killed, you bastard?"

Miller shrugged. "Maybe a couple, maybe none. It's Sunday night on Staten Island's North Shore. Think about that."

"Even one is too many."

In the fire's glow Miller's expression was serene. "Hey, we're making a world-saving omelet here, know what I mean? You gotta step back and see the big picture. You can't do that, you don't deserve to be the Sentinel."

Davis bared his teeth. "You shit!"

Jack wanted to take Miller's head off.

"You just vaporized five assets that could have been squeezed for intelligence—could have led to more creeps like them. Might even have given up info on Wrath of Allah."

"What's with you and this Wrath of Allah? That's like the third or fourth time you've brought them up. You got some kind of hard-on for them?"

Jack wasn't about to explain. He didn't owe Miller anything.

"You remind me of them—killing noncombatants for what they think is a higher cause."

Miller sneered. "Now I know you're not the Heir. You're too much of a pantywaist to be the Sentinel."

Jack stepped closer to Miller. Davis grabbed his arm.

"Don't. That's just what he's looking for."

Jack shook him off. Miller's opinions meant nothing to him.

"I'm cool." He stopped a foot or two before Miller and looked up into his flat gray eyes. "Tell me something, Miller. You've said a couple of times that you thought the Heir should come from the yeniçeri, right?"

"Yeah."

"Let me guess which one of the yeniçeri you think it should be. You?"

Miller's expression lost some of its bravado. "Maybe."

"Okay, Miller. Tell you what: You can have it. I don't want it. It's yours. I now officially declare you the Heir."

Miller looked even less sure of himself. "It doesn't work that way."

"Really? Okay, then, here's a deal: Find a way to transfer it from me to you and it's yours. No strings. How's that sound?"

Miller's mouth worked but he had nothing to say. He looked flummoxed, as if he couldn't conceive of anyone not wanting to be the Sentinel. Pretty obvious he hadn't expected anyone to offer it to him.

"My only reservation about giving it to you is I worry you'll be worse than the Adversary."

Miller telegraphed his move by a shift in his gaze and a tightening of his lips. Jack ducked the roundhouse right and kicked him in the left knee. Like kicking a concrete pillar.

"Hey-hey-hey!" Davis said, jumping between them. "Maybe there's a time and a place for this, but it's not here! We're done. Let's get back Home."

Jack eyed Miller and Miller glared back. Davis was right. Not the time or the place. Jack wondered if there was any right time or place to face this behemoth. His bulk made him slow, but it also made him hard to hurt.

But not impossible.

Jack noticed with some satisfaction that he showed a trace of a limp as they took the stairs down from the roof.

13. Davis smacked his lips as he slammed down his empty beer mug.

"Man, did I need that."

The ride back to Red Hook had been tense and silent. Along the way Jack had called the FBI. He gave them the address of Shabbir's apartment and fingered him as being behind the explosion.

After dropping Miller off at Home, Davis wanted to go out for a beer. Jack's first impulse had been to refuse. The night had left a bad taste in his mouth and he wanted to get back to his apartment and be alone. He'd had enough of yeniçeri and visions and weirdness for one night. But Davis had practically begged him, saying he wanted to talk. Jack liked Davis, sensed a core of dedication and decency in him, so he finally gave in.

They drove separate cars back to Bay Ridge and found a pub down the street from Shabbir's place. The widescreen TV over the far corner of the bar was running a continuous stream of aerial video of the blast area. No football tonight.

They chose a window booth where they could watch the local frenzy of activity.

The whole block had been taped off. Dozens of FBI-labeled flak vests milled through a delirium of flashing lights.

Jack finished his own beer. He'd needed one too.

"Let's do that again."

As Jack signaled the waitress for another round, Davis leaned across the table and lowered his voice.

"The Fibbies will be all over that place. Make *CSI* look like a food fight. You and Zek didn't leave any trace they can latch onto, right?"

Jack shook his head and took no offense.

"Kept the cigarette butts outside, wore gloves inside. Taught me that in Heir school too."

Davis didn't smile. "Good. If the Oculus's vision was accurate—about loading the vests there—they should find traces of Semtex in the apartment. They can analyze its composition and maybe trace it to the source."

"So? Five'll get you fifty it's Iran." Abe had told him the Iranians were turning out Semtex like pita dough. "What help is that?"

Davis leaned back and sighed. "Not a lot, I guess." He shook his head. "The borders are sieves."

"You think that's the way the Otherness is going? Terrorism?"

A shrug. "Anything that causes terror strengthens the Adversary." He leaned forward again. "And don't forget, this isn't just about America. Terrorism anywhere—Ireland, Iraq, Malaysia—is all food for the Adversary."

"Well then, don't you think that explosion tonight is causing its share of terror?" He nodded toward the TV. "That feed is going nationwide."

Davis nodded. "Yeah, well, I'm sorry about that. It wasn't supposed to go down like this. Miller is—"

"A menace. Something wrong with that guy—sick bad wrong. He's got a piece missing."

"Yeah, but he's loyal and fearless."

"So's Zeklos, but he's being sent to Idaho."

Davis's gaze shifted. "Zek isn't exactly fearless."

"Yeah? How so?"

"Let's leave it at that."

Jack could respect that. He leaned back as the waitress brought them fresh beers. He didn't feel like talking about tonight anymore.

"Okay," he said when she was gone, "honest now: Do you think Miller will ever accept me—not as the Heir, just my presence?"

"Well, he feels only yeniçeri should be in the MV."

"That doesn't answer my question. Will he ever accept me?"

After a long pause, Davis shook his head. "Maybe when they stop rerunning *I Love Lucy*."

That pretty much said it all. Jack turned to a couple of questions that had popped up during the day.

"Do you guys, you yeniçeri, have any lives?"

Davis nodded. "Yeah. It's called Militia Vigilum."

"I mean outside of that."

"You mean a home away from Home. Wife? Kids?" He shook his head. "Forbidden. No *Ozzie and Harriet* scene. Not even a girlfriend. The MV is all the family we need or get."

Jack couldn't see how that was possible.

"You mean you're some sort of monastic order?"

"In a way. But not celibate."

"You said no girlfriends."

Davis smiled. "We're an ancient order, and we take our comfort from a profession even more ancient."

"But how do you spend your free time? I get the feeling it's not fasting and meditation."

"We play cards and checkers and chess while we're on duty. I've become a pretty decent chess player. Want to play sometime?"

Davis's wistful tone prompted a little epiphany: This man was lonely. He'd sacrificed just about everything so he could devote himself to saving the world. Something to be said for that kind of dedication, that sacrifice, that singleness of purpose. Jack had met some rabid environmentalists who thought they were saving the world, but at least they had real lives on the side.

Jack felt for Davis, but not enough to take up chess again.

"Sorry. Gave it up."

His eyebrows lifted. "You're kidding. It's a wonderful game."

"Don't have the patience for it."

Jack had learned that he was too reckless, too impulsive to be a good chess player. Could last only so long before his patience ran out and he started making crazy moves—anything to get a little action going and break the game open. All the care and detail he put into his fix-its deserted him on the chessboard. Maybe it was a matter of real life versus a game.

If he gave into impulses on a fix-it, his skin was at stake; in chess, only some little chunks of wood.

"What else do you do?" he said. "Besides put out fires?"

"We track the Adversary. Sometimes that involves putting out fires, sometimes starting them."

"How so?"

"Well, for instance, in sixty-four A.D. we fought the great Rome fire alongside the official Militia Vigilum. That was when we started thinking of ourselves as a different sort of MV. We'd tracked the Adversary to Rome. To this day we're sure he started the fire, simply to feed on the chaos. But he wound up with a bonus when Nero blamed the Christians and started throwing them to the lions."

"But what about starting fires?"

"The library at Alexandria—we burned that because the Adversary's followers were secretly gathering a collection of dangerous texts there."

Jack wondered if the Compendium of Srem had been among them.

"But those were the old days," Davis said. "Now we watch a lot of TV. Too much, I think."

Jack remembered his references to *Lucy, Father Knows Best, Ozzie and Harriet,* and *Leave It to Beaver,* so he took a stab.

"Let me guess: *TV Land.*"

Davis's eyes widened. "You psychic? Or is that something else you learn in Heir school?"

Jack smiled and shrugged. "Tell me this: Can you quit the MV?"

Davis smirked. "Obviously they don't teach you everything in Heir school."

"Can you?"

Davis shook his head. "Nope."

Jack didn't buy that.

"You expect me to believe that after all this time, all these centuries—"

"Millennia."

"—not one person has quit? Come on. *Somebody* must have."

"Have you ever read an exposé of the MV or the yeniçeri, or even a news story hinting at our existence?"

Jack hadn't.

"Nobody has *ever* quit? Not even one disgruntled ex-member wandering around?"

Davis's face was a mask. "You are either loyal to the yeniçeri code, or you are not."

"And what if you're not?"

"Then you are . . . not." He blinked and shrugged. "But let's talk about something else. As I said, I'm sorry about tonight. But I like the way you handle yourself. Next time we go out—"

"Not going to be a next time."

Davis stared at him. "What? You can't be serious."

"Dead serious. This isn't going to work. Call me anal, but I like doing things my way. I do *not* like other people making decisions for me, even if they mean well, even if our goals are in tune. How I score is as important as the scoring."

"Look. I'll see to it that you never get teamed with Miller again. I can—"

Jack held up a hand. "Won't matter. It simply isn't going to work."

Davis leaned so far over the table he looked as if he were going to climb on it.

"This isn't about you, Jack. It's about everybody. I'm sorry your sensibilities took a beating tonight, but this is too important to let your ego get in the way."

"Nothing to do with ego."

"Then what? We're in the fight of our lives and we're losing. Every day the Otherness encroaches just a little bit more. Each little increment doesn't seem like much at the time, but if you look back you can see how far it's come. Stalin used the tactic in Eastern Europe. He called it 'salami slicing.' In other words, if you grab the whole salami, there'll be hell to pay. But filch a slice at a time and it's barely noticed; and even if it is, no one gets too upset. But keep on filching those slices and eventually you'll have—"

"The whole salami. I know."

"That's what the Otherness is up to. And it's winning. You

know why? Because it's more motivated. The Ally doesn't eat salami, it wants it simply because owning it is part of winning. But the Otherness loves salami—it doesn't just want us, it *needs* us. It'll feed on the negative emotions it can create once it takes over."

"Well, your pal Miller served up some snacks tonight."

"But it would have been so much worse if we hadn't stopped them. And say what you want about Miller, he's out there sweating in the firebreaks, doing whatever's necessary to keep the Otherness from spreading."

"That doesn't excuse—"

"We *need* you, Jack. We've been falling apart since we lost the Twins. Tonight was a perfect example. Miller wouldn't have dreamed of pulling that stunt if the Twins were still around. We need a new center. You—the Heir—you can provide that. You can get us back on track."

Jack felt the walls closing in. Davis was right about the Otherness winning—he felt it in his bones—and the importance of keeping it at bay, but he'd hated tonight. And yet, he wanted access to the Oculus to keep tabs on the big picture.

Things had been so much easier before he'd heard of these people.

He fished out a twenty and threw it on the table as he rose.

"I'll think about it. I'll be away on some business for a while. I'll contact you when I get back. Maybe."

He didn't give Davis a chance to reply.

MONDAY

1. Jack awoke to the blather of 880 AM, one of the city's all-news radio stations.

Last night, after checking his street to see if the mysterious stranger was hanging around—he wasn't—he'd turned on the radio and fallen asleep listening. He'd awakened a few times during the night but heard no mention of new explosions.

Same thing this morning.

So far so good. But the morning was still young.

No one was commenting yet on exactly what had exploded and who might have been killed. And no word about an apartment in Bay Ridge. The feds were playing it silent and savvy.

He checked his clock. Not quite six yet. Manhattan's rush hour wouldn't be in full swing for another hour or so. Still time for terror to start.

Yeah, they'd blown one group of cockroaches and their stash to hell, but he couldn't help worrying: What if more than one cell was involved? And what if that other cell had its own stash? Were they saving it for another day or were they planning to use it this morning in a two-pronged, coordinated attack? Compound the terror with a second strike?

That was why he'd wanted to feed the slimy bastards to the feds. But goddamn Miller . . .

He should have called the feds the instant he saw the drums of Semtex.

Screw the team approach.

Then again, if not for the Oculus and the MV, he never would have known about the plot.

He hated this.

He showered, got dressed, then went out. Not too cold. He decided to walk over to Gia's instead of grabbing a cab.

Wanted to get a feel for the mood of the city. The Staten Island explosion, located as it had been in a storage facility, had terrorist written all over it.

He saw a lot of wary faces along the way. Not worried, not frightened, just . . . cautious. Be a whole different story if subways and bridges and tunnels started blowing up.

Which was why he was headed to Gia's. It was early, yeah, but he wanted to be with her and Vicks if bombs went off.

2. Jack had an idea as he watched Gia zip up Vicky's blue winter coat before taking her to wait for the school bus.

"Hey, why don't we give Vicky the day off and the three of us go out for breakfast?"

Vicky's blue eyes lit. "Yeah! Pancakes!"

Gia didn't look up as she wrapped a red-and-white striped scarf around her daughter's neck.

"Skip school? We need an occasion for that."

"How about my last day in town for a while?"

Now she looked up at him. "You mean . . . ?"

He hadn't had a chance to tell her yet; had planned to as soon as Vicky was gone, but the thought of Vicky on a bus this morning gave him a crawly feeling in his gut. He didn't want either of them out of his sight.

He nodded. "Abe says everything is ready."

Her face fell. "Oh."

"I thought you'd be happy."

"I did too."

"Where you going, Jack?" Vicky looked worried. "To Shangri-la like you said?"

Jack had told her that last month when he'd thought he was going somewhere with no road back. This time it was to a boat slip in a Fort Lauderdale marina. He planned to stop by Abe's later this morning for the exact address.

"This is a lot closer, Vicks. Florida. And it's not for long. Less than a week."

She grinned and jumped up and down. "Can I go? Can we all go to Disney World?"

"Maybe in the spring," Gia said as Jack helped her rise to standing.

"But I wanna go now! It's hot all the time there, isn't it? I can go swimming!"

Jack wondered how an offer for breakfast had turned into a trip to Disney World. Things happened so fast with kids.

"How about breakfast first?" He looked at Gia. "She gets straight A's, so one day of hooky won't matter. Please?"

Gia shrugged. "Why not? We'll make it a family breakfast." She patted her swelling tummy. "All four of us."

"Great. Where?"

"How about Kosher Nosh?"

"Again?"

She patted her tummy again. "Baby wants lox."

Though something of a vegetarian—she'd eat eggs—Gia had added fish to her diet during the pregnancy.

"Then Kosher Nosh it is."

The small deli-restaurant up on Second Avenue was only a few blocks away, so they walked.

"I still don't get this kosher thing," Jack said as they ambled west on 58th. "How'd this happen?"

She shrugged and lapsed into Abe's accent. "You want I should explain taste? I'm talking apricot ruggalach, poppy-seed twists, onion bialys. What's not to like?"

Jack laughed. "Hey, that's good. You could move to Boro Park. The weird thing is, Abe was raised in an orthodox home and he won't touch the stuff."

Gia gave him a dubious look. "You mean there's something Abe won't eat?"

"That's what he says."

"So if I put a cheese blintz in front of him he wouldn't eat it?"

"Well, I guess he'd make an exception for that."

Kosher Nosh had an old-time luncheonette look, with Formica-topped tables and chrome napkin dispensers. They took a table near the back. A harried, scowling, middle-aged waitress brought them menus. A younger woman usually waited this table.

"Where's Aviva?" Gia said.

The waitress ran a hand through her hair. "Didn't show up."

She took their drink orders—coffee, tea, and milk—then hustled away.

Vicky made a face. "She's not very nice."

"She's overloaded today, hon," Gia said. "Take it from someone who's waited her share of tables. You can get frazzled."

Jack felt a warm glow as he watched mother and daughter study their menus. Two years ago, this situation, these feelings would have been unimaginable.

"They still don't have bacon," Vicky said.

She had a way to go before she grasped the kosher thing. Jack knew a little, but it still made no sense to him.

"Oh, look," Gia said. "Here's something I haven't tried: sauerkraut pierogies."

Jack grimaced. "For breakfast?"

"Hey, I'm pregnant. That means I get a special dispensation from the rules." She put down her menu and looked at him. "I can't read you this morning, Jack. What are you feeling?"

"I'm feeling I don't want to see someone eating sauerkraut pierogies for breakfast."

"Seriously."

He thought about that.

"I feel strange. Really strange. Like I'm giving up the real me, but the real me is really someone else. So I'm really giving up the fake me who's become more real than the real me. That make any sense?"

"From anyone else, no—I'd think you'd been smoking something. But from you? Perfect sense."

The waitress returned, pencil poised over her pad.

"Figured it out yet?"

"I'll have the sauerkraut pierogies," Gia said.

"Boiled or fried?"

"What's the difference?"

The waitress deadpanned her. "One's boiled, one's fried."

Jack rubbed a hand over his mouth to hide a smile. On any other day he might have been annoyed, but no bombs had gone off this morning, so a grumpy waitress was something of a joy.

"I'll have the boiled," Gia said. Then she looked at him and laughed. "Don't you love this place?"

3. Jack couldn't bring himself to go back to LaGuardia, and the Ashe brothers were both booked for charters, so he decided to fly Spirit out of Atlantic City. A longer drive than to Kennedy, but lots more scenic. And he was in no hurry.

Last year's flight to Florida—the first and only commercial flight in his adult life—had convinced him that his fake ID could pass muster with airport security, so he approached this flight with a lot more confidence than the last. But the prospect of getting tagged still gave him the willies.

He'd stopped by the Isher where Abe made a big deal of bidding a sad farewell to Repairman Jack—"I'd say a kaddish but I don't remember the words"—before giving him the marina address. Then Jack powered up the Crown Vic and headed south. He wore his yeniçeri shades. He liked their clarity, and their wraparound style.

AC International proved hassle free. He had no trouble parking. The identity check at the ticket purchase counter—one way to Fort Lauderdale, please—gave him a few moments of anxiety, but no problem. The line at the security checkpoint was short and efficient. He felt much calmer going through than the previous time—not carrying a concealed weapon this trip might have had something to do with that.

Being weaponless, especially on a plane, gave him a naked feeling. Not helpless, just naked.

With half an hour to go before his flight, he checked his voice mail and found a message from his brother-in-law, Ron, asking Jack to call him.

Ron Iverson, MD, was Jack's sister Kate's ex-husband. They'd met only once, at Dad's funeral, and that hadn't been pleasant. He'd never forgiven Jack for missing Kate's funeral. Not a bad guy. And since Jack had never explained why he hadn't been there—he'd loved Kate and if there had been any way on Earth he could have made it, he would have—Ron had a right to his anger.

This was the first time he'd ever called Jack. Had to be something important.

Curious, Jack punched in the number Ron had left. After some stiff obligatory pleasantries, Ron got down to business.

"Look, Jack. I know you're not interested in family matters but your father's estate needs settling."

"Oh, man . . ."

"Not for me," he added quickly. "Kate's third goes to Kevin and Lizzie and their college funds are already in good shape. I'm in no hurry, but Tom's wives . . . I've got to tell you, Jack, your brother married three doozies."

"So I've been told."

Tom had called them the Skanks from Hell.

"Well, let me tell you, ever since they discovered your father's net worth—surprised the hell out of me, too—they've been all over me to contact you and settle the estate so they can get their hands on the cash and divvy up the proceeds from selling the place in Florida."

"Must be hell."

"Damn near. You know . . . that Florida place . . . he asked the kids down a dozen times at least, but they made it only once. Had a great time. They miss him. Lizzie's still in the dumps."

"She's not alone."

"Yeah, well, he was a good guy. But, Jack, help me out, will you? Tell me when you can make it down here for a reading of the will so we can get this over with."

"I don't want any of it. Split it two ways instead of three."

After a long silence Ron said, "What is it with you, Jack? I thought you were back on track with your father. Why won't you take what he left you, what he wanted you to have?"

Because he couldn't. The Jack named in the will no longer existed. He hadn't filed a tax return since he went off official-dom's radar fifteen years ago, so no way could he claim an inheritance. And the real, live, government-sanctioned man who Jack was going to become was not named in the will.

But he couldn't tell Ron that. Had to give him another reason.

"Because I don't need it. I'd rather see it go to Kevin and Lizzie, and maybe filter through Tom's wives to his kids."

Another pause, then, "That's . . . that's very generous of you. I talked to your uncle Gurney last week. Your father left him a small amount but he didn't want it either. Said the same thing."

That didn't surprise Jack. He hadn't seen Uncle Gurney in ages but remembered him as an odd character. Jack couldn't count how many times his mother had told him, *You're just like your uncle Gurney.*

"Yeah, well, get some papers drawn up for me to relinquish my share. I'll sign and get them notarized and that'll be that."

Ernie the ID man was a notary. He'd take care of that end.

Ron sounded like he wanted to say more but Jack's flight called for boarding.

"Gotta go. Give my best to Kevin and Lizzie."

He doubted they'd remember who he was. He'd met them only once.

No problem boarding. No queue for the plane to take off: The doors closed, the plane lumbered onto the tarmac, and off they went.

Jack leaned back in his coach seat and figured he could get used to this. And once he became an official person, he'd have no worries at all. He could get a legit passport and see the world.

Yep, citizenship definitely had some advantages.

Still . . . he looked out the window and saw the spires of Manhattan in the hazy distance and felt a wave of ineffable sadness. Repairman Jack had left the building and wasn't coming back.

A cold, hard lump formed in his stomach as he pulled down the window shade and closed his eyes.

4. Jack stood in the doorway and sniffed the air of his father's Gateways home. The musty odor was no surprise: The place had been shut up for more than a month.

The real surprise was that he was here. Talking to Ron had got him thinking about Dad's estate. This house was part of it and would be pillaged by Tom's ex-wives before it was sold. And so Jack decided to do a little preemptive pillaging himself.

He'd packed the same gym bag for this trip as the last. As soon as he'd debarked at Fort Lauderdale airport—officially Fort Lauderdale/Hollywood International—he combed through the bag and found the front-gate passkey Anya had given him when he'd visited his father.

So instead of a local motel, he'd rented a car and headed south and inland toward the Everglades and Gateways.

He stepped inside and closed the door behind him. The shades were drawn and a wave of sadness eddied around him as he stood in the cool darkness. His father had left here figuring he'd be back to finalize its sale and pack up to move back north. His first try at selling the place had fallen through when the buyer died. He'd found another buyer, but this time it was the seller who hadn't made it to the closing.

As he moved through the front room he decided to leave the shades drawn. He was going to be here maybe twelve hours, most of them dark. No point in raising them—especially since he wasn't supposed to be here.

He went to the kitchen, opened the fridge, and smiled at the sight of four bottles of Ybor Gold. He'd discovered the brand on his previous trip and it looked like he'd made Dad a convert.

He popped a top and wandered back through the living room/dining room area. He noticed that the paintings had been stripped from the walls and the trophy shelves were empty.

Readying to leave.

He stopped at the door to Dad's bedroom. All the family photos had been removed from the walls. The only ones left sat on his dresser: Tom's three kids, Kate's two, and an old family photo of Mom, Dad, Tom, Kate, and eight-year-old Jack—or "Jackie," as they'd all called him.

His throat tightened as he stared at those smiling faces.

I'm the only one left.

He went to the closet and found the ugly Hawaiian shirts still present. Leaning in the rear corner was the M1C sniper rifle he and Dad had bought last trip to take care of a little business. But he was more interested in the old gray metal box on the shelf above. It had been locked the first time he'd found it. Not now.

He flipped it open, sorted through the photos of Dad's old army buddies from Korea until he reached the small jewelry box. He popped the lid to reveal the Purple Heart and Silver Star. Jack stared at them a moment, then snapped the lid shut. The photos and the medals would mean nothing to Ron, and even less to Tom's Skanks from Hell. They'd probably put them up on eBay first chance they had.

But they meant something to Jack—meant a *lot*. They were all he had left of his father, reminders of the part of his life Dad had hidden from his family, the war he'd tried to put behind him.

Jack closed the case and carried it to the kitchen as he went for another beer. But as he opened the door he spotted a green bottle sitting atop the fridge. He pulled it down. The label read THE SCOTCH MALT WHISKY SOCIETY, CASK 12.6. A gift to Dad from Uncle Stu. Jack remembered Dad's toast when they'd shared a glass.

To the best day of my life in the last fifteen years.

Jack recalled the burn in his throat, but now the burn was in his eyes.

He poured himself a shot and sipped. Just as good as he remembered. No, good didn't quite do it. Exquisite was more like it.

He placed the bottle atop the metal box. No way the Skanks from Hell were going to get their hands on this either.

He felt too melancholy to watch TV. He'd sit and drink a little, then hit the sack early. He had to get back to Fort Lauderdale and find that boat slip by six a.m.

TUESDAY

I. Jack awoke with a start and looked at the red LED on his father's clock radio: 3:15. Had he been dreaming? Or had something else pulled him out of a sound sleep?

And then he heard it: a faint scratching from the living room. He slipped out of bed and padded to the bedroom door. The sound came from his right—from the front door.

The top half of the door was glass, divided into nine panes. He saw the silhouette of a man crouched on the far side. The scratching sound continued.

Some son of a bitch was trying to pick the lock.

A slew of thoughts raced through Jack's brain. First off, what was he after? He was making no attempt at discretion, so obviously he expected the place to be empty. A little homework and he'd know that Gateways was a gated community with regular security patrols, and so only the most paranoid residents had alarm systems. But if he knew Dad's place was empty, why was he picking the lock? Much easier to cut a hole in one of the panes, reach through, and unlock the door. Jack kept a glass cutter and a suction cup in his bag of tricks for just that purpose.

The only benefit to picking the lock was to hide the fact that the place had been broken into.

And why would he want to do that?

Jack turned and started toward the night table for a pistol—then realized he wasn't home. No weapon.

No, wait. The M1C.

He stepped to the closet and pulled out the sniper rifle. He didn't know if it was loaded and didn't much care. The WWII–vintage piece had a walnut stock and a steel butt plate.

Why wake up the neighborhood with a shot when you have a ten-pound club?

He padded back to the living room, positioned himself so he'd be behind the door when it opened, and raised the rifle.

He waited.

Took a while—the guy wasn't adept—but he finally turned the cylinder and pushed open the door. When he stepped inside, Jack rammed the rifle's butt plate against the back of his head. Not too hard—didn't want to crack his skull or put him into a coma—but hard enough to subtract a hand-to-hand confrontation from the equation. Wasn't in the mood for any rough and tumble.

The guy gave a soft *"Uhn!"* as his legs gave out. He dropped his little gym bag—very much like Jack's—and went to his knees. He knelt, swaying, looking like a churchgoer with vertigo. Jack was pondering whether or not to administer another tap when the guy fell forward and landed face first on the carpet.

Okay. Next step?

Duct tape. Dad always had been a firm believer in the wonders of the stuff and Jack was sure he'd seen a roll of it somewhere during his last trip. The porch—that was where he kept his tools.

Jack slammed his hip against the kitchen counter on his way to the rear of the house. Wouldn't have happened if he'd had the lights on, but he didn't want the security patrol to wonder why a supposedly empty house was lit up at three in the morning.

The light in the parking area behind the house pushed enough illumination through the porch jalousies for him to locate his father's toolbox. In the bottom compartment he found a roll and hurried back to the living room.

2. Jack sat on the toilet-seat cover and watched the guy in the bathtub stir and blink his eyes. He was young—maybe late twenties—and dressed in khaki shorts, a burgundy golf shirt, and Topsiders. He'd gelled his dark brown hair into little spikes—a style Jack had always found baffling—and had grown his sideburns down to earlobe level. Looked like a million other twenty-somethings in South Florida. He lay on his back, his wrists duct-taped in front of him, with more tape around his ankles and knees. Not a foolproof taping job by a long shot, but Jack wasn't worried about that.

He was holding the guy's pistol.

After finishing the taping, Jack had hung a towel over the bathroom window and turned on the light. Then he'd dragged the guy in and rolled him into the tub. That done, he'd opened the gym bag—a High Sierra model with an empty water-bottle sleeve—and the first thing he'd found was a Luger.

Okay, a guy sneaking into his father's supposedly empty house was a deal, though not a terribly big one. But finding a pistol, even if he wasn't wearing it at the time, changed the picture and upped the threat level a few notches—maybe to orange. But then Jack noticed that the front sight had been filed off and the end of the barrel threaded. And when he discovered a dark blue MX Minireflex moderator in the bag, the situation went deep into the red, sending one thought clanging through his head like a gong.

Hit man. Or assassin. Whatever he called himself, he was geared for a close-range, silent kill.

Jack's first thought was that somebody wanted him dead and had hired this clown to make it happen. Then he realized that that couldn't be. No one had known he was headed here.

Jack hadn't known himself. Hadn't made the decision until he'd landed.

So who was he after? And why had he come here?

The guy groaned. He'd been doing that and opening and closing his eyes for about ten minutes. This time they stayed open and focused on Jack for a few seconds, then up and around at his surroundings.

"What the fuck?"

He tried to sit up but then grimaced and slumped back to his original position.

"Headache?"

Jack had been through the post-concussion thing a few times. Early on, every movement sent a bolt of pain through your head.

The guy fixed on Jack again.

"The fuck am I?"

"Who, what, or where?"

"Where."

"A nice little house in Gateways. The one you broke into just a short while ago.

"And who the f—?"

Jack raised the pistol. "That's my question. One of many I'm going to be asking you."

Jack saw fear race through his eyes at sight of the Luger, but only for an instant. Then the hard-guy look returned.

"I checked your clothes and your bag," Jack said. "No ID. So tell me: What's your name?"

The guy sneered. "John Smith."

"Very funny." Jack hadn't expected a straight answer but felt obligated to ask. "Okay, Smith, what's going on here? What are you up to?"

Another sneer. "The Motel Six was full up and I needed a place to stay."

Jack had an urge to wing a slug past Smith's nose but didn't want to mess up the tile. He hadn't looked but assumed the pistol had a round in the chamber. He worked the toggle anyway—for effect. The ratcheting sound echoed off the tiles as a cartridge spun through the air and bounced along the floor.

Jack gestured with the pistol. "Now we'll try again, Smith. What are you doing in my father's house?"

The tough-guy façade cracked a little. "Your father? Shit, I heard it would be empty."

"Heard from whom?"

"No one and nobody." He stared at Jack. "You mean you and your father live here?"

"Nope. My father's gone and I'm just visiting."

"But why are you a day early?"

That came from so far out in left field that it knocked Jack off balance.

"What?"

"You weren't supposed to be here until tomorrow."

"I wasn't supposed to be here at all. You sure you're talking about me? Did someone show you a picture of me?"

His tone turned uncertain. "No . . . never seen you before in my life."

Smith put his head back and closed his eyes. "Shit! I just can't believe he could screw up like this."

"He who?"

Smith's eyes snapped open as if he'd received a shock. He glanced at Jack with a worried look.

"No one. No one at all."

Jack studied his face. *He thinks he said too much. And maybe he did. But about what?*

Jack waggled the pistol at him.

"This is a hit man rig."

The sneer again. "How would you know?"

"Oh, I know. I know." Jack turned the pistol over in his hands. "An American Eagle Luger. Not the original—this is the Stoeger recreation—but a pretty piece, no less. Put a couple of hollow points through the back of the head, let them bounce around inside the skull to make Swiss cheese of the brain, and that's all she wrote, right?"

He saw a look of worry and wonder ripple over Smith's face. Seemed it was finally dawning on him that he'd broken into the wrong house at the wrong time and wound up at the mercy of the wrong guy.

"I'm not with the mob."

"Okay then, an assassin. Am I right?"

"You have no idea."

"Who were you supposed to hit?"

Jack hoped the "were" got through to him.

"Nobody." He raised his taped wrists and knuckled an eye. "That's just for self-defense."

"Yeah, right. Who sent you?"

"Nobody. Like I told you, just looking for a place to crash."

Jack had a feeling he'd learned all he was going to from this clown. Unless he applied a little pressure. He rummaged through the gym bag until he found the suppressor. He pulled it out and held it up.

"Nobody needs one of these for self-defense. So come on, Smith. Let's stop dancing around and put a few facts on the table."

"Told you all I know," he said as he rubbed his eyes again.

"We'll see about that. And keep your hands down."

With studied deliberation, Jack began threading the suppressor onto the end of the barrel, glancing at Smith with every turn.

"My, my . . . I do believe you're starting to sweat."

"Hot in here."

Yeah, it was kind of close in here, but not hot.

"Afraid of dying, Smith?"

"Not really. I'd regret it, but it doesn't scare me. Put one in my head and get it over with. You're boring the shit out of me."

" 'Boring the shit out of me.' " Jack had to smile. "I'll have to add that to my list of favorite last lines."

He hoped the subtext wasn't lost.

"You kill me, you get double nothing."

Jack offered what he hoped was a sadistic smile. "Who said anything about killing you? As long as you've got knees and ankles and elbows—"

Jack didn't know what type of smile Smith was going for. Whatever it was, it looked pretty sick.

"Same difference. You shoot me anywhere, I stop talking."

Those words, combined with the look on his face, struck a sour note in Jack. He looked around for the bullet he'd ejected and found it. His stomach dropped when he saw the tip: The hollow in the point had been filled with something and sealed over.

His thoughts flashed back a month—to a figure lying dead on the floor of the LaGuardia baggage claim area . . . dead of a flesh wound in the thigh that should have caused pain and some blood loss but no more.

Dead for one reason: He'd caught a cyanide-filled hollow point.

This looked like the same thing, except it was a 9mm Starfire instead of the 5.56 NATOs used at the airport.

Still . . . an assassin's bullet.

He held it up. "Cyanide tipped?"

Smith's mouth tightened into a thin line, but he said nothing.

"You connected to Wrath of Allah?"

Smith frowned. "Who the fu—oh, those Islamic assholes who did LaGuardia?" He looked insulted. "You gotta be kidding."

Jack set the round on the edge of the tub, point up.

"Those Islamic assholes used cyanide hollow points to do the job. You sure you're not connected?"

"Absolutely. On my mother's grave—wherever that is."

"Then who *are* you connected to?"

"No one."

Jack sighed. "You're pushing me. That bullet puts a whole new spin on this situation. Someone very close to me was killed by a similar round. Before the night's over I'm going to know who sent you. We can do it easy or we can do it nasty. My father left a well-stocked toolbox out on the back porch. I'm especially fond of his variable-speed electric drill. Do I have to go get it?"

Smith paled and broke out in another sweat. But he wasn't backing down.

"I've told you all I can."

Jack made note of the fact that he didn't say all he *knew*.

He wondered if his bluff would work. He wasn't in a black enough mood to drill into someone's shinbone. This jerk most likely broke into the wrong house. Under other circumstances

Jack might have loaded him in his trunk and dumped him in the swamp, leaving him to get out of the tape himself and find his way home. But that cyanide-tip changed things. Jack wanted more. Maybe plugging in the drill and revving it a few times as he brought it toward Smith's kneecap would prove a tongue loosener.

"Okay. You're going to make me hate myself in the morning."

As he rose he reached for the round, but Smith got there ahead of him. His taped hands darted up and grabbed it, then raised it to his mouth.

"Jesus!" Jack shouted. "What are you—?"

He leaped forward and grabbed for the hand, but too late—the round went into his mouth. Jack dropped the pistol and tried to pry Smith's jaws apart but the guy was struggling and thrashing and twisting his head back and forth to prevent Jack from getting a grip.

Finally Jack felt Smith's throat work, and then the man stopped struggling and smiled at him.

"You jerk!" Jack shouted. "What you do that for? As soon as that seal melts, you're a goner."

Jack imagined Smith's stomach acid working on the seal right now.

Smith shrugged. "You were going to torture me, then kill me, so I decided to skip the torture part."

Jack shook his head. "I was just kidding about that—trying to scare you. Sadism isn't my bag."

Smith stared at Jack. He must have seen the truth there because he hung his head and sobbed. Once.

Jack leaned forward. "You think you could puke it up?"

Smith shook his head. "No. Too late."

"Well, all right then. Since there's no turning back, why not come clean? Who were you supposed to hit?"

Smith hesitated, then said, "I don't know."

"Come on—"

"I never get a name. Just a description and a time and a place."

"Do I match the description?"

"Close enough, but you look like anybody."

"Yeah, well, I work at that. When was this supposed to go down?"

"Tomorrow afternoon, but I was supposed to get here early and set up."

"Who sent you?"

Before Smith could answer his eyes rolled up and he started flopping around in the tub like a hooked fish. He made grunting noises as he flailed his taped arms and kicked his legs.

Jack could do nothing but watch as his face turned blue and he arched his back to the point where it looked like he'd snap his spine.

And then he collapsed into a flaccid, silent lump of flesh.

Jack watched him a full minute for signs of life. None. He sat back on the toilet cover and wondered why these things happened to him. All he'd wanted to do was pick up his father's war medals, catch a few hours sleep, and be on his way.

Now he had a body to dispose of.

Shit.

He picked up the pistol and popped the magazine: eight more cyanide-tipped rounds within. Starfires were perfect because of their big cavity. He worked the toggle to eject the chambered round. Now he needed a way to dump the nine cartridges without poisoning someone.

He took a towel from the rack, unscrewed the suppressor, wiped it down, then wiped down the pistol too. He went to stow them back in the High Sierra bag but decided to give it one last, thorough search.

He upended it and dumped everything onto the bathroom floor. He checked all the end and side pouches and felt around inside for hidden compartments or a phony bottom panel.

Nothing else.

Just a change of underwear, a shaving kit containing an electric razor, toothbrush and toothpaste, a jar of Bed Head hair gel, a box of Starfires, yesterday's Miami *Herald*, a battered old John D. MacDonald paperback, a Manta Ray baseball cap, and sunglasses.

The banality of the pile depressed Jack. Who was this guy? Who'd sent him? And for whom?

Probably never know.

Jack used the towel to replace the pistol and suppressor in the bag. Since the sunglasses would take fingerprints, he picked them up with the towel as well. He was about to drop them back in when he noticed that they looked familiar. Too familiar.

Forgetting about prints, he held them up and stared through the lenses. No darkening—he could see the shower head perfectly. Yet when he flipped them over . . . impenetrable tinting.

A band of cold iron tightened around his gut as he jumped up and hurried to his own gym bag. He pulled out the shades Davis had given him and held them side by side with the dead guy's.

Identical.

Unless he'd stolen or found these, the guy in the tub was a yeniçeri.

3.   Jack drove along South Road until he came to Pemberton Road. The intersection lay on the outer limits of Novaton and, because this was the site of the hit and run on his father, he'd become well acquainted with it during his last visit.

The roads crossed in the swamps on the border of the Everglades and the area was as deserted now as then. More so now since the sun still had two hours to go before it cleared the eastern horizon.

Jack pulled over, got out, and popped the trunk. He grabbed Smith by the armpits and hauled him out. Then he dragged him to the shoulder and rolled him into a drainage ditch. No water, so no splash. He tossed the gym bag—pistol and all—in beside him.

He kept one round.

He'd looked up the number of the Novaton PD before leaving his father's house, and when he reached Route 1 he called it on his TracFone.

"Yes, I'd like to report a crime. I saw what looked like a body being dumped near the intersection of South and Pemberton. Thank you." He cut the connection.

There. That ought to set Novaton's finest into motion.

If not for the cyanide-tipped slugs he might have left Smith there as gator food. He could have disassembled the pistol and tossed it piece by piece into the swamp as he drove along South Road, but he didn't know what to do with the bullets. Anya had instilled a deep respect for the embattled Everglades, and he didn't want to add even a small amount of cyanide to its woes.

This way the Novaton cops would find him before anyone else; the cyanide hollow points would become their problem.

The big question now was, where to from here?

If he pushed it he could make it to the Fort Lauderdale rendezvous on time. His head told him to go there. Who knew when all the stars would again be aligned this way on the road to Bosnia? If he blew this, he might not have another chance before the baby was born.

But Smith's sunglasses added a major wrinkle, urging him to forget all that and find out what the hell a yeniçeri assassin was doing in his father's house.

So which was it? The marina or the airport?

Whatever his final decision, he had to head north on Route 1, so he kept driving, hoping he could resolve this by the time he reached Fort Lauderdale.

4. The pain awakens him.

Another Alarm—and so soon after the last.

Then he plunges into that other place, the flashing gray space where he is shown things yet to be—things that must be prevented, and things that must be done.

The pain knifes through his brain and the lights flash. He is aware of his bed under him and he grabs the mattress as he feels it begin to spin. The flashes cycle faster and faster until they coalesce into a vision . . .

A restaurant . . . a copy of *The New York Times* lies on the counter where an attractive woman is paying the cashier . . . the headline concerns a Bay Ridge apartment linked to terrorists and runs above a photograph of a building.

The woman has short blond hair and carries another life within her.

The Oculus has seen this woman before. She appeared in another Alarm . . . two months ago . . . in November. In that one she was standing on a curb, waiting to cross Second Avenue when a truck went out of control and struck her, killing her. He saw the driver of the truck: Zeklos.

That Alarm was stomach turning, but nowhere near as painful as the one that followed a month later.

But real life had not mimicked the November Alarm. Zeklos missed the woman—some of his fellow yeniçeri said on purpose due to a lack of resolve—and crashed into another truck instead.

Now the same woman, still with child, but not alone. A dark-haired little girl stands beside her, holding a candy bar. She appears to be pleading but the Oculus cannot hear what she's saying.

The clock behind the counter says half past one.

The vision fades to gray, then lights up with the woman standing on the exact same corner as the last time, only now she is holding the child by the hand while the child munches happily on the candy bar.

As the light changes, they step off the curb . . . and then, without warning, a white panel truck runs the red light and slams into the two of them, sending them flying. If he were seeing this with his eyes, the Oculus would have squeezed them shut. But since the scene is playing inside his head, he is compelled to watch. And in the driver seat of the truck he sees one of his yeniçeri: Cal Davis.

The vision fades to gray, and then the gray fades, and with it, the pain.

The bed stops its vertiginous whirl but the Oculus doesn't move.

A yeniçeri in an Alarm means the Ally needs this done.

Why? he wonders. Why does the Ally want this woman dead? The little girl wasn't in the previous Alarm. Does it want her life too, or is she merely collateral damage?

How will their deaths affect the fight against the Otherness?

And why must it fall to him to order their deaths?

He wonders if the Otherness is behind an Alarm like this, if it somehow taps in from time to time. But that can't be. He's tuned in to the Ally, and that's where the Alarm came from.

But although the Ally has never in his experience been cruel, he knows it can be merciless.

5. "Hi, Abe."

"Jack? From the boat you're calling?"

"I'm not on the boat."

"There's been a problem?"

"No. I changed my mind."

"A joke, right?"

"Afraid not."

"*Gevalt!*"

In the ensuing silence, Jack reevaluated his decision. It hadn't been an easy one. During the drive back, every time he'd lean toward boarding that boat, he'd think about those sunglasses and those bullets. In the end it all had come down to those damn cyanide-tipped bullets. They kept reminding him of the LaGuardia Massacre. It made no sense, he knew. Different caliber, and carried by someone who was anything but an Arab. If he'd found a Koran in Smith's bag instead of a novel, the decision would have been made right then and there. But John D. MacDonald didn't incite the slaughter of innocent people.

Then he'd remembered Joey Castles's dying words after they'd hit the Islamic center.

"It's bigger than them. Something else going on."

That had done it. The "something else" left him no choice but to head back to New York.

He'd waited till he'd reached the airport and bought his ticket before calling Abe. He didn't want to disappoint his oldest and best friend, but . . .

"I'm sorry, Abe. I know you spent a lot of time—"

"Months I spent."

"I know. And I know you called in some favors, but I just can't leave the country right now."

"People have been put in place, schedules have been re-arranged, space has been made . . ."

"I know, I know, and I'm awfully sorry, but something important has come up."

"What could be more important than this trip?"

"I'll explain when I see you."

He heard Abe sigh. "This I've got to tell you, my friend, a re-play may not be easy. May not be possible even. Someone's go-ing to be very upset that he went to all this trouble for nothing."

"I'll pay him for his time and trouble—cover all expenses and then some. He'll have his profit."

"Profit isn't everything. There's the matter of respect, which is very important to this man. I'll call him. Maybe he'll be less upset if he should have advance notice, although much in advance this is not."

"Thanks, Abe. I'll make it up to you some way."

He broke the connection and glanced at the departure board. Still had half an hour before takeoff. Should he call Gia?

Probably best not to. Better to explain in person instead of a cryptic phone conversation. He didn't think he was unrea-sonably paranoid. With his pay-as-you-go TracFone, calls were traceable to his number but not to him, since all sub-scribers were anonymous. But his calls weren't encrypted and were traceable to whomever he called. With Homeland Secu-rity and the Patriot Act in swing, no telling who might be lis-tening in.

He'd wait till he was ready to stop by, then call Gia to give her a heads-up that he was back in town, and tell her he'd ex-plain everything in a few minutes when he got there.

He wondered how she'd take the news. She'd been ambiva-lent about his new identity, but would she see the sudden change in plans as a lack of commitment to the baby?

No. She knew better. And she'd understand once he ex-plained his reasons.

The call came over the speakers that his plane was board-ing.

6. Ybarra, one of the yeniçeri on duty, placed a folded copy of the morning *Times* on the Oculus's desk.

"As requested, sir."

"Thank you."

As Ybarra left, the Oculus picked up the paper but did not unfold it. He feared the headline. If it said nothing about the Bay Ridge apartment, the woman and the child would have another day, perhaps more, to live. But if the story was there . . .

He took a breath, held it, then unfolded the paper. The air blew out of him in a choked *whoosh* when he saw a headline identical to the one in the Alarm.

He closed his eyes and lowered his head. He'd have to gather the yeniçeri. He'd have to tell them about the Alarm. He'd have to send them out to kill that woman and child.

The Oculus rested his elbows on the desktop and pressed his eyes against the upturned palms. At times like this he wished he hadn't been born with the gift. Because, in its own way, the gift was a curse. The Alarms could not be ignored—the Ally saw what was to be and demanded action. The enormity of the responsibility was appalling. If he kept the Alarm to himself, what would be the consequences? The Ally was not capricious. If it told him that a situation had to be addressed, then that was what must happen. To ignore it would be tantamount to aiding and abetting the Otherness.

He wished he were like any other man, wished he could wake up in the morning and go about his business without the crushing burden of the gift, without worrying about when the next Alarm would sound.

But the only escape from the Alarms was death. At times

he'd considered that option, but then he'd think of poor Diana, and of how his mantle would fall on her shoulders when he was gone. He wished to spare her for as long as possible. For that reason alone he vowed to live to a ripe old age.

But now he had to deal with the matter of the Alarm.

He buzzed downstairs. Ybarra answered.

"Gather the yeniçeri. We've had an Alarm."

7. Gia hung up her coat and rubbed her hands together. Cold out here.

She'd put Vicky on the school bus and had scurried back to the warmth of the house. She filled the kettle and turned on the TV. A little tea, a little news, and she'd get to work on the studies for that dust jacket.

Over the years Gia had developed good working relationships with the art directors of a number of publishing houses. Sometimes she received detailed instructions on what they wanted; other times, like this one, she received no directive beyond, "Something bucolic, with a house in the woods."

She'd dipped into the manuscript they'd sent her—a dreary tale about a middle-aged college professor's extramarital affair with a student—until she found an obsessively detailed description of the woodsy retreat that served as their trysting place.

Now all she had to do was come up with a couple of rough ideas, dab a little paint on them to show the color scheme, and bring them in. The art director would choose one, make his comments on composition and color, and then Gia would begin the actual painting. Sometimes it was a chore, sometimes it was fun, but either way, commercial art paid the bills, leaving her time for her personal paintings.

But working on anything today would be difficult. Maybe impossible. Jack hovered over her thoughts. She wondered how he was—*where* he was—and if everything was going as planned. He'd sailed off into the unknown not for himself, but for the baby. He was trading everything he'd struggled to become, everything he was, for fatherhood.

She blinked back a tear and flipped through the channels

until she came to *Headline News*. She stopped there for a quick rundown of what was going on in the world. Too-familiar footage of the smoking crater in the Staten Island storage facility flashed on the screen. She was raising the remote to switch the channel when the scene shifted to a view of a brick-fronted apartment house. "Bay Ridge" popped onto the upper left corner of the screen.

"*—BI officials have revealed that traces of the same compound that caused the Staten Island explosion were found in an apartment in this building in Brooklyn along with Arabic writing on the walls.*"

Gia felt her gut clench—and that seemed to spur a kick from the baby. The so-called "terrorism expert" who followed didn't make her feel any better.

"*From the amount of plastic explosive estimated in the Staten Island blast, I think we can assume that these individuals were out to do a lot of damage. Nothing like nine-eleven, of course, but considerable.*"

Gia rose and turned off the kettle. What if there were other "individuals" with other caches of explosives? If so, she didn't want Vicky locked down in a school if all hell broke loose.

She hurried to the closet. It wasn't rational, and it was most likely an overreaction, but she didn't care. She wanted her little girl with her today.

Looked like Vicky would get a second day off this week.

Gia's hand stopped in midreach for her coat.

A second day off . . . like yesterday. The explosion had occurred the night before, and Jack had been intent on keeping Vicky out of school. He'd said it was because he was leaving, but had there been more to it? In the demimonde he moved through he often picked up rumors and tidbits of news before they hit the papers.

She'd have to ask him when he got back. Right now she was going to catch a cab and head for Vicky's school.

8. As Jack waited for his bag, he couldn't help thinking of the last time he'd been in a baggage-claim area . . . how he'd left to get the car . . . how he'd returned to a charnel house.

But that had been LaGuardia and this was Atlantic City International: pretty far down on the list of terror targets, he imagined. Still he couldn't wait to get back to the car and wrap his fingers around the grip of his Glock.

He found his bag and carried it to his car. He dropped it in the trunk, opened it, and removed the Altoids tin he'd bought at a convenience store near the airport.

The first thing he did when he got behind the wheel was check for the Glock in the clip under the front seat. Still there. He patted it. Welcome home.

Then he opened the tin and tipped out the Starfire within. Here was why he'd checked his bag instead of carrying it on. If the security folks at the gate were doing their job, they'd have wanted to examine the contents of a metal case they couldn't see through, small though it might be. But checked bags weren't put under that kind of scrutiny.

He turned the round over in his hand a few times, then pocketed it.

Next up, call Gia.

He'd planned to wait until he was back in the city and just a few minutes from her door. But en route he'd seen the headline about an apartment in Bay Ridge in his neighbor's Miami *Herald*. He'd borrowed the front section and learned that the FBI had broken the story about the connection between the apartment and the explosion. The article also mentioned the Arabic scrawl Jack had seen on the wall. It translated as, *God is Great. Jihad forever.*

Swell.

The mood back in the city would be tense—only a tiny fraction of what it would have been had the cockroaches succeeded—but Gia might be worried for herself and Vicky and the baby. He figured she'd be more comfortable knowing he was around.

He tapped in her number.

No answer at home. He didn't leave a message but called her cell phone instead. Again, no answer. This time he left a message.

"Hi, Gi, it's me. Things didn't work out with the trip so I'm headed home. I'll explain everything when I get there. See you in a few hours."

He broke the connection and sat there.

Odd. He could usually get hold of Gia at one of those two numbers. She wanted to be always available should the Vick-ster need her. The only time she'd leave it home or turn it off was when she was with Vicky.

A vague unease settled on him. He started the car and gunned it toward the exit. A two-hour drive lay ahead of him, longer if he hit construction.

The unease grew stronger.

9. "A woman and a child?" Cal said.

The thought turned his stomach.

"Not just a woman," the Oculus said, his expression bleak. "A pregnant woman."

Cal groaned. Even worse.

He and about a dozen other yeniçeri had gathered on the first floor and stood in a semicircle before the Oculus. Miller had been called but wasn't answering his phone.

What was happening? Cal wondered. Some of the Ally's Alarms over the past few months had been pretty damn strange. More than strange—disturbing. The young girl, the Arabs—okay. That was the sort of thing he expected, the kind of work that made him proud to be a yeniçeri. The girl and a lot of New Yorkers were alive today because of those two Alarms.

But this . . .

"Are you sure we aren't supposed to stop this from happening?"

The O shook his head. "I was shown a yeniçeri behind the wheel."

Cal looked around for Miller but he hadn't arrived yet.

"I don't get it. First that woman back in November, then—"

"It is the same woman."

Cal heard Zeklos's voice whisper, "Oh, no."

He looked at him. Zek's face was ashen, his lips trembled.

"Thanks a lot, Zek," Hursey said. "Now one of us has to pick up after you."

"Shouldn't even be here," Jolliff muttered.

Both were Miller buddies.

"Let's not get sidetracked," Cal said. He turned to the Oculus. "If this is the second Alarm about this woman, the Ally must think she poses a serious threat. Any idea what?"

The O shook his head. "None. Perhaps the baby . . ."

Yeah. Maybe the baby.

"Any idea about the father?"

Another head shake. "Again, none. But for all we know . . . maybe it belongs to the Adversary."

There was a scary thought. But . . .

"Yeah. And maybe not." Cal thought of something. "These Alarms aren't infallible, you know. Look what happened last time. You saw a truck hitting this same woman, but it didn't. Zeklos missed her."

Everyone looked at Zeklos, some with naked hostility. The little man took a step back.

"It doesn't show *the* future," the O said. "It shows a possible or probable future. It shows me near things and far things, little things and momentous things. On Sunday it showed me explosions on buses and bridges—a future it wanted stopped. And we stopped it. But as you all well know, every so often it shows me a future it wants us to *make* happen. Like this one."

"So none of this is carved in stone."

"I don't think it can be. Because there's always the unforeseen, unpredictable variable of the human factor."

Again a number of the yeniçeri glanced at Zeklos.

But Cal couldn't stop wondering about the Ally's methods. In fact, the methods used by both sides. Neither employed full frontal attacks, no shows of naked force. Both pulled occult strings from behind the scenes, manipulating events through human agents.

Why? Why no overt aggression? Did they save that for elsewhere—pitched battles in interdimensional space? Were there rules for dealing with sentient species?

Cal had come to the conclusion that this cosmic game—and that was what it seemed to be—had no hard and fast rules, but rather guidelines that compelled each side to act without revealing itself. Perhaps they had a scoring system that awarded style points to the side that could gain or keep the upper hand with the most elegant medley of obscurity and élan.

And perhaps he was way off base. Maybe the human mind was incapable of making any sense of the forces in play here.

He did know he was a pawn—but a willing, enthusiastic pawn. If he had to be part of this game, he preferred to know the score than be an unwitting puppet.

The door chimed. Jolliff stepped to the monitors and checked the front door camera. He pressed the unlock button and smiled as he looked up.

"It's Miller."

Miller stepped inside and closed the door behind him.

"Sorry I'm late. Didn't get the message till a few minutes ago."

Probably with one of his hookers, Cal thought, knowing Miller alternated between two favorites.

More power to him. A night of heavy sex usually left him mellow. Well, relatively so. Cal sensed that a truly mellow Miller might violate some law of nature.

The Oculus gave him a quick rundown of the Alarm.

That done, Cal looked around at his fellow yeniçeri.

"All right. You've heard the Oculus. The Ally wants this woman gone. Does anybody want the job? If not, we draw straws."

Miller said, "Maybe we should give Zeklos another chance." Then he smirked. "Not."

This earned a few laughs.

Then Miller said, "I'll take it."

Cal wasn't often thankful for Miller's heart of stone, but this was one of those times. He was about to hand him the job when the O interrupted him.

"The Alarm showed you at the wheel."

At first Cal thought the O was simply confirming the obvious choice, but then noticed that he was looking at him.

His stomach plummeted.

"Me?"

The O nodded.

"You don't look so hot, Davis," Miller said with what passed for a grin. "What's the matter? Getting a case of Zeklositis?"

Members of his little faction yukked it up as Zeklos reddened. Shaking his head the little man turned toward the door, raising his middle finger over his shoulder as he left.

Cal watched him go, then forced his face into a neutral expression. Inside, he wanted to run from the room.

Why me when Miller gets off on this kind of thing?

His tongue felt like tortoise hide as he spoke. "All right. I'm in the hot seat. So be it."

"Put me down for pickup duty," Miller said. "That way, if Davis misses, I'll close the deal."

Cal glanced at his watch—10:25—then at the yeniçeri.

"We've got three hours to steal a truck and the cars and put everything in place. Let's move it."

He half hoped a car would hit him as he crossed the street outside. He'd take the pain if it meant he'd be spared what was to come.

10. "Gia?" Jack said as he stepped into her front foyer.

He'd made good time from A.C. and had rushed across town to Sutton Square. When she hadn't answered his ring, he'd let himself in.

The old townhouse felt empty but he did a quick search of all floors—even the never-used fourth—and found no one and nothing out of place. Nothing suspicious. No sign of a struggle. Her winter coat and her handbag were missing from the front closet.

What he did find, however, was Gia's cell phone in its charging cradle in the kitchen.

So, only one conclusion he could make: She'd gone out and forgotten her cell phone. Wouldn't be the first time. No sign of foul play, so why this vague feeling of dread?

Jack headed for the door. He'd catch up to her later. This cyanide-tipped Starfire was burning a hole in his pocket. He needed a little yeniçeri info, and knew just the man to provide it.

11. The Oculus called Davis aside as Miller and the rest prepared to debark.

Of all the yeniçeri, he felt closest to Davis. He trusted them all, knew each was ready to die protecting him, but the yeniçeri life had hardened many of them. Inevitable, he supposed. Not every Alarm involved violence and death, but the vast majority did. Which meant that these men were, in many ways, contract killers with one client: the Ally.

Difficult for anyone to retain his humanity under those circumstances, but the rest of their quotidian existence—no family, no permanent ties to people outside their MV unit—exacerbated the situation.

They were weapons—the Ally's spears. And spears had no branches.

The Oculi were insulated from the violence. They didn't order it, merely passed on the content of the Ally's Alarms. And they had children. Nothing was so grounding as a child. He cherished his relationship with his daughter. Diana was his jewel. Just as the yeniçeri would die for him, so he would die for her.

But Davis, despite everything, had managed to maintain more of his human core. He had a hard shell, but traces of warmth and compassion remained in the heart beating within it.

"I'm sorry it had to be you," he said when Davis came to his side.

"We do what we have to do. It's all for the greater good, a cause bigger than any one person—or any three persons, right?"

The Oculus sensed that this must be the soul-saving mantra

Davis would be repeating over and over to get him through this.

"We must trust the Ally."

Davis's expression was bleak. "Yeah. Trust the Ally."

"You have the vehicles?"

Davis nodded. "Snatched from the LaGuardia long-term lot. Doubtful they'll be missed too soon."

"Very well. When you return, come to my office—come alone—and we'll talk."

He had a feeling Davis would need a sympathetic ear after this ordeal was over.

The Oculus saw them off, then trudged up to his office. For what, he didn't know. He didn't want to sit and brood. Better to spend the time with Diana, drilling her on her studies. At least that would take his mind off what was about to happen.

12.   "I *neeeed* this one Mom look at the cover isn't it neat can I have it please-please-please?"

Gia looked and saw Vicky holding up a copy of *Science Verse*.

She'd had a bit of a hassle taking her out of school. Seemed she wasn't the only parent who wanted to keep her child close today. But after a careful ID check and confirmation from Vicky that this woman was indeed her mother, they'd let her go.

The question then was what to do? She didn't want to take her out of school just to lock her in the house. Since Vicky had outgrown most of her spring clothes, the obvious choice was to shop. But that presented potential problems too.

Gia had decided that if they stayed away from the iconic stores—she couldn't afford Saks, Gucci, or Bergdorf's anyway—and avoided Fifth Avenue, they'd be safe.

Gia didn't expect anything to happen, but she felt more in control with Vicky at her side on Madison Avenue. Plenty of great stores for kids on Madison. They came upon a bookstore called The Tattered Page. Vicky loved books and this one sold both new and used. Who could resist?

"You want a book about science?"

Vicky's tastes usually ran to fantasy and funny wordplay. Nobody liked puns more.

"But he wrote *The Stinky Cheese Man*!"

"Oh, well, in that case, we'll take it."

"Neeeat!"

Gia watched as she opened the book and began reading, watched her smile, watched her eyes dance. She had her father's hair . . .

The thought brought back memories of Richard Westphalen. A rich, handsome, suave Englishman whose sparkling wit had swept her off her feet when she'd first come to New York. If only she'd known the man within. They'd married and she'd looked forward to a happy future. She'd been overjoyed when she learned she was pregnant, but not Richard. He revealed his true nature—"a bounder and a cad," according to his aunt Nellie—by virtually walking out on her. He hadn't wanted to be a father and told her flat out that he'd married her for the tax breaks he'd receive by becoming an American citizen.

He was out with one of his bimbos the night Gia went into labor. Her folks were back in Iowa, she had no close friends, and she still remembered that cab ride to the hospital as the lowest, loneliest moment of her life.

But when the pain was over and she'd cuddled her daughter, the loneliness vanished and the world became a wonderful place.

God, she'd loved that little girl then and loved her more now. In fact she loved being a mother, plain and simple. Even loved being pregnant.

She tried to imagine what it would be like having two children, and wondered for the zillionth time what the new baby would be like. If she—and she couldn't think of her any way but as a *she*—had only half of Vicky's intelligence and joie de vivre, she'd still be a joy.

The baby gave her a good kick, then another. She'd been pretty active for the past hour or so. Maybe she sensed that her mother was hungry. Gia looked at her watch: 12:30 already.

"Ready for some lunch?"

Vicky looked up from the book. "This is so funny!"

"Hungry?"

"Yeah. I'm starving. Can we go to Burger King? Pleeeeease?"

"Not today." The thought of burnt meat—blech. "How about Kosher Nosh?"

"But we were there yesterdaaaaay."

Vicky was in full whine mode.

"You can have that hummus and pita platter. You liked it last time."

"Can't I have a cheeseburger?"

"They don't make cheeseburgers there. Remember the hummus? You said it was the best you've ever had."

"Oh, okay. But can I get a big pickle too?"

"You can have two big pickles if you want."

Vicky headed for the cash register. "Let's go!"

Gia followed her with a kicking baby and a watering mouth. Not for the pickles. For herring . . . pickled herring in sour cream. Yum. She could almost taste it.

13. Cal stepped into the Kosher Nosh and looked around.

The O had described the woman and the child and had said they'd be crossing the street shortly after leaving the deli. Cal just wanted to make sure they were where they were supposed to be.

"To eat in or to go?" said the bearded man behind the counter.

Eat? With his stomach feeling like it did? Out of the question.

"Just looking for a friend."

"Look away."

The place was three-quarters full, but he spotted her short blond hair almost immediately. Couldn't tell from here if she was pregnant, but she was sitting with a dark-haired little girl that fit the Oculus's description. The kid was reading to her from a book and they both were laughing.

Cal felt the room sway around him. Mother and daughter—had to be. Out together and enjoying each other.

His legs felt unsteady as he saw what might have been. He grabbed a chair and dropped into it.

That woman . . . that child . . . had things been different, had his parents not left him to die in a cold squatter's building, the Twins wouldn't have had to rescue him. He might have had a normal childhood, might have married a woman like that and had a child like that.

This wasn't the first time he'd thought of this, but most times he could lock it away—dreaming about might-have-beens was a form of self-torture. Useless. Destructive.

But today, now, at this moment, he could not sweep them under the rug. He was going to destroy a family.

"Find your friend?" the bearded man said.

Cal shook his head. "No."

He could say no more. He turned and staggered back to the sidewalk.

Miller stood on the corner, waiting.

"They in there?"

Cal nodded. "They're there, but I can't do it."

"What?"

"I can't. I just . . . can't."

"Shit." Miller spit into the gutter. "You're turning into a real pussy, you know that?"

Cal didn't care what Miller or anyone else—including the Ally—thought, he wasn't getting behind the wheel of that truck.

"Let's just call it off, okay?"

"Call it off? We can't call it off! It was an Alarm, an order straight from the top."

"You sure about that?"

"What's that supposed to mean?"

"I mean, it doesn't feel right. Something's wrong, Miller. It felt wrong when she got the bull's-eye put on her the first time, and it feels even more wrong now. And December—I don't even want to think about December."

Miller's features hardened. "We're soldiers, Davis. We've sworn to follow orders."

"Which means we'd make good little Nazis, right?"

"Don't try that hot-button shit on me."

"Well, why don't we grab her, take her to one of the safe houses, and grill her about her connection to the Otherness?"

"Did the O see us grilling her? No, he saw us offing her. So that's what we're gonna do."

"What if there's been a mistake?"

"Shit, Davis. The Ally don't make mistakes. We see only a tiny piece of the picture. These orders come from a source that's got the widescreen view and knows and sees a helluva lot more than we do. We do what needs to be done and we move on. No looking back."

Cal shook his head. "I'm saying it feels wrong."

"Don't matter what you feel. We've got to trust that what's

good for the Ally is good for us. We can't do that, we might as well go Home and gather everyone together for a Kool-Aid party."

In the rational part of his mind Cal knew Miller was right: If they started second-guessing the higher wisdom that had recruited them, they'd be ineffective against the Otherness. But emotionally he felt as if he should be protecting that woman and child, not plotting their deaths.

Cal shook his head again. "I can't do it."

Miller leaned into him and spoke through bared teeth. "Then I guess it's up to me, just like it was in December. And if I'd been behind the wheel in November we wouldn't be having this argument. It would have been a done deal. But the O said he'd seen Zeklos behind the wheel, so the pussy got the gig. And fucked it up. Well, no more fuck-ups. *I'll* take the truck, you drive getaway."

He stomped off, leaving Cal standing on the corner.

Cal didn't want to drive getaway either, didn't want to have anything to do with this. In fact, he wanted to go back to that deli and tell the woman to stay put, or stay away from 58th Street, or call an armored car to take her home.

But he didn't.

14.   After Jack pressed Zeklos's call button for the second time, a tiny voice came through the mini speaker.

"Who is there?"

Good. He was home.

"Jack. You know, the Heir head. We need to talk."

The door buzzed open and Jack pushed through. Upstairs, on the second floor, he found Zeklos waiting in his apartment doorway.

"I am surprised to see you. Davis told me you were going away."

"Change of plans." He held up a grease-stained White Castle bag. "Hope you're hungry. Burgers and coffee. Best burgers in the world."

Jack meant that. He'd come over by way of the Manhattan Bridge so he could stop at the White Castle on Willoughby. Only about half a dozen stores in the city and Jack knew them all. Gia called them ratburgers, but he loved them. Figured they might be a treat for Zeklos. Nothing like sharing food to lull someone into opening up.

And Jack needed him to open up. What he really wanted to do was hog-tie him and grill him, but he'd learned last Friday night that Zeklos wasn't easily pried. He'd have to be teased open.

Zeklos gave him a wary look. "Why do you bring me food?"

Jack was close enough now to smell the scotch on his breath. Going on another bender?

"Because I'm hungry and I don't like to eat alone. You telling me you've had lunch already?"

Zeklos shook his head. "No. No lunch. I have no appetite."

Jack pushed past him and headed toward the kitchenette.

"Cool. That means more for me. I could eat these suckers all day."

He set the sack on the counter next to a bottle of Dewar's scotch.

"Liquid lunch? Did I come at a bad time?"

Zeklos closed the door and waved his hands.

"No-no. I am just mashing the potato of happiness."

Huh?

Jack decided not to ask. He unpacked the sack as he spoke.

"You mean about being moved down to the minors?"

More suspicion in his eyes. "How do you know this?"

"Miller was laughing about it."

Not exactly true, but it worked. The suspicion retreated, replaced by a fearful resentment.

"Miller is glad to see me go. He hates me."

"I'd look on being hated by a jerk as a badge of honor." He held out a burger in its stiff-paper squarepants container. "Here. Try one."

The combination of hearing Miller called a jerk and the aroma of a White Castle burger seemed to do it. Jack saw the tension go out of his shoulders as he examined the burger.

"So small."

"Yep. That's why you buy lots of them. Bet you can't eat just one."

Zeklos took a bite. Then another. A third bite finished it.

He spoke around a mouthful. "This is good. This is very good."

"Have another. I bought plenty. And here's a coffee."

As they ate Jack debated his next step. Too early to bring up cyanide-tipped bullets. Better to stick with Zeklos himself.

"You know, one thing you never told me is why Miller's got it in for you."

Zeklos swallowed a big bite. "I do not think I should talk about that."

"Why not? I'm the Heir, aren't I? You heard Doc Oc say so himself."

Zeklos frowned. "Doc . . . ?"

"The Oculus. The O."

"Oh, yes, I see. But—"

"But nothing. They want me to hook up with the MV. Before I do that I need to know what I'm getting into. So come on. Give."

"I don't know . . ."

"Look. Maybe I'll become the Sentinel one day, maybe I won't. But if I do, I'll remember those who helped me when I was the Heir. And believe me, they won't be languishing in some training camp."

Jack couldn't believe the crap he was spewing, but he wanted answers and he'd take them any way he could.

And the crap seemed to be working.

Zeklos thought a moment, then said, "Very well. Since you are the Heir . . . I will tell you that I am in disgrace." His eyes flashed at Jack. "Partly because of you."

"You mean because I got the jump on you Friday night?" He shrugged. "Don't take it personally. I'd have done the same to Davis or Miller."

"Yes-yes, I know. But I was already in disgrace because I did not complete a duty given to me by the O."

"Which was . . . ?"

He looked away. "I was to kill a woman."

"When?"

"Last November. The Ally said she was to be struck by a truck."

That didn't sound very Ally-ish. It disturbed him that the Ally would send a yeniçeri out to run down a woman . . . disturbed him a lot more than he would have expected.

"Did the O tell you why?"

Zeklos shook his head. "He is never told. He sees only visions of what must be done or what must be prevented."

"I take it you missed her."

Zeklos nodded but kept his gaze averted. "Yes. I told them I hit the curb and lost control, but in truth I . . . I could not do it. And my brothers know that." Finally he looked up and locked eyes with Jack. "Do you too believe that I should be eating the corn of humiliation?"

"I don't know about the corn of humiliation"—whatever that was—"but I think—"

"What make my failure worse is that Ally has sent second Alarm about this woman. Because of me, it must be tried again."

Sounded like the Ally really had it in for this lady.

"Maybe you're just too human to make a good . . . hit man."

His own word sucker-punched him. He'd said it without forethought, without calculation, and yet here it was . . . here was the connection.

He reached into his pocket and pulled out the Starfire. He set it upright on the counter between them.

"What do you know about this?"

"I've never seen—"

"The hollow point here is filled with cyanide. That mean anything to you?"

Zeklos didn't have to answer. His expression said it all. Yeah, it meant something. Meant a whole lot of something.

Joey's dying words re-echoed . . .

"Something else going on."

Jack grabbed Zeklos by the throat and squeezed.

"Did the MV have anything to do with LaGuardia?"

Zeklos's features hardened as he struggled to get free.

"No! Let me go!"

Jack couldn't read his eyes so he tightened his grip.

"You're lying! You—"

He would have said more but another thought slammed its way to the forefront, pushing everything else aside.

Gia . . . a couple of months ago she'd mentioned how a truck had come within inches of hitting her.

He let Zeklos go.

"This woman . . . the one you were supposed to run down . . . what did she look like?"

Zeklos rubbed his throat and looked at him as if he'd gone nuts. He hadn't. Not yet.

Jack leaned into his face and shouted. *"What did she look like?"*

Zeklos backed away as he spoke. "She had short blond hair and—"

A blast of cold shot through him.

"Where did you almost run her down?"

"Fifty-eighth and Second Avenue. Why do you want to know this?"

"You said the same woman is targeted. When?"

"Today. At one-thirty."

Jack's voice locked. The words wouldn't come. He glanced at Zeklos's kitchen clock: 1:14.

Oh shit, oh hell, oh—

Finally he found the words. "Where?"

"Same place. Fifty-eighth and Second. Why do you care?"

Jack jumped to the door, pelted down the steps, and ran for his car. Along the way he yanked his phone from his pocket.

He stopped at his car door and called her home.

Please answer, Gi. *Please.*

Four rings and then Vicky's voice came on with her leave-a-message routine.

Praying that she'd check her voice mail, he said, "Gi! If you get this, go inside. I mean that. No matter where you are, step into the nearest doorway and call me back. I'm not kidding! This is life or death!"

He slipped behind the Vic's steering wheel and started her up. As he got rolling he dialed her cell number. Maybe she'd come home and retrieved it. But the cell rang and rang until a canned voice-mail message came on.

"You have reached 212 . . ."

With his heart battering against his ribs he left the identical message and gunned the car toward the highways. Which way to go? The BQE to the Manhattan Bridge or jump into the Battery tunnel? His dashboard clock read 1:25.

Either way he'd never make it. Even if he could fly.

Wanted to cry, wanted to vomit. Pounded his steering wheel and screamed at his windshield. So helpless, so goddamn helpless.

Where was she? What could—?

Lunch—lunch time. If she'd stopped to eat . . . where . . . ?

Kosher Nosh.

Jack thumbed 411 and asked for the number. The operator offered to dial it for him.

"Do-it-do-it-do-it!"

Two rings and a man's voice announced that he'd reached

the Kosher Nosh. Jack remembered the name of the owner, the guy who ran the cash register.

"Is this Dov?"

"Who else should it be?"

"Listen, do you know Gia, the woman with short blond hair who comes there a lot? You know who I mean?"

"Know? Of course I know. Pickled herring with sour cream she had. A whole plate." He laughed. "These pregnant wo—"

"Is she still there?"

Say-yes-say-yes-say-yes.

"She and her little girl just walked out."

Little girl? Wasn't Vicky in school?

"Stop them!"

"Already they're gone."

"Go get them! Call them back! I'm begging you! It's an emergency! Life or death! I've got to speak to her right now!"

"Okay. I'll see if I can catch her."

Jack heard the phone hit the counter, heard the voice say, "Aviva. I'm running out for a minute and you shouldn't hang up the phone."

Jack drove on, dying by inches as he waited for Gia's voice to come on the line.

15.

Cal idled his stolen Camry on 58th, downstream from Second, and watched the street corner in his rearview mirror.

Hursey and Jolliff waited down near First in their stolen cars. They'd pull out in Cal and Miller's wake and run interference should anyone come in pursuit.

He fidgeted in his seat. Hard to sit still. Hell, he could barely breathe. Inside his gloves, his palms were slick with sweat under his death grip on the steering wheel.

This shouldn't be happening. The yeniçeri were warriors—trained to fight evil. Usually that meant men. He had no illusions that males had a lock on Otherness-related activity, but executing a pregnant woman and her daughter . . .

He knew the Ally wasn't *good*, per se, but these days—especially after last month—its ends and means seemed indistinguishable from the Otherness's. He'd begun to wonder if good existed.

Take this woman. Yeah, yeah, he'd be the first to admit that looks could deceive, but he'd seen the way she smiled, the way her eyes sparkled as she listened to her little girl reading to her. He didn't give a damn what the Ally said, this woman was *not* evil.

He needed a bathroom.

16. Miller idled the truck in an empty fire hydrant space west of Second Avenue. He had the last spot on the corner and an unobstructed view of the intersection. Second ran uptown, moving from his right to his left.

He shifted his attention between his watch and the traffic light. He'd been timing the sequence. The green came in consistently at an even sixty seconds, followed by five seconds of amber. He'd have to time this perfectly. Wouldn't be easy, but it could be done.

And he could do it.

Shit, he hoped so. One thing to play hard guy with Davis, but something else entirely to have to live up to your own press and—

Suddenly she was there—short blond hair just as the O had described—and heading for the corner, guiding a kid.

Why'd there have to be a kid along? Kids were noncombatants as far as he was concerned, but the O said the Ally wanted them both. Miller trusted the Ally. He had to. Without that trust, he had nothing. His life would mean nothing.

He watched the light switch from red to green and began timing. He put the truck in gear and waited. He noticed he'd broken out in a sweat. What was wrong with him?

He watched her standing at the curb, waiting for permission to walk. Miller always ignored those signals—wasn't going to wait for anyone's permission to cross a street—but he guessed it was a different story with a kid along. Set a good example and all that.

At the fifty-five-second mark he started inching the truck forward. He waited for the amber, then counted down. With a second left to go he hit the gas and roared into action, picking up speed as the light turned red. He saw the woman and the kid step off the curb.

The only thing that could stop him now was some asshole getting a jackrabbit start on the green.

17. The Oculus was sitting at his desk, taking a break from schooling Diana, when the room darkened.

His head snapped up as he realized this wasn't simply a fluctuation in the current—this dimness originated in the room, in the air around him.

As the darkness deepened he reached for his call buzzer to summon a yeniçeri but found he could not move. His hands had rooted to his desktop, his body to the chair, his feet to the floor. He opened his mouth to shout for help but his throat locked before he could utter a sound.

He watched in helpless terror as the darkness enveloped him. It didn't block the light, it absorbed it.

In half a minute, perhaps less, the formless darkness became complete. No up, no down, just fathomless blackness.

And then he knew he was not alone in the room.

A pair of eyes appeared before him, floating in the otherwise featureless void. His mind, desperate for orientation of any sort, grasped at them, then recoiled.

The whites were cold and hard as crystal, the irises dark, verging on black. But the pupils . . . the pupils were windows into a writhing, hungry chaos, inviting him in.

Why not go? Why not leave behind this weight of responsibility? It would be so easy . . . so easy . . .

He shook it off.

And then he heard the music . . . if it could be called that. A choir screaming a discordant cacophony. But no human voices had ever made sounds like these.

"So," said a soft voice, "you are the local Oculus. I'd introduce myself, but I believe you've figured out who I am."

The Oculus knew and the realization threatened to empty his bladder.

Rasalom . . . the Adversary.

"I've put off meeting you because I wanted to wait until certain events had transpired. I was about to pay a call last November but plans went awry, didn't they. This time, however, all will go as planned—no second reprieve for this woman."

He spoke so casually, with no more emotion than someone ordering cold cuts at a deli. Yet the Oculus sensed a mix of hunger and malicious glee bubbling beneath the façade.

But he had no time to wonder why. His brain buzzed with the question of how Rasalom knew about the woman and that the Ally had marked her for death.

Unless . . .

His mind reeled at the possibility that the Otherness had sent those Alarms. The idea had occurred to him this morning but he'd discarded it as impossible. He had a direct link to the Ally, a dedicated line, so to speak.

But what if the Otherness had tapped in and sent a false Alarm?

What if this woman was being run down not at the Ally's behest, but at its expense?

And he had been the instrument.

Why me?

"I'm sure you have a thousand questions," Rasalom said. "We have some time, so why not pass it with a few explanations. Not a Q and A, I fear. More of a soliloquy. What I'm going to tell you will upset you, make you doubt yourself and your calling, but that's all to the good. It will serve as an appetizer to what is to come."

The Oculus knew many things could upset him, but nothing could make him doubt himself and his calling.

But as Rasalom told his tale, he realized he was wrong.

18. The WALK sign flashed the go-ahead green to cross 58th. Gia was just stepping off the curb when she heard a voice calling from somewhere behind.

"Miss! Oh, Miss!"

Calling her?

She turned and saw Dov, the owner of Kosher Nosh, hurrying toward her, waving his arms.

Had she forgotten something?

"Phone call!" he said, pointing back toward the deli. "Emergency phone call!"

Emergency? Who—?

Her chest tightened as the possibilities raced through her mind. Had something happened to her parents? No, they wouldn't know about Kosher Nosh. Only Jack knew of her fondness for the place, and no one in her family had a way to contact him.

It had to be Jack.

She signaled to Dov that she'd heard him, then turned to take Vicky back. She was surprised to see her a third of the way across the street, her nose in her new book. Probably thought she was right behind her.

Then things began to happen.

Hearing the roar of a big engine . . .

. . . turning to see a truck of some sort running the red light and bearing down on Vicky . . .

. . . seeing the hulking shadow behind the wheel . . .

. . . realizing he wasn't going to stop . . .

. . . knowing Vicky was going to be hit and nothing she could do would change that . . .

. . . leaping into the street . . .

. . . pushing Vicky to get her out of harm's way . . .
. . . seeing the truck's grille rushing at her . . .
. . . feeling an instant of awful, bone-crushing impact . . .
Then nothing.

19. Cal saw it all—saw the kid step off the curb, saw the mother run to the child, saw the impact, saw two human projectiles that looked like rag dolls.

And then Miller came to a screeching halt behind him, blocking the view. He hopped out of the truck and into the passenger seat.

"Let's go!" He pounded on the dashboard. "Go-go-go!"

Fighting a wave of nausea, Cal flipped the Camry into gear. The tires chirped as he hit the gas.

Neither spoke as they accelerated the half block down to First Avenue and turned downtown. Though the FDR might be faster, they'd opted instead for local streets, figuring they'd offer more options.

Somewhere in the forties, Cal gave in to the need to say something.

"Are we proud of ourselves yet?"

He expected a typical Miller reply—like "Fuck you"—but it didn't come.

"Almost missed her," Miller said in a low voice. "For some reason she stopped at the curb. I mean I could have driven up on the sidewalk to take her out, but probably would have wrecked the truck and me along with it."

Cal glanced at him. Something odd in Miller's voice.

"But that didn't happen," Cal said, and added a silent *unfortunately*.

"No. I was figuring I'd have to settle for just the kid when the woman sees me coming and jumps out to try and save her when there was no way in hell she could. They both looked at me. I saw their eyes—they had the same blue eyes—staring at me just before . . ."

As Miller's voice trailed off, Cal shook his head. He was feeling worse and worse.

"So . . . the mother knows it's going to cost her life but she tries anyway?"

"Yeah. She was in the clear."

"But her kid was more important." Cal gave his head another shake. "Does this sound like someone involved with the Otherness? Someone who's a threat to the Ally? What did we just do, Miller? What have we *done*?"

Miller said, "Pull over."

"What do you mean? We've got to keep moving."

"Pull over, goddammit!" His voice sounded strange. Strained. No questioning the urgency in the tone.

So Cal pulled to the right and stopped midblock. Miller opened his door and leaned out. Cal heard retching and the splat of vomit hitting the pavement. Twice.

Then he straightened and wiped his mouth on his sleeve as he closed the door. He looked pale and sweaty.

Cal stared at him, astonished. "What the—?"

"Just something I ate, okay? Shut up and call the O. Tell the fucker it's done."

Then he leaned back and closed his eyes and took a deep, shuddering breath.

20. Jack shouted into the phone as he steered the car into the maw of the Brooklyn Battery Tunnel.

"Hello! Hello, goddammit!"

Where was she? Where was Dov? Had he missed her? Why wasn't one of them back?

His blood chilled when he heard a commotion on the other end, cries of alarm.

Oh, please . . . please . . .

After a seeming eternity—long enough for Jack to near the far end of the tunnel—he heard a voice. Not on the phone, but near it.

Not Gia. Dov.

Jack's blood began to sludge as he heard him wailing, *"Oh, dear God! Oh dear God!"* in the background.

"Pick up! Pick up!"

Finally a clatter and then the guy's voice, sounding strained, shaky.

"You are still there?"

"What happened? What's wrong?"

"A terrible thing! A terrible thing! The lady and the little girl—by a truck they were hit!"

Jack forced the words past a locking throat. "Are they hurt? Are they alive?"

"They're hurt terrible is all I can tell you. I don't see how they could live through such a thing. Emergency has been called. Help is on the way but I don't know . . . I don't know . . ."

Jack dropped the phone without cutting the connection. Dov might have been still talking but he couldn't hear.

The tunnel wavered before him, went out of focus. A blaring honk brought him back in time to keep his car from drifting into the next lane.

He searched for an emotion but he felt nothing—no rage, no fear, no sorrow. He'd flatlined. All that kept him sane was the conviction that this couldn't be . . . couldn't be . . .

Sunlight ahead. He aimed for it. Then he was out and pointed toward the FDR Drive. As he raced uptown he felt his insides turning to stone.

21. The Oculus's insides jumped as the ringing of the phone jangled through the enveloping darkness. With each passing minute the temperature had dropped, but his body was nowhere near as cold as his soul.

For as he'd sat in this black neverwhere he'd been forced to listen to the Adversary as he whispered his insidious, serpentine soliloquy.

What I'm going to tell you will upset you, make you doubt yourself and your calling . . .

The Oculus hadn't thought that possible, and had listened through a wall of iron confidence. His calling was his heritage, in his genes.

But now . . .

As Rasalom had talked on, his words rang true, resonating with the Oculus's own questions about the Ally's recent alarms. And toward the end, as he saw how it hewed to a certain frightful logic, he realized that Rasalom might very well be telling the truth.

It sickened the Oculus to his soul to realize that he might have been involved in—

He heard the phone's receiver rattle off its cradle and a voice say, "Hello?"

Rasalom had picked up the call and . . . it took the Oculus a few heartbeats before he realized that Rasalom was speaking in a perfect imitation of his voice.

"Very well. Good work . . . You sound upset. I can hear it. I feel your pain . . . Yes, well, we answer to a higher calling, don't we? You must take solace in that."

Then the sound of the receiver returning to its cradle.

"And there it is," Rasalom said softly in his previous voice.

"Confirmation from the yeniçeri themselves. A bit late calling back, don't you think? Perhaps because they're upset. I sensed their inner turmoil. They aren't yet aware of what I've told you, and perhaps they never will be, but they sense that something is not right, that something is askew. It's causing confusion. And confusion is . . . delicious."

And then those eyes with the unblinking stare hovered before him again.

"Well, now that the Alarm has been answered and the mission complete, I don't see that I have any further use for you. The important question is, how to dispose of you?"

The Oculus's bladder clenched. The yeniçeri—what were they doing? If only one of them would call, or stop in, or—

"But another question is, what to do with your daughter?"

Not Diana! No, please!

If only he could speak, shout . . .

Rasalom's tone became mocking. "Ah, the concern of a loving parent for the safety and well-being of his beloved offspring. I sense your terror, your dread, your plummeting self-worth because of your helplessness. Tasty."

The Oculus's mind screamed for help. Where was the Ally in all this? Where was the Sentinel? Or even the Heir? Why was this being allowed to happen?

"On the other hand, I may let her live. Give those lackeys you call yeniçeri someone to rally around after they work through their loss, their sense of impotence and worthlessness. After a suitable period of self-flagellation, they'll recover and move on to a renewed purpose, a sense of hope, a search for redemption after having failed you so. Let them feel they've succeeded in protecting their new Oculus, then crush them again."

Bastard.

"I know what you're thinking: Why do this piecemeal? Why not go from Oculus to Oculus—say, one a day—and kill each in a serial massacre? Perhaps because all the pieces of the elaborate clockwork I've been assembling are not yet in place. And although the deaths of the Oculi are necessary to the plan, they are but one facet. So it amuses me to spend the intervening time—and you may trust me that it will not be long—removing you poor excuses for prophets at random intervals. The human mind is comforted by patterns, but I shall offer none.

"Now, a question you're probably asking—besides why must I face this alone?—is why is he telling me all this? Well, call it a weakness, but the truth is, my existence does not allow me much opportunity to talk about these things—at least with someone who knows the truth."

The Oculus wished he could shout his own take on the truth: *You want to gloat!*

"I used to have a companion. I called him Mauricio, but that was not his name. I could discuss anything with him— even argue with him. I miss that. He died along with your beloved Twins. A mutual tragedy."

The Twins? Dead?

The Oculus had been all but sure that their absence meant they were dead, but now to hear it from the Adversary himself . . .

If he'd had a voice he would have sobbed.

Rasalom heaved a sigh as heavy as it was artificial.

"But enough talk. Time to get down to business. Your demise must occur in a way that causes the most consternation, evokes the most revulsion in the survivors. I'm good at that. An artist, you might say. I've already done my masterpiece— hard to believe it's been four years already. I tailored it for a certain man—to drive him to his knees, to crush him into the dirt. I thought I'd succeeded, but I've learned he's still standing. I intend to remedy that. As for you, however . . . you shall be an acceptable lesser work."

And then the cold, silent, wrenching, tearing agony began . . .

22. Jack rushed down Second Avenue but slowed as he reached 58th Street and saw a flashing cop car blocking the entrance. He spotted other units farther east, clustered around a double-parked truck. But no ambulances, no EMS rigs.

He'd already stowed his Glock under the front seat, so he double-parked and ran to the nearest uniform.

"Was—?" He cleared his throat. It was almost too tight for speech. "Was there an accident here?"

The cop was waving away cars that wanted to turn onto 58th. He turned and gave Jack the patented NYPD who-the-fuck-are-you? stare.

"Move on, sir."

A vision of his hand shooting out and grabbing this lard-assed bastard's throat and slamming his head back against the roof of his unit flashed through Jack's brain, but he let it remain a fantasy.

"I got a call that my—my wife and little girl had been hit right here. Is that true?"

The cop's features softened. "Oh. Sorry. Yeah, we had a hit and run here. Woman and child hit at high speed. The driver took off."

Jack felt himself swaying—or was it the world? He looked around.

"But where . . . ?"

"On their way to the hospital."

Hope jumped in his chest. His heart starting up again? For the first time since his call to Kosher Nosh, he sensed a trace of life inside.

"You mean they're alive?"

The cop's expression turned bleak as he became more interested in moving the traffic along.

"Can't say. Been up here since the git-go."

"Did you see *any*thing?"

"I saw a couple of pretty banged-up people."

Aw no.

"Where'd they take them?"

"New York Hospital, up on—"

"I know where it is." Jack ran back to his car. Ten blocks uptown on York Avenue—he could be there in minutes.

23. The first indication Miller had that something was wrong was when no one answered the doorbell. He rang it three times and still no one buzzed them in.

Angry and puzzled, he said, "What the fuck?" and jabbed the button for a fourth try.

They'd dumped the stolen cars one at a time along the way. First the Camry. Miller and Cal then piled into Hursey's car, which followed Jolliff until he dumped his. Then all four drove to where they'd left the Suburban. No one had said much along the way.

Miller kept seeing that woman's face as he'd hit her. He kept telling himself it had been for the cause, for the greater good.

But the memory of that face made him want to puke again.

He looked up at the two overhead cameras. Both had their red indicator lights lit, which meant they were operating.

Creeping concern blanked out the soul-deep malaise that had gnawed at him all the way back.

"I don't like this," Cal said.

"Neither do I. I'm going to let us in."

He fished his keys from his pocket while Cal, Hursey, and Jolliff pulled their pistols and hid them under their coats. He heard hammers being cocked. Miller's own H-K would be out in a moment, but first he had to unlock the entrance.

Home was protected by an Electrolynx steel door, set in a steel frame—no way of breaking in—and secured by three bolts. Each yeniçeri had a set of three keys but were supposed to use them only in dire emergency. Each key turned one bolt. Manually unlocking any of the three set off an alarm.

Miller inserted a key into the top lock and heard the warning bell begin to clang as he turned it. At least the alarm worked.

When no one responded, he quickly unlocked the next two, then pocketed the keys and replaced them with his pistol. He looked up and down the street. He felt so exposed out here on the sidewalk in daylight, but no one seemed to be paying them any attention.

"Okay," he said. "Stack."

They quickly divided into pairs on either side of the door-frame. On the left, Miller stood and Jolliff crouched; Cal and Hursey took the right.

"Ready?"

When he had three nods he grabbed the knob, twisted, and pushed the door in. Wilco's "Pot Kettle Black" was playing within, but he heard nothing else: no warning shout, no shots. Just . . . Wilco.

A strange, disturbing odor wafted out along with the music.

Miller chanced a look, tilting his head forward for a peek inside, then ducking back with closed eyes as his stomach did a roll.

Ybarra . . . mouth gaping, eyes wide and staring . . . draped over the monitoring console . . . his head twisted at an impossible angle . . . and blood . . . blood everywhere.

Miller didn't know whether to be angry or afraid. He liked anger—so much cleaner and sharp-edged than fear—so he pumped it up. Not hard to do. One of his brothers, probably more, had been slaughtered right here at Home.

Davis's voice: "What's going on?"

Miller looked at him. "We've been hit."

24. The hospital's official title was New York Presbyterian Hospital–Cornell campus, but no one called it anything but New York Hospital.

Jack pulled into the semicircular entrance drive at the eastern end of 68th Street. The complex had a classic medical-center look—twenty or so stories of vaguely art-deco design with a clean granite face and tall arched windows. He was ready to abandon his car in front of the canopied entrance. If they towed it, so be it. But if they checked the tags first and found Vinny the Donut's name, they might leave it alone.

Then he saw the valet parking sign and screeched to a halt in front of the Latino attendant.

"How long you gonna be?" he said as Jack hopped out of the car.

"Forever. Where's emergency?"

He pointed over Jack's shoulder. "Right over there where it says EMERGENCY."

Jack looked. How had he missed that?

He ran inside and came face-to-face with a uniformed security guard.

"Can I help you?"

"I need to check on two emergency patients."

He jerked a thumb over his shoulder at a windowed alcove. "There you go."

Jack fairly leaped toward it and slid back the glass.

"A woman and a little girl! Just brought in by ambulance! Where are they?"

The mocha-skinned clerk behind the desk took her time looking up from her computer screen. Her name tag read MARIA.

"What are their names, sir?"

"DiLauro and Westphalen."

He spelled both for her and watched as she did some tapping on her keyboard. He couldn't keep still. His fingers kept up a chaotic tattoo on the counter, his feet shuffled back and forth.

She shook her head. "No . . . no one by that name. But we did have two Jane Does brought in, an adult and a child. MVA."

Jack looked around. "Where are they? How are they?" He had to force out the next question. "Are they alive?"

"I can't say."

He felt his fingers stop fidgeting and ball into fists.

"Why the hell not?"

A look of alarm flashed across her face—maybe she'd heard something in his tone.

"Because I don't have that information. They were taken directly to the trauma unit."

He pushed away from the counter.

"Where's that?"

"You can't go there, sir."

"Why the hell not? I'm their husband and father!"

He prayed they wouldn't ask him to prove that.

"You still can't go. Not until they've been worked up and stabilized. No non-staff can be present during resuscitation. You can't—"

"Resuscitation?"

She checked her screen again.

"CPR was under way when they were brought in."

The room did a quick spin. He folded his arms on the counter and pressed his head against them while he quelled a surge of nausea.

He felt a hand on his wrist and when he glanced up he found the clerk looking at him with sympathetic eyes.

"Have faith, Mr. Westphalen. They're in good hands."

Westphalen? Oh, right—he'd said he was the child's father and her name was Westphalen. Gia had dropped her ex's name.

"We have a level-one trauma center here," she was saying.

"Trust that everything possible that can be done for your wife and child is being done."

"I've got to see them. Just once. Just for a second."

She shook her head. "I'm sorry. Please have faith."

Faith? Faith was why they were getting CPR. Men with faith who thought they were doing the right thing because they believed some supposedly unimpeachable source had put Gia and Vicky here.

No more faith. He had to see them. He had to know that a mistake hadn't been made. Two Jane Does? Could be anyone. He had to stick his fingers in their wounds—figuratively, anyway—before he could accept this nightmare as real.

Maria frowned at him. "Don't even think about it."

What was she—a mind reader?

"What?"

"Don't try to sneak up. Security is tight there. And if you cause a ruckus you'll be arrested. And *then* where will you be?"

If she only knew. Arrest would involve a lot more than a fine and a warning. Once the cops learned he didn't exist, he'd be spending his time in a jail cell instead of the waiting room.

Shit.

"Here's what I can do," she said. "I'll call the trauma unit and let them know you're down here. Once your wife and daughter are stabilized, one of the doctors will come down and talk to you."

He nodded, silently thanking her for not saying *if* they're stabilized.

He realized he had no option but to wait.

With limbs of lead, he did a slow turn and looked for a waiting area. He saw three, but only one—the nearest—was unenclosed. He shuffled toward that. He felt a hundred years old.

Not many seats left, but that didn't matter much. Doubted he could sit anyway. The only thing a chair would be good for right now was tossing through a window.

25.

Numb with shock, Cal turned in a slow circle amid the carnage.

They'd entered as they'd been trained, pepper-potting in alternating pairs. Not until they were sure the main floor was secure did they risk a good look at what had been done to their fellow yeniçeri.

Ybarra and the other three who'd been on first-floor duty had all suffered similar fates: necks and backs broken—in how many places Cal could only guess—and their bodies arranged in positions that made them look like spineless rag dolls. Each had a gaping hole in the center of his chest, right where the heart would be. Except the cavities were empty.

Where were the hearts?

Cal wandered around like a dazed bomb survivor. He found their pistols—main carries and backups—spooned together in a line in the center of the floor. But where were their hearts?

Four well-armed men had been slaughtered in broad daylight. How does that happen? He could see if it had been night and a well-trained team with night-vision goggles cut the power and broke in. But the lights were on. How could anyone get close enough—

He heard a faint sob and recognized the voice.

"Diana!"

He whirled. Not here. Couldn't be here. Upstairs—

He wasn't alone as he raced to the stairway. The rest of them had come out of their horrified trances and remembered their primary purpose for being here.

The Oculus.

He heard Diana sob again as he took the steps two at a time.

He skidded to a stop in the Oculus's doorway. The others collided with him from behind, crowding him into the office.

Cal choked back a surge of bile. The carnage downstairs had been only a prelude to this.

Except for the blood spattered everywhere, the office was in perfect order, as if the O had stepped out for a cup of coffee. Only he hadn't stepped out. He was still here, nailed upside down to the wall behind the desk.

In pieces.

His limbs had been torn from their sockets and rearranged so that his arms jutted from his hip sockets, his legs from his shoulders, in a spread-eagle fashion. Like the yeniçeri downstairs, his chest had been ripped open. His head rested on his bloody crotch with his penis jutting from his mouth. Cal noticed that his wide, staring eyes were blue now, the color they must have been before he became an Oculus.

But that wasn't the worst of it. As a finishing touch, his killer—and Cal had little doubt who that was—had used the O's intestines to create a circular border in a hideously grotesque inversion of Da Vinci's Vitruvian Man.

When Cal could drag his gaze from the obscene tableau, he noticed an array of crimson objects on the desk. He took a wobbly step closer and realized they were hearts, eight of them—seven arranged in a perfect circle around the eighth. Looked like some sort of grisly parody of Stonehenge.

He closed his eyes. It confirmed what he'd already guessed: The three yeniçeri upstairs had suffered the same fate as those below.

And then a sob . . . to his right . . . from behind the door to the private quarters.

Diana—still alive. Why? Why would he do that to her father and spare her? It didn't make sense.

Here was one more item to add to Cal's lengthening list of things that didn't make sense.

He rushed to the door but found it locked. No. More than locked. Jammed.

"Diana?" he called. "It's Davis. You're safe now. Stay away from the door. I'm coming in."

He looked back at Miller and the others, all slack-faced with awe and horror.

"Hey! Cover me."

They snapped out of it and stacked up around the door while Cal threw his shoulder against it once, twice, and then broke through on the third. As he stumbled in he found Diana crouched on the floor, head down, face buried in her hands, her body shaking with sobs.

Cal's first reaction was to grab her and drag her to safety, but he wanted to protect her from the charnel house in the outside room. So he broke procedure and made a quick one-man search of the room.

When he was sure it was secure, he knelt beside her, wanting to put a comforting arm around her, but she was only thirteen and he didn't know how she'd react.

"You're safe, Diana."

"My dad," she said through her hands.

Oh shit.

"Did you see?"

"No, but I know he's dead."

"How . . . ?"

She looked up at him with tear-filled eyes . . . all-black eyes, as black as her father's had been.

"Because I am your Oculus now."

26. "Mister Westphalen?"

Jack heard the voice but didn't react. He'd heard at least a hundred names in the past few hours, none of them his. He'd seated himself at the rear of the waiting room and dropped into a barely functioning state just this side of suspended animation.

"Mister Westphalen?"

Then he realized the voice was calling for him. He shot out of his chair, looking around.

"That's me!"

He saw a middle-aged woman standing at the front of the waiting area. She held a clipboard and wore an expectant look. He'd watched the shifts change and she was the new head honcho.

His heart pounded in his throat as he bulled through the waiting area, bumping people left and right, barely aware of an occasional "Hey!" and "Watch it!" His mind was consumed with thoughts of Gia and Vicky, knowing he couldn't expect good news, but praying he wouldn't hear the worst.

Finally he reached her.

"What is it? Something wrong?"

Her face gave nothing away. Most likely she didn't know a thing.

"Doctor Stokely would like to speak to you."

Jack looked over her shoulder. "Who's he?"

"*She*. She's one of our trauma specialists—the attending on your wife and daughter. She's waiting for you in one of the treatment rooms. I'll show you where."

Jack followed her to a small cubicle, windowed on three sides. The curtains were open. Through the glass he saw a dark-skinned woman in green, sweat-stained scrubs. She looked about Jack's age—mid thirties—but the extra twenty or thirty pounds she carried might have taken off a few years. She wore no makeup and kept her kinky black hair short and natural.

She stepped forward and extended her hand as he entered. She introduced herself as Dr. Malinda Stokely.

"Call me Jack," he said as they shook. She had a good grip. "How are they?"

"Let's sit down over here."

Sit? He didn't like the sound of that. The last thing he wanted to do was sit. He'd been sitting for hours. But he didn't argue with her. He took the chair she offered. She sat opposite him.

"Just tell me: Are they alive?"

She said, "Yes—"

Jack slumped in a warm wave of relief.

"—but they're in very serious condition."

He straightened in his seat. Aw, no.

"What's that supposed to mean?"

"I don't know how much you know—"

"I know they were hit by a car, but beyond that . . ."

He couldn't say more. He had a pretty good idea who'd been driving. A score to settle there. A monumental score that dwarfed all scores before it. But it could wait. Had to wait. Nothing more important now than getting Gia and Vicky through this.

"They both suffered trauma to the abdominal viscera, the chest, and the head. We've stabilized them but . . ."

His tongue felt like sand. "But what?"

"The head trauma was severe, especially in your wife. We had to evacuate a subdural hematoma."

Maybe on a good day the words would have made sense, but today, now, they might as well have been Swahili.

"Come again?"

"A pocket of blood inside the skull—between the skull and the brain. It was putting pressure on her brain so we drained it."

"How—?" Jack waved off her explanation. "Never mind." Some things were better left unsaid.

"Your daughter had intracranial bleeding that stopped on its own."

"I guess that's good news."

"Well . . ." She looked him square in the eyes. "They're both comatose."

After a slap of shock and a quailing of his heart, he recovered. Okay. Comatose. He could deal with that. His father had been in a coma down in Florida and he'd come out of it fine. He was up and walking less than a week after his hit and run—

Hit and run . . . was there a pattern here? A connection?

No. Couldn't be. He'd found out who'd run his father down and they were very literally sleeping with the fishes.

"What're their Glasgow scores?"

She blinked. "You know about the Glasgow scale?"

The Florida experience had taught him that there were different levels of coma.

"A little." He steeled himself for the answer. His father had started out a seven, which his neurologist had considered pretty bad. "Scores?"

"Both eight—the same eight: E-two-V-two-M-four."

Well, better than Dad had been.

"What's the E-two stuff?"

"It explains the score. In their cases their eyes open in response to pain—that's a two; any sounds they make are incomprehensible—that's another two; they withdraw from pain—that's a four. And I guess you know that any score of eight or below means severe brain injury."

"What are their chances?"

"It's too soon to say."

He shot out of the seat and circled it. Couldn't sit still.

"I've got to see them, doc. I need to see them."

She nodded as she rose. "Of course. But only for a minute or two."

Feeling as if he were walking underwater he followed her to the elevator. He was pretty sure she was talking to him as the car rose but he couldn't make out the words. Trying to deal with the realization that the two most precious people in his world were comatose crowded out everything else.

The elevator stopped at some floor or another and again he fell in behind Dr. Stokely, following her down a hallway to a pair of double doors. He felt her hand grip his upper arm and stop him just outside.

"I need to warn you that what you're about to see will come as a shock, so be prepared."

"How do you prepare for something like this?"

"Just remember that you're here to look and no more. Whatever you do, don't interfere."

"Why would I interfere?"

"We've had people scream and throw themselves onto the bed. You don't look like the kind to do that, but I just want you forewarned that the first look can be very upsetting."

"You're telling me it gets better with time?"

He couldn't imagine that.

"Let's just say it gets more tolerable."

She elbowed a large button on the wall and the doors swung open. Dr. Stokely started ahead but Jack held back. He saw beds, he saw curtains, he saw tubes and bags, he heard the whoosh of respirators and the beep of heart monitors. The combination paralyzed him. His legs wanted to turn and run, but he forced them forward.

He created a sort of tunnel vision by focusing on the spot between Dr. Stokely's shoulder blades as he followed her. She led him to the feet of two beds and stopped.

"We put them in adjoining beds. Mother and daughter . . . it seemed right."

She stepped aside, giving Jack an unobstructed view.

His first reaction was a wild thought that it was all a horrible mistake, that these two . . . *things* in the beds couldn't be Gia and Vicky. They didn't look anything like either of them. The larger thing lay to the right. He didn't recognize the purple swollen face. It lay on its back with a clear green tube squirting oxygen into its nasal passages. A thick bandage encircled the head. Fluid from bags hanging on both sides ran through tubes into each arm. A blue fiberglass cast encased the left leg. A thicker tube snaked from under the sheet down to a large transparent bag quarter filled with reddish-yellow fluid.

No. This couldn't be Gia.

And to the left, the smaller thing looked like a mirror image of its larger counterpart, except that the cast was on its right arm instead of a leg, and bandages swathed the left side of the face. But no bandages on the head, leaving the hair exposed.

And Jack knew that hair.

The little thing was Vicky.

He heard someone moan and it took him a second to realize the sound had come from him.

He stepped closer and reached out a hand to touch her. Her left palm lay facing up. He placed his index finger across it, expecting it to close and grip him as it always did. How many streets had they crossed with Vicky's little hand gripping that finger? Too many to count.

But the skin of her palm felt unnaturally cool, and the fingers remained inert.

Without turning, he pointed to the bandages on the left side of her face and moved his lips. The words came out sounding like a nail scraping on concrete.

"Why the bandage?"

"Abrasion from the street. She has a fracture of her left zygomatic arch—one of her cheekbones—but it's undisplaced so we're leaving it alone. The bandages are for facial abrasions from when she hit the pavement."

Jack's brain automatically tried to picture it but he shut it down. Instead he leaned over and spoke in her ear.

"Vicky? It's Jack. I'm here. You're gonna be all right. Jack promises."

Stupid thing to say. Irresponsible, even. But the words had come out on their own. Maybe because he'd come to see himself as her protector, and she probably felt the same. After he'd pulled her off that freighter a couple of years ago, she probably assumed nothing bad could happen to her as long as he was around.

But he hadn't been around this time.

He moved over to Gia. Facing her was even harder. Her swollen face was almost unrecognizable. He pointed to her bandaged head.

"The surgery?"

"Yes."

As he squeezed her cold hand he feared he might explode. He touched her purpled cheek, then leaned closer.

"Gia, this is Jack. I'm here and I'll be here as long and as often as they let me. I'm sorry. God, I'm so—"

His voice broke and so instead of trying to say more he kissed her hand. Then he turned to Dr. Stokely.

The doctor looked at him and backed away, her face a mask of fear.

"What?" she said, a tremor in her voice. "I'm not to blame."

"I didn't say—"

Then Jack knew what she was talking about. He closed his eyes and relaxed his facial muscles. He must have had that look. Gia had seen it once and called it "murder incarnate." But he had no grudge against the doc. Just the rest of the world.

Dr. Stokely said, "For a second there I thought you were going to . . . never mind."

"I'm pretty strung out right now, doc. But I need you to tell me flat-out true, no sugar coating: What are their chances?"

"I told you: too soon to say."

"I'm not asking for a percentage, just . . . good or not good?

"Not good."

Jack stared at her—for how long, he didn't know—until he could find his voice. Even then it took a massive force of will to push the next words past his frozen lips.

"You mean they might not make it?"

Her round face revealed no emotion, gave no hint of what she was thinking. He knew that look. He'd seen it on old cops and on the demimonde's bottom feeders. The look that comes from seeing too much human damage, the accidental and the intentional. So much damage that, in the interest of self-preservation, certain circuits shut down. Someone like Dr. Stokely couldn't allow herself to think about the private lives of the people she cared for, couldn't allow their hopes and dreams, the people they loved and the people who loved them to matter. If she did, she'd burn out like a meteor. She had to reduce them to problems to be solved. Which wasn't so hard since the vast majority of her patients were comatose; and the ones who weren't hadn't come to her willingly and wanted to escape as soon as possible.

Here was a woman who was used to giving bad news.

"I've learned not to make predictions, but it's a dire situation."

"Come on, doc. You've been around the block a few times—a *lot* of times. You must have an instinct for these things. What do your instincts say about their chances of coming back?"

She locked her gaze on him and said, "Fifty-fifty."

Fifty-fifty? That was no help. Even odds they'd live or die. Or die . . .

Slowly, forcing his locked knees to turn him back toward the bed, he looked at the loves of his life and wanted to scream. But he couldn't give in to that. If he caused too much of a ruckus they might not allow him back.

What he really wanted to do—*wished* he could do—was rip out their tubes and grab their shoulders and shake them and shout that the game was over and they could stop fooling around now. They'd won, he gave in, they'd scared the hell out of him and ha-ha what a sick, sick joke, but now let's all stop fooling around and go out and laugh about it over a pizza.

Instead he stood there and felt his heart break. He'd always assumed it a figure of speech, a hoary cliché in hackneyed prose and Brill Building tunes, but here it was. Something in his chest turned to glass and shattered.

He bent and kissed Vicky's hand, then bent over Gia and kissed her swollen lips.

As he slowly straightened he noticed that the sheet over her abdomen was flatter than it should be.

He spun to face Dr. Stokely.

"The baby! What about—?"

She shook her head. "I'm sorry. She lost the baby."

27. Davis left Diana in her bedroom in the private quarters. He knew he should be thinking of her as the Oculus now, but he'd known her since she was seven. Hard to think of her by any name other than Diana.

Hard to imagine that this girl, barely into her teens, was going to be their new conduit from the Ally.

He put all that aside as he called the off-duty yeniçeri to give them the awful news and tell them to pack and report to Home: They were moving.

While he was on the phone, Miller, Jolliff, and Hursey began the grisly task of prying the former O's body from the wall and hiding the pieces under a bedspread.

After finishing the last call, Cal leaned his elbows on the monitoring console and rubbed his temples as he tried to get a grip on the situation, on himself.

What's wrong with me?

He should have felt grief, terror, rage, *something.* Instead he felt empty, damn near dead inside.

He thought he knew what it was: The cold-blooded killings recently ordered by the Ally had put him on the down slope, and now this. It wasn't so much that the O was dead, or the appalling manner of his death, it was the *ease* with which it had been done. It seemed as if the Adversary had simply strolled in, slaughtered everyone, and then strolled out.

He heard a noise to his left and looked up to see Miller dropping into a nearby chair. He was drying his hands on a paper towel. He looked as empty as Cal felt.

"Where are we in the cleanup?"

Miller jerked his head toward the stairs. "Last one coming down now."

Cal looked and saw Jolliff and Hursey maneuvering a sheet-covered body down the steps. Blood had seeped through in a couple of spots.

"Who?"

"Kenlo."

"Shit."

He'd liked Kenlo. Cal remembered his easy laugh—the guy had never heard a punch line he didn't like. He'd been their computer geek. Probably the brightest guy in the whole crew.

"What are we going to do with the hearts?"

Cal thought about that. "Stick them back in their chests."

"But we don't know which belongs where."

"I know, but we'll do it anyway. Better than leaving them in a baggie somewhere, and sure as hell better than leaving them arranged in a circle up there on that desk. Each of our guys deserves to be buried with a heart, even if it's not his own."

Miller nodded. "Yeah. I suppose you're right."

The door chime sounded. He checked the monitor and saw Lewis, luggage bags flanking his feet, giving the all-clear sign at the front door. Cal buzzed him in.

He heard Miller sigh and glanced at him. "You okay?"

"Not even close." Miller shook his head. "I mean, is it worth it to move her to the safe house? Will it make any difference? I mean, this guy seems to pick us off as he pleases."

His words mirrored Cal's thoughts.

"The safe house is a little different. You've been there. It's on an island, it's got water on two sides, and only one access road. Nobody's going to be sneaking up on that place."

Cal didn't mention that the location's biggest asset—its isolation—had its downside. At this time of year it offered no distractions for the men during their down time. Cabin fever—or island fever—would set in pretty quickly.

Well, no one had said the job would be easy.

"I wonder," Miller said. "Don't you get the feeling this guy's playing with us? Like he could take us all out any time he pleases but he'd rather play cat and mouse?"

"You mean like leaving Diana alive."

"Exactly. And if he can take us out when he wants, then everything we're doing is useless. We're not even delaying the inevitable because he's got us plugged into his calendar, and when the time comes"—he drew a finger across his throat—"we're cooked."

"Maybe that's why he didn't kill her. To get us thinking it's all an exercise in futility but keep us on the string. He feeds on hopelessness. Maybe we're snack food. But maybe not. Maybe—"

The chime again. This time it was Geraci. Cal buzzed him in, then turned back to Miller.

"You ready to give up?"

Miller gave him a hard stare. "Me? You should damn fuck know better than that."

"I do. Just checking."

Another chime. Cal looked and saw Zeklos. He'd called the little guy back in because they were so shorthanded. He'd meant to tell Miller in advance so he'd be prepared, but hadn't had the time.

He buzzed him in and then tapped the heel of his fist on Miller's knee.

"I called Zek in."

Miller stiffened in his chair. "You what?"

"We need every warm body we can get, so just put aside your—"

He shot to his feet. "No fucking way!"

Zeklos came through the door then, rolling a wheeled suitcase behind him.

"This is terrible, terrible!" he said. "How did such a thing—?"

"You!" Miller shouted, pointing at him. For a crazy instant he reminded Cal of Ralph Kramden. "Out!"

Zeklos stopped and stared, shock in his eyes and his expression.

"But Davis—"

"I don't give a shit what Davis said, I'm not working with you ever again!"

"Easy, Miller," Cal said. "We need him."

"Fuck we do! He's a Jonah! He loses his Oculus, then shows up here and we lose ours."

Zeklos stood his ground.

"The other day you say to me, 'the fact remains that your Oculus is dead and you are not.' " He held up his index finger. " 'Strike one.' Remember? Well now *I* say to you that your Oculus is dead and you are not." Now the index finger pointed at Miller. "Strike one on you."

Cal couldn't believe his ears. Neither could Miller, apparently, because he stood staring at Zeklos with a slack, drop-jawed expression.

Cal recovered first. Knowing what would happen next, he grabbed Miller's upper arm with both hands and held on as Miller started toward Zek.

"Why you little piece of—!"

"Cool it!" Cal shouted. "We just lost seven brothers and our Oculus! This is not the time to start fighting among ourselves! This is exactly what the Adversary wants. You're playing right into his game."

Miller dragged him a few steps, then stopped, red-faced, panting.

"He's not coming along!"

"We need—"

He whirled on Cal. "If he comes, I stay. And I'm pretty sure I won't be the only one."

"You'd sabotage our whole operation over some personal vendetta?"

"It's not personal. He's a menace. And I mean what I say. Him or me and others. Choose."

Miller knew damn well he'd left Cal with only one choice.

The door chimed again. Cal glanced at the monitor, saw Portman, and hit the button.

"Well, what's it gonna be, Davis?" Miller said.

Cal was looking for a way out when Portman walked up and dropped a newspaper on the monitoring console. The headline of the *Post*'s late edition leaped out at him.

HIT & RUN
HORROR!

The subheading read: MOTHER AND DAUGHTER MOWED DOWN BY RED-LIGHT RUNNER.

Cal's stomach clenched as he looked up at Portman. "Yeah, we know. We were there, remember?"

Portman had a funny expression. "Check out page three."

Cal did just that. He recoiled at the grainy black-and-white photo of EMTs loading a small figure on a stretcher into an ambulance.

"So?"

Portman tapped a fingertip on one of the paragraphs.

"Says here she's still alive. Looks like we missed again."

Cal felt a burst of elation.

He heard Miller mutter, "Shit."

Behind Portman, he saw Zeklos raise two fingers.

"Strike two, Miller."

28.   Jack found himself at the corner of a park he hadn't known existed. Looked to be about two blocks long and one deep. He stared up at the street sign: 78th AND CHEROKEE PLACE.

Where the hell was he?

He vaguely remembered Dr. Stokely telling him that his visiting time in the trauma unit was up but he could come back later. Until then he could wait in the family lounge. But that meant more sitting, and Jack couldn't sit.

The baby . . . on top of everything else, the baby . . . gone.

Had to get out, had to move. He'd fled the hospital and walked into the night. Must have turned uptown, then turned east at some point because he could hear the roar of racing traffic ahead of him, and see twinkles of distant lights across the water. The traffic had to be the FDR, the water the East River, and the lights Queens, or maybe Roosevelt Island.

The cars made the only sound. The park lay deserted to his right. No surprise in that. Nobody with any sense would be looking for a park bench on a night as cold as this. And even if they were, the eight-foot, spike-topped wrought-iron fence would keep them out.

A nearby plaque read JOHN JAY PARK.

He'd heard of the place but had never been here.

He spotted a ramp ahead, leading to what looked like a pedestrian bridge over the FDR. He started moving again. Midspan he stopped and looked through the high, tight, chain-link fencing at the cars below.

If the NJ Turnpike had had this sort of fence on a certain overpass fifteen years ago, he'd be leading a different life now. He never would have met Gia and Vicky, and he'd be so much poorer for that. But at least they wouldn't be fighting for their lives now.

He didn't know exactly how, but he had no doubt this was all his fault.

A crushing fatigue settled over him. Feeling as empty as the promenade on the far side of the overpass, he stumbled down the ramp, found a bench, and dropped onto it.

He'd never been here before, but could imagine the concrete path packed with joggers, strollers, and bike riders during the warmer weather. A low wrought-iron fence on the far side of the promenade separated him from the water running a dozen feet below. He noticed huge dock cleats, painted black like the fencing and spaced every twenty feet or so along the edge. That told him boats used to dock here. Maybe they still did.

Baker Street–style lampposts lined the walk, augmenting the wash of light from the FDR's overhead lamps.

He sat and stared at Roosevelt Island, a long clump of land plopped in the center of the East River. The lights of the apartment buildings blazed, blocking his view of Astoria and Long Island City on the far side. He watched a jet glide into LaGuardia. To his right the lights of the graceful Queensborough Bridge twinkled in the night while the Roosevelt Island trams shuttled to and from Manhattan on their wires.

On any other night he'd have thought it a beautiful sight, but beauty is better when shared. He'd have loved nothing more in the world than to be sitting between Gia and Vicky right now, an arm around each of them. He could almost hear Gia saying that she'd like to come back to this spot tomorrow night and paint the scene.

And then he thought about the baby, his lost child. He remembered all the times in the past few months he'd imagined himself bouncing his little boy on his knee, tickling him to make him laugh, teaching him to throw and catch and—

Christ, he didn't even know if the baby was a boy or a girl. His mind had been so numb he'd forgotten to ask.

But even if it turned out to be a girl, no matter. She'd still need bouncing and tickling, and even throwing and catching lessons. And she'd have been beautiful, with blond hair and blue eyes like her mother's.

This time last night he was starting a new future, one crammed with possibilities. Now he had nothing. Not even hope.

That was the worst of it. *Where there's life, there's hope.* Yeah, right. Maybe. But not in this case. Gia and Vicky might go on living, but not as Gia and Vicky. No, don't call it living. Mere existence was not living. The two people he'd loved would be gone while the blobs of protoplasm they'd inhabited survived.

He clung to the possibility that Dr. Stokely had understated the possibilities. She'd probably learned a few hard lessons about giving families hope and then not being able to deliver. False hope worked for a while, but in the end it was worse than no hope.

No hope . . . that certainly fit the baby's case. No coming back for him. Or her. He'd imagined a little piece of himself and Gia continuing beyond their time, their place, aimed toward infinity.

Now . . . never happen.

But the very worst was knowing the reason why Gia and Vicky and the baby were where they were.

Him. Jack.

The Otherness was toying with him, trying to break him down. First Kate, then his father and brother, and now his child and the two people on Earth who meant the most to him.

On the face of it, flat-out killing him and having done with it made more sense. Why target those around him?

Last fall, in a Florida swamp, Rasalom himself had provided the answer.

"Killing you now might be something of a favor. It would spare you so much pain in the months to come. And why should I do you a favor? Why should I spare you that pain? I don't want you to miss one iota of what is coming your way.

"Physical pain is mere sustenance. But a strong man slowly battered into despair and hopelessness . . . that is a delicacy. In your case, it might even approach ecstasy. I don't want to deprive myself of that."

Being on intimate terms with the Otherness, Rasalom had known exactly what was coming.

Jack hadn't.

He didn't know how to deal with this. Did anyone? He wanted the ground to crack open and swallow him.

A sob tore loose from deep, deep inside. His head fell back as he let it loose and screamed into the night—all the pain, all the shattered dreams, all the frustration . . .

He straightened and wiped his eyes. Had to get a grip. Had to—

The lamp above him winked out. Then the one to his right, thirty feet away, did the same. Then the one to his left.

What the hell?

Then the overheads on the FDR began dying, up and down the road.

Some sort of power failure.

So what?

As he continued to stare across the water he saw a round shadow slowly rise on the far side of the railing. At first he thought it was a balloon, but as it continued to rise it broadened into a pair of shoulders, then arms straight down its sides.

A man . . . a floating man.

The languorous way it rose, without moving its arms . . . had to be a balloon, an inflatable doll.

But when its feet reached the level of the top rung, it moved, stepping forward to stand on the railing. Then it crouched with its arms about its knees and perched there like some sort of gargoyle. Jack couldn't see the face, but he knew its eyes were fixed on him.

"What the—?"

"Hello, *Heir*," it said in a mocking tone. "How's life?"

Jack knew that voice.

Rasalom.

With a howl he went to leap off the seat and wrap his fingers around the throat that housed it. And if the two of them tumbled to the river below, so be it. He'd go to his grave strangling this son of a bitch.

But he never left the seat. He could move his arms, but not

his feet or his legs. His body wouldn't budge. He clawed the air and howled again, sounding like a madman. At that moment he was.

Rasalom put his head back and sniffed the air.

"Mmm. The nectar of desolation, the liquor of devastation, the elixir of despair, the wine of disheartenment. This is a fine, fine vintage. If only I could bottle it."

Jack felt his rage cooling. Not lessening, simply mutating from hot to cold.

"Why?" he managed to say. "Am I that much of a threat to your all-powerful boss?"

"Boss? Oh, you must mean what you people so quaintly call the Otherness. No, it's not my *boss*, so to speak, but we do have arrangements—promises that have been made—for when certain ongoing operations and processes run their courses."

"So you sent a false Alarm through the Oculus, made the yeniçeri think they were doing the Ally's work."

"A false Alarm is very difficult. Only once have I been able to send one. I prefer more indirect stratagems. For instance, to make you cross paths with the yeniçeri, I encouraged a cretinous cult I'd started—just for this purpose, by the way—to kidnap the niece of someone who frequents one of your environs—"

"Cailin?"

"Yes. Her. Well, they thought they were going to 'sacrifice her to the Otherness.' Of course, I'm far more interested in torture sacrifices than is the Otherness, but they didn't know that. The 'Otherness' part set off the Alarm—a genuine Alarm—and three yeniçeri were sent."

Jack was baffled. "Why would you want me in contact with the yeniçeri?"

"So you would wind up right where you are now. But you almost escaped me. I had to send a false Alarm—a very brief one, and quite a strain it was. It went through a Florida Oculus. I wanted to bring you back."

"The yeniçeri assassin? You sent him? Why did you want me back?"

"Because I didn't want you in Europe when your last two loved ones were removed."

Last two loved ones . . . the filthy—

Jack exerted every fiber of muscle, every ounce of will to lever himself from the bench, but he might as well have been trying to stop the freighter making its way down river behind Rasalom.

"Is your boss so petty it stoops to killing mothers and children? How did they even get on its radar?"

"Let's not forget the deaths of your father and siblings. You're wondering why something as vast as the Otherness would concern itself with these seeming trivialities?"

"So you could have this moment, I suppose."

Rasalom laughed, and the genuine amusement in the sound puzzled Jack.

"The Otherness leaves me to create my own amusements."

"Then *why*? Does it think I'll be so discouraged and beaten down that I'll crawl into a hole and die? Well, guess what— it's backfired. It's made an enemy for life who'll do anything and everything to get in its way. So you'd better kill me now."

Jack realized then that for the first time in his life he was reaching a point where he wouldn't mind dying. If Gia and Vicky didn't make it, he couldn't think of a goddamn thing to live for . . . beyond revenge. And revenge wasn't enough.

Rasalom said nothing.

"Why, goddammit?"

A dramatic sigh. "Well, I was saving this for later but I suppose telling you now will have just as much effect: The Otherness is not behind the tragedies that have befallen your loved ones."

"Don't lie to me. I *know*!"

"Have you ever heard the expression, 'A spear has no branches'?"

Jack had—a number of times. But what—?

And then the realization came crashing in on him, crushing him like an avalanche.

"The Ally?" He could barely hear his own voice.

The silhouette nodded. "Who else?"

Jack sensed the glee in the tone and his mind reeled. Had

the side that had drafted him been systematically eliminating everyone who meant anything to him? It couldn't be.

"Aaahhh . . . the broth of betrayal. Spicy, delect—" Jack saw the silhouette straighten, saw the head swivel. "What?" It dropped to the pavement and stood looking around. "Where are you? Come out!"

"I'm over here," said a woman's voice to Jack's right.

As he looked around, the lights flickered to life, but weak, sickly life. He saw a tall slim woman in a long, stylish, camel hair coat. She had patrician features and wore her long, glossy black hair up in a knot, Audrey Hepburn–style. A dog—an Akita, maybe—strained at the leash she gripped.

"You!" Rasalom gritted. "What are you doing here?"

"Halting your feast." Her tone was cultured, just this side of Long Island lockjaw. "And clearing the table."

A lady with a dog, Jack thought. Again.

"Since when do you interfere in my business?"

"Since now. Be on your way." Her voice betrayed no emotion. She could have been ordering alterations on a dress. "I'm sure you can find a child being molested somewhere and slake your thirst there. You'll sup no more here."

"No? We'll see about that."

He turned back to Jack and stepped toward him, arms extended, fingers curved like claws.

The dog growled.

"Don't force me to release him."

Rasalom hesitated.

"That thing can't harm me."

"He can't *kill* you, but he can certainly *harm* you. Or did you forget that you still inhabit human flesh?"

"I can harm him as well."

"I know. And I wouldn't want to see that, so that is why I still hold the leash. But if you force my hand . . ."

"Why are you doing this?"

The words sounded as if they were being driven through clenched teeth. Jack could sense his rage.

"Because it pleases me. And because I can. You are of this Earth, and nothing of this Earth can harm me. Move along, Rasalom. You're finished here."

"You do not order me about."

"I just did. I can't make you go, of course. And you can't drive me away. But I can keep you from feeding. I believe this is what is called a stalemate."

He took a step toward her but stopped when the dog growled.

"I'll put an end to you eventually," he whispered. "It's inevitable and you know it."

"I know nothing of the sort."

"I've already hurt you and weakened you."

"Not you. That in no way guarantees you victory."

Jack noticed a drop in the assurance of her tone.

"Not yet. But I'm growing stronger while you are not. I'll weaken you again. And after that . . ."

"My-my, what confidence. Aren't you forgetting someone?"

Now it was Rasalom's turn to lose a little self-assurance.

"I'm not worried about him."

Jack gathered they were talking about Glaeken—the Sentinel.

"You should be," the Lady said. "The last time you underestimated him you wound up locked away for half a millennium."

"That will not happen again."

"Are you sure?" Her tone turned taunting. "You've never been able to defeat him."

"Those were different times. This time I'm restructuring the battlefield to my liking. When I'm ready to make my move, I will have the high ground and he will be powerless to stop me."

She shook her head. "Hubris . . ."

"Where is he then?" Rasalom said, and Jack heard anger in his tone. "I might already be too powerful for him. That's why he doesn't show himself."

"Why don't you show *yourself*? Why do *you* hide? Why do you sneak through the shadows, never showing yourself? You fear him."

"Perhaps he fears me."

Probably right, Jack thought. One of the Ladies had told

him that the Sentinel was nothing but a powerless old man now. Obviously Rasalom did not know that.

"I doubt that very much," the Lady said. "I believe he's watching you, toying with you, letting you think you're gaining the upper hand, waiting until you're almost ready before he moves in and crushes you—just as he's done before."

Good for you, Jack thought. Keep him off balance, keep him looking over his shoulder.

Rasalom said nothing.

"One thing you can be sure of," the Lady said, pointing to Jack, "is that he has his eye on this one. Harming him will be like setting off a beacon as to your whereabouts. And then the hunt will begin in earnest—and *you* will be the prey."

Rasalom straightened his shoulders. "My time is near. I know who will win our Ragnarok. But you won't be there to see it."

He hopped up onto the top rail where he turned toward Jack. Through all this he'd not had a single glimpse of Rasalom's face.

"And neither will you."

With that he took a step back and slowly sank from sight.

29. Cal couldn't drag his eyes or his attention from the newspaper.

"What do we do?" Miller said.

Cal looked up at him. This was the first time in recent memory that Miller had asked his advice.

They stood at the monitoring console, an island of tranquility in a sea of furious activity. Back in the lounge area he could see Lewis and Geraci emptying the contents of the lockers into heavy-duty black garbage bags.

"I don't know that we do anything."

"Get off it. We were supposed to take them out but they're not—down, maybe, but not out."

"We don't know that they were supposed to be killed. The Oculus saw us hitting them with a truck—"

"Not us—you. He saw *you* driving. But it didn't turn out that way, did it."

Cal didn't reply. No need to.

Miller leaned closer. "Let's cut the bullshit, okay? The Ally didn't show you running down those two because it wants them laid up for a while. It wants them out. Gone. Kaput."

Cal looked at the paper again. "Says they're in critical condition. Maybe they won't last."

" 'Critical condition' don't mean shit. You ever read about anyone going into a hospital in less than critical condition? Yeah, it means someone's bad hurt, but I bet nine out of ten walk out of there."

"You hit them awful hard."

"But not as hard as I could've. If the lady had stepped off the curb with her kid, yeah—they'd've been goners. But she held back—talking to someone, I think. Don't matter why. Bottom line was I had to swerve toward her, and then when she ran out to her kid I had to swerve back again. If they'd stayed together we wouldn't be having this conversation."

They stood in silence. Cal glanced at Miller and saw a pensive look on his face. He seemed to have regained some of his usual bravado, but not all.

Then Cal thought of something.

"Maybe we *shouldn't* be having this conversation."

Miller gave him a questioning look.

"I'm saying, what if they didn't make it. What if they're already gone? Then we can forget about them."

Or try to anyway.

"How do we find out?"

Cal looked at the paper. The woman's name was given as Gia DiLauro, the little girl as Victoria Westphalen. His stomach gave a lurch. He wished he hadn't read that. They had names now. That made it worse.

"Says they were taken to New York Hospital. Okay . . ."

He picked up the phone and called information which gave him the hospital's main number. He dialed in and got shifted around until he wound up with Patient Information. He decided on a backdoor approach.

"I'd like to send some flowers to two of your patients. Can you give me the room numbers of"—he checked the article—"Gia DiLauro and Victoria Westphalen?"

Miller gave him a thumbs-up.

After spelling both names twice, he learned what he hadn't wanted to hear.

"I'm sorry, they're in the trauma unit. No flowers allowed, I'm afraid."

He thanked her and hung up.

He didn't look at Miller as he spoke. "They're still hanging on."

Cal jumped as something crashed behind him. He turned and saw Portman smashing one of their computer towers. Zeklos was helping him. They both wielded heavy hammers to crack open the case. Zeklos pulled out the hard drive and together they began smashing it into an unrecognizable lump of metal and plastic.

Transporting the computers risked disaster if they fell into the wrong hands, so they'd leave them—but not in useful condition. They'd run a shredder program on each drive but Cal felt it foolish to underestimate the ability of some hacker to peek under the overwrites. He didn't have a degausser to do a magnetic wipe, so he told the men to smash the drives as well. The MV had other computers at the safe house and secure backups of everything that mattered.

Zeklos saw him looking and approached.

Miller snarled. "What do you want?"

"The Heir came to my apartment today."

Miller looked at Cal. "Didn't he say he was going out of town?"

Cal nodded. Yeah, he had. He turned to Zek.

"Why would he want to see you?"

"He talk about MV. He say if he is to join, then he wish to know about it."

"Why didn't he come to us?" Miller said.

Zek eyed him. "You have not been very welcoming."

That was true in Miller's case, but Cal thought he and the guy had connected in some way. He was getting a bad feeling about this. The only reason to go to a guy on the outs with a group was to hear the dirt.

"What exactly did he want to know?"

Miller added, "And what exactly did you tell him?"

"Very little. But I do not think that is why he come." He reached into his pocket. "He brought this."

He held out his hand. Cal felt an electric jolt when he saw the Starfire's filled hollow.

"Oh, shit," Miller said. "Where the fuck did he get that?"

"He did not say. He ran out before I could ask him."

"When was this?" Cal said.

"A little after one o'clock."

"Why did he run out?"

"I do not know."

Zek's eyes said that wasn't quite true, but that would keep

till later. Cal didn't want to get sidetracked from the Starfire. Cyanide tips were what the yeniçeri had been taught to use for a hit. And the Starfire was favored because it had such a large hollow.

"One o'clock," Miller said. "Diana says she heard the commotion of a fight around one-thirty. The guy's in the neighborhood, pumping Zeklos, then he leaves, and a little while later the O and everybody else are slaughtered." He looked at Cal. "You thinking what I'm thinking?"

"I can't imagine what you're thinking."

Miller leaned closer. "Maybe this 'Heir' wasn't anything of the sort. For all we know he could have been the Adversary in disguise, and we invited him in. Hell, we dragged him in like a Trojan fucking horse."

"The O would have known."

"Yeah? He didn't know he was going to be torn to pieces. Maybe he got fooled."

Cal didn't want to think that, but he had to admit the timing was suspicious.

Miller pounded a fist on the console. "I never trusted that fucker. I smelled something wrong from the git-go."

Cal took the Starfire from Zek and pointed back to the computers.

"Finish up so we can get out of here."

He pocketed it as he turned back to Miller.

"We'll worry about the bullet later. Right now we need to decide about the woman and the girl. What do you think we should do?"

He hesitated, then shrugged. "Finish the job."

"How are you—?"

"Uh-uh." Miller was shaking his head. "Not me. I'm not letting our new Oculus out of my sight."

Cal felt the same way. Who knew how many were left in the world?

"So who? It'll be a kamikaze mission."

Miller had that pensive look again. "Kamikaze . . ."

"What are you thinking?"

"I know just the guy." He straightened and called over Cal's shoulder. "Hey, Zeklos—want to redeem yourself?"

30.   As soon as Rasalom disappeared, Jack felt the bench release his body. He sprang to the railing and peered below, but saw only dark, churning water. No sign of him.

Gone.

So what?

He stepped back and slumped into the seat again. He glanced right and saw the lady and her dog still standing there.

"How many of you are there?" he said.

She stepped closer.

"As many as need be."

Women with dogs had been dropping in and out of his life since last year. They all knew more about what was going on in his life than he did. They seemed to be a third force in the shadow war. One had told him that if they had their way, both the Otherness *and* the Ally would be chased off to do their interfering somewhere else.

"What did you mean about preventing him from feeding?"

"I blocked his access to your pain."

"You can do that?"

"Only on a one-to-one basis. If I could block him from all the world's pain, he'd shrivel up and blow away."

Jack sat in silence, wondering at the sick nature of what had become his reality.

Finally he looked up at her. "Is it true what he said—that all this is the Ally's doing?"

She nodded. "I am afraid so."

He felt weak, as if life were oozing out of him.

"But I'm supposed to be on the Ally's side. Is this what it does to its people? Is this any way to treat your troops?"

"You've been told about the war: It's not a battle between Good and Evil, but more like a battle between the indifferent and the inimical. We cannot comprehend their scope, nor understand their motivations, so it's useless to try."

"But I thought the Ally would at least—"

"Obey the rules? Follow a code? Neither force has rules or morality. The concepts are alien to them. When you are so vast and so powerful, you've moved beyond the abstracts of right and wrong. Whatever gets you what you want is right, whatever impedes you is wrong. We can make rules for ourselves, but not for them."

"Then we're pawns."

"Only some of us. You are one."

"Great. Just great."

"The Ally regards us as nothing more than a possession. Let me give you an example. Do you know what sea glass is?"

"Of course."

What did this have to do—?

"Then you know it's simply broken glass that has been worn and rounded by time, tide, and sand. People collect it. The whitish sea glass is the most common and can be found every day on every beach. The colored glass—the red, blue, green—is much more rare and prized by collectors."

"I don't see what—"

"Just bear with me. I'm trying to put this in the most concrete terms possible. Different worlds, different realities are sea glass to the Ally. It collects them and gathers them under its cloak. But the most prized of these are the *sentient* realities—the equivalent of colored sea glass. Now let's suppose you have a collection of sea glass. How much would you care about the individual pieces? Would you take each out at every opportunity and examine it under a loupe for any new flaws? Would you love it and cuddle it and polish it every day?"

She waited for an answer, so Jack shook his head and said, "No. Of course not."

"Same with the Ally. It devotes only the tiniest fraction of its consciousness to us. But let's say there's a predator out there that *eats* sea glass and is always on the hunt for more.

You're going to protect that collection, aren't you? Not because you care for every single individual piece, but simply because it's yours."

"I've got the picture."

"Not quite. A full frontal assault by the predator won't work because you are virtual equals and you can repel it. That was tried back in the First Age, and it failed. But that doesn't mean the predator has gone away. It hasn't. And it never will. So you've got to worry about sneaky, backdoor moves and—" She shook her head. "I feel I'm trivializing this, and I don't mean to."

"I'm following."

"Good. So they battle on a smaller scale."

"Who's winning?"

"The Otherness, I'm afraid. The Ally is an interested collector who wants this world, this reality. The Otherness *needs* it—needs *us*. It feeds on worlds such as this. Its hunger is a more insistent drive than the Ally's possessiveness."

"But how's it going to take us away?"

"Through subterfuge. By tricking the Ally into believing this is a nonsentient world—that it's dead white glass instead of the colored sort. That is what Rasalom meant about restructuring the battlefield to his liking. The Otherness is counting on the Ally losing interest then and withdrawing— effectively abandoning us."

"Can it do that?"

"It has already started. You know of Opus Omega?"

Jack nodded. "The columns Brady was burying."

"Yes. It began thousands of years ago and the project continues without Luther Brady. When that is complete"—she looked away—"and when other requirements are met, the Otherness will have this world to itself."

Jack swallowed. "No way to stop it?"

"Perhaps . . . if the Otherness's pawn is defeated once and for all by the Ally's. They look on their pawns as weapons."

"Spears." The word was acid on his tongue.

She nodded. "Yes. And spears have no branches."

The words hung in the air between them for a seeming eternity. Finally the woman broke the silence.

"A spear must be smooth and sleek—a weapon. A spear is cut from the straightest, toughest branches of a tree. But in order for it to be effective, its own branches must be removed."

"And Gia and Vicky and the baby are branches."

"Tragically, yes. Not so much Victoria, for she carries none of your blood, but certainly the baby, and Gia because she carries the baby."

"But the human cost—"

"Means nothing to the Ally. Would you ask a tree for permission to remove one of its branches to make a spear? No. Would you ask the branch permission to strip it clean? Of course not. That's the way the Ally views us: as natural resources, raw materials. No evil there, just pragmatism."

Jack began to see a pattern.

"Like the yeniçeri."

"Exactly. That is why they are recruited from abandoned children, so they start off without branches. They are human spears from childhood, ready for use. You weren't so lucky—if a fate such as theirs can be called luck. You came with many branches, and they all had to be cut off."

"But wouldn't I be a better spear if I was fighting to protect people I cared for?"

"The Ally views such people as branches, attachments that not only add weight to the spear, but interfere with its aerodynamics as well. It doesn't want its human weapon weighted with or distracted by family ties, by people he loves. Those are liabilities, vulnerabilities. If the enemy can threaten what the spear cherishes most, it will be hesitant in battle, will lose its edge, perhaps even break. A broken spear is useless."

"And here all along I've been thinking it was the Otherness."

"That was what you were supposed to think. Through direct and indirect means, you were pushed to this state for one reason. Tempered by tragedy, fueled by rage at the Otherness, you'd be a perfect weapon, more than ready to step into the Sentinel's shoes when the time came. And willing to do anything—anything—to destroy the Adversary."

Jack leaned his head back and stared at the pitiless stars. He sensed them staring back.

"Why me?"

"I can't say. Who can know the ways of something like the Ally? But I can surmise. I believe you were chosen young. I believe you were next in line behind the Twins. And when they died . . ."

Thanks to me. Shit!

"I became the heir apparent."

"Yes."

Something she'd said penetrated the fog enshrouding his brain.

"You said I was chosen young. How young? When I came to the city?"

She shook her head. "Long before that. As a child."

"Why? There was nothing special about me."

"There must have been. The Ally must have sensed something in you—the qualities it was looking for in a spear."

"But I was never a fighter. Christ, I was an English major in college. I'd probably be teaching modern lit in high school right now if it hadn't . . . been . . . for . . ." He bolted from his seat and stared at her. "My mother?"

She looked sad as she nodded.

"No!"

"I am afraid so. The man who dropped the block from the overpass and killed your mother was a common sociopath. The Ally simply arranged for your parents' car to be passing below when he released that block. Thus your mother was the first branch removed. And that created the turning point, the pivotal episode in your life that changed you from a typical college student to the man you are today."

Jack began stalking back and forth, swinging at the air. He didn't know what else to do. He heard the Akita growl. Maybe it sensed a threat. And with good reason. He wanted to hurt someone, something. The Ally most of all. But how could he strike back at a formless entity?

And though he knew it was true, he didn't want to believe it, couldn't accept it.

"So it's all been planned? Everything that's happened to me! Everything that's happened to my family—Mom, Kate, Dad, Tom! And now Gia and Vicky!"

It's too much! *Too much!*

"I am sorry. No more coincidences, remember?"

He stopped in front of her.

"You ladies knew this all along?"

She nodded.

"Then why didn't you warn me?"

"Not possible. Past events can be catalogued, plans can be deduced, but the future?" She shook her head. "It cannot be seen with any accuracy."

"But you could have warned me that they were targets. I could have protected them."

"Not possible. Sooner or later, despite your best efforts, no matter where you moved them, no matter what protections you used to shield them, they would be struck down."

"Were Vicky and Gia supposed to die?"

"Yes."

"Then why are they still—?"

"Alive?"

"If you can call it living."

"Human frailty, human error . . . that is something even the Ally can't predict."

"Can you help?"

She shook her head. "I would if I could."

"Anya helped my father."

"That was possible because of human error. The car crash did not kill him as intended—"

"It didn't kill Gia and Vicky either."

"It has left them gravely injured, though. Far more so than your father."

"But their Glasgow scores—"

"Do not matter. Your father could be helped because the Ally had no direct involvement after the accident, allowing intervention. That is not the case here."

Jack started stalking about with his hands pressed against the side of his head. Everywhere he turned he ran into a wall.

"You've got to try."

Another head shake. "The Ally is staying with this. It wants to bring this to a close and have done with it. Their condition will deteriorate. If the Ally steps back, I can help. But unless that happens . . . it is too powerful for me."

"So there's no hope?"

"I don't see any."

"All because of me."

"You can't blame yourself. You've had a say in your day-to-day choices, but no control over the overall course of your life. Events have been engineered to bring you here to this place at this time as a seasoned spear without branches."

"I can't believe this cosmic power has been paying attention to *me*!"

" 'Attention' is a relative term. I told you it devotes only the tiniest fraction of its awareness to this entire sphere, and only a fraction of that fraction is watching you—and not full time."

"Okay then. What are the chances they'll survive?"

Her face remained impassive. "Even though I cannot see the future, I see no future for them."

"Because they're going to be brain dead?"

"No. Because the yeniçeri will not rest until they have completed their assignment."

"Aw, no."

She nodded. "I think you had better return to the hospital."

"Why?" He couldn't help it. Nothing was going to keep him from going back to the hospital—especially now—but he had to ask. "If they're doomed, as you say, if they're as good as gone, what's the point?"

"Because as I told you: Nothing is carved in stone. The human variable—willingly or unwillingly, whether through frailty or fervor, torpor or tenacity, cowardice or courage—has the capacity to affect outcomes in the most unpredictable ways."

31. After hurrying home for a few essentials, Jack returned to the hospital. He was allowed another peek into the trauma unit. He knew his previous visit wouldn't lessen the shock of seeing them like that. He'd never get used to it. But though it crushed him to see Gia and Vicky in this state, he owed it to them to be at their sides whenever allowed.

But on his way to their beds he stopped at the desk where a young, twenty-something nurse with M. PEDROSA RN on her ID badge sat making notes in a chart.

"Excuse me," he said, "but I was told earlier that Gia Di-Lauro lost her baby after the accident. Do you happen to know if it was a boy or a girl?"

She looked at him with sad, brown eyes. "No, I'm afraid I don't, Mister Westphalen. And I doubt I can find out at this hour. But we can call Records first thing tomorrow."

Jack nodded. The sex wasn't all that important to him, but he wanted to know if he should be thinking of the baby as his son or his daughter.

Pedrosa accompanied him as he edged toward the beds. He didn't want to look, but when he did he stopped dead at the foot of Gia's bed. A ribbed plastic tube jutted from the mouth, connected to another tube that ran to a *shhhhh*-ing respirator.

He turned to the nurse. "What-what happened?"

"Respiratory arrest. She stopped breathing."

Jesus!

A quick look at Vicky—relief: Still breathing on her own.

"But why?"

"Cerebral edema—swelling of the brain. It's not uncommon after a subdural. Doctor Stokely has increased her medications."

Jack had no idea what she was talking about but knew it couldn't be good.

Maybe he should have expected it. *Their condition will deteriorate* . . . that was what the Lady had said. But he couldn't accept it.

Soon it was time for him to go. He ran into Dr. Stokely in the hallway.

"So it's worse."

She nodded. "I'm afraid so. We've lowered your wife's score to a six."

"How long does she have?"

"I can't say. If the mannitol and dexamethasone reduce the swelling in her brain, her score will come up."

"And if not? How long?"

Dr. Stokely sighed. "If her brain keeps swelling it will herniate the brainstem—push it out through the opening in the base of the skull. When that happens . . . all the body's basic functions will cease."

Jack could only stare at her.

Finally: "If she doesn't respond, what? A day? Two?" The words sounded like croaks.

"Three at the most. We're doing everything that can be done, Mister Westphalen."

Jack nodded and told himself the swelling would go down. It had to. The human variable . . .

And that meant he would have to do everything possible to make sure the yeniçeri didn't speed Gia and Vicky on their way.

32. Jack sat in a small lounge reserved for families of patients in the trauma unit. Earlier he'd found himself faced with an agonizing decision. He hoped he'd made the right choice.

The trouble with New York Hospital was its size. It took up a couple of city blocks. He'd checked a layout map by the information desk and seen two main entry points: the ER and the main lobby. He couldn't cover both. Had to choose.

Then he'd learned of this special family waiting area off the hallway by the trauma unit.

So here he sat, holding up a paper and pretending to read it; a good way to hide his face. He'd switched to a red-and-blue reversible jacket. He had the red side out now. The Kel-Tec nestled in the right pocket; though tiny and easily palmed, the little pistol held eleven 9mm rounds. The final touch was a knit watch cap with two eye holes hidden in the rolled-up segment. If needed, he could pull it down to cover his face. He hoped that wouldn't be necessary. The last thing he wanted was to start a shoot-out in the hospital. But if it came down to that, he'd go for it.

He felt sweat trickling from his face and armpits. Hot in here. But he didn't dare remove anything. Had to be ready to move on an instant's notice.

Out in the hallway, the elevator and stairway door lay to the left. He or they would enter from there. The restroom doors sat directly across from the lounge entrance, the trauma unit doors to the right. Whoever the MV sent would have to pass between him and the restrooms.

He hadn't yet decided his moves when the time came, though the restrooms presented possibilities . . .

The big question: Who would they send? And when?

Jack guessed Miller, and probably late. After one, at least: Patients asleep, visitors gone, doctors home, and only a reduced late-shift nursing staff to deal with.

He glanced at the clock. Hours to go till then. He yawned. He'd had maybe three hours of sleep during the last forty-eight. He needed some coffee but didn't dare leave this spot.

He looked around at his fellow lingerers. Maybe he could pay one of them to get him a cup.

WEDNESDAY

1. The elevator chime jerked Jack from his semidoze. He looked up and saw two nurses coming back from their break.

He stretched in his seat. One a.m. and he had the trauma unit's family lounge pretty much to himself. Just a disheveled woman who seemed to live here—he'd overheard that her husband was in the unit—and a hollow-eyed couple on vigil for their son.

His bladder was sending pleading messages. He'd been putting it off because it meant leaving his post. But sooner or later . . .

He guessed he could risk a quick trip. He rose, pushed through the men's room door, and was approaching a urinal when he heard the elevator *ding* again.

He stepped back to the door and pulled it open a few inches. He palmed the Kel-Tec and waited.

The shock of seeing Zeklos, dark glasses and all, step into view delayed his reaction time. He shook it off and reached through the doorway, grabbing the little man by the coat collar as he passed and jerking him into the restroom. Zeklos struggled but Jack had size and strength on him. He rammed his gut against a sink, knocking off his shades. Zeklos's face blanched when he saw Jack in the mirror.

"You!" he said and reached for the pistol in his shoulder holster.

Jack put him in an arm lock and bent him over the sink while he removed a now familiar suppressor-equipped H-K Tactical. He stuck his Kel-Tec in a pocket, then pressed the nose of the H-K against Zeklos's spine at midlevel.

Jack kept his voice low. "I thought you couldn't kill a woman."

Zeklos glared at him in the mirror and said nothing.

"You're here to finish off a helpless woman and child, right? Proud of yourself?"

Again no reply.

"If you don't open up, you're no good to me, so there'll be nothing to keep me from pulling this trigger."

Finally a response. "I am not afraid to die."

"Who said die? Know what a nine-millimeter hollow-point can do to a vertebra? It smashes it and severs the spinal cord in the process. You'll live, pal, but you'll never walk again."

Of course he might die if one of the fragments severed a good-size blood vessel, but so what?

"So give. Why'd they send you? I thought Miller kicked you out."

Zeklos's hard expression wavered. "He . . . he does not think I come back alive. But . . . why are you here? The woman you ask about?"

"Never mind that."

He glanced at the door. Any second now someone could walk through, see Jack's pistol, and shout for security.

He bent Zeklos over the sink and patted him down. Found a Kahr K9 in an ankle holster. He traded the H-K—which went into his waistband—for the smaller Kahr, then yanked him up straight.

"We're going for a little walk."

"Where?"

"Outside, where we can talk." He turned him toward the door and prodded him with the Kahr. "No funny stuff. Behave and you'll come out of this in one piece with both legs working. Act up and I'll shoot you down like a mad dog."

2. Jack didn't want to be seen too much with Zeklos. No such thing as a dark and private place around the hospital—not with all those HSP lamps lighting up the night like day—so he walked him up to John Jay Park.

Marched him along Seventy-eighth, over the FDR, and down the steps toward the waterfront promenade where Rasalom had caught up with him earlier. The stairway ended in an alcove under the ramp. Smelled like urine. Chain-link fencing penned them in on two sides.

Uptown-bound traffic roared past just ten feet away but Jack positioned them out of sight. He kept the Kahr buried against Zeklos's spine as he leaned him against the alcove's rear wall.

Zeklos said, "If you are going to kill me, please do it swiftly."

"What makes you think I'd do that? I've got no beef with you unless you were driving the truck."

"Truck?"

"The one that ran down the woman and the child. Was it you?"

"No."

"Who was driving then?"

When Zeklos shook his head, Jack jammed the pistol harder against his spine.

"*Who*? It was Miller, right?"

A long hesitation, then Zeklos nodded.

Jack closed his eyes. How do you reach a point where you can do something like that?

He felt the darkness bloom from its cellar room, looking to take over. He beat it back. Later maybe. But not now.

"Do you know who that woman was?"

"All I know is that O say Ally want her dead."

"I was going to marry her. And the little girl with her . . ." Jack felt his throat clench. "She was going to be my daughter. And the baby she was carrying was mine."

Jack felt Zeklos stiffen, then sag. He started to turn and Jack stopped him, then stepped back and let him. In the faint light he saw his expression migrate from disbelief to acceptance to sadness.

"This is truth?"

"I wish to hell it weren't."

Zeklos dropped to a squat.

"I am so sorry. This is terrible." He looked up at Jack. "I do not understand."

"I do. And I've got scores to settle."

"You will not kill me then?"

"Only if you get in my way. My beef is with the O and the guy who was behind the wheel."

"Is that why you killed him?"

"Who?"

"The O."

Jack felt as if he'd been punched. The Oculus . . . dead?

"Christ! When did that happen?"

"This afternoon—shortly after you left me—and left that bullet."

The Starfire. He'd forgotten all about it. Damn. But he'd had only one thing on his mind at the moment.

"Why would you think I did it?"

"Miller does."

Yeah. Miller. Figured.

"I was racing to Second and Fifty-eighth. Care to guess why?"

Zeklos hung his head. "I am so sorry."

"What are you guys going to do without an Oculus?"

He looked up. "Oh, but we have one. We have the daughter, Diana."

"She becomes the Oculus—just like that? What about her eyes? Hers were blue and her father's—"

"Hers are black now."

Jack tried to imagine how she'd look. The picture he conjured creeped him out.

Zeklos said, "What are you going to do?"

"About your pals?"

He nodded.

"Well, I was going to wait in that little room in the hospital until I knew whether my ladies were going to live or die. But I can't do that now, can I. Your rotten yeniçeri friends have made that impossible, because they'll keep trying. Am I right?"

Zeklos looked down again. "I do not know."

"You do know. Miller won't let this go."

Zeklos didn't reply.

"Your people leave me no choice. I've got to make sure no one else tries to finish your job."

"You will kill Miller?"

"And anyone who gets between me and him."

Zeklos rose. Jack raised the pistol and backed away a step. Never let anyone get too close.

"You must not! We fight Otherness!"

"You know, at this point, I don't give a rat's ass. And what do you mean, 'we'? They demoted you to the farm team."

"It does not matter! I am still yeniçeri!"

With the last word he leaped. Jack had been half expecting him to do something stupid, but the little man's speed surprised him. He got under Jack's arm, grabbed his wrist, and threw his right side against him while trying to twist the Kahr free. Jack chopped at him with the edge of his left hand but Zeklos was well padded in his winter coat and kept his head down, giving Jack no angle. He'd locked Jack's pistol hand in a death grip.

"Don't be an idiot!" Jack said.

"You attack one yeniçeri, you attack us all!"

"You're going to lose this one. Back off."

"No!"

Slowly, inexorably, Jack rotated Zeklos's body to the right and angled the little pistol leftward until it pressed against the little man's chest.

"I'm not looking to kill you." True. Zeklos wasn't one of the bad guys. "So don't force my hand."

With that Zeklos bent and sank his teeth into Jack's wrist.

Jack pulled the trigger. Zeklos's coat muffled the report. He sagged to his knees and toppled over onto his side. His eyes were open. Jack could see his breath puffing into the air.

Jack stood over him. "What'd you have to go and do that for?"

The puffing stopped. The little man's dark eyes remained open.

"Shit."

So goddamn unnecessary. Just like everything else that had gone down today.

He pocketed the Kahr and looked around. No one in sight. He needed a place to hide the body—didn't want the yeniçeri to know just yet.

When they heard no news of a hospital shooting, and Zeklos didn't show up or report in, they'd suspect he'd lost his nerve and bailed. At least that was what Miller would think, and he'd sell it to the others. Zeklos turning up dead would put them on guard.

The park with its locked gate and pool and spiked fencing would be the perfect spot—not exactly a busy place in January—but that meant carrying the body over the FDR. Too risky. Yeah, he might make it unseen, but the odds were against it.

Then he realized he was standing just a few feet from an almost-perfect spot. He slipped his hands under Zeklos's arms and dragged him into the darkest, most sheltered corner of the alcove. He'd keep there at least until morning, maybe longer. He emptied his pockets of everything, especially anything that might identify him.

Jack noticed his crushing weariness had faded. Adrenaline, probably. Or maybe it was having a purpose again. He'd been drowning in helplessness, unable to do anything for Gia and Vicky. Now he could. Now he had to. It might be an empty exercise. Maybe the outcome would be the same whether someone pumped cyanide-tipped slugs into them or not. But he couldn't let that happen.

Jack took the walkway back to 78th Street and headed for York Avenue to catch a cab home. He had four pistols on him now. He wanted to dump two before going back to the hospital. He'd bring back a pad and pencil, sit in the family lounge as before, and start making plans.

3. Jack stood between the beds, arms stretched to either side so he could hold their hands. A one-way hold—theirs lay limp in his. He was standing there, staring at the oscillating dials on Gia's respirator, listening to its rhythmic wheeze, when Vicky's hand moved. He turned and gasped.

"Nurse!"

Her back was arching and dropping, her arms thrashing about, her legs kicking in violent spasms.

A heavyset, late-shift nurse bustled over—Jack didn't know her name and didn't give a damn at the moment—took one look and called to the desk.

"Three's seizuring! I need five of diazepam stat!"

Jack stood frozen, horrified, helpless as he watched Vicky convulse. Finally he shook off the paralysis and went to grab her arms so she wouldn't hurt herself.

The nurse put out an arm to block his way.

"Please, sir. You'll have to wait outside."

"But I can—"

"You'll only be in the way. For the sake of your child, please get out of the way and let us do our job."

For the sake of your child . . .

Jack couldn't argue with that. Feeling useless, he backed toward the doors, watching until they closed in front of him.

4. "What are we going to do with the bodies?" Miller said.

Cal looked up from his checklist. He needed to be sure that anything that could give a clue as to who they were and where they'd gone was removed.

They stood by the security console on the first floor. The air still reeked of blood. All around them the yeniçeri combed every crack and crevice for anything that might connect them to this place.

The bodies . . . he'd been wrestling with what to do about them.

Portman squatted at the rear of the space, moving from corpse to corpse. He'd been assigned the distasteful task of emptying the pockets of the dead. Not of just what might be used for identification—*everything*, no matter how seemingly inconsequential.

"Got to leave them. I don't see that we have a choice."

Miller shook his head. "Never leave anyone behind. It's the code. You know that."

"Never leave anyone *living* behind."

"You interpret your way, I'll interpret mine. But either way, the O and those guys deserve a decent burial."

Cal felt a spike of anger. The stress of being in charge of this move, making sure every *i* was dotted, every *t* crossed, was eating him alive. But Priority Number One was moving Diana—the Oculus—to safety ASAP.

"You think I don't know that? Don't you think it's tearing me up as much as anybody to have to walk out on them? But what choice do we have? We can't risk driving up the Connecticut Turnpike with seven mutilated corpses in our cars."

Miller looked down. "Still . . . it's not right."

Cal slammed his hand on the counter. "Then you come up with a plan! You figure out how we can get them upstate, dig seven graves in frozen ground, and still protect Diana. Go ahead. Tell me. I'm all ears."

Miller sighed and said nothing.

"Here's what I think we can do," Cal said. "What we *have* to do. They stay here, but only temporarily. We turn off the heat—and turn off the water too, in case the pipes freeze—and leave them. The cold will preserve them. Pretty much like being in a cooler at the morgue. When we get settled at the new place, some of us come back and bury them."

For centuries the MV had owned a hundred acres of wooded land upstate in the Putnam County wilderness. The final resting place of all the New York yeniçeri.

"But right now, soon as we're packed up, we're out of here. I want to catch the first ferry out tomorrow morning. That means we've got to be in Hyannis before nine."

"All right, then," Miller said. "But I'm coming back—for them and for him. Some day, some way, he pays."

5. Jack sat in his car and rubbed his burning eyes. The wan dawn light drove knives into his brain. Good thing it was overcast. No telling what direct sunlight would do.

He hadn't been able to sleep since Vicky's seizure episode. It had taken a while for the nurses to calm the convulsions. But she needed so much medication to keep them under control that they had to put her on a respirator as well.

Gia and Vicky were safe until the yeniçeri learned Zeklos had failed. So about an hour ago he'd roused himself and headed for Red Hook where he'd parked again along the park, facing the warehouse. His plan was to wait and watch and see who came and went. He wanted to see Miller leave. Wanted to follow him. Wanted to settle a debt.

A drive-by wouldn't do it—for a number of reasons. On the practical end, too many chances for someone to see it go down and report his license plate. On the personal end, it wouldn't satisfy Jack. He needed a face-to-face confrontation. Needed to look in Miller's eyes before he put a bullet between them.

But . . . something not quite right here.

He rubbed a hand over his chest. The rakosh scars felt cool, numb. None of the itching and burning sparked by proximity to the building in past trips. He'd driven by this morning and felt nothing.

He opened his shirt and checked. The three ridges of scar tissue were their usual pale white instead of the angry red of the last time he'd been here.

Was that because the Oculus was dead? But Zeklos had said

they had a new Oculus in the daughter. Had they evacuated the place?

He'd have to sit and wait.

Jack hated to wait.

6. Almost eleven o'clock and Jack hadn't seen one damn person enter or leave.

Between calls to the trauma unit—no change in either of his ladies—he received an incoming call at quarter to eight: Abe. He'd seen the papers and was almost speechless with grief. Anything he could do, any way he could help, just ask. But Jack had known that. He'd said he'd get back to him.

To kill time he scanned the FM and AM bands. Heard a lot of crummy music and learned the weather forecast by heart: Big storm in the south, coming up the coast, scheduled to slam the city with a blizzard late Thursday or early Friday.

Yeah, well, so what? Couldn't come close to the winter in his heart.

During the wait he'd realized that Gia's folks out in Iowa didn't know about any of this. And Jack didn't know how to get in touch with them. He'd have to go back to her place and see if she'd written down their number somewhere. Most likely not. She talked to her mom a couple times a week, so she didn't need it on paper.

Part of him hoped he'd never find it. Calling her folks . . . telling them what had happened to their daughter and grandchild . . . and how grim the prognosis . . .

The prospect made him ill.

Call me a coward, he thought, but I'd rather go mano a mano with Miller than have to relay that kind of news.

And worse, his husband-and-father cover would be blown at the hospital.

He refocused on the warehouse. Still no sign of life. The yeniçeri had either taken off, were entering and exiting by a different route, or knew he was out here and were waiting for him to make a move.

The second possibility seemed remote—from what he'd seen they'd focused all their security on the front door. The third seemed equally remote—unless they'd all spent the night there.

All of which left him with no recourse but to make a close reconnoiter on foot.

He grabbed Zeklos's keychain from the passenger seat. He'd found it in the dead man's pockets and had brought it along for the ride not knowing whether or not it would come in handy. If the rats had jumped ship, it would.

He removed the Glock from its SOB holster, chambered a round, and slipped it into his jacket pocket. With the grip in his hand and his finger on the trigger, he stepped out onto the sidewalk. He blinked as his eyes teared in the icy wind. Bundled into anonymity, he kept to the opposite side of the street as he walked past the three-story building. He looked for the same itching, burning sensation across his chest as before. No show.

At the end of the block he crossed the street and walked back until he came to the door. Even now, standing directly in front of it, his scars remained impassive.

This was risky—maybe stupidly so—but his gut told him the place was empty, and he'd learned to trust his gut. So he kept the Glock in his pocket aimed toward the door as he rang the bell once, twice, three times. No answer.

He pounded on the steel door. Same response.

Okay. Time for the keys. About a dozen of them on the ring. He began trying one after the other in the top lock. Number four fit and turned. Inside, an alarm bell began to *clang*. Only inside. Nothing outside. That meant the alarm was to warn the inhabitants, not bring help. Which meant it wouldn't be hooked up to a monitoring service. He couldn't see the MV getting involved with outside security.

After that it was quick and simple since all three were neighbors.

Now . . .

He stood to the side, turned the knob and pushed the door open. He peeked in. Nothing moving.

He stepped inside. As he did a quick four-wall scan he saw the smashed computers on the floor. Either someone had tossed the place or the yeniçeri were burning bridges.

The space smelled strange and felt empty. And cold. The heating had failed, or maybe been turned off.

Didn't look like they were planning on coming back. He closed the door and, keeping his eyes on the ransacked room, keyed the three dead bolts shut.

No sense in letting someone surprise him from behind.

The ringing of the damn bell was getting to him. He stepped to the monitoring console to look for a button or a toggle labeled BELL OFF or KILL THE GODDAMN BELL but stopped when he spotted the smears of dried blood. He spotted more on the floor near his feet.

What the hell had happened here?

Before finding out, he had to stop that bell. He found nothing that mentioned "Bell" but did find a RESET button. He jabbed it.

Silence . . . the blessed silence of a . . .

He turned and spotted the sheet-draped figures lined up against the far wall.

. . . tomb.

Zeklos hadn't mentioned any other deaths beside the Oculus. Looked like the yeniçeri had wound up on the wrong side of a massacre.

Jack's first impulse was to check out the bodies, but he made himself search the lounge area and upper floors first. The building might feel empty, but it never hurt to be sure.

The O's office stank of dried blood. It splattered all four walls, but was especially heavy behind the desk. It pooled so thick on the desktop that it wasn't completely dry yet.

He checked the personal quarters and found two closets. One full of men's clothes—the Oculus's, no doubt. The other was mostly empty except for a couple of feminine shorts and a halter top.

The third floor sported its share of blood too, but no corpses.

He relaxed a little. He was the only living person in the building. No one around to catch him by surprise.

He hurried down to the first floor and approached the sheet-wrapped figures. He squatted and uncovered the first one. Despite the blood-spattered face, Jack recognized him. Didn't know his name but had seen him around.

Where had the blood come from?

He pulled the sheet farther down and swallowed when he saw the hole in the man's chest. Yeah, he had a heart, but it had been ripped from all its vessels.

Who the hell had done that? And how?

He had a pretty good idea.

He pulled the sheet down to knee level. He'd intended to search the clothing for some hint as to where the surviving yeniçeri had fled, but when he saw the out-turned pockets, he realized someone had preempted him.

He worked down the row and found each corpse in the same condition. By the time he reached the last he'd grown used to the human carnage, but the eighth was something else again: the Oculus—with an empty inch between his head and the base of his neck. He'd been savagely decapitated, not by a blade . . . his head had been ripped off.

Jack walked a meandering path through the carnage, stepping around the smashed computers as he looked for something, anything that might offer a hint as to where they'd gone. He picked up a battered hard drive that had been all but flattened across its middle. He didn't know much about computers, but he couldn't see this giving up anything.

But he collected all the drives he could find anyway. He'd give them to Russ Tuit and see what he could do. Russ was something of a cybergenius but Jack doubted even he could squeeze anything out of these.

He turned in a slow circle and wondered where in hell they'd gone. He combed his memory for some dropped remark that might offer a clue, but came up with nothing but Idaho, and that seemed unlikely. They'd want to keep their Oculus in the Northeast.

Their Oculus . . . Diana. He had an idea . . . the thinnest shred of a hope . . . but if it was to come to anything he'd have to find her.

How? A secret organization, used to clandestine operation,

on the run. They wouldn't leave a trail. Maybe the FBI could track them, maybe not. Jack knew he couldn't.

What to do? Gia and Vicky would be safe until the yeniçeri realized Zeklos had failed. Then they'd try again. Jack knew he might not be so lucky next time.

He saw only one option: Divert them from Gia and Vicky by giving them another target they'd want to hit even more.

Him.

And Jack knew just how to do it.

7. Portman rose and asked if anyone wanted more coffee.

Cal, simultaneously tired and wired from all the caffeine he'd already poured down his gullet, shook his head. He watched Portman's lurching retreat across the tilting deck.

They'd made it to Hyannis in time for the first ferry and had commandeered a corner of the main cabin. No one protested. Not enough passengers aboard to care.

Not enough yeniçeri to matter.

Their ranks had been thinned to an even dozen. They'd needed only four vehicles—the Suburban, the Humvee, and two SUVs—to transport them and the new Oculus. The cars sat below in the ship's huge drive-in/drive-out bay.

Uneasiness wound through his gut. They'd abandoned Home too quickly to allow for a meticulous sweep. He was sure they'd left things behind. He just hoped whatever it was didn't point to the safe house.

Diana sat next to him, her black eyes hidden behind dark glasses and her arm hooked through his as she stared out the window at the rolling, wind-whipped swells. She seemed calm on the outside, but that was probably shock. She had to feel lost without her father and terrified of the responsibility his death had thrust upon her.

She turned her pale face to him. "I don't feel good."

"You're a little seasick. Don't worry. We'll be in the harbor soon."

From there it would be a trip to a narrow strip of land on the eastern edge of the island. The house there had water on both sides and nothing behind it except a lighthouse. A pair of sandy ruts offered the only access. Whoever approached them would have to come in slow or break an axle.

"For now, the best thing is to keep your eyes on the horizon—what you can see of it."

She turned back to the window.

He patted the back of her hand. "You'll be safe soon. And you'll stay safe. I promise."

He prayed it was a promise he'd be able to keep.

8. Jack sat at the MV monitoring console in the warehouse and went over his list. He'd given all three floors a close inspection in a hunt for ways to deal with the yeniçeri who'd be sent after him. He'd found a number of possibilities, but wanted a couple more as backup.

He rose and wandered back to the bunk/lounge area at the right rear. He'd already given it the twice over but it might yield something. The old TV offered possibilities. And the lockers, though they'd been swept clean, might trigger inspiration. He started there.

A couple of dozen or so stood against the wall, all their doors agape. He closed one and stepped back. Its incongruity might trigger curiosity, which wouldn't be a bad thing—for Jack, at least.

He dropped to his hands and knees and checked out the two-inch gap between the locker bottom and the floor for a place to hide a surprise. Nothing but dust bunnies and—

Something metallic gleamed a dull yellow behind one of the bunnies. He snaked his hand under and grasped it between his fingertips. He identified it on contact: ammo.

He pulled it out and dropped it into his palm. A hollow point with a long, slim cartridge. The hollow was filled and sealed. And the caliber . . . it looked like a .223 Remington, but a closer look told him it was a 5.56mm NATO round.

Jack leaned against the lockers as his heart went into overdrive.

The killers in the LaGuardia Massacre had used cyanide-tipped 5.56 NATOs.

His mind raced to a barely justified conclusion: The killers hadn't been Arab terrorists. Joey Castles's last words had hinted that LaGuardia was bigger than the Arabs he and Jack had shot up, that something else was going on.

Not Arabs . . . yeniçeri. Had the Ally showed them what to do, and they'd done it? Killed more than fifty people in order to kill one: his father?

Dad had been a branch . . . and a spear has no branches.

The Lady's words came back to him.

That's the way the Ally views us: as natural resources, raw materials. No evil there, just pragmatism.

No evil unless you were on the receiving end.

He drew up his knees and rested his forehead against them.

Okay, we're natural resources to the Ally. It can't show compassion because it has none. It can't be held to human moral standards because it makes its own rules and answers only to itself.

But none of that exonerated the yeniçeri from following through with the "Alarms" it sent—not when it involved the slaughter of innocent lives, especially lives close to him.

"I was just following orders" . . . or . . . "I was doing it for the greater good of humanity" . . . that bullshit carried no weight here.

Sick and disgusted, Jack pushed himself to his feet and pocketed the round. He had work to do.

Time to adjust the calendar.

Judgment Day would be arriving early for the yeniçeri.

9. Midafternoon, after leaving the warehouse, Jack stopped by Russ Tuit's place and showed him the hard drives. Russ told him they were ruined way beyond repair. Maybe some NSA code-head geek could coax something out of them, but he doubted even that. The drives were useless.

Disappointed, he'd returned to the unit to check in on Gia and Vicky—no change. Normally that might be good news, but not in this case.

Then Jack set about tracking down someone who knew about the baby. He found that someone in the Records department. Wilma Dryden appeared about fifty and wore a blue skirt and blazer. She looked efficient and officious.

"Oh, Mister Westphalen," she said, looking up from her desk. "I'm so glad you stopped by. You're a hard man to find."

"I've been pulled in a lot of directions. Where's my baby?"

"I'm so sorry for your loss. She's in our morgue."

Jack closed his eyes as his throat constricted.

She . . . that meant the baby's name was Emma.

Emma . . . his . . . their Emma was in the morgue.

Jack knew lots about morgues—more than he wanted to. The thought of Emma in a bag in a cooler somewhere in the cellar sickened him.

"I suppose you've come to make arrangements for burial," Ms. Dryden said.

Burial? It had never crossed his mind.

"No . . . not really."

"Well, by law any miscarriage past the twentieth week must be buried or cremated."

Cremated . . . Emma? He wanted to scream.

"I can't think about that now. My . . . my wife's in a coma. I'd like to see our baby."

Wilma Dryden frowned. "Do you think that's a good idea? I mean, before the mortician has had a chance—"

"I don't know when that will be and I don't want to wait that long. I need to see her."

"Well, I don't—"

Jack spoke through his teeth. "I want to see her. Now."

"Really, Mister Westphalen, there's no need for—"

He slammed his hand on her desk.

"Now!"

She flinched and rolled her chair back.

He lowered his voice. "Please."

10. The morgue attendant was a kind-looking old gent. He checked the pass that Ms. Dryden had arranged for Jack, then led the way toward a row of drawers. Jack felt his feet dragging of their own accord. He didn't want to do this, but he had to. He owed it to Emma . . . to Gia . . . to himself.

"Terrible thing for a baby to die before it gets a chance to take even a single breath," he said. "My condolences, mister."

Jack said nothing.

They stopped before a drawer. The gent slid it out to reveal a black, zippered body bag. A little lump pushed up the center of the plastic.

Emma.

Jack stared but could not move.

The gent said, "Do . . . do you want me to open it?"

Jack could only nod.

The zipper was pulled down, the edges were parted, and there she was, lying on her side.

Emma was a tiny thing, maybe the size of a kitten, and pale, almost blue white. About a foot of the umbilical cord was still attached. Her eyes were closed but her mouth was open; her knees were drawn up and her tiny fists were clenched under her chin . . . as if she'd died in pain.

Jack leaned over and touched her. He ran a fingertip across the eyelids, down past her lips and along one of her arms. Her skin felt nothing like a baby's—cold, thick, almost hard. He wanted to say something, something as simple as *Hi, Emma*, but he was incapable of speech.

He saw a drop of water on her shoulder. He touched it. It felt warm. Then another appeared. And another.

He realized they were tears.

11. Jack sat in the family lounge. His body craved sleep, his brain screamed for a time-out, but it wasn't in the cards. Every time he closed his eyes he saw Emma lying cold and white in that body bag.

He shook himself and checked his watch. A little after eleven. Time to go see another corpse.

He exited the hospital and headed uptown. John Jay Park and its environs were fast becoming a familiar haunt. More familiar than he wished. He hoped this would be his last visit.

He trotted across the overpass and down to the promenade. A swift reconnoiter showed a couple of hardy old souls strolling the riverside, gloved hand in gloved hand. He waited until they passed, then he ducked into the alcove under the steps.

Zeklos's body was where he'd left it, but stiff as a four-by-four. As he'd hoped, none of the sparse passersby had ventured into the alcove today.

Now came the touchy part—the *really* touchy part. He wriggled into a pair of latex gloves, then pulled out the Yarborough knife he'd brought along. He used it to slice away Zeklos's shirts. The black blade slipped easily through the fabric, exposing the pale, sparsely haired chest. Jack took a deep breath, hesitated a second, then crunched the blade through the right upper ribs. Using both hands he sawed down, angling toward the midline. No blood spurted—it had long since congealed and frozen. He repeated the process on the left, then grabbed the lower tip of the breastbone with both hands and yanked it up with a sickening *crack*. The exposed heart seemed to contract within its fat pad as the icy wind found it.

Without allowing himself any time to think or reconsider, he cut the heart free and set it aside. When he'd wiped the knife clean on Zeklos's shirt, he pulled out the note he'd written earlier and pinned it to the dead man's coat.

Then, after checking again to make sure no one was in sight, he hauled Zeklos out and laid him next to the telephone. No one walking by could miss him, but the lights of one of the passing cars on the FDR might pick him out first.

Jack then grabbed the heart and tossed it into the East River. He couldn't see it land in the dark, but heard the splash.

He removed his gloves and stored them in a Ziploc, then dashed up the steps and crossed back to 78th Street. He stopped at the corner of York Avenue and leaned against a wall. He'd dreaded that grisly task, but at least it was done. Poor Zeklos deserved better than that, but Jack had to work with the materials at hand. Zeklos was one of those materials.

As he started down York he took out his phone and dialed 911. After three rings a woman answered.

"Emergency services."

"Look, I was just on the riverside walk near East Seventy-eighth Street and I think I saw something that looked like a body by the overpass."

"Could I have your name, sir?"

Jack hung up.

The rest was up to the papers. He knew the note and the condition of the body would earn front-page coverage.

12. When he got back to the hospital, the trauma unit's head nurse told him he'd have to wait before he could see his family. Dr. Stokely was with Vicky who was having more seizures despite all the medication.

Helpless, he sat. And waited. And thought. Had to be some way to fix this. Not from here in the hospital, but from another direction.

He simply had to find it and make it work.

THURSDAY

1. Cal accompanied Grell and Novak to the supermarket. The little island had only two. Since Grell was the best cook among the survivors, he landed the task of filling the larders. And since that was no little task, they'd taken the Hummer and one of the SUVs and brought Novak to help carry.

They didn't need Cal, but he wanted to get the lay of the land. He'd known of the safe house for years—and had hoped never to have to use it—but this was the first time he'd stayed here.

The place had a stark kind of beauty. Rolling hills and moors near its center, dunes protecting the shore, thick underbrush, scrub pine, and oak; two-lane blacktops alternated with winding sandy paths, and not a single traffic light to be found. It measured fifteen miles east-west and half that north-south, but seemed bigger. Only locals here this time of year. Summer, he'd been told, was a wholly different story.

They pulled into the Stop & Shop, the closest supermarket. A Grand Union was cross island in the town that cozied around the harbor. Someday this week he'd get downtown and do some wandering. They'd passed through it on their way from the harbor and it looked quaint and friendly.

The Stop & Shop seemed fairly crowded. The low, leaden, late-morning sky and the promise of a big snow on the way probably had something to do with that.

He grinned and nudged Grell, a tall, gangly redhead with a long reach. "Storm coming. Better stock up before the hoarders grab it all."

He nodded. "Good idea."

Cal sighed. Sailed right over his red head.

"I need a Pringles fix," Novak said.

Cal eyed the stocky man's expanding waistline but said nothing.

"You guys do your thing. I'll wander."

He'd have preferred to do his wandering outside, explore the island a little, but the icy, straight-razor wind robbed the outdoors of any appeal. Maybe some other day.

He grabbed a little shopping basket and picked out a few things for personal use. He liked food that crunched, so he picked out bags of carrots and celery. He liked to dip his crunchies in guacamole, but the store had only Marie's guacamole dip. Well, that would do in a pinch.

He saw newspaper racks ahead and made a beeline for them. Today's papers should have reached the island by now. News-wise, the satellite TV at the house offered only the national channels and Boston locals. He wanted to keep an eye on the goings-on in New York, especially for news about eight mutilated bodies being found. Did *not* want to hear that.

The headline of the *Post* stopped him dead in his tracks. Even at ten feet the stunner headline screamed at him.

YENIÇERI?
WHO DAT?

And then the *Daily News*:

"HEIR" TO
WHAT?

What the hell?

He hurried to the rack and grabbed a copy of each, found a ledge by the front window, and sat down to read. His fingers trembled as he turned the pages.

The stories were pretty much the same. Someone had reported a body alongside the FDR Drive. The man had been shot once—in the heart, they suspected—but his heart was missing. He carried no identification but was short, slight of build, with dark hair and brown eyes. Anyone with information should call the given number. Then the reporter got to the puzzling note found pinned to the body.

"*I* ❤ *yeniçeri* ❤*s. The collection is 8 and growing. The Heir*"

The *News* asked, "Is the Heir a new serial killer?"

Cal sagged back against the window. The Heir . . . Jack . . . yeah, he might be just that.

Zeklos . . . the dead man had to be him. Poor Zek, his heart ripped out like the rest . . .

Cal shook his head. He'd liked Jack, hadn't had an inkling he would or could do something like this. Especially to someone as innocuous as Zek.

And then to be so blatant about it, to announce it to the world. And announce to the yeniçeri that he was the one who'd killed their brothers.

Rage surged but quickly died. Something about this didn't sit right. He couldn't put his finger on it, but something seemed askew.

"Davis!"

He looked up and saw Novak giving him the high sign from one of the cashier lanes.

He'd have to tell them. He fought an impulse to buy all the New York papers and throw them away. They had to know. They had a right to know. Even though Zeklos was on the outs, they'd be enraged.

And Miller . . . Miller would go ballistic.

2. "It's terrible, Jack. Terrible. So awful I can't believe. Like a knife in the heart it hurts. And you . . . how you must feel . . . unimaginable."

Jack could only nod.

Exhausted, he leaned on the scarred counter at the rear of the store, with Abe seated across from him. In a way he didn't understand, he took comfort in the familiar clutter, in the sound of Abe's voice, his proximity, his uncharacteristic mother-henning. This was a side of his old friend he'd never seen.

"Also you look terrible. You should be resting. And eating. Are you eating?"

Jack shrugged. "Not hungry."

"You must eat already. You'll collapse if you don't. I have cake. I'll make us some coffee and—"

"Food is the furthest thing from my mind, Abe."

"Some chicken soup then? I can go around the corner—"

"Please, Abe."

Silence hung between them.

Finally Abe said, "And the latest report?"

"Deepening coma for Gia, Vicky's still seizing off and on. And it wasn't an accident."

Abe's pale, never-seen-the-sun skin blanched further.

"They were targeted? No, you've got to be wrong. Why on Earth should anyone want to hurt those two sweet people?"

Jack explained what he'd learned from Rasalom and the Lady.

Abe's expression went slack during the telling. He rubbed a pudgy-fingered hand over his face and continued on to the balding pate above it.

"All this time you've been blaming the other side, this Otherness thing."

"Exactly what the Ally wanted me to do. It wasn't just stripping my branches, it was heating me to the point where I'd do anything to get back at the Otherness."

"When all the while . . ."

"Yeah. My side was doing the shafting. But wait. It gets worse."

He pulled the NATO round from his pocket and set it upright on the counter.

Abe stared at it for a few seconds, then picked it up for a closer inspection. An instant later he stiffened, his head snapped up, and he stared at Jack with wide eyes.

"LaGuardia? These yeniçeri schmucks did LaGuardia?"

Jack nodded. "That's where all the signs are pointing."

"But it's *meshuggeh*!"

"No. It's pragmatic."

God, he'd come to hate that word.

"The Ally has worked all this circumspectly, so much so that I still don't know how it managed Kate's and Tom's deaths. The Ladies know. I wish I could sit down with one of them for a couple of hours and find out."

"How would that help?"

"I guess you're right. The *how* doesn't really matter. It's the *what* that counts. And what the Ally has done is backfiring. Now I want to get back at it. Now I hate it more than the Otherness. I'm crazy mad enough to sign up with the Otherness."

"No."

"I need to get back at it, Abe. But how?"

Abe shrugged. "I should know how to take revenge on an amorphous cosmic entity? Like fighting air already. Besides, the rest of us need the Ally to keep out the Otherness."

Jack knew he was right.

"It's really got me, hasn't it."

"Yes. You can't join the other side, you can't even declare yourself a noncombatant, because you're not the type to sit idly by and watch everyone and everything you know destroyed."

Trapped. He wanted to scream, throw things, break things.

But he held back. For Abe's sake. Not fair to decimate his stock.

"We may not like this *farkuckt* Ally, but we need it. And it needs you."

It needs you . . . that struck a chord in Jack. He'd been thinking along similar lines . . .

He pulled a piece of paper from his pocket and handed it to Abe.

"How much of these can you get me?"

Abe scanned the list, nodding. "Some I have here, some I can get without too much trouble." He looked up at Jack. "You planning on starting a war already?"

"Yeah."

"You think you can beat this Ally?"

"No. But I need to get its attention."

"For what?"

"To make a deal."

3. Miller surprised Cal. He'd expected a wild outburst, but instead he handed the paper to Geraci and stared into space. He remained that way as the papers circulated among the others.

Cal heard cries of rage and alarm from the other yeniçeri, but nothing from Miller.

Cal found that unsettling. He'd have preferred a foot-stomping, arm-swinging rage. This was kind of scary.

The uproar from the yeniçeri escalated, and still Miller remained silent.

Cal walked to one of the big windows and stared out at the harbor. The safe house's design was what the locals called "upside down." Unlike most two-story houses which have the living room, dining room, and kitchen on the first floor and the bedrooms on the second, upside-down houses reversed that. The living area was up and the bedrooms down.

It made sense in a location like this. The floor-to-ceiling windows on the second floor offered magnificent views of the surging, gray Atlantic to the east, and the harbor—mostly frozen at this end—to the west. A huge great room, including the kitchen and a dining area, dominated the center of the level. The master bedroom—given to Diana—occupied the south end, while a sunroom filled the north.

The whole deal sat on pilings to protect it from storm flooding. Wouldn't help in something like a tsunami, of course. The place would be washed away with most of the rest of the island. But though an Atlantic tsunami was supposedly possible, Cal wasn't going to lose any sleep over it.

Cal gave his brother yeniçeri some time for venting, then turned and raised his hands.

"All right, everybody. Let's settle down."

It took them a while but eventually the room was silent.

He cleared his throat. "From the nature of the note and since we haven't heard a word from Zeklos, I think it's obvious to everyone that he's the dead man."

More rumblings.

"What's less obvious—to me, at least—is who killed him." He held up his hands again to cut off any outcry. "Yeah, I know the note is signed by 'The Heir,' but anyone could write that. Could have been the Adversary himself, for all we know, trying to turn us against the Heir."

"And the Heir could have been the Adversary," Portman said.

"I'm not denying that possibility, but think about it: The O sensed his identity. And then we had to *drag* him into the Home. He fought like a tiger, as some of you well know."

He nodded toward Jolliff.

"So what?" Jolliff said and rubbed his still-swollen nose.

"So, whoever could kill the O and our brothers, without them firing a shot, has powers way beyond human. Anyone or anything with that kind of power didn't need to trick us."

"Maybe he's like a vampire and has to be invited in," Novak said.

"Let's be serious. I think even Miller would agree: We know from the time we spent with him Sunday night that the guy is very human."

"Maybe you do," Miller said. "I don't. Told you from the start I thought the guy was playing us."

"Yeah, you did. But step back and look at the situation. We sent Zek in to finish the job. Only we knew about that. But he winds up dead—*before* he completes his mission."

Geraci frowned. "How do you know that?"

"Because two comatose patients being hit in a major New York hospital would have pushed everything else off the front pages. But just to be sure, I called the hospital soon as I got back. They're listed as no change: still critical."

"What the hell's going on?" Hursey said.

"I don't know any more than any of you, but I think what's gone down is a pretty good sign that this woman and child are very important to the Adversary and the Otherness. The Ally wants them gone, and the Adversary is protecting them."

Silence as they absorbed this. No one could argue the logic.

"So Zek walked into a trap," Hursey said.

Call nodded. "Yeah. And we sent him."

"What about this Heir guy?" Grell said. "Where does he fit in?"

"As far as I can see, he's a wild card. He's got no connection to the woman and the girl—"

"None you know of," Miller said.

"Right—none any of us has even a hint of. So despite what the note said, I don't see how he's got any reason to off Zek and cut out his heart."

Miller said, "Does if he's working for the enemy."

Cal turned to him. "Makes no sense if you remember what Zek said yesterday. The Heir had dropped in on him. They were talking, then he ran out. If he had Zek on a hit list, why wouldn't he do it then and there?"

Miller shook his head. "Poor Zek."

Everyone in the room stared at him, a few with dropped jaws.

" 'Poor Zek'?" Cal said. "You couldn't stand the guy. You made his life hell."

Miller looked at him. Was that a hint of sadness in those cold eyes?

"Yeah, I guess I did. Maybe I shouldn't have let it get so personal with him. But none of that matters now. What does matter is he's dead, killed in the line of duty. That can't go unanswered."

Cal didn't like the sound of this.

"You're not thinking—"

Miller nodded. "We go in and finish the job. We owe it to Zek." He looked around.

The surrounding yeniçeri nodded, their expressions grim.

"You mean go back to the city? And leave this place unguarded? That's crazy!" Cal closed his eyes for a couple of seconds to compose his thoughts. "Doesn't it strike you as odd for whoever killed Zek to taunt us by leaving that kind of note? Like maybe it's an attempt to get us so riled up we do something stupid—like what you're suggesting."

"I'm not saying we all go. Just me and a few others."

"We're shorthanded as it is!"

"I'll do it alone if I have to, but some extra eyes and legs would help shorten the trip."

Hursey said, "I'm in."

Jolliff: "Me too."

Miller's buddies—no surprise there.

"Count me in too," said Gold.

"Oh no," Cal said, pointing at Gold. "I've got to draw the line there. We need you for the computers."

With Kenlo's death, Gold had taken over the computer chores.

"Portman knows as much as I do. I'm going."

Discipline . . . organization . . . chain of command . . . all gone to hell. No wonder the Otherness was winning. But Cal could see from Gold's set features that he'd be wasting his time arguing.

"All right then, but absolutely no more. As it is, this leaves us with only eight."

"But only for a little while." Miller glanced at his watch. "We catch the noon ferry, we can be in the city by seven, eight o'clock. We'll hit the hospital in the wee hours and be back in time for the first ferry out in the morning. Besides, this place is a cinch to guard. It's a security wet dream."

"And if you're ambushed like Zek?"

Miller's steely eyes hardened further. "Let him try. In fact, I hope he does. Taking down Zek is one thing. Taking me and these guys down is something else entirely. Best-case scenario: We finish the job and get some payback for Zek along the way. Hurt one of us, you hurt us all. Blood demands blood, right?"

Cal shook his head. "And worst case: You end up like those guys back in the Home and—"

"Speaking of our fallen brothers, what did that note mean by 'the collection is eight and growing'?"

"Shit!" Hursey said. "He went back and got the hearts!"

Miller nodded. "First thing we do we get to the city is check." He slammed a fist down on an end table, almost upsetting it. "Knew we shouldn't have left them!"

Cal looked around at Hursey, Jolliff, and Gold. "You realize, don't you, that some of you won't be coming back."

"You don't know that," Miller said.

"If you get out of the hospital after you've done your work—and to do that you'll probably have to kill a few innocent security folks who're only doing their jobs—you'll be the target of a citywide manhunt."

"We'll run the getaway just like we ran it yesterday. After we do the car switches, we can be out of the city and on Ninety-five in no time. No problem."

Cal didn't buy that for a nanosecond, but the message was clear: He'd been overruled.

Still, something didn't sit right. Killing Zeklos . . . cutting out his heart . . . pinning the note to him . . . it almost seemed specifically designed to set Miller off. Was someone setting a trap for him?

The uneasiness nagged at him.

4. Jack knew the yeniçeri would send someone—more than one someone, most likely—to take up where Zeklos had failed. Knew he'd have to face them but didn't want to do it in the hospital.

So he'd done what he could to draw them to the warehouse first. It made sense for them to stop off in Red Hook to get their act together and wait until the wee hours before making their move anyway. But he'd used Zeklos to give them added impetus to check the place out.

He still needed a little insurance at the hospital end, so he'd called the chief of security. He told him a terrorist group had targeted someone in the trauma unit and he'd better pass everybody heading that way through a metal detector. The terrorists would be wearing sunglasses—*sunglasses*, at night, indoors, during the winter. Got it? Stop anyone wearing sunglasses in the hospital.

And then he'd hung up.

On the off chance the yeniçeri tried the hospital first, the heightened security would chase them back Home to work out another plan of attack.

Just where he wanted them. Because he'd made some alterations in the warehouse.

So now he was back in his old spot down around the corner and next to the park, sitting in the dark, watching, waiting, and having trouble keeping his eyes open.

He got out, walked through the park and back again. The frigid air revived him a little. He woke up the laptop Russ Tuit had lent him. It had some sort of little card with an antenna plugged into its side. Three windows lit on the screen, each taking a video feed from one of the warehouse levels. Nothing to see yet since all the lights were out, but it still amazed him how easy this had been to set up.

Russ had told him what software and hardware he needed, then he'd rigged the computer to receive signals from the wireless spy eyes Jack had bought. After that, Jack let himself into the warehouse and installed the eyes in upper corners of the first and third levels, plus the O's office.

Using the materials he'd secured from Abe, he made a few other modifications while he was there.

Now the waiting.

At 7:52 a black Suburban rolled to a stop in front of the warehouse. When Jack recognized Miller's hulking form step out, he tightened his fists.

Yes!

He'd worked hard on the Zeklos note, phrasing it so that Miller would have to respond. The big guy had sent someone less competent to clean up after him, and now that guy was dead. The note and missing heart had left Miller no choice but to come back and finish the job himself.

Then three more men stepped out. The glow from the nearby streetlight glinted off their sunglasses.

Four yeniçeri in all. Looked like they weren't taking any chances this time. No problem. He'd prepared for a crowd.

Jack felt his pulse pick up.

Show time.

He grabbed the small, battery-powered FM transmitter, lowered his window, and placed it on the car roof. He closed the window on the wire of the attached microphone and readied himself to start talking.

5.   Miller brought up the rear as the group approached the Home door—check that: former Home.

He wasn't looking forward to seeing the remains of his fallen brothers again, especially with their hearts missing, but even without the Heir's note they'd have been stopping here— the team needed a break from the road before they began hunting up cars to steal.

They'd made good time on 95, and during the long trip they'd batted around various ways to get this done.

The timing was clear: halfway through the late shift—say, two or three a.m.—when patients were quiet and staff was minimal.

The big question was how. Miller had decided on a direct approach and, since nobody could come up with anything better, that was the way it would go down. He'd pose as a family member and learn the location of the trauma unit. When he was allowed in for a visit he'd use his silenced H-K and put one cyanide-tipped nine into each. Then he'd run like mad.

He'd be on his own getting out of the hospital, but after that—what?

They kept coming back to their tried-and-true escape sequence—same as they'd used after the hit on the woman and the kid. Gold would have a car idling outside the ER. Miller would jump in, Hursey and Jolliff would run interference in their wake. A few minutes later they'd all be back in the Suburban and on their way to Hyannis.

Miller took a deep breath and let it puff his cheeks as it escaped. The getting-out part would be dicey. He could count on up to a minute of shock and confusion before the staff would realize what had happened. Their first concern would be their patients and they'd start resuscitation before doing anything else. But someone would eventually make a call, and then security would be mobilized.

Nobody had promised him an easy time in the MV. The risks came with the territory.

"Hey," said Gold. He stood in the doorway with his keys in his hand. "Didn't we lock this before we left?"

Miller's pistol seemed to jump into his hands with a life of its own. Nerve ends jangling with alarm, he pushed to the front of the group.

"Damn right we did."

The fucker had been here and stolen the hearts. Miller wanted to scream.

Gold gripped the knob and jiggled the door without opening it. Even in the poor light Miller could see that it wasn't latched. Whoever had killed Zeklos had no doubt stolen his keys.

Big question: Was he waiting inside?

Jolliff was on his wavelength. "Think he's in there?"

Miller thought not.

He said, "If you had an ambush set up inside, would you leave the door open?"

Jolliff shook his head. "No way. I'd've relocked it. That way we'd walk in thinking the place was as empty as we'd left it. We'd be sitting ducks."

"Okay, but why leave it unlocked? It's like a neon sign saying someone was here."

"Because that's just what it is. He *wants* us to know he was here. He's thumbing his nose at us, just like he did with that note on Zeklos. He's taken the hearts."

"Bastard," Gold said.

Miller's sentiments exactly. Still . . . nose thumbing or not, in a case like this it never hurt to be too careful.

"Okay. We need someone to go in low and slow and find the light switches. We'll stack up here; soon as the lights go on we'll ease in and secure the first floor. Anybody want to volunteer?"

"I'll go," Gold said. "Haven't seen any action in a while."

Miller took one side of the door, Hursey and Jolliff the

other. Gold eased it open and entered in a crouch. Miller tensed to respond at the first hint of trouble, but none came.

Light flared from within, then he heard Gold say, "So far so good. Except for the bunk area, this level looks clear."

Miller entered in a crouch, pistol held before him in a two-handed grip. He found Gold squatting by the monitoring console.

Gold said, "I'll check the bunk area. Cover me."

They did just that as he zigzagged toward the open doorway. He reached inside and the lights came on. After a quick peek he entered, then came out a minute later.

"Nobody home," he said. His breath steamed in the cold air.

Miller relaxed, but not completely. He lowered his pistol but did not holster it. He couldn't see anything wrong, but some extra sense was on high alert.

He walked over to the far wall where they'd left the fallen brothers. He pulled the sheet off the closest. The heart was where they'd left it. No signs of further desecration, no notes.

The good news—if any news about this scene could be called good—was that the cold appeared to have stalled decomposition.

Then why that note about a "collection"?

Miller did a slow turn. The other three, pistols in hand, had spread out, checking the nooks and crannies. The place looked exactly as they'd left it. What had the intruder wanted here?

Maybe they'd find something on the upper floors.

"Look for a note," he said.

The others nodded and split up.

Seconds later Hursey said, "Found something!"

He stood by one of the outer walls of the bunk area, just to the right of the doorway. He pointed to the floor.

"I'm pretty sure that wasn't there before."

Miller squatted for a better look. Two words . . . hand printed in red at the base of the wall.

Bad Move

"You're right. It wasn't." At least he was pretty sure it wasn't.

"What the hell's it mean?"

Miller shook his head. "Damned if I know."

"Here's another one," Gold said, pointing to the floor to the left of the door. "Same thing. I don't get it. What—?"

"Hey!" Jolliff called from the far side of the room. He stood by the stairs, his head cocked toward the stairwell. "I hear something."

Miller joined the migration to the doorway. The four of them clustered, listening.

Miller heard nothing at first, then . . .

A voice.

Jack held the transmitter in his left hand, the mike in his right as he crossed the street and approached the warehouse door.

"Yeniçeri," he said. "Calling all yeniçeri. I know you're here. Come out, come out wherever you are. Don't be afraid. I won't hurt you. I'm even less dangerous than unsuspecting women and children."

He'd intended to repeat the taunt immediately, but choked on the rage and grief evoked by those final words.

He swallowed hard and kept moving. When he reached the door he was able to start again.

"Yeniçeri. Calling all . . ."

Miller strained to make out the words. The voice, blurred by distance, distorted by static, had a tinny quality. That told him that it was either a recording or a transmission.

He nodded. Knew it. The guy couldn't resist leaving a pee stain on yeniçeri turf. What was it this time? The electronic equivalent of a note?

Gold turned toward him.

"Well, I don't see any way around it. We'll have to go up and find out what's going on."

"Yeah," Miller said. "But not all of us." No way he was going to leave their rear flank exposed. "Gold, you came in first, so you stay down here and take our backs. Watch the door. I don't want any surprises."

Gold nodded, but didn't look happy about it.

Miller hit the light switch as he put his foot on the first step. The stairwell lit up. Nothing unusual there.

He motioned Hursey and Jolliff to follow, then started up. No hurry. They had plenty of time. The door on the first landing stood open. He kept his pistol trained on the dark rectangle.

The voice became louder as he ascended but no more distinct. No question—coming from the third floor. But he wasn't going there. Not yet. Level two had to be cleared first.

He stopped on the landing and reached around the door frame. He found the light switch and flipped it. As the ceiling fluorescents in the O's office flickered to life, he peeked into the space. The desk and the furniture were as they'd left them. The stains on the splattered walls were the same—no messages written in blood there.

He motioned to Jolliff to stay where he was and for Hursey to follow as he moved in.

A quick check confirmed the empty feel of the office. The only hiding place was the desk's kneehole, and that proved empty.

"Jolliff," he said. "Get in here and watch the door while we check out the living quarters."

A search of the O's apartment—the closets, the pantry, even under the beds—yielded nothing.

"One more stop," Miller said as he led the way back to the stairwell.

". . . Calling all yeniçeri. I know you're here . . ."

Jack stood in the cold, repeating his mantra over and over.

What was taking them so long? They should have reached the third floor by now. The only reason for the delay he could think of was a stop on the second floor to check that out.

Good move.

Now—up to the third floor to get this circus going.

As they went up the steps, Jolliff's view was pretty much restricted to Miller's big butt. He leaned around and noticed that the door to the third level stood open as well. But unlike the second, the lights here were already on.

As he followed Miller's slow ascent, the voice grew louder with every step. But he still couldn't make out what it was saying.

At the top he and Hursey squeezed up beside Miller, pistols at ready.

A quick peek showed the level as they'd left it except for one detail: The black, elongated oval of a boom box sat on a table against the front wall. It was plugged into the wall socket and attached to an FM antenna taped to the bricks behind it. It had a CD and cassette player; the radio dial glowed.

Here was the source of the voice, but accompanied by too much static to be understood.

"Be careful," Miller said. "Could be just a distraction. Spread out and secure the space."

The third level offered fewer hiding places than the first and Jolliff figured the other two could complete their sweep in less than a minute without him. As Miller and Hursey moved away, he stepped up to the box. Not understanding the words was making him crazy. After all, he'd been the first to hear it. That made it his discovery.

He bent close. The voice seemed to be repeating something over and over. Closer. One of the words sounded familiar.

He bolted upright when he recognized it.

He called out, "It's coming over the radio. I'd swear I just heard it say 'yeniçeri.'"

He looked around at the others. Miller and Hursey had stopped and turned to stare.

He leaned forward again and reached for one of the knobs.

"Maybe if I tune it in better . . ."

Jolliff heard Miller say, "Wait."

But why wait? He wanted to hear what the voice was saying.

As he gripped the knob to adjust it, a small corner of his brain let out a silent shout of warning. But he ignored it.

Miller again: "Jolliff, maybe you shouldn't—"

Then the boom box exploded.

Leaning against the outer wall, Jack felt the blast more than heard it. Little chunks of mortar rained from the bricked-up windows on the third floor, but all the bricks remained where they were. He'd planted a small charge—deadly at close range but not overly destructive. He didn't want officialdom here just yet.

He dropped the microphone and reached for the brand-new set of keys he'd had made this afternoon.

Earlier in the day he'd picked open the three locks and then removed them. After taking them to a locksmith to be rekeyed, he'd replaced them but left the door unlocked. Wouldn't do to let Miller and company learn too early that their keys were no good.

Sure now that no one would hear him, Jack inserted each new key and turned it, triple-locking the door. Then he left the keys in place and waited. Would have loved to trot back to the warmth of his car and keep track of events on his computer, but he had one more thing to do here.

He raised his fist and swung it toward the door.

The sound of the blast paralyzed Gold for a few unbelieving seconds.

An explosion? Here? At Home?

Had someone booby-trapped the third floor? He couldn't wrap his mind around it.

Finally he reconnected to his limbs and got his body moving toward the stairwell. He stopped at the bottom step and cupped his hands around his mouth.

"Miller! Hursey! Jolliff! What happened?"

No answer. No sound. Not even a groan. Just fine plaster dust drifting from the upper level.

He pulled his pistol. He'd have to go up.

But as he put his foot on the first step, someone began pounding on the front door.

He froze. Who the hell—?

He looked up the stairwell, then at the door. Maybe the bricked-up windows had blown out and this was a cop, or a fireman, or a neighbor.

Shit!

Couldn't let anyone in—not with eight corpses lined up against the wall here and maybe three more upstairs. The fact that they were knocking instead of entering was a good sign. He'd left it unlocked and they could have walked right in.

Another look up the stairs. He heard voices now—loud, echoing down the stairwell. Whatever had happened up there, they were still alive.

But he couldn't go up just yet—whoever was out there eventually would try the knob and then the MV would be in even bigger trouble—if that was possible. He had to see who it was, and the best way to do that was a peek through the camera over the door.

He ran back to the monitoring station. They'd shut it down before leaving.

As he hit the ON switch he had a premonition—an instant before the explosion—that he'd made a terrible mistake.

The blast slammed against the inner surface of the steel door like a giant fist. Jack had placed himself to the side as he'd pounded on it—just in case it blew. But it held. So did the bricked-up windows—sort of. He saw bricks bulge in the frame of the nearest, but only one fell out. He hurried over, grabbed it, and forced it back into its slot. It would go only partway in, so he left it like that.

He stepped to the curb and looked up and down the street. Only a couple of pedestrians out in this cold, and they seemed oblivious to the muffled booms from within the warehouse. No one in the park. The passing cars were clueless.

All praise nonresidential neighborhoods.

He headed back to the car to watch.

Miller pushed himself up from prone to his knees. He shook his head to clear the ringing in his ears. For a few dazed heartbeats he wondered where he was and what had happened. The air was smoky, and what was that smell? Almost like burning . . .

Then he remembered.

Jolliff!

He turned as he struggled to his feet. Movement to his left: Hursey rolling over and groaning. Something—some*one*—sprawled in the middle of the floor, burning. Miller stepped closer for a better look. Bile rose in his throat. If he hadn't known it had to be Jolliff, he never would have recognized him.

The man lay spread-eagle in a pool of blood. His face was gone. Crisped. Blown off. No skin, no eyes, no hair, his broken jaw twisted at an angle. The blast had ripped open his throat as well. Blood still oozed from the torn arteries within. His jacket was on fire.

Miller took off his own jacket and beat out the flames, then stepped back and watched for movement in the chest. He couldn't see how anyone could look like that and still live, but you never knew.

But no movement: not a twitch, not a breath.

Beyond Jolliff's remains he saw Hursey stagger to his feet and wag his head like a dog trying to shake off a fly. He gave Miller a dazed look, then his gaze dropped to Jolliff. He paled and moved his lips.

At first Miller thought Hursey had lost his voice, then realized it was his hearing. He couldn't make out a word over the whine in his ears. He stepped closer.

"What'd you say?"

No problem hearing his own voice, though he sounded like he was under water.

Hursey's surprised look said he'd just realized that his hearing was on the fritz as well. He cupped his hands around his mouth and shouted. "Don't tell me that's . . ."

Miller nodded.

Without speaking they both skirted the body and approached the spot where the boom box had been. The table still stood, though its top was scorched. Tiny bits of black plastic lay scattered everywhere.

Hursey leaned close to his ear. "Jesus!"

Miller was studying the wall behind the table. It looked unscathed—not even scorched. That meant only one thing.

He turned to Hursey and pointed to the wall. "Shaped charge."

Hursey stared a few seconds, then said something. Miller didn't have to hear him—he could read his lips.

"The fuck!"

Right. The fuck. But a smart fuck.

A shaped charge—the basis of armor-piercing rockets and antitank grenades—focused the energy of the explosion. It allowed a lot of bang from a small amount of plastique. The guy hadn't wanted to blow out the walls, so he'd used an inverted cone-shaped charge to do most of its dirty work directly in front with the least amount of collateral damage.

Miller wanted to kick himself for being such a jerk. He'd let this guy play them like hooked fish. He'd counted on one of them adjusting the knob to fine-tune the reception.

He grabbed the table, lifted it, and hurled it across the room.

As the table landed, the building shook with a muffled boom. Miller stared at it a few seconds before realizing the boom had come from below.

The sound of Gold buying it?

"Fuck!"

He pointed to the doorway, motioned Hursey to follow, then started for the stairwell. He wasn't going to rush. No telling what else was rigged. He faintly heard Hursey's footsteps through the hum in his head and realized his ears were recovering.

"Damn!"

First thing Jack had done upon returning to his car was to check the third-level view. It looked empty except for an unidentifiable body in the center of the floor. He could tell from its size that it wasn't Miller, but nothing more.

But on the second floor—trouble. The explosion above must have jostled the camera out of position. It still worked but instead of its fish-eye lens taking in the O's office and the stair door, it had angled so that he saw only the O's desk.

His first-floor view was still okay and now showed Miller and Hursey, pistols held before them, warily entering from the stairwell. They approached the remnants of the monitoring console and the smoking remains of whoever had activated it. Jack figured that was the newcomer he hadn't recognized.

He watched Miller and Hursey approach the body.

Scared, Miller? Terrified? Hope so. But don't think you've seen it all. Still a few surprises left.

He pulled out two cell phones—one labeled LEFT and the other RIGHT—and accessed a preprogrammed number on each. With his fingers poised over the SEND buttons, he watched and waited.

Hursey had to pee something fierce. He was ready to wet his pants, but bit his upper lip and held it back.

Don't let me end up like Gold and Jolliff . . . please-please-please.

Jolliff . . . gone. He couldn't believe it. They'd been buds since boot camp. But missing him would have to wait till later. Right now priority number one was getting his ass out of here in one piece.

He followed Miller to Gold's body. Not much left of him,

just an unidentifiable, human-shaped mass of bloody, steaming, burnt flesh.

Miller said something about another shaped charge, but Hursey couldn't follow him. He hadn't seen Jolliff this close up. Now, looking at Gold, not only did his bladder become more insistent, but he wanted to hurl as well.

This was a dream . . . a bad dream . . . and he'd wake from it soon.

"We're getting out of here."

Miller's voice again—faint, but the words recognizable.

Hursey could only nod. He looked at Miller and saw that he was pale and sweaty, even in this cold. Miller . . . scared . . . confused. Never thought he'd see the day.

The big guy pointed to the front door and said, "Ease over there and don't touch anything—I mean *anything*—along the way."

Hursey didn't have to be told twice. He was closer so he led the way. He started tiptoeing and stopped himself. That wasn't going to do any damn good.

Finally, the door. He hesitated before grabbing the knob, afraid for a second that it might be booby-trapped like the others. But no . . . they'd come in through it, right?

Still . . . his heart was banging away a thousand miles an hour as he closed his fingers around the knob . . . and very slowly turned . . . and oh so gently pulled—

It didn't move. He pushed and shoved but it wouldn't budge.

"It's locked!"

Miller pushed him aside and tried it himself with equal success. He cursed and pulled out a set of keys.

"Gold must have locked it."

Yeah. Poor Gold. Locked the door to stay safe, never knowing the real danger was right in front of him.

Hursey watched Miller shove a key into the top lock and twist. It wouldn't turn. Miller shot him a concerned look and tried again with another key. Same result. He noticed Miller's hand trembling as he wiggled the third and last key into the lock.

No luck.

Miller turned to him, his face white. "He changed the locks."

"No way." Hursey took a closer look at their scratched surfaces. "Those are the same locks. I swear it!"

"Try your keys."

He dropped them as he fumbled them from his pocket. He tried them all in all three locks.

"I don't get it."

Miller's expression was grim. "They've been rekeyed."

Hursey reached for his cell phone. "I'm calling for help."

Miller grabbed his arm. "Yeah? Who? The cops? The fire department?"

Hursey saw what he meant.

"How about the MV? A couple of them could come down here and—"

"And nothing. They couldn't get here till tomorrow afternoon. You want to sit in this mousetrap till then?"

"Then what do we do?" Hursey hated the queer quaver in his voice, but he couldn't help it. "How do we get outta here? Even if we had a crowbar—and we don't—we couldn't get through that door."

"Don't need one. We unscrew the locks and take them out—just like he did."

Hursey studied the locks' faces and saw each was fastened to the door by two Phillips-head screws. So simple. Why hadn't he noticed? But then he remembered—

"I hope you've got a screwdriver on you, because we moved all the tool boxes out."

Miller glared at him. Why? For wet-blanketing his idea?

"No. No screwdriver. But I've got this."

He reached into his pocket and pulled out a knife. He opened it and went to work with the four-inch blade. In less than a minute it became clear that a knife—at least this one—wasn't the answer: the point couldn't get enough traction in the screw's cross-hair grooves to turn it.

Miller slammed his fist against the door.

"The son of a bitch must have used a power screwdriver." He folded his knife and looked around. "Okay, start looking for something, anything that'll loosen those screws. But don't—repeat: *don't*—go pulling open any doors or drawers."

"Then how are we going to—?"

"Just find what you can without getting yourself killed. Check the second floor. I'll take the third."

Hursey made his way upstairs, looking for trip wires across the steps. They'd already tramped up and down this route, so he doubted he'd find one, but he wasn't taking any chances.

He searched through the O's office and then the living quarters. The dresser drawers were all closed and he wasn't about to try them, but the closets were open—and empty but for a bunch of coat hangers.

When he returned to the first level, Miller was already there, scouring the area around the ruined console. Hursey wandered into the bunk area. The beds were stripped, just as they'd left them, and the lockers were open and emp—

He stopped and stared. All open except one.

He took a step closer. The door wasn't completely closed. Something jutting from the bottom was holding it open. When he saw what it was he took a quick step back.

"Miller! Want to take a look at this?"

When he entered Hursey gestured to the closed locker door.

Miller shook his head and almost smiled. "Now *that's* insulting. He must think we're idiots."

"Maybe, but look what's sticking out the bottom."

Miller looked, squinted, and said, "The bastard."

Together they approached the locker. Miller squatted and stared at the business end of the protruding Phillips-head screwdriver.

"This is like being in a fucking video game." He looked up at Hursey. "I used to be a pretty good RPGer. Let's see if we can find some string or twine, or anything we can use to open this from a safe distance."

"We've already been through the place. You see any string? I didn't. I—" He remembered that closet. "Wait a minute. There's a bunch of wire coat hangers upstairs. If we hook them together . . ."

Miller nodded. "Worth a try. Good thinking. Go get them."

Hursey hurried upstairs. He couldn't help smiling. They'd

beat this sucker yet. And Miller had paid him a compliment. Must be the stress. Miller never complimented anybody.

He fairly ran to the closet, grabbed the hangers—had to be twenty or so—and rushed back to the first floor. They devised a quick and easy method. If they pulled down on the middle of the horizontal section, they could stretch the triangle of the hanger into a narrow diamond shape with a hook on one end.

They had nineteen. At a foot and a half or so apiece, hooked end to end in a daisy chain, the hangers gave them a thirty-foot head start.

To keep the locker door from opening prematurely they gingerly rested the back of a chair against it. Then they looped the hook of the last hanger into the handle and retreated to the chain's opposite end.

Miller shook his head. "Not as long as I'd like."

Hursey had been thinking the same thing. The best place to be was behind what was left of the monitoring console. Not a great place, but pretty much the only game in town. Problem was, it was still ten feet away.

"Well," Miller said through a sigh. "Gotta do what you've gotta do. When I pull, run like hell."

And then, with no further warning, not even a countdown, he yanked the goddamn chain.

Hursey saw the chair start to topple as the door swung open. He saw no more because he spun and dashed to the console, fell as he slid to a stop, and scrabbled behind it. He covered his ears—didn't want to lose any more hearing—and waited.

And waited.

After nearly a minute he lowered his hands and looked at Miller.

Miller shrugged. "Let's not get fooled. Could have a long delay to suck us in. We'll just sit here and wait."

So they waited.

After a good twenty minutes Miller reached into his pocket and pulled out a quarter.

"Could be a misfire. Someone's got to check."

Hursey had a bad feeling about who that someone would be.

"Let's wait a little longer."

"Uh-uh. We need that screwdriver. Heads or tails? Call it in the air."

Miller flipped the coin but Hursey found his voice locked. He couldn't utter a sound.

Miller gave him a shove. "Come on, dammit. You wanna flip?"

He nodded. Miller handed him the coin. His hands shook but he managed to toss it into the air.

Miller said, "Heads."

The coin landed, rolled, came to a stop with George Washington's head showing.

"Looks like it's you. Get moving."

Hursey let out a shuddering breath. "I don't want to end up like Jolliff."

"Don't be a baby. Look, it'll be okay. I'll walk you halfway there."

"If it's so okay, why not walk me all the way?"

Miller's lips turned up at the corners. "Well, if I'm wrong, one of us has to escape this dump and get to the hospital to finish the job."

Hursey took a breath. Now or never.

"Okay. Let's go."

He rose and started walking toward the bunk area. True to his word, Miller came along. But he stopped at the doorway.

"Look," he said, pointing to the screwdriver that had fallen out of the now open locker onto the floor. "It's right there. All you've got to do is hustle over, pick it up, and bring it back. After that, we'll be out of here in twenty minutes, tops."

Hursey stared at the screwdriver. Seemed easy enough.

He swallowed. "Okay, here goes."

He dashed toward the locker, stooped, and grabbed the screwdriver. But before making the return trip, he couldn't resist a peek inside. And there in the locker he saw a timer sitting atop a bulging backpack. Numbers flashed on its LED readout.

. . . *6* . . . *5* . . . *4* . . .

"*Bomb!*" he screamed.

He turned and ran with everything he had; his feet slipped

on the floor as he fought for traction. When he reached the doorway, he saw Miller hightailing it for the console. Not enough time for that. Neither of them would make it.

One thing Hursey knew he had to do was get clear of the doorway. The blast would funnel through it. He cleared the door and dove to his left, flattening himself on the floor and wrapping his arms over his head.

But just before he closed his eyes he saw the handwriting on the floor.

Bad Move

Hursey screamed.

❖

The blast caught Miller from behind, slamming him against the ruined console. He felt ribs crack. As he bounced off, his knees buckled and he dropped to the floor. He landed prone. He lay there and rode the spinning floor. Finally it slowed, then stopped.

He opened his eyes and found himself facing the bunk area. A gaping hole had been blasted through the bottom half of one of the walls. What was left of Hursey—a charred, smoking lump of flesh—had been blown ten feet away.

The explosion . . . what triggered it? Not opening the locker—they'd waited too long after that. And the bomber couldn't have known that Hursey would wind up in that spot.

Or maybe he could have.

Miller remembered the signs on the floor to the right and left of the door. BAD MOVE. And it sure as hell had been a bad move for Hursey to wind up on one of them. But how had the bomber known he'd end up there?

Unless he'd put something in the locker to make Hursey think a bomb was going to go off any second. Then yeah, the only thing to do was get to the other side of the wall and dive for cover.

And the rat bastard had counted on that. The signs on the floor were his way of flipping them the bird.

But what if Hursey had turned right instead of left? Miller could understand if the walls on both sides of the door had exploded, covering either contingency, but only Hursey's side had blown. Which meant there was some sort of detector—

—or the guy was watching.

Miller pounded his fist on the floor. That had to be it.

Gritting his teeth, he pushed himself up. Christ, he hurt everywhere. The best he could do was roll over, and that started the building spinning again. Must have a concussion too.

He waited until things steadied, then looked around, concentrating on the ceiling.

And there he found it, in the right upper corner of the room: a little black box with a lens in the middle.

The fucker had been watching the whole time. He could pick and choose which side of the wall to trigger, and when.

Miller repressed an urge to pound his fists and kick his feet like some spoiled brat in a tantrum. He was furious with himself. This guy had played them like a tin flute. And he'd allowed it.

He calmed himself. Anger was no good here. Had to be cool—at least as cool as the guy playing him. Cooler even.

Because this guy was a pro. Got the drop on them in their own car, sent them on a wild goose chase by palming his tracer off on a taxi, slipped by them at the bar. And now this.

Had to admit he had style. Could have blown the whole building as soon as they'd stepped inside. Instead he'd done surgery, taking them out one at a time. His style said he was a thinker, a planner. And a guy who knew people. He'd known someone would not be able to resist tuning the radio. And he'd known someone would eventually turn on the monitoring console. And he'd known they'd be suspicious of a single closed locker door. Could have closed them all, but no. He'd known they'd be suspicious about just one.

But all that aside, the most important question facing Miller now was what to do.

At the most basic level, he had two options: get up or stay put.

In his present condition, if he got up now he'd be staggering around and might blunder into another bomb.

But if he stayed put . . .

If he just lay here and played dead or badly wounded, maybe he could suck the guy in. And maybe not. Maybe the guy would figure he'd done his day's work and run off to whatever rat hole he called home.

Either way was okay. If he didn't deal with the fucker now, he'd do it later. The end was going to be the same: payback. He'd hunt him to the ends of the Earth, and sometime before his dying day he'd collect for Jolliff, Hursey, and Gold.

But for now, he'd have to put on a show.

He rolled over and pushed himself to his hands and knees. This time the room held steady. He made a show of trying to straighten up, then let himself fall back to the floor.

He'd give it an hour like this. If the guy didn't show, he'd risk ducking into the bunk area to grab the screwdriver, then he'd get to work on those locks.

If the guy did show . . . he'd have to leave wherever he was receiving that camera feed and unlock the front door. Miller would listen for the sound of those locks, and when he heard the first bolt click back he'd be up and moving. By the time the third was open he'd be at the door and ready to kick the shit—

Wait. He'd never hear the locks over the roaring in his ears. How was he going to work this?

He'd figure something.

Jack watched Miller's prone form on the laptop's screen and waited for him to move again. He didn't.

Dead?

Jack hoped to hell not. He'd planned to leave one man standing, or at least alive enough to answer a few questions. The answers were of critical importance to Jack.

He watched a little longer. The camera's lens didn't provide enough resolution to see if his chest was moving. From here Miller didn't seem to be breathing, but he could be simply knocked out.

Or faking it.

Always that possibility. But if so, he'd deal with it. At least he wouldn't be walking in blind.

He disconnected the laptop from the cigarette lighter socket. The screen flickered as it switched to battery power, then stabilized. He cradled it as he opened the car door and kept an eye on the screen on his way to the warehouse.

When he reached the door he pulled out his keys and began unlocking the deadbolts. One . . . two . . . three.

Miller didn't budge.

Jack pushed the door open and stepped inside.

The place reeked of burned flesh. A thin layer of white smoke, disturbed by the open door, undulated in the air. Jack eased it closed behind him, then placed the laptop on the floor and drew his Glock.

Slowly he stepped toward Miller with all the caution of a lost camper approaching a sleeping bear.

Miller felt rather than heard the footsteps—a vibration from the floor into his skull. He hadn't heard the door, but no question about it, someone was here.

He snaked his right arm under him where he could grip his H-K. Then he waited, tensing his muscles. Closer . . . closer . . .

A work boot edged into view, but not close enough to grab. Then a second. Someone in jeans and steel-toed boots stood about four feet away, probably staring at him, wondering if he was dead.

Come on . . . just a couple of feet closer.

But the shoes didn't budge.

Okay. Right time or not, he had to make his move *now!*

He pulled the pistol, rolled as he brought it out and up and then the *crack!* of a shot and a stab of blinding pain in his arm. His fingers went numb and he dropped the pistol.

The fucker had been waiting for just that move.

Miller ignored the agony in his bloody arm and lunged for those jeans. He grabbed air instead. Where'd he go?

He scrambled to his feet, spun about and saw him. Yeah. Him. The Heir . . . or Jack . . . or whatever his name was. He had Miller's H-K in his left hand and what looked like a Glock in his right, but he had them pointed toward the floor. He stood by what was left of Hursey, and the thought of what had happened to him and Jolliff and Gold turned the air red.

With a roar he charged.

But the guy wasn't there when he arrived. He felt an explosion of pain in his left knee, and then he was losing his balance, tripping over Hursey to land by the blown-out wall.

He checked his knee. He hadn't heard a shot. No blood. Must have kicked him.

Miller fought to his feet but the knee barely held him. He found the guy standing about a dozen feet away, silent, expressionless, looking like someone waiting for a green light so he could cross the street.

He charged again, but it was an ungainly, limping charge. The guy easily ducked to his right, and though Miller saw the kick coming, he could do nothing to avoid it. The heavy work boot rammed the side of his other knee. He felt ligaments rip and cartilage tear. He crumbled to the floor.

Two blown-out knees. Goddammit! He was playing with him, just like he'd played with the bombs. Surgery. Carving out one life at a time—only here it was one limb at a time.

Miller tried to rise but he had the use of his left arm and nothing more. He wanted to scream. He wanted to cry like a baby. He'd lost. Goddammit he'd lost.

The guy squatted half a dozen feet away and stared at him. He still hadn't said a word.

"All right. You got me, asshole. No way that'd happen if you hadn't softened me up with your bombs. So do your worst. Come on. Get it over with."

And still the guy said nothing.

"You had the O fooled, and Davis too, but I was on to you. Knew from day one you were a phony. Have to admit, though, I didn't think you were working for the other side."

The guy shook his head and said, "I'm not."

The words seemed to echo down a long tunnel through the ringing in his ears.

"You gotta be. You've got no reason to do all this. You gotta be working for the Otherness."

Another slow shake of his head.

Miller gave him a closer look and noticed his eyes. This wasn't the same guy who'd tagged along when they did the Arabs Sunday night. That guy'd been a nothing, a schlub. This guy was scary. On the outside he looked like a cross between a stone-cold hard-ass doing some extermination work. But from somewhere in his eyes, his face, his voice came a whisper that this was all personal. Very personal.

"Then why? Who do you work for?"

"I work for me."

"Why, dammit! What did we ever do to you?"

"I had no beef with the MV at the start. Didn't want to join, but I was perfectly content to live and let live, let you go your way and me go mine. And that's the way it would have stayed. But then you and your crew effectively killed the two most important people in my world."

What was he talking about?

"Who? When?"

"The woman and child you ran down."

"You *knew* them?"

A nod. "I was going to marry the woman; I was going to make her little girl my own. The woman was carrying our child."

He pulled something from a pocket and held it out.

Miller squinted at what seemed to be a black-and-white photo, but he couldn't make it out.

"That supposed to mean something?"

"It's a sonogram of my daughter. We were going to name her Emma. But now her mother and sister are vegetables and Emma's dead. Because of you."

Miller tried but couldn't quite grasp what he'd just been told. It was too far out, too crazy.

"But the Ally wanted them dead. The only reason for that would be they were connected to the Otherness."

His head did a slow shake. "No. No Otherness connection. Because they're connected to me."

"Then you must be Otherness connected."

Another head shake and a sigh—a tragic, despondent sound, weighted with incalculable grief.

"No, I'm Ally connected."

"Make sense, dammit!"

"Too late for that. But I've answered your questions, you answer one for me."

"If it's about the new O—"

"We'll get to her in a minute." He pulled something from his pocket and set it on the floor between them. "It's about La-Guardia."

Miller's gut tightened when he saw what it was: a cyanide-tipped 5.56mm NATO round. He'd filled the hollow with cyanide himself.

"Where'd you get that?"

"Found it under one of the lockers. That was an MV operation, wasn't it."

"Fuck you."

"Might as well tell me. It's not going to change the outcome here. And confession is good for the soul."

"I repeat: Fuck you."

The guy shook his head. "How do you do that? How do you stand there and mow down fifty-odd innocent people?"

"You should know. Between yesterday and today, look how many yeniçeri you took out."

"I had nothing to do with yesterday, but I take full credit for tonight."

For some reason, Miller believed him, but he wasn't about to admit that.

"So you say."

"I'll ask again: How do you stand there and mow down fifty-plus innocent people just to get to one man?"

He knows! How the fuck does he *know*?

"You figure it out."

"Okay. My guess is you got an Alarm from the Ally that showed you mowing down everyone at that particular baggage claim at that particular moment. Right? So you became Wrath of Allah."

Miller could only stare. He'd nailed it—except the Wrath of Allah part. He and Hursey had done the deed, yeah, but didn't make any calls to the media. Hadn't even thought of that. He'd been shocked when he heard some group calling itself Wrath of Allah was claiming credit for the attack.

He had to say something. "You don't second-guess the Ally. It sees the big picture, you don't."

"You'd have been a hit at Nuremberg."

"This isn't a game, goddammit. Human rules don't apply."

"Yeah, maybe. Who helped you—who was the other gunman? Jolliff or Hursey?"

"You can go to hell."

Suddenly he looked sad. "Do you know the name of the man you were supposed to kill?"

Miller shook his head. "No. Just that he'd be in the crowd."

"I knew him," the guy said. "I called him 'Dad.' "

Miller thought—no, was *sure* he'd misheard.

"What did you say?"

"My father. You killed my father that day."

Miller could only stare. If this guy was telling the truth, that meant that the yeniçeri—him most of all—had pretty much clear-cut his life. *If* he was telling the truth. A big if, but the look of loss on his face said he was.

What the fuck? Why did the Ally have such a hard-on for this guy? What had he done to get a cosmic being so pissed at him?

He'd probably never know the answer to that, but he did know that if positions were reversed, he'd have been planting bombs too.

Other things he knew were that he could expect no mercy from this guy, and that he had only minutes left to live.

Strangely enough, that didn't bother him as much as he would have expected. Not like he was leaving a wife and kids behind. As he'd been told half a million times, a spear has no branches.

And then the answer hit him: The Ally was pruning this guy's branches, making a spear out of him. Miller could see only one reason for that.

"You *are* the Heir after all."

He nodded glumly. "So I've been told. But enough about me: Where's your new O?"

Miller shook his head and looked longingly at the NATO round, just out of reach. A foot closer and he'd have been able to grab it and use it to make a quick exit.

"Can't have you planting a bomb under her too."

"I just want to talk to her."

"Yeah, right."

"You're going to tell me."

Miller shook his head again. "Ain't gonna happen."

He waggled his Glock. "I could make your last hours seem very, very long. Eternal."

Torture . . . Miller's gut clenched at the prospect. Would he be able to hold out? He didn't know. Everyone had their limit. Where was his?

He hoped he never found out.

He hid his dread and said, "Do your damnedest. I ain't saying shit."

The guy sighed. "You know what? I believe you."

He picked up the NATO round as he rose and walked around to Miller's left side.

"Don't take this personally. It's simply to keep you out of trouble."

He lowered the stolen H-K until its muzzle was only two inches from Miller's left elbow and fired. Miller screamed— he couldn't help it—and rolled onto his back. At which point the guy shot him in his right elbow.

The guy used his foot to roll him over onto his belly, then went through his pockets.

"You won't find anything there," Miller gritted through the pain.

Soon enough the guy realized he was right.

"Don't go away," he said as he walked off.

6. Shit!

Jack wanted to kick something, but he drew the line at kicking a helpless man. Even if it was Miller.

He'd planned to leave one yeniçeri alive—for questioning. Had to find out where they'd taken Diana, had to talk to her. She was Gia and Vicky's last hope. Maybe. An infinitely long shot, but a shot.

He hadn't wanted the survivor to be Miller. He'd been pretty sure he could get one of the others to crack, but sensed Miller would be too tough.

On the other hand, he'd wanted to go mano a mano with Miller, wanted—*needed*—to make it personal.

And he had.

Miller's pockets had been virtually empty; his wallet hadn't yielded a clue. Jack still had no idea where they were hiding their new O.

Okay, try the others. A grisly task, and no more fruitful than Miller. The only thing of interest was a dark blue doodad hanging from a lanyard around Gold's neck. It was lozenge-shaped, a couple-three inches long, imprinted with PRE-TEC and 8GB.

Looked like a flash drive.

He hurried over to his laptop and plugged it into a USB port. But when he accessed the drive, all he found was gibberish. Maybe the explosion had scrambled its memory. Maybe Russ Tuit could unscramble it.

He pocketed the drive and the car keys Jolliff had been carrying. One place left to search.

Outside, he combed through the Suburban's interior, emptying the glove compartment, checking all the storage pock-

ets. He hit pay dirt atop the driver's visor: a round-trip
Steamship Authority ferry ticket for a car and three extra passengers from and to Nantucket.

Okay. That had to be it. The new safe house was on Nantucket. But where on Nantucket? All he knew about the place
was that it was an island off the Massachusetts coast, somewhere near Martha's Vineyard. But he'd know more real soon.

7.   The guy came back and squatted before him. He held out a slip of paper and waggled it. Through his fog of agony Miller saw a ferry pass.

Shit.

"So she's on Nantucket. Care to tell me where?"

"Fuck you." It came out like a groan.

"I'm not out to harm her—anything but. Unlike you, I don't target women and children. But I *am* going to find her. You can make it easier by telling me where."

"You gotta be kidding me. The fuck would I do that?"

" 'Cause maybe it'll help undo what you've done."

Undo? Was this guy crazy?

"No way."

The guy raised the pistol in his other hand—Miller's own H-K—and said, "Then you're no good to me."

Miller had known this was coming. To his surprise, he felt no fear. Torture he feared. Dying clean and quick . . . not so bad. He'd sworn to die for his Oculus if necessary. Now it was necessary.

He looked the guy in the eyes and said, "Things'd be different if we'd had a fair fight."

The guy looked sad. "No such thing as fair. You of all people should know that."

He saw the barrel come level with his face.

Saw the cold eyes behind it.

Saw the muzzle flash.

Then saw nothing.

Ever again.

8. Jack wished he could have found more satisfaction in standing over Miller's fresh corpse. But he felt nothing—too dead inside to feel anything but grief and loss and rage.

Straightened and looked around. Time to get out of Dodge.

He did a sweep, removing the three undetonated bombs, then the newspaper-stuffed backpack and the battery-operated timer from the locker. He'd had Russ reset it to flash a count-down from ten to zero in a continuous loop so that whoever saw it would think they had only seconds before an explosion. The bombs and timer went into the backpack, as did his laptop. He stepped outside and looked around. All quiet.

9.   Back at the hospital he left his hardware in his car on the chance that Security had taken his warning seriously. They had: Made him pass through a metal detector before being allowed upstairs. Good for them.

He found Dr. Stokely charting at the nursing station.

"Dare I ask?" he said.

Her expression was grim as she shook her head. "I wish I had good news for you, Mister Westphalen."

"Call me Jack."

"If you wish. What *I* wish is that I could tell you there's been no change in Gia and Vicky, but . . ."

He leaned against the wall.

"Oh, no."

She nodded. "Gia's showing signs of the brain stem herniation I warned you about. And Vicky . . . well, we can't seem to stop her seizures. We've thrown everything we have at her and it works for a little while, but then she starts convulsing again. She's quiet now, but I've never seen anything like it."

I'm sure you haven't, Jack thought.

"What happens if she doesn't stop?"

"Status epilepticus will, for want of a better term, fry her neurons. Cause cerebral edema. She'll herniate her brain stem, just like her mother."

"Brain death . . . like the Schiavo thing?"

"No. That was different. That was a persistent vegetative state. Schiavo still had her brain stem intact, and thus the basic brain functions that keep the body alive—circulation, respiration, and so on. That won't be true in the case of your wife and daughter."

"You mean . . . ?"

She nodded. "With significant herniation . . . total shut-down of vital systems . . . the end."

She might as well have slapped his face.

Numb, he said, "What Glasgow score have you got them at now?"

"Three."

He felt himself swaying. "That's as low as you can go."

Another nod. "Yes, it is."

"How much longer?"

"At this rate . . . twenty-four hours. I wouldn't get too far from here, Mister Wes—Jack."

But he had to go far. Probably to Nantucket. It was the only chance they had.

He walked over to their beds. When he saw the gauze patches over Gia's eyes he did an about face and returned to Stokely.

"What's with—?"

"The eye patches? That's to keep them from drying out or being injured. Gia has lost her corneal reflexes."

Goddammit he *had* to find the new O. The previous one had said something about being one of the Ally's eyes. Jack was counting on that . . . praying it was an open connection.

10. In a black fog he walked over to Russ Tuit's place on Second Avenue in the east nineties. Smelled like they were frying tortillas in the Tex-Mex restaurant below.

Russ greeted him at the door.

"How'd that timer work out?"

"Perfect."

Russ, a redheaded code head with pale skin that most likely had not seen the sun in the thirty-odd years of his life, had garbed his pear shape in a flannel shirt and old corduroys worn almost smooth. No matter what the season, he wore flip-flops.

"Still not going to tell me what you used it for?"

"Probably better you don't know."

Jack handed him the flash drive.

Russ's eyebrows shot up. "Eight gigs. Cool. But what's this crud on it?" He scraped at the crusty stains with a thumbnail. "Hey this looks like—" His head shot up and he stared at Jack. "—blood. Is it?"

Jack said nothing.

Russ nodded, looking a bit queasy. "Yeah, yeah. Probably better I don't know, right?"

"Probably. Thing is, I think it may be messed up. I can't make any sense of what's on it."

"Let's take a look."

Russ plugged it into his computer and hit a few keys. Jack watched his screen fill with the same gibberish he'd found.

"See?" Jack said. "It's screwed up."

Russ turned to him. "Yeah, it's screwed up, but in a special way: It's encrypted. Probably one-twenty-eight bit."

"And that means?"

"Means we need a decryption key."

"Where do we get that?"

"From the mother computer that encrypted it, or . . ." He smiled.

"Or what?"

"Or I run it through my own personal decryption program."

"What do you mean, personal?"

"It means I wrote the code. It's the reason—all right, one of the reasons— I'm not allowed online for the next twenty-two-point-two years."

Russ had done a two-year, soft-time jolt in a fed pen for a shopping list of Internet crimes, most of them bank related. One of the conditions of his parole had been a quarter-century ban from the Internet.

"Okay. How long and how much?"

"Can't say how long. Can't even say I'll succeed."

"I need it yesterday, Russ."

"Okay, okay, I'll crank on it. As for how much: two-fifty just for trying, five hundred if I break it." As if anticipating a protest, he quickly added, "The two-fifty is for my time and the use of my proprietary software." He gestured around at his front room, furnished in contemporary crummy. "I need cash to maintain this lavish lifestyle."

"Deal."

Russ rubbed his chin. "Got a feeling I low-balled myself."

Jack grabbed a pad off his desk and scribbled his cell number, then wrote "Nantucket."

"I need anything and everything on that drive that has to do with Nantucket. And I need it fast." He peeled five fifties from his cash roll. "Here's the down payment. Another two fifty later and a five-hundred bonus if you get it done before six to-morrow morning."

Russ grinned—he really needed a new toothbrush. "*Awright*! I'm on it. If it's doable, I'm the guy to do it."

11. Back in his apartment, Jack Googled Nantucket. He found a boomerang-shaped island thirty miles south of Cape Cod. Small: only fifty square miles. Only? That was twice the size of Manhattan. Not good. But year-round residents numbered just under ten thousand. Much better, but still a lot of people. Loads better though than the forty to fifty thousand on the island in the summer.

He figured the islanders would be, well, insular, and the kind who knew everybody's business. They'd sure as hell know if a bunch of sunglass-wearing outsiders and a teenage girl had moved in among them. But would they tell another outsider? Jack had his doubts.

So he needed Russ to ferret out a name or address or anything involving Nantucket from that flash drive. Otherwise he'd have to tackle the island on his own and find some locals to chat up, see if they'd come across with any hints as to the whereabouts of the yeniçeri.

A very iffy proposition since Jack had little time and no illusions about his chatting-up abilities. They stank.

In the meantime, he'd hang at the hospital and hope for the best . . . hope he wouldn't have to go to Nantucket at all.

He realized what an idiotic hope that was, but he wasn't giving up on Gia and Vicky. Not ever.

FRIDAY

1. Cal lay in bed in the dark and listened to the wind howl around the house. He had one of the eight downstairs bedrooms to himself. Each could sleep four, but the MV's butchered numbers didn't require that sort of crowding.

He checked the clock again—4:11—then grabbed his cell phone from the night stand and checked that: Yeah, it was on, but still no call from Miller or any of the others.

The plan had been for Miller to call once they were on their way back to Hyannis.

Cal hit his speed-dial button for Miller—only the tenth or twelfth time in the last hour. He listened to a long series of rings before the leave-a-message voice came on.

Realizing sleep was impossible, Cal slipped out of bed and padded into the hall. To his left he saw a figure silhouetted in a glowing window. He walked toward it.

"How's it going, Grell?"

In the wash of light from the security floodlamps outside, he could make out the binocs hanging from Grell's neck and the twelve-gauge shotgun, the Bushmaster, and the sniper rifle leaning beside the window. The super-bright lights automatically turned on at dusk and stayed on until dawn.

The silhouette nodded. "All quiet on the southern front. What're you doing up?"

"Waiting to hear from Miller."

"No call yet?"

"Nope."

"Shit."

Yeah. Shit.

Cal headed upstairs to the computer that occupied a small study off the great room.

"Just me," he said as he spotted Novak in the sunroom where he had a view of both the harbor and the ocean, as well as north.

He lit up the computer and started searching the news services for stories of gunfire in a New York hospital.

Nothing.

Acid seeped into his stomach, burning, gnawing. This looked bad. Worse than bad. This had the makings of a catastrophe. If Miller, Jolliff, Hursey, and Gold had wound up like Zeklos . . .

He shook his head. What would he do? What *could* he do? Diana—had to get used to calling her the Oculus now—and the others would be looking to him for answers, and he had none. This isolated house on this spit of land bordering the Atlantic offered more safety that anyplace else they might have chosen, but it hamstrung them as well. Even if they had the manpower to answer Alarms, they were too far from just about anywhere of importance to act on them.

Militia Vigilum . . . the words mocked him: They could be vigilant, but not militant.

He almost felt as if the Ally might be mocking them as well: No matter what I tell you to do, no matter how heinous, you run to it. I say, "Jump," and you say, "How high?"

He'd never felt the slightest confusion about his relationship to the Ally. It had always been the vast, wise commander, and he had always been the small, fleshy appendage that did its bidding. But on his last outing he hadn't been able to—had outright refused.

Was he losing faith?

He hoped not. Because that would make his whole life a waste, an empty exercise. A lie.

Feeling lower than he could ever remember, Cal turned off the monitor but remained seated. If only Miller would—

A sound.

He straightened in the chair and listened more carefully. It came from the far end of the great room . . . from the master bedroom suite.

A girl's voice . . . sobbing.

They'd ensconced Diana in the suite because it was where

she would have stayed if her father were still alive, and because she'd be safer on the second floor.

Safer, yes, but more isolated.

Cal rose and slowly, carefully crossed the great room. The door to the suite was ajar but the room beyond lay dark. The sobs grew in volume as he approached.

When he reached the door he hesitated. She was thirteen, her father had been murdered just days ago, and she was vulnerable. Very vulnerable.

Damn me.

With everything else going on—arriving in a rush, learning about Zeklos's death and the note, then Miller and his crew taking off, he'd completely forgotten about the kid and how she must be feeling.

They needed a grown woman here, someone Diana could talk to, confide in, cry on her shoulder. Being an Oculus was a hellish responsibility for an adult. It had to be crushing for a teenage girl.

Teenage girl . . . oh, hell, had she had her first period yet? Who'd talk to her about it? Who'd go to the store for tampons or whatever they were using these days?

We need a woman!

But female yeniçeri didn't exist. The MV was strictly Old School in that regard. Women had never *been* members and therefore women would never *be* members.

Maybe not a bad idea. Imagine the turmoil and distractions they'd cause in the training camps.

Poor Diana. She couldn't go to school or have even one friend. Not with those eyes. They'd give rise to too many unanswerable questions.

So it was up to Cal.

Had to tread carefully here. Couldn't let her think he was interested in anything but her well-being, that he was knocking on her door at this hour with any agenda other than to see if he could help. Her world had fallen apart. She had to be crushed, terrified. He didn't want to add to that.

He knocked on the doorframe.

"Diana?"

A startled gasp, then a teary, hesitant, "Yes? Who's there?"

"It's me—Davis. Are you all right?"

Louder sobbing answered his question.

He leaned next to the door, unsure of what to do. He knew a hundred ways to kill, but hadn't the slightest clue as to how to comfort a newly orphaned teenage girl. Maybe if he'd been a father at some time, but . . .

"Want to talk?"

A sniff. "That's okay." Another sniff. "No, wait. Yes."

"Okay if I come in?"

"O-okay. But just to talk. Just for a minute."

Yep. Had to tread *very* carefully here.

He stepped into the room but didn't turn on the lights. He figured she'd rather not be seen with tears on her cheeks. And to be honest, he'd rather not see those black eyes of hers. Her father's hadn't fazed him, but Diana's . . . he'd watched her grow up with normal blue eyes. Seeing them now as glossy black orbs disturbed him. The little girl had mutated into something else.

He was glad she wore shades day and night—but he doubted very much she wore them to bed.

Enough glow from the floodlights seeped through the blinds to allow him to make out the huddled shape sitting in bed with the covers pulled up to her neck, held there by little hands protruding from the sleeves of one of her long flannel nightgowns. He knew about those because he'd packed them for her.

He found a chair and pulled it up next to the bed, then seated himself facing her.

"I can't imagine what you're going through," he told her. "None of us can. You must be frightened half out of your mind."

A whimper. "I am."

"I hope you know that we're here for you, ready to die for you. But I've realized that's not enough. You need a family. We'll be that family. You've got a dozen uncles." Only eight, he thought, if Miller and company didn't come back. "We'll make time for you whenever you need it. We'll school you, play games when you want us to, leave you be when you want time to yourself. The important thing you've got to realize is that you're not alone in this, Diana."

She began crying again—deep, wracking sobs this time. The sound tore him up.

Without realizing he was doing it, Cal reached out and took her hand. He was ready for her to pull away, and that would be okay, but instead she clutched it with both tear-slick hands.

"I'm so-so-so scared!"

"It's all right to be. You didn't choose this life, I know, and it won't be easy, but we'll all try to make the best of it."

"You don't uh-understand. I'm scared of an Alarm. I don't want to get an Alarm."

Cal could understand that. He'd seen her father when they hit him. They didn't look pleasant. Diana undoubtedly had seen it too. He didn't blame her for being frightened.

But what to say?

"All I can tell you is we'll help you in any way possible."

Lame-lame-lame.

"But what if one comes at night?"

Cal didn't have an answer for that beyond an even lamer, "We'll come as soon as you call." Then he thought of something. "Maybe you won't have any Alarms."

"Why not?" She sounded almost offended.

"Well . . . what good would they do? Unless they concern something right here on Nantucket, what can we do about it?"

After a few heartbeats she said, "You really think so?"

He had no idea but felt compelled to ease her fears any way he could.

"It's a possibility."

"Can't you stay with me?"

He temporized. "I can stay here now while you get some sleep. Lie back down. I'll stand—I mean sit watch. You'll be okay."

She removed one hand from his but kept a tight grip with the other. She slid further under the covers and lay prone. In minutes she was asleep.

Cal sat and held her hand. Maybe after she'd experienced an Alarm or two she'd feel more at ease. Until then, he'd do what he had to do. If it meant holding her hand all night, then so be it.

With his free hand he switched his cell to vibrate.

Where the hell was Miller?

2.   Jack was dozing in the family waiting room when his phone started vibrating. He recognized the caller's number—Russ—so he roused himself, stepped into the hall, and hit SEND.

"Jack? Did it. Decryption accomplished. Made the deadline, right?"

Jack glanced at his watch: 5:47.

"Just barely. Any mention of Nantucket?"

"Yeah. A few. Don't know what you're after, but what I've found doesn't look like much. Something like a Quicken file."

Quicken . . . money-management software. If the MV was making mortgage payments on the Nantucket place . . .

"Be right over."

He decided to hoof it. Russ was only a mile and a half or so away. Jack had garaged the car and by the time he got it out on the street or found a cab he could be there. Besides, the cold air would revive him.

Christ, he was tired.

The air, the exercise, and the cuppa Joe he grabbed from an all-night coffee shop on 81st combined to revive him, leaving him alert and fairly energetic by the time he arrived at Russ's.

Jack had seven-fifty in bills ready in his hand when Russ opened the door. He didn't want any jive—he wanted info.

"Here." He handed Russ the wad. "Show me."

Russ stared at the bills, then at Jack. He wore a stunned expression. "That was quick."

Jack pushed past him and stalked toward the computer. He was not in a chatty mood.

"Show me."

Russ pocketed the cash as he scooted ahead. He hung over the chair and started banging the keyboard.

"It's right about—*here*." He pulled out the chair and motioned for Jack to sit. "There's six gigs of data on that drive. I searched high and low but this was the only mention of Nantucket I could find."

Jack saw bar graphs and calendars but no mention of Nantucket.

"What am I looking at?"

"It's a bill management program. Let's you know if and when you paid a recurring expense." He ran his finger along a line. "See these numbers. They all went to a guy named Darryl Heth on Pocomo Road in Nantucket—or should that be *on* Nantucket?"

"And who might he be?"

"Well, he's listed under 'Maintenance,' so I'd guess he's some sort of handyman or caretaker."

"Does it say where he does his maintaining?"

Russ shook his head. "That's about it: name, address, and 'Maintenance.' That what you're looking for?"

"Not quite. No mortgage payments listed?"

"Maybe. But if so, they're not linked to Nantucket." He reached over Jack's shoulder and entered a few bursts of typing. He shook his head. "Nope. No mortgages at all."

Jack stared at the screen. He hadn't learned any more about the location of the new MV home, but he'd bet the ranch that Darryl Heth could tell him.

"Print out his name and address for me."

"Gonna write him a letter?"

"Nope. Going to pay Mr. Heth a visit."

3. Jack was dozing in his car outside the Twin Airways hangar in the wilds near a Long Island burg with the improbable name of Muttontown, when Joe Ashe pulled up in a very retro, very bright yellow Chevy SSR pickup.

"Thank God," Jack muttered, rubbing his eyes.

He'd been having trouble hooking up with the Ashe brothers the last two times he'd needed to fly. He hadn't been able to get past their voice mail earlier so he'd driven out to wait. He hoped Joe wasn't here to get ready for another charter.

Joe, tall and skinny, stepped out of his truck and ambled toward Jack's Vic, a curious expression on what little was visible of his face. He wore shades and a cowboy hat low over his fair, shoulder-length hair. The lower part of his face hid behind a short beard just the far side of stubble.

Jack stepped out and waved.

Joe grinned when he recognized him. "Hey, Jack," he said in a molasses-thick Georgia accent. "How're they hangin, boy?"

Jack had borrowed that accent last week when he'd braced the yeniçeri from the rear of their Suburban.

"Need your help."

Joe laughed. "Some more larkin like that tire-dumpin gig? Man, that was so fun it oughta be illegal." He struck a pensive pose with a hand to his chin. "Hey, wait a minute. I do believe it was."

"Got to get to Nantucket, Joe."

"Not a problem. Long's you don't need to go today."

"I need to be there now. As in yesterday."

"Shoot, man. I got a charter scheduled for midday." He

looked at the gray clouds lidding the sky. "Course that might not happen. Got a heap of weather on the way. A snowy nor'easter, they say."

"What about Frank?" Frank was Joe's twin brother.

"On a charter to Tampa. Lucky bastard. He'll probably stay there awhile to wait out the storm."

"This is really important, Joe. Please. I'll pay you anything."

"Ain't a question of money—question of time. Why'nt you just go commercial? And if you can't do that, I reckon I can call on some folks'll be glad to take you."

"The *how* is as important as the where and the when. I need to bring along some hardware."

Joe stared at him a moment, then said, "C'mon inside where it's warmer."

He led Jack to the hangar, unlocked the door, and deactivated the alarm. Inside Jack saw a Gulfstream jet and a few small prop models.

In the cozy office in the front corner, Joe started a pot of coffee. Looked like he'd set it up the night before so it would be ready to go.

Jack said, "How long will it take you to get me there?"

"Do 'er in half an hour, tops."

Jack glanced at his watch. "It's only a little after eight. You can be back by nine-thirty."

"Whoa-whoa-whoa." Joe held up his hands. "This here ain't like jumpin inna pickup. You gotta do all sorts of checks'n shit."

"Well, let's get started. I'll help."

He opened his mouth and Jack expected another refusal, but Joe caught himself. Maybe Jack's desperation had seeped through.

Finally he sighed. "Shit. What the fuck. Let's do 'er. How long you plan bein there?"

"Overnight. Less if you can hang out and—"

"'Fraid you're gonna have to get back on your own. Last thing I need is to get snowed in at ACK."

"Ak?"

"A-C-K—Nantucket Memorial's ID code. Come on. Let's get doin if we're gonna do this."

Jack wanted to hug him but figured Joe wouldn't appreciate that.

4. The sleek little four-seat, two-prop Diamond Twinstar had a bumpy time in the cloud-filled sky.

"Unsettlement in the air," Joe told him through the headphones.

"Long as we don't do a John-John."

"Gotta few more hours under my belt. Just a few."

Jack knew the Ashe boys had uncountable hours of flight time, but still he hung on and prayed.

He hid his relief when, at a little after ten, he was able to step out onto the tarmac of tiny Nantucket Memorial Airport. He pulled his duffel bag from the rear and shook hands with Joe.

"I owe you one, man."

"Hell, you paid me."

"You know what I mean."

Joe smiled through his beard. "Yeah, I do. Hope things never get to the point where I have to call you up and collect."

"You've got my number."

Joe looked at the sky. "Don't reckon I'll be able to come back here for a while. Once that nor'easter hits—and it looks to be real soon—I'll be snowed in. We ain't commercial or even municipal. Takes time to get our strips plowed."

Since Jack wasn't sure he'd be able to go back tomorrow—or ever, for that matter—he took the news in stride.

"I'll work something out."

Joe rubbed the arms of his sweatshirt. "God damn, I swear it's even colder here than back home. I gotta get back inside."

Jack waved, then hurried through the razor-edged wind to the solitary, cedar-shake-sided building where he found a

Budget counter. After renting him a Jeep Liberty, the woman there gave him a map and outlined the route to Pocomo Road.

Pocomo, it turned out, was a section of Nantucket whose main artery was—surprise—Pocomo Road. The area lay northeast of the airport as the crow flies, but no road ran the crow route. He'd have to follow a roundabout course that took him west and then back eastward.

A small annoyance, but still an annoyance. It meant delay, and time was a fist against his back, kidney punching. If the doc had been right last night about Gia and Vicky having twenty-four hours left, damn near half of that was already gone.

If Darryl Heth didn't want to tell him what he needed to know, what then? Getting rough with him would be counterproductive—might alert the yeniçeri that someone was asking questions about their place. He'd have to use an oblique approach—make Heth tell him about the house without Jack asking about it.

He thought he knew a way. But first he had to find the place.

Due to multiple wrong turns, the ten-mile trip along winding, rolling roads took forty minutes. He detected a conspiracy in the lack of road signs out here. The first three or four miles had been fine, everything clearly marked. But the farther east he moved, the spottier the markings. This was the less populated, untouristy half of the island. He sensed the residents saying, if you can't find your way around here, maybe you shouldn't *be* around here.

All of which he understood. And sympathized with. But not when he was working against the clock.

As he drove, following a line of canted telephone poles, Jack noticed that almost every house, no matter what the shape or size, had a dark roof and cedar-shake siding. No tile-roofed, stucco-walled, Tara-columned, bright-colored, vinyl-sided McMansions here. No McDonald's either, for that matter. Or Wendy's or Burger King. A chain-free oasis that discouraged the look-at-what-I-can-buy parvenus. A suburb of heaven.

Finally, Pocomo Road. He followed it, marveling at the

huge houses on either side, until he ran out of pavement. He kept going. He found "Heth" on a mailbox on the right and followed a winding pair of sandy ruts through the six-foot-high brush to Chez Heth, a tiny, cedar-shaked ranch on the north side near the end of the road. *Head Case* had been carved into the wood of a canoe paddle fixed over the front door.

Hardly encouraging.

Jack parked in front, walked to the door, and knocked. A thin woman, in her sixties, wearing a house dress, answered the door. Her pale blue, wrinkle-caged eyes took his measure as she stood and stared at him.

Jack said, "Can I find Darryl Heth here?"

"Who's asking?"

"Someone who might have some work for him."

"He's 'round back, chopping wood."

He walked around and found a sixtyish man splitting logs with a long-handle ax. Reminded Jack of a Charles Bronson scene from *The Magnificent Seven*.

Jack introduced himself as John Tyleski. Heth took off his gloves and they shook hands. His palm and fingers were tortoise-shelled with callus. His face was as wrinkled as his wife's.

"Beautiful piece of property you've got here."

Jack was burning to shake the info out of this guy, but he held back. Never hurt to soften up a source. Besides, Jack wasn't lying. Heth's house sat on a bluff overlooking a huge expanse of ice—square miles of it. He imagined how beautiful it must look in the summer with sun sparkling on the water.

"Yeah. Been in the family forever. If I wanted to buy this property now, I couldn't afford it. Hell. I couldn't afford a corner of it. The price of land on the island . . ." He shook his head in disgust.

"Don't I know. I'm looking to buy and it's, well, it's just incredible." He pointed toward the ice. "What am I looking at here?"

"The head of the harbor." He pointed a gnarled finger leftward. "See that low shore on the far side over there? That's the coatue; it keeps out Nantucket Sound."

Jack saw a sandy colored strip capped with a fuzz of vegetation—scrub brush, most likely.

He pointed straight ahead across the ice. "And there to the east, that line of dunes you see keeps out the Atlantic."

The same kind of strip, but this one sported a single large house midpoint.

"Does the harbor always freeze up like this?"

"Not the whole harbor, not down by town, though sometimes that happens and an icebreaker has to come through so we can get food and heating oil. But here, well, the head of the harbor's something of a backwater. Freezes over most every winter. This year's no exception."

Jack nodded toward the stack of split wood. "Doesn't look like you'd miss the oil much."

"Been burning a lot more of that since the price of oil went outta sight." He eyed Jack. "But I gather you didn't come here to admire the view, nice as it is, or talk about oil. Just to save us both some time, let me tell you flat out that this place ain't for sale."

"I appreciate that." Jack dropped an oceanfront street name he'd picked off the map: "I've been looking at property along Squam Road—"

"Weather can get rough over there."

"So I've been told. That's why I'm leery of leaving the place to the elements for nine or ten months a year."

"And you're looking for someone to keep an eye on your house."

"You got it."

Heth narrowed his eyes. "Well, just so happens I do a bit of that. But how'd you know?"

Jack shrugged. "Someone in one of the realty offices gave me your name. Would you be able to fit another place into your schedule?"

"Sure. What did you have in mind?"

"Well, let's not get ahead of ourselves here. I don't wish to offend you, but before we come to an agreement, I'll need some references. I hope you understand."

"Course I do. Only a damn fool would hand his house keys to a stranger without knowing something about him."

"So you can provide references?"

"Sure can. Come on inside."

Okay, Jack thought. So far, so good.

He was burning clock here, but he reminded himself that he wouldn't be able to make a move on the safe house—wherever it was—until after dark.

The ranch was cramped inside and smelled of fried fish, but its pine walls and floor were clean and polished. Mrs. Heth poured coffee as they sat down at the dining table. Heth pulled a ledger from a drawer and began thumbing through it.

"I caretake nine places—all shapes and sizes, from a brand-new oceanfront in Surfside to the old Lange place over on Cliff Road. I charge a monthly retainer."

He seemed pleased to be able to say that he received retainers.

"Can you provide contact numbers for your clients?"

Jack figured a guy who liked receiving retainers would also like the idea of having clients.

"All nine?"

"Well, I'll need only a couple of responses, but who knows how many will reply?"

Heth nodded. "Good point. I'll write 'em down for you." He reached for a scratch pad. "Matter of fact, you can ride over to one of the places right now and ask them in person."

Jack kept his tone casual. "Is that so?"

"Yep. It's on the other side of the harbor head. This is the first time I've known them to show up since I been working for them."

"Really."

"Interesting history to the place. You can see it from here—sitting by itself on that strip of land I pointed out to you, you know between the harbor and the Atlantic. Been there fifty-sixty years or better but the present owners done some strange modifications."

Jack's ears pricked up.

"Such as?"

"Well, you see, the house sits over a wash-away garage."

"I'm not familiar with that term."

"Means the living space of the house proper sits on a bunch

of pilings. The under part is enclosed as a garage, but not all that sturdily built. That's so, in a real bad storm, should the ocean have a mind to jump the land and pay a visit to the harbor, the walls of the ground level will wash away, leaving the flood waters swirling around the pilings while the house sits safe above it all."

Jack was disappointed. "Not such a strange modification."

"That was the original design. I'm talking about other stuff. The original design also had a set of stairs running from the garage up to the first floor. But these folks tore that out and covered the opening with steel plate. In fact, the entire flooring of both levels is reinforced with steel plate." He shook his head. "That's not gonna protect you from no storm."

Jack agreed. But it would protect from anyone shooting through the ceiling below.

Jack leaned forward. "So how do they get in?"

"You gotta go up an outside stairway to a door. Get that? No matter what the weather, you've gotta leave the garage and go outside to get inside. Don't make sense."

Made lots of sense if you wanted to limit access.

"Who are these strange folks?"

"Nice people. Said they won't need me coming around while they're here but they're gonna keep paying me my retainer. Lucky thing they're here, too, otherwise you might have trouble getting hold of them."

"Why's that?"

"The place is owned by some sort of foundation." He checked his ledger. "The MV Foundation, whatever that is. It hired me and pays me."

Jack resisted pumping a fist. He'd just taken a giant step closer to the new O.

"I'll put these folks first on my list."

5. Over Darryl Heth's objections, Jack left him with a Ben. The man might have protested more if not for the take-the-money-and-shut-up look his wife was giving him. A man's time was worth something. He'd taken up some of Heth's, and Heth in turn had saved Jack a lot of his own. A hundred bucks for that seemed the deal of the century.

He'd given Jack directions, warning him that he'd need four-wheel drive to reach the house. So Jack took Pocomo back to Wauwinet Road where he made a left and followed the harbor head's shoreline.

He had no intention of bracing the yeniçeri in daylight, but he wanted to get a look at the house, scope out its shape and size and possible routes of access.

Far along he passed a little guard shack with a stop sign and a warning that only residents and four-wheel-drive vehicles were allowed past this point. But the shack was empty and Jack kept going.

Past the shack he found a hotel of sorts on the left: THE WAUWINET—AN INN BY THE SEA.

Past that the pavement narrowed, then vanished, replaced by sandy ruts. Jack levered the Liberty into four-wheel drive and pushed on. Eventually the scrub pines vanished, leaving nothing but sand and brush. About half a mile out on the isthmus between the wind-whipped, white-capped Atlantic and the frozen head of the harbor sat a big lonely house.

Was this the place? He looked down at Heth's directions. He'd followed them to the letter. And the house looked just as he'd described it: two stories atop a two-car garage.

Shit.

The isthmus looked about four hundred feet wide—

certainly no more than five hundred—and had no access other than the sandy path that passed it on the ocean side. Jack's map called the path Great Point Road, named he guessed after the finger of land that jutted out from the island's northeast corner.

The perfect safe house. No way to sneak up on it during the day; if they had floodlights—which he assumed they did—no way to sneak close enough to matter at night. They could zero in on any approaching car and keep it covered until it was well past. Same with hikers, although Jack doubted there'd be many of those in this weather.

He pulled out his compact binoculars and focused them on the place. Two garage doors faced him. The set of stairs Heth had mentioned ran up to a door on the harbor side of the second level. Two decks jutted from the top level, one facing the harbor, the other the ocean.

Jack imagined the views in the summer must be fabulous. Be great to rent it some day. Gia and Vicks would love—

What was he thinking? They weren't going to see another summer if he didn't find a way into that house for a little face time with the O. And even then . . . if she couldn't put him in touch with the Ally . . . or if she could but the Ally wasn't into making deals . . .

So many ifs . . .

He focused on the stairway landing and the deck not quite directly above it. From this angle he couldn't tell how much space separated them.

It began to snow. Small, scattered swirling flakes, but the sky promised more. Much more.

Shit.

He seemed to be saying that a lot lately.

6.   Cal had given up on calling Miller or hearing from him. He sat at the kitchen island with Novak, watching the hulking, dark-haired man spread Skippy super-chunky on Ritz crackers and shove them into his mouth. Grell stood at the counter over by the window, whipping up some sort of chicken thing to cook later for dinner.

Lewis and Geraci had another half hour to go on their guard shift. Come four o'clock, Cousino and Finan would be on till midnight, after which Cal and Dunsmore would take over. Three eight-hour shifts covered by four teams of two allowed everyone to rotate through each shift.

A few hours earlier Cal had driven to the Stop & Shop and stocked up on nonperishables like canned chili and Spaghetti-Os, bottled water and soft drinks and such. He'd also bought lots of crackers and peanut butter. And a hand-powered can opener. The house had an electric model, but that wouldn't be much use if the storm knocked out the power. Yeah, they had a generator, but it never hurt to be prepared for anything.

Diana was taking a nap—she hadn't got much sleep last night. Cousino and Dunsmore were playing cards. Finan was reading. They'd spread out the thousand pieces of a puzzle of one of Monet's lily ponds on the dining room table. Diana spent a lot of time with it, and everyone else tried to fit in at least one piece as he passed.

He looked out through the sliding glass doors at the inch of snow that had already collected on the top-floor deck. The Boston TV weathermen were predicting a bad one. Who knew how long they might be stuck here? Days, or maybe not at all. Either way, none of what he'd stocked in would go to waste.

Novak washed down a cracker with a mouthful of Pepsi and said, "What're we going to do, Cal? Nice as this place is, we can't stay here forever."

Cal knew what he was feeling. He felt it too. Only a couple of days here and already island fever was setting in.

"You're right. We can't, and we won't. But this will have to be Home until the camps send reinforcements."

Grell turned from the counter. "And when will that be?"

"I talked to Idaho. They're stretched pretty thin already. Everyone they've got is green and raw."

"Did you tell him we're down to eight?" Novak said around a mouthful or Ritz and PB.

"Of course. He's going to do what he can."

"Which is?"

Cal shook his head. "Wish I knew."

Grell rinsed his hands and perched his long, angular body on a stool at the counter.

"Welcome to Cretaceous Park."

Cal looked at him. "What's that supposed to mean?"

"Obvious, don't you think? Yeniçeri are dinosaurs and the big meteor that's going to make us all extinct is breathing down our necks."

"Well, aren't you Mister Cheerful," Novak said.

"Just stating the facts. No use in kidding ourselves about Miller and Gold and Jolliff and Hursey. They're not coming back. We started off the week with twenty guys. Now we've got eight." He shook his head. "The writing's on the wall. All you've gotta do is read it."

Cal knew what he meant. They were losing—losing big. He looked for a way to put a positive spin on it, but couldn't find one. If Oculi kept dying at the present rate, by this time next year they'd be extinct. And that would leave the surviving yeniçeri—assuming any remained—adrift, with no purpose, no place in the world.

Ronin.

He looked at Grell. "So what do you think we should do? Give up? Walk away and leave Di—our Oculus unprotected?"

Grell stared at a corner of the ceiling. "Well, why not?

Might be the best thing for her. With no yeniçeri to answer her Alarms, there'd be no reason for the Adversary to bother with her."

"Don't count on that. She's one of the Ally's eyes."

"Until she gets her heart torn out."

"But what if the Adversary's plan is to blind the Ally? Okay, I doubt he can do that, but taking out all the Oculi could sure as hell make it myopic."

Grell shook his head. "I still think she'd have a better chance—"

"Forget that she's an Oculus. She's a scared little girl, terrified and alone. Who's going to take care of her? She was crying last night. I went in and sat with her and talked to her. Since I've got the midnight shift, I won't be able to do that tonight. One of you might have to."

Grell looked uncomfortable. "What do you say to her?"

"You say what I did: That she should think of us as family and that we're always here for her and that we're ready to die protecting her."

Grell nodded. "Oh. You mean like the truth."

Cal loved him then.

"Yeah. The truth."

7. Jack checked the weather through the dormer window of his second-floor hotel room. Dark as night. His watch said it was almost five, which meant that it pretty much was night. Or twilight. Not that it mattered a whole lot. The clouds had lowered even further and the local weatherman said the snow was falling at better than an inch an hour.

Good.

He'd picked the Wauwinet Inn because it sat on the head of the harbor just a few hundred yards from where the pavement ended, and about half a mile due south across the ice from the yeniçeri place. Like every structure elsewhere on the island, it had cedar-shake siding and white trim. Could have been any of the oversized two-story houses he'd seen, only much larger.

He'd taken a second-floor room to see if he could spot the yeniçeri house. Early on he'd found it with the field glasses. As the snow had thickened, it disappeared, but not before he'd been able to determine that the third-floor deck was not over the stairway landing.

Bummer. That would have made things easier.

Easy or not, the house was going to have an uninvited guest tonight. What he had to decide was when: Now, with relatively little snow but everyone in the house up and about? Or fight the deeper snow later to arrive when all but the guards were asleep?

He couldn't see that it mattered. No one would stay asleep for long once he made his presence known. Besides, the clock was running.

He stepped to the bed and surveyed his day's purchases spread out on the flowered coverlet.

After finishing his long-distance survey of the house, he'd

driven into town to do some shopping, scouring Main Street and the surrounding area for any kind of white clothing. Not many stores open, and the ones he found were closing early because of the snow. He did find a place with a skiwear section, but the men's sets were all red or blue or yellow or a combination of the three.

Lots of white on the women's rack, though. He checked out the largest sizes he could find and garnered strange looks when he tried them on. He settled on a white parka with a fur-lined hood, and white ski pants, both too small but big enough to squeeze into. Then he bought a white king-sized down comforter. As a final touch he picked up twenty feet of half-inch nylon rope from a marine outfitter near the docks.

To all that, he now added the two H-Ks he'd picked up over the past couple of days. He'd have preferred his trusty Glock, but these babies came fitted with high-quality suppressors. He wanted to keep the noise to a minimum.

One last thing before he left: a call to the trauma unit. Stokely was there.

When he asked her his perpetual question, she said, "Not good, I'm afraid. Your wife has developed an arrhythmia and—"

"Her heart?"

"Correct. We're keeping it from getting out of hand, but it's only a matter of time."

"I hope you're not asking me to pull the plug."

"No. That won't be necessary."

A deep, shuttered part of Jack had suspected that, but to hear it put into words . . .

"No hope?" He could barely hear his own words.

"There's always hope, but . . ."

Jack knew what she'd left unsaid: . . . *but not enough to matter.*

"I don't know where you are," she said, "but I advise you to get here while you can, before the snow keeps you out."

He wanted to be there—she'd never know how much. But Dr. Stokely and all her staff offered no hope. And maybe that house out there on the isthmus didn't either, but it offered a *chance* of hope. So that was where Jack had to go.

"I'll be there. Soon."

He hoped.

Jack's sense of urgency couldn't push to a higher level, so he blanked it out and concentrated on the moment. He wound the rope around his waist, then wrapped his purchases plus a few other goodies in the comforter and hauled everything out to the Jeep in the lot across the road. He knew his furry white parka would attract attention in the hotel so he put it on in the car.

As for the rest of the night, he very much doubted that whatever went down at that house—whether yeniçeri deaths or his own—would ever be reported to the police. The yeniçeri had their own laws. So did Jack. Neither would bother with anyone else's.

Still, he wanted to avoid attracting attention. It wasn't a strategy; it was a way of life.

All geared up, he rolled up the comforter, stuck it under his arm, and stepped out of the Jeep. He opened the double gate that led to the lawn. Not until he reached the north side of the hotel did he feel the full force of the storm. A blast of snow-laden wind staggered him. He leaned into it and pushed forward.

The ferocious gale made it hard to tell how much snow had fallen. Some areas of the front lawn were bare down to the dead grass, others had drifts eighteen inches high. And the storm was barely five hours old.

Jack had heard of a whiteout; this was the first time he'd been in one.

He followed the sloping lawn down past a raised deck that sat like a wooden island in the dune grass, then to the water's edge. No problem telling where land ended and harbor began: The wind had buffed the ice virtually clean of snow.

Jack pivoted and looked at the Wauwinet. All he could see was the glow of its outdoor spots. Could have been a hotel or a beached commercial fishing boat with its running lights on.

He turned back toward the head of the harbor and felt his heart pick up its pace when he saw nothing but darkness ahead. He knew the angle he had to travel from the hotel to reach the house, but after moving a hundred feet out on the ice he'd lose the hotel as a landmark. Without bearings he could wander around in circles out there until he froze to death. He needed a compass but hadn't brought one—who could have imagined this situation?—and hadn't been able to find one in town.

Shit.

The only way of surprising them was to come in off the harbor. They wouldn't be expecting anyone from that direction. Probably weren't expecting anyone from anywhere in this storm. But after everything that had gone down this week, they had to be paranoid as all hell. They'd keep their guard up no matter what, especially where the road was concerned.

He stared out at the impenetrable darkness of the ice. Suicide to go out there without a compass. He kicked at some drifted dune grass. God *damn* it!

He'd have to try the road. He could keep the Jeep's lights off and work his way out along the isthmus until he saw the house lights, then go the rest of the way on foot—head out onto the ice and approach the house at the same angle he would have if he'd been able to cross the harbor.

Yeah. That would do it.

He hurried back up the slope to the lot, started the Jeep, and put it on the road. He kept it in four-wheel drive. The pavement was much like the hotel lawn: drifted in some spots, bare in others. But a hundred feet past the end of the asphalt he had to hit the brakes.

A fallen pine blocked his way.

Jack jumped out and tried to push it aside, but couldn't budge it. The way it was wedged across the road, he'd need a power saw to get past. And there were no side paths out here—hell, there were barely *sides*.

Back in the Jeep he banged the steering wheel and let his head drop back against the safety restraint. How the hell was he—?

And then he saw a pair of LCD letters in the overhead console: NE.

A compass—the Jeep had a built-in compass.

He slumped back. So what? Not as if he could rip it out and carry it with him across the ice.

Unless . . .

Did he dare?

He didn't see that he had any choice.

He flipped the Jeep into reverse, turned around, and headed back to the Wauwinet.

8. "Gin," Diana said as she slapped three eights and an eight-high straight of clubs onto the table.

Dressed in an NYU sweatshirt, jeans, and her shades, she said it with little enthusiasm. Cal hadn't expected her killing time with him to relieve the pain of her loss, but hoped the distraction would dull it.

He smiled for her and shook his head. She'd just learned the game—apparently her father hadn't believed in card games—and already had beaten him five out of the last eight hands.

"Luck. Pure luck. Okay, total up your points."

He was getting creamed in the point tally. He fancied himself a fairly decent card player, but his strength had always been in reading his opponent. That wasn't possible with Diana—even if she had her shades off he doubted he'd be able to suss out anything in those black eyes.

She leaned back. "I'm hungry."

Only five-thirty. Kind of early, but he took her hunger as a good sign. She hadn't eaten much the past couple of days.

He craned his neck to find Grell and spotted him in front of the TV.

"Yo, Grell. What's dinner?"

"Chicken *française*. Hungry?"

Cal glanced at Diana. "Yeah."

Grell rose from his seat. "It's all set to go. Gimme half an hour. In the meantime, take a look at this storm. It's *big*."

Diana rose from her seat. "I think I'll take a shower before dinner. I'm kind of rank."

He smiled. "Could've fooled me."

She turned away, then turned back. "Thanks for staying with me last night. It was . . . nice."

He shrugged. "You needed a friend."

"Do I have to call you 'Davis' all the time? What's your first name?"

"Yeniçeri never use first names."

"Couldn't you make an exception for me?"

He shook his head. "Not even for you."

He saw her lips tighten, then she turned and strode to her room.

Cal closed his eyes and let out a breath. *I'm not cut out for this.*

Maybe Grell was right. Maybe she'd be better off without them.

He wandered over to the TV where the Weather Channel was showing satellite images of the storm. The reception kept breaking up as gusts of snow peppered the dish on the roof. But the feed held together enough to display a swirling mass of white running north along the coast. Accumulation predictions ran from two to four feet, depending on location.

He gave a mental shrug. Long as the ocean didn't act up too much, a blizzard was a good thing for them. Not much chance of anyone making a move on the place during weather like this.

On the other hand, someone might think they'd lower their guard because of the storm. He had to warn the men not to slack off.

He crossed to the big picture window and stared out at where the harbor was supposed to be. He heard the wind pelting the glass with snow. He could see nothing but swirling white. The bright security lights made the whiteout even worse. The house could have been moved to Siberia or Antarctica or Jupiter for all he knew. He had to trust that the rest of Nantucket was still out there.

And hope that no one was foolish enough to be heading their way.

9. Jack had figured driving down the hotel lawn to the ice would be the easy part. And he was right. No sweat with four-wheel drive. And no one around to raise a ruckus.

Now the hard part: Did he dare roll out there in this thing? He had no idea how thick the ice might be. Yeah, it had been cold lately, and the ice had looked thick in daylight, easily capable of supporting a single man. But how would it hold up under a couple of tons of SUV?

He shook his head. What was he stalling for? None of that mattered. Gia and Vicky were at stake here. And having no other options made the decision simple. He was going.

But slowly.

The ice would be thickest and safest near shore, most likely frozen all the way to the bottom. Farther out, he couldn't say. He knew nothing about the head of the harbor and hadn't had any time to learn.

He took his foot off the brake and let the Jeep ease down the last few feet of the slope and onto the ice.

It held.

Watching the overhead compass readout, he turned off the headlights, angled the wheels to the right, and gave her a little gas.

A little proved too much. Even in four-wheel drive, the wheels spun and the Jeep side-slipped. Zero traction out here. He put it into first gear and tried again. Better. He began to move ahead. He adjusted his direction until the compass read N, and kept rolling. But just barely. If the ice wasn't going to hold this baby, he wanted to find out before he was too far from shore.

He watched in the rearview as the snow swallowed the

lights of the hotel. And then, only blackness behind, only blackness ahead. Like driving through ink. No moon, no stars, the only light coming from the dashboard. He couldn't see the snow, but knew from the crinkling sound it made against the windows that it was out there.

The wipers squeaked across the windshield. At first he thought to turn them off—nothing to see out here anyway—then he remembered that there soon would be. Or so he hoped.

He seemed to be traveling an awfully long time. Had he got off course? Was the gale causing the Jeep to side-slip?

And then he saw a faint blob of illumination at one o'clock, but only for an instant—as if someone had lit a candle in dense fog and then blown it out. As he angled toward where he'd seen it, it flashed again through a break in the snow. A few feet more and it became a steady glow.

Yeniçeri-ville. Had to be.

He stopped the Jeep and shut her off. If he needed to return, he could find her by using the remote to flash the headlights. He hoped.

A lot of hoping going on.

He'd been running through what Heth had told him about the place. Breaking in at ground level would do no good because it gave no access to the living space. The only way in was through a single door atop an outside stairway. He'd bet the ranch the place was alarmed up the wazoo. A soft entry seemed impossible. So he'd come prepared to go in hard.

He'd loaded the two H-Ks with Devastators—so-called exploding bullets—each with an aluminum tip and a lead azide center designed to detonate on impact. He checked to make sure each had a round in the chamber. Then he filled his pockets with the various goodies he'd brought along. When he was loaded up, he slipped on a pair of safety glasses, grabbed the white comforter, and stepped out into the storm.

The wind hit him like a fist, driving the tiny hard snowflakes against his exposed skin. Good thing he'd thought of the goggles. His face felt like it was being sandblasted.

He grabbed the comforter and started walking—

And then froze as he heard a booming *crack* and felt a

shudder run through the ice. He made out the vague outline of the Jeep, still safe and sound where he'd left it. He couldn't see a break anywhere, but that meant nothing. He couldn't see much of anything.

Just a noise. Maybe the infrastructure of the ice was adjusting to the two tons of car perched on its back. Or maybe this was what frozen lakes and harbors did whether or not anyone was on it.

If a tree falls in a forest . . .

He heard-felt a second *crack* boom through the ice. As he stepped back to check the Jeep he heard something else.

A splash.

He pulled off a glove and squatted to check the ice. Wet. Covered with at least half an inch of water. And more gurgling up through a half-inch crack.

Quelling a surge of panic, fighting the urge to run, he shuffled back to the Jeep and eased inside. He started her up, put her into first, and began a slow right turn . . . to the east . . . toward the nearest shore.

Hang on, he told the ice. Hang on.

His only consolation was his assumption that the closer he got to land, the safer he'd be—the ice would be thicker and more stable in the shallows along the shore. He just had to make it there. But how far was *there*?

Finally the Jeep nudged against something. He put her in park and stepped out. He had the headlights and a flashlight but didn't dare use them—not with the house lights visible to his left.

He knelt and felt piled snow. He dug through and sighed with relief when he found sand.

Made it.

He rose and looked around. His original plan had been to approach the house from the west. He didn't want to change that, so he'd have to walk out onto the ice and loop back to the house.

The big question was how safe was the ice out there. He weighed a hell of a lot less than a Jeep, but was it too unstable even for a single man? He wished he knew.

What he did know was that falling through the ice would be

the end of him. Even if the frigid water didn't throw him into shock, even if he didn't drown and managed to drag himself to thicker ice, a water-soaked man would die of exposure in this frozen wind long before he reached warmth.

But he had to risk it.

He pulled the comforter from inside the Jeep and held it up ahead of him where it served as a shield while blurring his human outline. He started walking, peeking over its upper edge to make sure he was on course.

No more ice booms. Small comfort. He felt it could crack open under him any second.

He kept the glow to his right and slowly it began to take shape. He'd arrived. And he was facing the house's western flank.

He crouched and draped the comforter over his head like a shawl, then pulled out his binocs. He picked out the stairs leading up to the only door: solid, no glass, probably steel. He'd been hoping for but not expecting a few panes of glass. Solid steel offered the best protection. The only glass needed was a peephole.

He'd worry about the door later. He first had to cross a hundred feet of ice and a couple of hundred feet of snow to reach it. Those last two hundred feet were well lit. Very well lit.

Like Shea Stadium.

Lots of light inside too. He shuffled closer and scanned the windows: regular casements on the lower level; big picture type centered in the top, with sliding glass doors onto the deck up there. The big window was the major threat to his arriving unseen.

No one there now. Maybe he should—

He spotted movement in a top-level window to his right. He focused on it. Just a silhouette . . . but it was brushing long hair.

The new Oculus—Diana.

That settled it. He knew where he had to go, and knew it had to be now.

Stuffed the binocs into a pocket. Then, staying in a crouch, held the comforter before him and let it flap in the wind as he charged the house. Got off to a slow start on the bare ice, but that changed as soon as he hit the snowy shoreline. His sneakers dug into the calf-high powder and he sprinted a zigzag course across the two hundred feet toward the base of the house. Felt the ground change as he crossed the road; stumbled in one of the ruts, but kept his balance.

When he reached the wall he flattened his chest against it and pulled one of the H-Ks. Then he waited for an outcry or a commotion.

Nothing.

Except for the howl of the wind, all remained quiet.

His scars itched like they had at the warehouse when the Oculus was present. That clinched it: She was here.

Turned to face the way he'd come and—

Footprints . . . a trail of them winding from the icy shore to the house.

Damn. He'd known he'd have to leave some, but the lights cast shadows along their edges, making them stand out. As he watched, though, the wind began to fill them with snow. In a little while they'd be gone—before anyone spotted them, he hoped.

His back to the siding, he inched around to the steps and inspected their undersides. Risked a few blinks of his flashlight—doubted they'd be noticed in the flood of light from the spots—but couldn't find any wiring. As expected. Early warning sensors might make sense in a city, but out here the salty air would strip the insulation from exposed wires in no time.

Made his way up the steps—slowly, carefully, hugging the cedar siding all the way. When he reached the landing he inspected the door. Just as he'd expected: steel, secured by a knob lock and a dead bolt. Gave the knob a try—you never knew—but it held fast. Would have been nice simply to push it open and let them think the wind had done it.

But that would have been too easy. Had a feeling nothing was going to be easy tonight.

Opened his parka and uncoiled the rope from around his waist as he studied the top-floor deck. It sat a couple of feet above his head and five feet north. On a good day he could stand on the landing's railing and jump, grab the edge of the deck, and pull himself up. This was anything but a good day. Grab and hold on to a snowy deck? Good luck.

Thus the rope.

Tied a slipknot and made a two-foot loop. Brushed the snow off the landing's two-by-four railing and climbed atop it, spreading his feet to shift most of his weight to the ends of the board. Leaning against the cedar shakes for support, he threw the loop at the deck's corner post. The wind blew it back. Tried again, throwing harder. Same result.

Made it on the fifth try.

Tightened the loop, then knotted his end of the rope around the base of the landing's inner post. Now he had a makeshift rope ladder to the deck. But he wasn't leaving the stairs just yet.

Pulled off the white parka. The wind sliced him as he stuffed the comforter into it, even up into the hood, then zipped it closed. Using his Spyderco he cut off a length of the remaining rope and used it to tie the parka to the top step, back to the door.

Flattened himself against the siding and pulled out one of the three M84 flash-bangs he'd brought along. He yanked the safety pin but held the clip in place as he drew one of the H-Ks.

Then he pounded his fist on the door.

With the dish reception shot due to the storm, Diana had started the DVD of her favorite film, *Napoleon Dynamite*. Cal tried to watch but found it a lost cause. He saw why she might identify with a movie about geeks who simply can't fit in with the rest of the world. She probably saw herself as the ultimate geek.

He glanced at the other two occupants of the room: Lewis was dozing on the couch while Geraci fiddled with the puzzle.

He wandered over to the harborside picture window. No letup in the snow. At least the ocean wasn't acting up.

He was turning away from the window when the snow suddenly thinned and revealed what looked like a winding trail of indentations through the snow. Instantly the storm thickened again and hid it from view. Wind could sculpt weird patterns in snow, but this had looked like footprints.

Crazy. Couldn't be. But he stayed at the window and waited for another break. And when it came he was ready.

There—a zigzagging line of shallow depressions. Had to be footprints. Goddamn! Someone had come off the harbor!

He ducked away from the window and yelled, "We've got company!"

Geraci leaped to his feet. "Where?"

Lewis mumbled a "Huh?" from the couch.

"Footprints outside. Go down and tell Cousino and Finan"—this was their watch—"and wake up Dunsmore and tell Grell and Novak."

As Geraci pounded down the stairs, Cal pointed to Lewis.

"Get these lights off."

He hurried over to where Diana sat lost in her movie. Nothing he'd said had registered. He grabbed her under an arm and pulled her from the TV.

"Hey!" she said with no little indignation. "What're you doing?"

"Taking you to your room. Someone's here who shouldn't be!"

The indignation vanished in a gasp. "Oh, no!"

Keeping himself between her and the sliding glass deck doors, he guided her to her room.

"Keep the lights out and sit in the closet until we straighten this out."

He left her, closing the door behind him. When he came out he found Geraci bounding up the steps.

"You won't believe this. Someone's knocking on the door."

"Knocking?" That was just about the last thing Cal had expected.

Geraci started for the sliding glass doors. "I'm gonna go out on the deck and have a peek."

"No! That might be what they want. They could have a sniper out there waiting for us to do just that. Stay low and stay ready. I'm going downstairs."

All the bedroom doors had been closed so it was safe to leave the center hallway lit. Cal raced to the laundry room that served as the house's vestibule. He found five of his men clustered around the entrance, weapons out and trained on the door. He pushed through and took a look through the peephole. At the very edge of his view he saw someone in a hooded white parka sitting on the first step. Looked like a woman leaning on the newel post.

He pounded on the inside of the door.

"Hey! Hey, you!"

No movement—no sign of life, for that matter. He turned to the men.

"All right. We've practiced this. You know what to do. You see anything at all suspicious, do not hesitate to shoot. I'm going upstairs to cover the O."

As he turned and hurried back to the stairs, he saw Cousino, Finan, Grell, and Novak stacked high and low on either side of the laundry room, their pistols trained on the door. They would stay covered while Dunsmore unlocked it, then he would stay behind it as it swung inward.

Cal had just reached the top of the stairs when he heard a deafening *BOOM!* from behind; a bright flash stretched his shadow before him.

Flash-bang!

Jack watched the door swing inward. Popped the clip on the grenade and started counting.

One thousand and one . . .

"Who's there?" said a voice from within.

. . . one thousand and two . . .

"You out there—what do you want?"

. . . one thousand and three . . .

Tucked the H-K into his belt as he tossed the grenade through the opening, then turned his back to the door, closed his eyes, and held his ears. The M84 exploded with a 180-decibel boom and a million-candela flash. Anyone in the vicinity was going to be deaf, blind, and disoriented for the next few minutes. Certainly in no shape to get in his way.

After the detonation, Jack grabbed the rope and hauled himself up to the deck. As soon as he slid over the railing he brought out another M84 and reclaimed the H-K. Pulled the pin with his teeth, flipped the clip, and started another count.

One thousand and one . . . one thousand and two . . .

Fired a vertical line of five Devastators down the center of the sliding glass door. As the explosive bullets shattered the glass into countless fragments, he tossed the second grenade inside.

Cal hung over the railing and listened. He heard cries from the men but couldn't understand them.

"Who's down?" he called. "Anyone still mobile come to the stairs and—"

He heard a fusillade of shots behind him as the glass door exploded inward. He turned, pistol raised, and started firing at the door. Then he saw the silhouette of a canlike object float through the air into the room.

"Flash-bang!" he shouted as he dropped his weapon, squeezed his eyes shut, and jammed his fingers into his ears.

The room must have gone bright as the sun because the light blinded him through his eyelids. And then a noise louder than anything he'd imagined possible spiked around his fingers and into his eardrums.

After the flash-bang, Jack leaped through the hole in the window into a large dark room. The room he wanted—he prayed he'd figured this right—lay to the right. In the wash of light from the outside spots he made his way to the door. He was reasonably sure Diana was in there, but who else?

He dropped to the floor, rolled onto his back and kicked the door open.

No shots, no one even asking who was there. Just the whimper of a frightened child. Again, he had enough light from outside to make out the outlines of the furniture. He followed the sound to a closet. When he pulled the door open he found Diana cowering on the floor. He flicked on his flashlight and saw her black, tear-filled eyes staring up at him.

She screamed.

It took Cal time to reorient himself. He'd been knocked to his knees. Now he staggered to his feet and looked around. Through the huge purple blob of afterflash floating in his vision he made out Geraci and Lewis writhing on the floor. Over the roar in his ears he heard them moaning about being blind and deaf. They hadn't been able to react in time.

Cal stood swaying, shaking his head to rid himself of the buzzing in his skull, blinking to fade the afterflash, and wondering why he and the others were still alive, why their attackers hadn't finished them when they were down and defenseless.

Then he heard a high-pitched scream. He whirled toward Diana's room and saw her open door.

No!

He dropped to the floor, found his pistol, then charged the doorway.

"Diana!"

He lurched into the room, found the light switch and, dreading what he'd find, turned it on.

At first he wasn't sure what he was seeing. Diana knelt in the doorway of her closet, looking alive and well but terrified. Behind her, in the closet, crouched a man in a flannel shirt and white ski pants. Cal had to blink a few times before he recognized him.

"You!" He started to raise his pistol—

"Uh-uh. Put that down."

The words sounded far away. Then his bladder clenched as he saw the muzzle of one of the yeniçeri's own H-Ks pressed against Diana's throat.

He looked at Jack and saw the eyes of a stone killer. How had he missed that before? How did he hide it? Almost as if another person had moved into his skin. Another thing about those eyes . . . here was someone who didn't care all that much whether he lived or died. Nobody more dangerous or unpredictable than a guy like that.

"Don't, Jack . . . she's just a kid . . . please don't hurt her."

Cal searched for a way to get a clear shot without hitting Diana, but couldn't see one.

"If I were here for that, I'd have done it and been gone by now. But that's not the plan."

"Then what *are* you here for?"

"To talk."

"Talk?" Cal felt a flare of anger. "You didn't have to do all this just to talk!"

"Really?"

"Yeah. You have my number. You just had—"

Jack was shaking his head. "I don't need to talk to you. I need to talk to an Oculus. You going to tell me you'd have let me if I asked you?"

No . . . of course not.

Cal sensed Geraci and Lewis staggering up behind him. He glanced around and saw they had their pistols out before them.

Geraci said, "What the—?"

Cal raised a hand. "Easy."

"Get them out of here," Jack said. "There's been enough killing. And close the door after them."

Cal turned and motioned them back, closed the door, then stared at Jack. Something he'd said . . .

" 'Enough killing' . . . what's that mean?"

"Just what it says."

"Zeklos?"

He nodded.

The son of a bitch.

"And Miller and the others?"

Another nod.

Fuck! Cal felt his trigger finger spasming.

"And the O?" He steeled himself for the answer.

Jack shook his head. "You'll have to look elsewhere for an answer to that."

"Why Zeklos, of all people?"

"I tried to prevent that. Didn't work out."

"You cut out his heart?"

"Only his, and that was for effect. It brought Miller and his posse where I wanted them."

"You took them out? All four of them?"

A nod.

"Who the hell are you?"

"Just a guy. You hurt me, I hurt you back."

Just a guy? Obviously the wrong guy to hurt.

"But why? How did we hurt you? We were going to take you in."

"You people—you, your Oculus, the Ally . . . especially the Ally—killed my baby and put the woman I was going to marry and the little girl I was going to adopt into a coma."

"No!" Diana wailed. "My father would never do that!"

Cal felt his knees soften. The woman and kid on 58th Street . . . no. Couldn't be.

"But the Alarm said . . . it showed . . . why would the Ally want them dead? It had to have a good reason."

"By its standards it did. You've heard the expression 'a spear has no branches,' I assume."

"Of course I—oh, no."

"Oh, yes. But that's not all of it. One of your LaGuardia victims was my father."

Cal felt weak. He stepped away from the door and sat heavily on the bed.

Diana stared at him with wide onyx eyes. "What is he talking about?"

Everything that hadn't made sense about the ops now became diamond clear. They'd been Jack's branches.

"Is it true?" Diana cried. "Is it *true*?"

"Not the kind of thing I'd make up," Jack said.

Cal stared at Jack. "Then you really are the Heir."

"Seems to be the case. And there doesn't seem to be one goddamn thing I can do about it."

Cal shook his head. "I'm sorry. Man, I am so sorry."

"Sorry doesn't quite cut it."

Cal nodded toward Diana. "Killing her won't make things better."

"Haven't you been listening? I'm here to talk."

"To her?"

"No. To the Ally. I want to make a deal." He waggled his pistol at Cal. "Now get out of here. I don't want you hanging over us while I do this."

Cal looked at Diana and saw her black eyes pleading with him.

He shook his head. "No way. I'm not leaving her alone with you."

Jack raised the pistol and leveled it at Cal's face so that he was looking down the barrel.

"Out."

Cal shook his head again. "Shoot me if that's what you've got to do, but staying with her is what I've got to do."

"No-no-no!" Diana whimpered to Jack. "He's my friend!"

Jack sighed and lowered the pistol. "Like I said, been enough killing."

Cal saw something else in his eyes now—a sense of urgency.

"All right, Diana," Jack said. "Turn around and face me. No funny stuff. Just do as I say and this will all be over in a few minutes."

Cal watched as Diana shuffled a hundred and eighty degrees until her back was to him. Again he looked for a shot but couldn't find one. Oddly, he felt almost glad about that. What they'd done—what the Ally had done to this man . . . he'd been put through hell. No, not through . . . he was still looking for the exit.

"Now," Jack said to Diana. "Look at me. Look into my eyes, look at my face. Concentrate. Send a message or whatever you do to the Ally—Christ, I hate calling it that—and tell it—"

"I cuh-cuh-can't!"

Cal said, "It doesn't work that way. She's a raw feed. She can't send a message. She doesn't even know whether or not the Ally is tapping in."

Jack's eyes flashed as he glanced at Cal. "It damn well better be listening. I've got some news for it." He focused back on Diana. "Now just watch and listen. That's all you have to do."

"But I—"

"Shhh," he said softly, pressing a finger gently against her lips. "Let me worry about who's listening."

As he leaned back and raised the pistol, *NO-NO-NO-NO!* reverberated through Cal's brain. But then, to Cal's shock, he placed the muzzle under his own chin.

Diana cowered away, but Jack gripped her shoulder.

"Don't worry. No splattered brains here. Maybe later, but not yet." He cleared his throat. "Listen up, you son of a bitch. You've expended a lot of time and effort turning me into one of your spears. Maybe you plan on me becoming your big weapon. Well, get this: You could very soon be looking for a new Heir.

"So here's the deal. You bring back Gia, you bring back Vicky, and you bring back Emma. Or you step aside and let the Lady bring them back. I don't care which as long as all three are back.

"What do you get? You get me. I'll be your butt boy. I'll do your bidding. But only in return for getting them back. And don't try to pull a monkey's paw on me. I want them back the way they were before your clowns ran them down. If that doesn't happen, I pull this trigger. And I will do it. So it's simple: If they go—I go. Without them I won't have much to live for, and I won't have anything in this world to protect from the Otherness. So I'll opt out, and you can start looking for another guy to screw. Got that? Back the way they were or sayonara."

He looked at Cal over Diana's shoulder, then rose to his feet.

"Now what?" Cal said.

"Now I go home."

Cal stood and faced him.

"After what you did here, what you did to Zeklos and the others, you can't believe we'll let you go."

"Like I said: Been enough killing. I could have used frags

instead of flash-bangs. If I had, we wouldn't be having this conversation. You force me to shoot my way out, I probably won't make it, but . . ." He pulled another H-K. "These are loaded with Devastators. I'll take some of you with me. Guaranteed."

Explosive bullets . . . Cal didn't want to lose any more men.

Jack sighed. "And if that's not enough reason, I've got one more."

"Like what?"

"You don't really want to kill the Heir, do you?"

Cal let out a breath. Yeah. That was the kicker. They'd be undoing so much of what they'd worked for all their lives. He didn't know what to say or do.

"Feeling empty?" Jack said. "Helpless? Impotent? Welcome to my life since you blew a hole in it."

Cal knew he had to let him go, and not simply because he was the Heir.

Jack's father. And then that pregnant woman and her little girl . . . he remembered how they'd been laughing together at lunch . . . and what the yeniçeri had done to them a few moments later.

Yeah, Jack had killed five yeniçeri, and Cal mourned them, but it had been self-defense. He'd done it to protect his loved ones. And Zeklos and Miller and the rest would be alive still if they hadn't run down those two—no, three innocent people.

He owed this man something.

"I don't know if I can convince the others."

"Get them all downstairs. I'll handle the rest."

Cal wondered what to tell them. Maybe say they needed a strategy meeting out of earshot . . . by the laundry room. That might work, especially since he was sure now that Diana was in no danger. And he had a pretty good idea how Jack would get out.

"All right. I'll give it a shot, but no promises." He focused on Diana. "You'll be safe here. Don't leave the room till I come back for you."

"Don't leave me!"

"I'm not going to hurt you," Jack said. "And you'll be safer in here if things go wrong out there."

"He's right," Cal said. He stepped toward the door, then turned back to Jack. "Good luck with the woman and the girl. I hope they make it. The baby too."

Jack's lips tightened and he gave a small nod, but he said nothing.

Jack watched the door close behind Davis. He slumped back. Not in the clear yet. Getting out could prove harder than getting in.

He glanced at Diana and found her staring at him with her whiteless eyes.

"Are you really the Heir?"

"Not by choice."

"But it's an honor."

"Somebody else might see it that way. I don't. Might be different if I'd been asked first."

In that case, of course, the answer would have been a firm N-O.

Sensing a conflict within her, he said, "And how about being an Oculus? Is that an honor?"

She straightened her shoulders. "Yes. Of course."

"Wouldn't you have liked a choice?"

"It's not a choice—no more than the color of your skin is a choice. You are born an Oculus. It's my destiny and my duty."

Jack wondered how many times she'd been told that. Enough to have it branded on her memory.

"All fine and good, but wouldn't you have liked a say?"

"I—" The words choked off as her composed expression crumbled. She buried her face in her hands and sobbed. "I don't want this! I want to have friends my own age, I want to dance, I want to date!" She looked up at him with her red-rimmed black eyes. "I want a *life!*"

Jack cupped her chin in his hand. "No one can appreciate that more than I. We're in the same boat. I wish I could help you, but I can't even help myself." He rose and stepped past her. "I may not even be able to get out of here alive."

She looked up at him. "It's all true . . . what you said . . . what happened to you?"

"Yeah."

"I'm so sorry. I didn't know."

"Not your fault. And I'm sorry if I frightened you."

"And what you said about killing yourself, that was true? You'd do that because of them?"

Jack nodded.

Three years ago, before he'd met Gia, the idea of offing himself would have been . . . what? Inconceivable didn't even approach it. He'd been a self-contained unit, an island in every sense, thumbing his nose at John Donne.

Gia and Vicky had wrought a sea change. Before he'd met them he'd been unable to imagine sharing his life with anyone; now he couldn't imagine life without them.

"You're a good kid, Diana. I hope—"

"I'm not a kid!" she sobbed. "I'm an Oculus. I'm a tool. And so are you. But you've found a way out. Maybe I—"

"Don't say that. You—"

She held clawed hands around her onyx eyes. "I don't want to live like this!"

Jack didn't know what to say. What was left of his heart went out to her. Barely into her teens and her life had been appropriated. All her choices had been made. All except one.

"All I can tell you, Diana, is wait. These are dark days for you. Maybe you'll meet another Oculus your age and—"

"There's hardly any of us left!"

He had to get out of here.

"Just give it some time, Diana. That's all I can say." He gripped the edge of the closet door. "As for now, get back inside and lie flat. Things could get nasty in the next few minutes and I don't want you hurt."

"Maybe I don't care," she said, but complied.

Jack pushed the door closed. He heard a faint "Bye," just before it clicked shut.

He stepped to the door to the great room and eased it open for a peek.

Looked empty. Quiet except for distant voices.

The question of the moment was whether Davis would stay

true to his word, or if he and the remaining yeniçeri were waiting in the stairwell ready to open up on him.

Pulled his spare H-K. Since that had the fuller clip, he switched it to his right hand. Keeping both trained on the stairwell, he slipped out of Diana's room and padded along a diagonal path to the shattered glass door. Cold air and snow poured through.

Stepped through the opening onto the deck, stowed the pistols, then swung his legs over the railing. Grabbed the rope and slid to its lowest point where his sneakers were only half a dozen or so feet off the ground. Dropped, landing in a crouch. Then, steeling himself for a bullet in the back, dashed for the harbor shore.

No shots, not even a shout. Davis had delivered.

He stayed off the ice and ran along the shoreline. No need for secrecy now, and this was the most direct path to the beached Jeep. Good thing too. Couldn't afford to be too far off course. Although he still had his gloves and ski pants, he'd left the parka on the steps. The wind was scything through his flannel shirt like it was cheesecloth.

He pulled out the Jeep keys and started clicking the LOCK and UNLOCK buttons, but saw no flashes.

"Come on, come on."

He kept moving and clicking and freezing, then he spotted a flash ahead. He homed in on it.

10. When Jack reached the Jeep he jumped inside, started her up, and maxed the heater. He put her in gear and started back, hugging the shoreline. A longer trip, but safer.

As soon as he had the lights of the Wauwinet in sight, he picked up his cell and speed dialed the hospital.

"Trauma," said a woman's voice. "Pedrosa speaking."

"Maria," he said—he knew a lot of them on a first-name basis by now, and vice versa. "This is Jack. Any—?"

Light suddenly bathed the Jeep and then something crashed into its rear bumper, snapping his head back.

Jack didn't wait to find out what had happened—he had a pretty good idea. He hit the gas. Since he was already rolling from the impact, he picked up speed quickly, though the Jeep slewed and yawed this way and that. He glanced in the rearview and recognized the grille of a Hummer.

Davis? Jack doubted it, but it didn't matter who was behind the wheel. Probably followed his footsteps along the shore and come out on the ice after him.

He heard the crack of a gunshot but nothing hit the Jeep. Leaving his lights off he turned away from the shore—the Hummer would catch him before he'd cleared the Wauwinet property—and headed out on the ice as fast as the Jeep could manage. If he could lose them in the snow, maybe he could make it back to land unseen.

Then he remembered the cracking ice.

And that gave him an idea.

With the Hummer hot on his trail he headed due north as he had before. As soon as he saw the first glow of the yeniçeri house he slammed on the brakes and went into a sliding spin.

A second later the Hummer did the same. But it slid past and kept on going, its occupants firing wildly as it sailed by.

It had to weigh at least twice as much as the Jeep. Jack didn't know much about physics but knew more weight meant more momentum, and more momentum meant a longer stopping distance.

He turned on his lights so he could watch it slide into the area where the ice had cracked. If it had started to give way under a two-ton Jeep, what would it do under a four-ton Hummer?

Jack had the answer almost immediately. When the Hummer finally slid to a stop, it paused for a second as the driver spun its wheels to resume the chase. A second was enough: Its front end dipped as the tires broke through the ice. Then the rear sagged. Then it was gone.

Just like that.

Might have lasted a little longer if the windows had been up, but you need them down to shoot.

Jack watched the Hummer's headlights glow beneath the ice as it sank, then he turned the Jeep south and headed for land.

As soon as he was moving he called the unit again, and got hold of Pedrosa.

"Any news?"

He'd held a forlorn hope that he'd hear a wild commotion in the background and cries of wonder because Gia and Vicky had suddenly emerged from their comas.

But all sounded quiet.

"No, Jack. Still hanging on but . . ."

"No improvement? None at all?"

"Sorry. You coming in soon?"

"I'm stuck out of town in the snow."

"Get here as quick as you can, Jack. I don't think there's much time left."

He broke the connection.

If the Ally had heard the offer—a big if—it hadn't taken it. No deal. Jack's move.

His foot fell off the gas pedal and he let the Jeep roll. He closed his eyes as his head fell forward against the steering. He was tapped out. Nothing left. This had been his last chance, his last hope. He'd given it his best shot and had come up empty.

Nothing to do now but wait for the inevitable.

Get here as quick as you can . . .

For what? To stand by helplessly and watch them die? He didn't know if he could do that. And yet what else was left to him? He owed it to Gia and Vicky to be there when they were declared brain dead. So they wouldn't breathe their last among strangers when Stokely turned off the respirators.

He understood now why people went postal. He could see himself listening to the last wheeze of their powered-down respirators, watching the last rise and fall of their chests, flinching at the wail of their flat-lined cardiac monitors, then pulling out a pair of Mac-10s and starting to shoot, and keep on shooting until every living thing and every piece of equipment in the unit was dead, until he stood alone in the echoing silence.

And then he'd flip the Ally the bird and follow through with his threat.

But that had to remain an unfulfilled dream. He'd have to stand quietly by as his already crumbling world turned to ash. And then he'd have to hunt down Gia's folks and break their hearts. And then he'd have to stand and watch as Gia and Vicky and Emma were ushered into their graves.

Only after all that could he allow himself the luxury of bird flipping and promise keeping.

By that point he'd be looking forward to it.

SATURDAY

I. "New York Hospital on East Sixty-eighth. Fast."

Jack slouched in the cab's backseat and closed his eyes. He felt like hell.

The storm had blown out to sea around two a.m., heading for Nova Scotia, leaving behind a flawless winter sky for sunrise.

He'd paced the tiny Nantucket airport terminal all morning waiting for the plows to clear the runways. The Ashe brothers were snowed in, but the plowing in Nantucket proved to be less of a job than expected. The airport sat right on the beach, and the wind off the Atlantic had scoured the main runway—there were only two—while piling drifts along the tree-lined perimeter.

The real problem had been finding a flight. The commercials were either canceled or way behind. By noon LaGuardia had a few runways open and he found a charter pilot willing to take him.

All through the night and morning he'd made repeated calls to the unit. No change. Still hanging on by their fingernails.

Waiting for him?

I'm coming. Don't let go till I get there.

Fast didn't appear to be an option. The city had taken eight inches and was only partially plowed out. Good thing it was a Saturday. Anyone with a brain who didn't have to go out was staying home.

As soon as the cab neared the hospital, Jack felt a growing sense of urgency; by the time he stepped out at the entrance it had become an icy fist squeezing his heart.

Was he too late?

He ran inside and passed through the security check. The elevator ride seemed an eternity. When he stepped out on the trauma unit's floor he found a funereal silence. Three glum people sat in the patient lounge, staring either at the TV or into space.

Jack went directly to the unit's doors and stepped through—

—into a chaos of frantic activity as nurses and aides ran back and forth, shouting orders to each other.

Was this it? Had Gia and Vicky sensed his arrival and given up just as he'd arrived?

But the expressions on the staff—no grief, no concerned urgency, more like . . . joy and wonder.

Dr. Stokely spotted him just as he spotted her. She fairly ran up to him.

"Mister Westphalen—Jack—it's a miracle! A fucking miracle. I almost never use the f-word but that's all that fits: fucking miraculous!"

Jack's tongue turned to sand. "Gia? Vicky?"

Stokely nodded, her expression gleeful. "They came out of it—simultaneously! It's impossible, but a few moments ago they began moving their limbs and turning their heads. Their EEGs show increased and increasing brainwave activity. Vicky's seizures have stopped, Gia's cerebral edema has vanished, and her cardiac rhythm is normal sinus. And just before you walked in they simultaneously pulled out their endotracheal tubes—they're breathing on their own! I've never seen—I've never even *heard* of anything like it. It's un—"

Jack dodged around her and fairly leaped to the bedsides. He pushed the nurses and aides aside and stared down at Gia first, then Vicky. They looked peacefully asleep. Their color was good, and yes, they were breathing on their own.

Jack grabbed their hands and dropped to his knees, not in prayer, not in thanks, but because for a second there they wouldn't support him. When they regained their strength he was on his feet again, leaning over Gia.

"Gia? Can you hear me? Gia?"

Stokely laid a gentle hand on his back and said, "She may

very well be able to hear every word we say, but she's not yet capable of response."

Jack straightened and looked at her. "But she will be?"

"I hate to make predictions, as you know, but I'll go out on a limb and say yes. She'll have some neurological deficits—that's unavoidable—"

"Twenty-four hours ago you were telling me death was unavoidable."

"Yes, that's true, but no brain can undergo an ordeal like theirs and come away unscathed."

We'll see about that, Jack thought as he turned back toward the beds.

Obviously the Ally had accepted the deal, but why had it waited so long to do its part?

"When did you say they started coming around?"

"About half an hour ago, right after Gia's mother left."

Jack swung back on her. "Her mother?"

How had Gia's mother found out?

"Yes. Why, is something wrong?"

"I don't know."

"She said she was her mother. An elderly blind woman—looked old enough to be her grandmother, really."

Jack had never met Gia's mother but was pretty damn sure she wasn't blind.

And then he knew.

"Did she have a dog with her?"

"Yes. A big, beautiful, seeing-eye German shepherd. She wanted to bring him in with her but we couldn't allow that."

That was it. The Ally had withdrawn, allowing one of the Ladies to come in and work her healing.

"What did she do?"

"Just spoke to them. I wasn't close enough to hear myself, but one of the aides said she overheard her telling each of them that it was time to wake up and—" She broke off, frowning as she looked past Jack. "What on Earth are those?"

Jack turned and saw what she meant. Leaning against the head of each bed was a three-foot tree branch with a tin can painted with odd red-and-yellow squiggles resting atop it.

Jack had seen one of those before—behind his father's hospital headboard in Florida.

Stokely grabbed the arm of a passing nurse and pointed to them.

"Where did they come from?"

The nurse looked and shrugged. "I don't know. Never saw them before. Maybe the old lady—"

"Well, get them out of here."

"Don't touch them," Jack said.

Stokely and the nurse must have sensed something in his tone because they both stopped and stared at him.

Jack thought fast, looking for a way to keep those talismans or charms or fetishes or whatever they were in the room. He didn't know what they did but he knew that one of them had been nearby when his father had come out of his coma.

"They're religious—part of my wife's religion."

Stokely said, "What religion is that?"

Good question. He picked something she'd mostly likely know nothing about.

"Wicca."

"She's a witch? Well, whatever, those things have to go. God knows what kind of bacteria they're carrying."

"They *stay*," Jack said, letting an edge creep into his tone. "Does this hospital make accommodations for orthodox Jews and Muslims and vegans? You'd let a Roman Catholic keep rosary beads and a Virgin Mary statue at bedside, wouldn't you?"

"Yes, but—"

"No buts. Unless you want to be responsible for the hospital being slammed with a religious discrimination suit, they stay."

Stokely stared at him. "I thought you were a different sort of person."

"I am. I'm a very different sort of person. You'll never know how different. But the religious objects stay, right?"

Stokely sighed. "Okay, okay."

Jack smiled. "Great. Now, do you have any idea where I can find the La—Gia's mother?"

"As she was leaving I heard her mention something about a baby but—"

Good Christ! Emma! Could she . . . ?

Jack pushed past Stokely and hurried for the doors.

"Wait? Where are you—?"

And then he was out and running for the closing elevator doors. He caught them and pushed them open with such force that he frightened the old couple inside.

"Sorry."

The morgue was in another wing. One of those can't-get-there-from-here situations where he had to go down to the main floor and switch to another elevator bank.

He watched the descending numbers as they stopped on every goddamn floor.

Come on, come on, come on!

Finally the main level, a dash to the other elevators, another excruciatingly slow ride, and then he was on the morgue floor, running down the hall. He burst through the doors and headed straight for the coolers.

"Hey!" said the attendant—younger and stockier than the guy he'd met before. "Where's your pass?"

Jack ignored him. He beelined for the drawer where they were keeping Emma and pulled it open. The black bag was still zipped, the lump still settled in its center. But something new had been added: a stick with a decorated tin can at its end lay beside the bag.

Back to the lump: Was it—was that movement he just saw?

A hand grabbed his shoulder and pulled him back.

"Hey, buddy. You can't just walk in here. You gotta have a pass."

Jack turned on him, ready to rip his heart out and feed it to him.

"This is my baby!" he gritted through his clenched teeth. He gave him a shove. "Get out of here!"

The guy staggered back, his belligerent expression morphing to fear.

"I-I'm calling security."

"Knock yourself out."

Jack turned back to the body bag and reached for the zipper.

Emma, alive. Thank you, Lady, whoever, whatever, and wherever you are.

He pulled the zipper, spread the edges, ready to take her in his arms and wrap her in the warmth of his shirt.

He froze.

Emma lay exactly as he'd left her: stiff . . . white . . . lifeless.

"No . . . oh, no . . ."

He lifted her, held her against him. This couldn't be. He'd made a deal. All three of them back . . . as alive and as well as before. What had happened? The Lady had been here—the stick and the can were proof of that. Why wasn't Emma alive? Why hadn't she come back?

"Sir," said a gruff voice behind him. "You're going to have to leave."

Jack ignored him and held on to Emma.

"We're sorry for your loss, sir," said another, softer voice. "But we have to escort you out of here."

Jack realized he didn't have any fight left in him. Not trusting himself to speak, he nodded. He kissed Emma's cold, fuzzy scalp, then laid her back in the bag and zipped it closed. He let his hand linger on the lump that was his baby, then turned to let them kick him out.

2. He found the Lady in the main waiting area, sitting and seemingly staring at nothing through her dark glasses. A German shepherd in a seeing-eye harness sat at her feet, its tongue lolling. It looked at Jack as he dropped into the seat next to her.

"Thank you," he said.

She nodded. "You have questions. Let's walk."

Questions was putting it mildly.

They rose and Jack waited while she unfolded her white cane.

"Are you really blind?"

She turned her face toward him so he could see his reflection in her black lenses.

"What a question."

What a non-answer, but he let it slide.

He took her arm and guided her out into the cold, bright afternoon. They sat on one of the benches near the roundabout driveway. Neither spoke for a few moments, then Jack could wait no longer.

"Emma . . . the baby . . . I guess it was expecting too much to think you could raise the dead."

"Not too much. It has been done."

"She was dead too long then?"

"Perhaps. But even if not, the Ally would not allow her return."

Jack stiffened. "But the deal was—"

"I know about your threat."

"But how could you?"

"That does not concern you. What does is that you should know that you have some value to the Ally, but you are not irreplaceable. I think it may have amused the minor molecule of its being that pays attention to this sphere to partially comply."

"Partially . . ."

"Yes. Allowing me to return your Gia and your Victoria to you, but not the baby, was its way of sending you a message."

"That I don't call the shots."

"Precisely."

"But the deal was for all three."

"There was no deal. Only your threat."

Jack was beginning to see, and what he saw became a crushing weight on his shoulders.

"A threat I can't follow through on now that Gia and Vicky are back."

No way he could eat a hollow-point and leave them to face the coming apocalypse without him.

She nodded. "Yes. It has negated your threat without fully acceding to your demands . . ."

He felt his throat tighten. "Why not fully? Why couldn't it simply free Emma too? It would've cost it nothing and . . . and she's just a baby."

"You are thinking emotionally about a force with no emotion." She turned her dark lenses toward him. "You had to be shown who is boss."

Utterly spent, Jack slumped on the bench and stared at the naked trees within the roundabout, the steady stream of cars dropping off and picking up patients and visitors.

He'd been outflanked, but at least his battles with the MV hadn't been for nothing. At least he had Gia and Vicky back.

"How am I going to tell Gia?"

"She will know something is wrong as soon as she awakens and realizes there is no baby in her belly. Her first hope will be that it was somehow saved, that her infant awaits her in the neonatal ICU. You must be there to comfort her when she learns it is not."

She cocked her head as if listening.

"What?"

"They will be conscious soon. Do you wish to be there when they wake?"

"Of course."

He wanted to be the first person Gia and Vicky saw when they opened their eyes.

"Then you must go now."

Jack jumped out of his seat and helped her to her feet.

"You coming?"

She shook her head. "No. I have no place there."

She tapped her cane on the walk and she and her dog began to move away.

"Where are you going?"

"Not far. I am never far."

He watched her until she'd rounded the corner of the nearest building, then he turned and hurried back inside. He had to be there to tell Gia about Emma.

Guilt clung to him like a school of leeches as he headed for the elevators.

Tell Gia about the baby, yes, but he could not tell her everything, could not let her know that it was no accident, that she and Vicky had been deliberately run down because of him . . . simply because they meant something to him.

No. Couldn't tell her that. Not yet. She'd have enough to deal with as it was. He'd tell her someday when she'd gotten over the worst of losing Emma, but not yet.

At least they were safe now.

No, not quite. Safe from the Ally, maybe—Jack had made it clear that losing those two branches meant losing the spear. But what of Rasalom? Would he try to strike through Gia and Vicky? It certainly wasn't beneath him.

Only time would tell. Jack had an idea that he didn't rank very high on Rasalom's list of priorities. Nevertheless he'd have to keep his head down and stay on guard.

Always on guard.

Turn the page for a preview of

F. PAUL WILSON'S

BLOODLINE

(0-7653-1706-0)

Available October 2007 from Forge

Tuesday

*Someone said you might be able to help me. I need to keep my
daughter from making a terrible mistake.*
 Christy P.

Jack stared at the last of the messages forwarded from his Web
site, repairmanjack.com. None would have been of much interest even if he were working now. He'd blow them off later.

He'd looked into starting a site on MySpace because its sheer
size provided an anonymity of sorts, but he'd almost bailed
when he discovered that URLs repairmanjack, repairman-jack,
and repairman_jack were already taken. What the hell? He'd
finally had to settle for www.myspace.com/fix_its.

But after setting it up he realized only other MySpace members could contact him there, so he'd kept his original as well.

"Jack? Can I bother you for a minute?"

Though he was in the study and Gia upstairs, Jack could
hear the distress in her voice. He had a pretty good idea what
was wrong.

"Be right there."

He took a quick sip of coffee and glanced at the computer's
time display. Vicky was going to miss her bus if they didn't
hustle.

He took the stairs two at a time to the second floor.

"Where are you?"

"Vicky's room."

Figured that.

He walked in and found the two loves of his life sitting on

the bed, Vicky facing away, Gia behind her, holding onto her long dark hair.

"I can't do it," Gia said, looking up at him with American-flag eyes: blue on white with red rims. "I still can't do it."

Gia looked too thin. Her weight was still down since the accident. She'd lost a lot during the coma and the early recovery period, but wasn't regaining it now that she was almost back to normal. Though not exactly sunken, her cheeks weren't as full, giving her a haggard look. She still cried now and then but, despite her therapist's advice, resisted taking an antidepressant.

She'd let her blond hair grow to the point where it was now longer than he'd ever seen it, covering her ears and the nape of her neck.

But at the moment Vicky's hair was the problem: Gia had started weaving the back into a French braid but had botched it badly. Not as badly as she had in preceding weeks, but still . . . she used to be able to do this in thirty seconds—with her eyes closed. Now . . .

"Look at this mess."

Jack crouched beside her and kissed her cheek.

"You're getting better every day. Just keep at it. You know what Doctor Kline said."

"'Practice, practice, practice.'" She sighed. "But it's so frustrating sometimes I want to scream."

And sometimes she did. But never when Vicky was around. Jack would hear her in another room, from another floor. He wondered how often she screamed when she was here alone.

Vicky half-turned her head. "Am I going to be late for school, Mommy?"

"You'll be fine, honey."

Some things had improved in the three months since the accident, but by no means had life returned to normal. Jack doubted it ever would. The broken bones had healed, but scars remained, on the body, the brain, the psyche.

Vicky had the best chance of leaving it all behind. The unborn sister she'd been waiting for would not arrive, and she'd accepted that. Emma had been no more than a bulge in her mother's belly and an image on an ultrasound monitor, not a little person she could see and touch.

Not so Gia. Three months ago she'd stepped off a curb as a mother-to-be and awakened days later to learn she'd lost the baby. Emma had been very real to Gia, a little person who'd turned and kicked inside her. More real to Gia than to her father, Jack.

Gia's scars ran deep.

And not being able to care fully for Vicky slowed their healing.

Her motor skills hadn't returned to normal yet, though they were worlds better than when she'd come out of her coma. With physical and occupational therapy she'd recovered about ninety percent of her manual dexterity, but it was the missing ten percent that was killing her.

She couldn't braid Vicky's hair.

And she couldn't draw or paint—at least not like she used to.

Which meant she couldn't make a living. Graphic art paid her bills, but her personal paintings soothed her soul. She worked daily at both in her third-floor studio, but didn't like much of what she produced commercially, and wouldn't show Jack her private paintings. He worried she'd one day explode and he'd find her splattered all over her studio.

"Am I going to be late for school, Mommy?"

Gia said, "You just asked me that, remember?"

Vicky frowned, then nodded. "Oh, right."

Vicky's only deficit was her short-term memory, but that was steadily improving. The neurologist said she'd be back to normal in a few more months. Her teachers were taking that into account and cutting her some major slack.

Jack looked around at the bookshelves lining the wall of her high-ceilinged bedroom. The good news was that Vicky hadn't lost her love of books and was still a voracious reader. He glanced at her Jets banner—she remained a devoted a fan—and at the four too-handsome faces crowded onto her Boyville poster—still her favorite music group, unfortunately.

Gia was unraveling the botched braid.

"You'd better do it or she'll be late."

As she rose to let Jack take her place, he gripped her elbow. "Okay, but coach me. I still haven't got this down."

Not true. He'd helped so many times he could do it in his sleep.

So she stood over his shoulder and talked him through brushing out the hair, separating a nice fat lock, then poking his index and middle fingers through to divide it into three fat strands. Then the tricky part of keeping the strands in the webs of his fingers as he picked up new strands while braiding.

"Now . . . which one do I start with?"

He felt a gentle punch on his back and a soft laugh from Gia.

"As if you didn't know."

She kneaded his shoulders as he worked.

"Boy, if the guys at Julio's could see you now."

"Why do you say that?"

"Well, I doubt this is the guy they know."

"Maybe not. But you wouldn't hear a peep out of them."

"No? Rib nudging? No wise cracks?"

"Uh-uh."

"Why not?"

He looked up and winked at her. "Because of the guy they know."

He finished the weave—something very comforting about working with Vicky's hair—and tied it off with a blue elastic band.

"There. Not bad for a guy, eh?"

Gia bent and kissed his cheek. "Actually it's great. And thanks for being so patient."

He looked at her. "Patient? What's patient got to do with it?"

"Everything. It's not one of your strong points. Just . . . thanks for putting up with me."

As she hurried Vicky downstairs, Jack remained on the bed, staring out Vicky's window at the still-bare trees and feeling low. Worse than low. Like a rat. And a cowardly one at that.

Patient? Of course he was patient. He would be patient with her under any circumstance. And considering he was the cause of all the trauma that had befallen her and Vicky, how else could he be?

But she didn't know that. Because he hadn't told her. Yet.

Gia, the accident that killed our baby, that almost killed you and your daughter, that left the two of you with broken bodies and battered brains, was no accident.

When would be a good time to say that? When would it be okay to tell her it had happened because he cared for them, because they mattered to him, because the baby carried his bloodline?

Would there ever be a right time?

"Dollar for your thoughts?"

Jack jumped. "Hey."

Gia looked down at him. "You seemed a million miles away."

"Just thinking."

Her eyes bore into his. "Didn't look like happy thoughts."

He shrugged. "They weren't. Can you think of much to be happy about?"

She smiled. "I'm alive, Vicky's alive, and it's been great having you stay with us. So look on the bright side."

Yeah. The bright side: moving in here to take care of them after they were released from rehab. Not easy, but maybe the most rewarding thing he'd ever done.

She kissed the top of his head. "Okay, we're heading for the bus stop, then I'm off to OT."

"Want me to drive you?"

She shook her head. "A cab'll have me there by the time you degarage the car. See you for lunch?"

"It's a date."

"Got anything planned for the morning?"

"Probably hanging with Abe."

She looked down at him. "No business?"

"No business."

"What about that lady who wants help for her daughter?"

"Hmm? Where?"

"I just saw it on the screen down there. She sounds worried."

Jack shrugged. "I'm on hiatus."

"You're bored is what you are. You've made our troubles your troubles, but we're coming out of those troubles. You need a break."

Couldn't argue with that. The less and less Gia and Vicky needed him, the more restless he'd become.

Gia squeezed his shoulder. "Why don't you see what she wants."

He looked up at her. "I believe I'm having an out-of-Gia experience."

She laughed—a sound he didn't hear nearly enough these days.

"Seriously," he said. "This doesn't sound like you."

"Maybe it's a new me. I know spending all your time hanging around here or at Abe's isn't you. I know who you are. I thought I could change you but I realize I can't. I'm no longer sure I want to. You are who you are and I love who you are, so why don't you go out and be who you are?"

Jack stared at her. She meant it—she really meant it. A crack about the lingering effects of brain trauma leaped to mind but he quashed it. Not funny.

"Maybe I'm not so sure who I am anymore."

"You know. It's in your blood. See what the lady wants."

"Doesn't sound like my kind of thing."

"Maybe not, but it's her *daughter*."

The last word hung in the air.

Daughter . . . like Vicky was to him, emotionally if not legally . . . like Emma would have been if not for . . .

He remembered the message: *I need to keep my daughter from making a terrible mistake.*

Like what? Getting involved with a guy like me?

No . . . he wasn't going there again. He'd been there too many times.

"Maybe I'm not on hiatus. Maybe I'm retired."

A wry smile: "Then why are you checking the Web site? As a matter of fact, if you're retired, why keep it up and running at all?"

"Maybe I just haven't got around to shutting it down."

"And maybe you need a diversion, Jack. Go on, give her a call. If it's not in your ballpark, simply beg off." She kissed him and headed for the door. "Gotta run. Think about it."

He sat a moment longer. When he heard the front door close he forced himself to his feet. Lots of inertia lately. Too long since he'd awakened with his own agenda for the day.

He ambled downstairs and into the study where he stood and stared at the screen.

Someone said you might be able to help me . . .

She'd included her phone number.

What mistake do you think your daughter's going to make, lady? And why do you think a stranger will be able to do anything about it?

Okay. He'd bite. Couldn't see any downside to giving her a call.